Releasing Janet

Alex Banwell

BROAD PLACE
publishing
broadplacepublishing.co.uk

First published in Great Britain in 2025

Broad Place Publishing
https://broadplacepublishing.co.uk

British Library Cataloguing-in-Publication Data.
A catalogue record for this book is available from the British Library.

Paperback ISBN:	978-1-91-5034-63-2
Hardback ISBN:	978-1-91-5034-65-6
EBook ISBN:	978-1-91-5034-64-9

Cover images courtesy of Rodolfo Clix, Suzy Hazelwood and Conger Design at pexels.com

Books can be purchased from https://broadplacepublishing.co.uk

*This book is dedicated
to the wonderful women who shaped me.*

Titles in this series

Just Benny
Releasing Janet
Only Ola (a prequel novella)

1

The twinkling white lights on the Christmas tree and the gas fire's flames filled the living room with a cosy glow as Janet Wellander sat in an armchair cradling two-year-old Beth on her lap. Although the child's eyes were heavy with sleep, persuading her to take her afternoon nap had become a battle of wills. Beth was a curious little girl who insisted on inserting herself into the centre of everything that went on around her. She had a fear of missing out and an insatiable desire to learn. So different from Benny at the same age. Janet's mood was reflective as she enjoyed the familiarity of rocking a toddler, and she hummed to still Beth's over-active mind.

'Wanna see Benny.' Beth fought to be free of her embrace.

'He won't be long, sweetheart,' Janet crooned, tightening her hold on the squirming infant. 'Just close your eyes, and when you open them, Benny will be here.'

She glanced at the clock to confirm the validity of her promise. Her son would be home in just over an hour. Surely Beth would sleep until then? Janet continued rocking and humming, until Beth's body relaxed, and her breathing settled into a steady rhythm. The girl's nineteen-year-old mother, Nettie, often complained about her daughter's resistance to napping during the daytime, but Janet assured her it only took a little coaxing. She was always seeking to offer reassurance, and when she'd seen Beth's grandmother struggling when Nettie was at work, Janet had gladly offered her help. Mary had handed her granddaughter over gladly, confessing that she struggled with Beth's rambunctiousness even more than Nettie did.

Safe in the assurance that Beth was finally asleep, Janet carefully lowered the toddler onto the sofa, covering her with a blanket and tucking Beth's favourite white teddy in the space she'd vacated. Janet marvelled at her love for a child who wasn't related to her by blood. Yet Beth had stolen all their hearts, even Ola's.

Janet bustled out to the kitchen to prepare their evening meal. A casserole was ideal for a bitterly cold December day. Would Ola come home early if the weather turned? Probably not, she mused whilst chopping carrots. Her Danish husband was forever grumbling that a couple of flakes caused the whole country to *grind to a halt*. The stubborn man would fight his way home to prove his point. Meanwhile, their son was probably staring out of a classroom window, praying for enough snow to close school the following morning.

Poor Benny was finding his studies harder than ever during his final year of GCSEs. He had made himself so ill before the mock examinations in November, that he ended up spending over a week in hospital while they fought to bring his seizures under control. Although the school had made tentative noises about Benny doing his mocks again, Janet hoped he wouldn't have to face exams until May. She was already fretting over what might happen when May came. Struggles with basic learning had dogged her precious boy all his life. He longed to train as a mechanic at his father's garage, but Ola said that would have to wait until the summer.

The front door closed with a bang, and Janet ran to the living room, fearing the noise would wake Beth. Pausing in the doorway, she relished the sight of her cherished son bending over the little girl, kissing her forehead, and hushing her with tender words.

'Sorry, Bethy,' he whispered. 'I didn't know you were sleeping. Silly Benny.' He picked her up, and Beth tucked her head under his chin.

'Silly Benny,' she repeated, still half asleep.

Benny held her a little longer, then returned her gingerly to the sofa before tiptoeing to his mother with doleful eyes. 'Sorry, Mum. I forgot you had her today.'

'You're home early.' Janet pulled him into a hug. Now it was Benny's turn to receive her comfort. She registered his sadness, and what might have been the glint of tears.

'Headache,' he said, resting his head on her shoulder. Even though she suspected it was a convenient excuse to get out of the after-school tuition he was meant to have stayed for, Janet wouldn't question him. She hated seeing him struggle. 'They knew I wouldn't cope today so they let me go.'

'Go upstairs till your dad comes home.' She kissed his cheek, expecting him to head for the door.

'Can I stay with you?' Benny lingered in her arms. His vulnerability took Janet back to his early childhood, and she tried not to indulge in her memories. She was slowly adjusting to the fact that Benny needed her less.

'Of course.' Janet smiled and led him into the kitchen. 'I'll make us both a cup of tea, and you can talk to me while I work. Beth will be fine until she wakes up.'

'Thanks for helping with her.' Benny flopped into a chair while Janet filled the kettle. 'Nettie reckons she's happy when she's with you.'

'Nettie claims that's because I spoil her.' Janet's words contained no malice. She had a fairly good relationship with Beth's feisty red-headed mother, who oozed the confidence her shy and withdrawn son lacked.

'Yeah, you do.' He laughed. 'But you still spoil me as well, so that's cool.' He leaned his head on his arms as Janet turned to him with concern in her eyes.

'Do you think the headache is a warning sign of a seizure?'

Benny shook his head. 'It'll go away now I haven't gotta read no more. I hate reading. It's too hard.' He sounded younger than his 16 years as he fought not to cry. Then he pondered for a moment and added, 'Except for the Bible, but Pastor Tim doesn't make me read loads of that, and he says God understands when I can't read sometimes cos of my seizures.'

He drummed his fingers on the tabletop before continuing, 'I wish God was one of my teachers. I bet He wouldn't have a go at me like they do.'

'What happened today?' Janet sensed something had pushed him beyond his ability to cope.

'Mrs Grant said my English essay was so bad she couldn't mark it. I've gotta do it again. But I can't, Mum. I can't do no better than what I did!' He rose to pace the room, his agitation increasing with every word.

'It's okay, Benny.' She pulled him into her arms as he surrendered to tears. 'We know you're doing your best.'

'They don't,' he wailed. 'And I don't reckon Dad does either, cos if he did, he'd let me leave school and work with him at the garage.'

'That's all you want, isn't it?' Janet rubbed his back, and Benny nodded.

'Failing my GCSEs won't make me a better mechanic.'

'I'll talk to your dad,' Janet promised, though she knew her words would fall on deaf ears. Benny was technically old enough to leave school, but Ola was adamant that Benny should successfully complete his education despite his predicted grades being well below average.

Beth's voice calling his name had Benny rushing for the door. When he returned carrying her moments later, Janet's emotional little boy had transformed into Beth's loving and responsible father figure. After getting her a drink and biscuit, he sat playing with her at the kitchen table. With Benny at home, sleep was no longer an option, and Beth monopolised him until her mother arrived after a long day at work.

'You're welcome to stay for tea, Nettie,' Janet said, noticing the crumpled pharmacy uniform and exhaustion in Nettie's eyes.

Benny responded with a beaming smile. Nettie didn't need much persuading either, and the couple snuggled on to the sofa with Beth. With Nettie being older, Ola had been quick to establish ground rules when she'd begun dating his son, which Nettie had been careful to obey. There had been no further confrontations since the first time they were discovered alone together.

Janet heard Benny telling his girlfriend about his school day through the open kitchen door, and she was pleased by Nettie's reassurances. 'I keep telling you, you're not thick. There are plenty of things you're good at.'

A long period of silence elapsed, broken by Beth's demands for attention. Clearly, Nettie's daughter didn't appreciate her mother's need for romance.

Ola came home right on time. By then, it was snowing, and Benny claimed he was praying it would continue all night.

'Are you supposed to pray about things like that?' Ola reached for a second helping of casserole, while Benny fed Beth from his own plate.

'Tim reckons we've gotta pray about everything.' Benny alternated mouthfuls with Beth, the toddler waiting for hers like an expectant baby bird.

Janet was grateful for the way Pastor Tim had helped Benny the previous year but was unsure what to make of Benny's blossoming faith.

'She's got her own dinner.' Nettie pointed to the contents of an untouched tea plate.

'Mine's nicer, isn't it, Bethy?'

Beth nodded, and her exhausted mother sighed. She was likely grateful for the chance to enjoy a meal without interruption.

When they were done, Nettie offered to help with the dishes, while Benny and Beth raided the freezer for ice cream.

'You want ice cream when it's snowing?' Janet shook her head in bewilderment.

'Of course he does.' Even Ola was jovial tonight. Perhaps it would be the ideal time for Janet to broach the subject of Benny's education again?

Half an hour later, Janet's hands were still submerged in soapy dishwater when she heard a crash from the hallway. Nettie threw down the tea towel and ran towards Beth's cries.

When Janet rounded the corner, Ola was already kneeling beside their son as Benny's body convulsed with a seizure.

'It's okay, Bethy.' Nettie swept her whimpering daughter up into her arms. 'Benny's just icky. He'll be better soon.'

Nettie crouched beside Benny, assuming the role that had previously belonged to Janet. Still cuddling Beth, the beautiful young woman whispered endearments, and the love shining in her eyes brought Janet to tears. 'I'm here, Benny. I love you. You'll be okay. It'll be over soon.'

Seeing Benny in capable hands, Janet retreated into the kitchen to retrieve a bowl, returning just in time for her son to open his eyes and vomit.

'We caught it.' Nettie smiled, reaching for his hand as her worried-looking boyfriend gradually regained his focus.

Beth had calmed, so Nettie released her to help Benny into a sitting position, wrapping her arms securely around him, and soon Beth's little hands were clinging to Janet's legs.

'I love you, Nettie.' Benny whimpered, but the fear in his eyes had retreated. Nettie's calmness in the wake of his unexpected seizure had achieved its desired effect.

'Is it over?' she asked.

When Benny nodded, Nettie helped him to stand. 'You need to sit down.' She guided him into the lounge and sat beside him on the sofa, still holding his hand.

Janet followed, noting the trust in Benny's eyes as he fixed them on Nettie. As she and Ola took the two armchairs, Beth scrambled onto the sofa next to her mother and gradually inched her way onto Benny's lap.

'I'm okay now, Bethy.'

'Course you are,' Nettie hugged Benny with Beth between them. 'Want a drink?' she asked, and Benny nodded.

As Janet watched another woman expertly caring for her son, she experienced a momentary twinge of sadness, quickly replaced by love. She had been wrong in thinking no other woman could match her devotion to Benny.

Beth soon became bored while her companions chatted and enjoyed their warm drinks. Nettie had prepared coffee for herself and Ola, and tea for Benny and Janet.

'Those aren't for playing with, young lady,' Ola reprimanded as Beth's tiny fingers examined the decorations hanging from the tree.

'Some of them look old.' Nettie turned her attention to the glittering tree.

'A few go back to my childhood,' Janet admitted, 'but I bought most of them when Benny and Emma were little.'

Then her son rose and joined Beth. 'I made that one at school.' He lightly touched a rudimentary cardboard ice cream cone that had faded with age.

Nettie laughed. 'Why doesn't that surprise me?'

'The other kids made Father Christmases and snowmen, but they're boring. Ice cream is much better.'

Nettie's attention was caught by a photo album lying on a shelf near the tree. 'Are those pictures of Emma and Benny?' she asked. 'Can I have a look?'

'Actually, they're from my childhood,' Janet confessed. 'Cameras weren't commonplace back then, and my parents didn't have one. These are the photos their friends and other family members took.'

'I haven't seen that before,' Ola said.

'No, you wouldn't have.' Janet reached over to pick it up. 'I told you my parents have moved to a retirement complex?'

Ola nodded.

'My mother posted me the photos because she knows I'm sentimental over memories. It just arrived today.'

Janet opened the album, and Benny and Nettie crowded in. Even Ola put his coffee down and joined them.

'Oh, you were cute!' Nettie's attention was drawn to a black and white picture of a tiny Janet wearing a frilly dress and a sun bonnet.

'Not really.' Janet blushed. 'I was always a plain Jane.' She stopped herself from adding more whilst flicking through the sparse collection – such a minimal visual record of her childhood.

'You look happy in that one.' Nettie pointed at a picture in which Janet appeared barely four years old, and Janet agreed with a nod. She was relieved that none of them seemed to notice the whole years unaccounted for.

Long ago, the family album had contained more photos. When had her parents removed them? Was it within weeks of the tragedy that had fractured their unity forever? Or had they waited until later? And was it her mother or her father? Who had decided they needed to go?

'So, you've got two brothers?' Nettie asked, pointing at two teenage boys. She seemed set on finding out all she could about Janet's past.

'Yes, just Malcolm and David. And they're both older than me.' As the words escaped, the back of her throat constricted. A desire to close the album and hide it somewhere overcame her. Why was this happening to her now? Why did a photo album have the power to rake up long-buried memories? It was easier not to think – to pretend it hadn't happened. All her family needed to know was that she had lived an uneventful life, growing up with her parents and brothers...

'Did you ever wish for a sister?' Nettie probed.

Suddenly, Janet was powerless. Unbidden tears pricked and then fell. She tried to hold them back, but the dam had burst, and the trickle swiftly became a river.

'Mum? What's wrong?' Benny put his arms around her, and Nettie glanced helplessly at Ola.

'Jan?' Even her husband's tone was gentle, and Janet realised the time had come.

Safe in the circle of her loved ones, she spoke the long-forbidden words in little more than a whisper. 'I did have a sister. Her name was Sylvia.'

2

'Wake up, Jan.' Daddy's tender whisper dragged me back into the real world, jarring me away from dreams of fairies and angels with fluttering wings.

'Daddy…?' I cautiously opened my eyes. Why was he waking me up when it was still dark?

'It's okay, sweetheart.' Daddy folded back the pink knitted blanket, lifting me into his arms and cradling my head against his shoulder as he switched on a bedside lamp. 'I'm sorry. I shouldn't have woken you. I'm a mean old daddy. I just thought you'd want to hear the news.'

'What is it?' I blinked as my eyes adjusted to the light. I was suddenly wide awake. Daddy looked happy. His news might be more exciting than flying with angels and dancing with fairies.

'You've got a baby sister.' He kissed the top of my head.

'Have I?' My mouth fell open. 'I've been asking Jesus for a sister!'

'Have you indeed?' he laughed.

'Mrs Smith at Sunday school said we've got to talk to Jesus about everything, so I've been talking to Him about my sister.'

'Well, it seems He answered your prayers.'

'Where is she? Is she here?' My eyes searched the room, finding only my familiar collection of dolls and stuffed animals, arranged exactly as I had organised them before climbing into bed.

'She's at the cottage hospital with Mummy. They're going to stay there for a few days, but when they come home, you'll be able to help us look after her.'

'I will, Daddy.' I puffed out my chest. I wasn't the youngest child anymore and I felt the heavy, but joy-filled responsibility.

We had a new baby girl. 'I'm gonna help Mummy do everything for her.'

'Of course you will. You'll be a massive help. But you need to go back to sleep now.' Daddy lowered me into bed with another kiss.

'Do Malcolm and David know?'

'I don't think they'll be as excited as you, so I didn't bother waking them up.' He chuckled, tucking my blanket snugly around me and Billy, my favourite teddy. 'They'll find out in the morning. You're only the second person I've told.'

'Who was the first?'

'Mrs Harris from next-door. She's been waiting downstairs, because I had to ask someone to stay here while I was with Mummy.'

'When did you go?' I asked. 'You were both here when I went to bed.'

Daddy smiled. 'Mummy thought the baby was coming soon, so we waited for a while to make sure. Then I fetched Mrs Harris, and Mr Harris drove us to the hospital. I had to wait while the doctors and nurses looked after Mummy, but getting to hold your baby sister was worth it.'

'I'm glad you told me second, Daddy.' I reached for his hand and squeezed. 'I love you.'

'Love you too, Jan.' He turned out the light and padded from the room, closing the door behind him.

Alone again in the darkness, I couldn't sleep. I had a sister! Questions whirled through my mind. Would the baby have brown hair, the same as me, Daddy, and the boys, or blonde hair like Mummy? It would be nice if it was blonde, so Mummy wouldn't be the odd one out.

'Yes, I hope she's like Mummy.' Giving up on sleep, I tiptoed out of bed, pulled back my curtains and gazed up into a star-dappled sky. 'And she's got to have a pretty name. It needs to be better than horrible, boring Janet.'

I played quietly with my dolls and teddies until the sun rose. Then, at the first hint of the household waking, I rushed downstairs, eager for breakfast.

'My tummy's making funny noises.' I bounced into the kitchen and took my seat at the table.

'You're full of beans this morning,' Daddy said. He was making breakfast which seemed strange, because Mummy always did it. Malcolm and David were already munching slices of toast. 'Is it because of our special news?'

I watched my brothers, waiting for their reaction as Daddy told them about their sister. But they barely looked up!

'Aren't you excited?' I asked, completely confused.

'What's there to get excited about?' Ten-year-old Malcolm shrugged. 'It's only a baby.'

'No, it's not! She's our sister!' I turned to David, hoping for more enthusiasm, but my eldest brother only seemed interested in his toast.

'Ignore them, Jan,' Daddy said. 'They're boys, and boys don't care about babies.'

'You're a boy, Daddy. And you care. You woke me up to tell me.'

'Of course. She's my daughter.'

'She's just another sister,' 12-year-old David rose and scraped back his chair. 'And we know they're annoying because we've already got you.'

Protest was on the tip of my tongue, but before I could respond, Daddy successfully diverted the conversation.

After David and Malcolm had gone to find their friends, I cornered Daddy with the question that was uppermost in my mind. 'I know you said Mummy and our baby can't come home yet, but will you take me to see them?'

My nose screwed up as he ruffled my hair. 'I expect they'll let you in for a quick visit as long as you're quiet.'

'I will be, Daddy. I'm five now and I'm a big sister, so I'll be really grown-up.'

I returned to my bedroom in search of the ideal gift for the precious new arrival. I would make Mummy a card – Mummy loved home-made cards and drawings. But what could I give a baby? Even though my baby sister would have her pick of the old toys stashed away on the top of my wardrobe, her first present had to be extra special.

As my eyes roamed the room, I caught sight of Billy, the stuffed bear I slept with every night. There was nothing I loved or valued more than my oldest friend. Could I really give him up? Cradling Billy in my arms, I studied his well-worn fur. My sister should have something new, but nothing would show the depth of my love more than giving away my best friend.

'I'm not gonna cuddle you at night no more, Billy.' I spoke tenderly as I kissed the bear's velvety nose. 'Someone else is going to be your mummy now, and I bet she'll love you as much as I do. I'm sad cos I've gotta say goodbye, but we'll still see each other every day. When she's bigger, my sister will sleep in here with me, and you'll live on her bed, not mine.' I tucked the bear under my arm, then skipped downstairs in response to Daddy's call.

'Why are you bringing Billy?' he asked.

'I want to give him to my sister.'

Daddy's eyes welled, like when he watched the news sometimes. 'She'll have her own teddies. You don't have to give her Billy.'

'I want her to have Billy because I love him best of all, and now I'm gonna love her too.'

'That's so kind.' He scooped me up into a heartfelt hug, then said it was time to leave.

I held my father's hand as we waited for the bus and sat on his lap as we travelled. While watching the familiar streets speed by, I wondered how far it was to the hospital.

'What's it like, Daddy?' I pressed my nose to the glass.

'The hospital? It's a place where ladies go to have their babies. The doctors and nurses look after them until they're ready to come home.'

'Will there be lots of babies?'

'I expect so.'

'I bet ours is the prettiest,' I said, drawing a face in the steam on the glass. When Daddy tried to say that all babies were special, I was adamant. 'Ours is the specialist cos she came from Jesus.'

'Specialist...?' Daddy tweaked my nose.

We soon arrived at the red-brick cottage hospital in the centre of town, and a nurse guided us into the ward where Mummy sat up in bed cradling her newborn daughter.

'She's like my baby doll,' I whispered, clutching Daddy's hand more tightly.

'There she is. There's my Janet,' Mummy beamed. 'Have you come to meet Sylvia?'

'Sylvia...?' I breathed the beautiful word in a reverential whisper. 'Is that her name?'

'Your father told me to choose, and I like Sylvia.'

'I do too.' I crept closer to the metal-framed bed.

'What do you think?'

When Mummy held Sylvia out for closer inspection, my heart skipped. She had a tiny tuft of blonde hair! 'She looks like you, Mummy,' I said, gently stroking the top of her head. 'Hello, Sylvia.'

'Yes. We've finally got another blonde in the family. Would you like to hold her?'

'Can I?' I was awe-struck. What if I hurt the most precious bundle in the world?

'I know you'll be gentle. You're a very responsible girl,' Mummy encouraged.

Daddy lifted me onto the bed, ready to receive Sylvia in my arms. As Mummy showed me how to support the baby's head, she smiled indulgently.

'I wish we had a camera,' Daddy bemoaned.

'I don't need pictures,' Mummy murmured into my ear. 'I'm going to carry this scene in my mind forever. Our two girls having their first cuddle.'

'I'm your big sister,' I crooned, then leaned down to place a gentle kiss on Sylvia's forehead. 'I asked Jesus for you, and now you're here. I love you.'

As we returned home on the bus, I saw the surrounding beauty with new eyes. The spring flowers were in full bloom, their colours more vibrant than ever. I hoped my sister would love them as much as I did. The pink ones were my favourites, because I loved pink. Purple and yellow came next. I'd inherited my love of gardening from Mummy, and before leaving the hospital, I'd promised to remind Daddy and the boys to water the plants so they wouldn't die while Mummy was away.

Back at home, I took my dolls into the garden. Positioning them in a circle around me, I addressed them in sombre tones. 'I can't play with you and tell you stories anymore. I'll need to help Mummy take care of my baby sister. I'm big now. I'm not the baby. Sylvia is. You mustn't sulk and be naughty. When she's bigger, Sylvia will play with you too, and we'll give you tea parties and picnics. Mummy's going to teach me to knit, so I'll make you new clothes, and Sylvia will dress you up for parties. We'll have lots of fun, but I've got to make sure nothing bad happens to her. She's only little. She won't know when she's got to be careful. She might put things in her mouth. I'll have to stop her doing that, so she doesn't choke.'

I lay back on the lawn, gazing into the sun-dappled sky. Truly, this was the best day of my life. I would remember it forever. When Sylvia was older, I'd tell her how I'd visited the hospital and held her just hours after her birth. I would tell her about my prayers for a sister, and how Jesus had answered with a perfect miracle. The stories in the Children's Bible my parents had given me for Christmas were my favourite. Mummy read it to me at night, because of the big words, but by the time Sylvia was old enough to understand, I would be able to read.

As my eyes grew heavy, I planned the wonderful things me and Sylvia would do, and I drifted into a peaceful sleep. This time, there were no fairies and winged angels dressed in white. Instead, my dreams centred on a child with long blonde hair, laughing and swinging her hand as we danced together amongst the flowers.

3

'Sylvie? Sylvie?' I stood on the front doorstep craning my neck. My five-year-old sister was nowhere in sight. I spotted one of the neighbouring children and waved her over. 'Have you seen my sister?'

'She was playing with Will Sloane.'

I sighed and rolled my eyes. Although Sylvia knew our mother disapproved of the Sloane family with their rubbish-strewn front garden, the neighbourhood newcomers fascinated my imp of a little sister. She was especially impressed by their eight children.

'Where do they all sleep, Jan?' the curious girl had asked me some weeks earlier. 'Their house has three bedrooms like ours, and Mummy says that's too small for six people, never mind ten.'

'I don't know.' I suspected the Sloane children lay top to tail, squashed into their single beds. I didn't want to think about how uncomfortable that would be, so I quickly changed the subject.

If our mother found out Sylvia was at the Sloanes again, there would be trouble, and my self-appointed mission was to protect my adventurous little sister from our mother's wrath at all costs. Cupping my hands to my mouth, I called out our special rhyme. 'Sylvia Pew! Where are you?'

Within moments, a small, blonde-haired figure came skipping towards me, a huge grin lighting up her elfin face.

'Is it time for tea?'

I held the wooden gate open for Sylvia to pass through, then closed it firmly behind her. 'It will be soon. What have you been doing?'

'Something really exciting!' Sylvia's eyes danced with glee as she reached for my hand. 'Can I tell you?'

'You were at the Sloanes, weren't you?' I narrowed my eyes, and Sylvia's baby blues lost some of their sparkle.

Wearing my most earnest big-sisterly expression, I gazed down at her. 'Mum said she doesn't want you going there.'

'Why doesn't Mummy like the Sloanes?' Sylvia always pushed for explanations, whereas I accepted our mother's authority.

'Just because.' I hoped my stern glare would be enough to inform Sylvia the subject was closed.

'But they've got a cat,' Sylvia gushed, as if this was the perfect excuse for defying our mother's orders.

I fought not to smile, but the corners of my mouth betrayed me. 'I should have guessed there'd be an animal involved.' I gently squeezed my sister's shoulder. 'Any furry creature arrives in the neighbourhood, and you have to make a new friend.'

'I wish we could have a pet.' Sylvia's sigh reflected the uselessness of this oft-repeated wish.

'Mum will never say yes.' I tried to inject a note of sympathy into my voice, even though I agreed with our mother. Animals were messy. 'You'll have to make do with visiting other people's pets.'

'Except that boring tortoise.' Sylvia laughed. 'I'm not gonna bother going to see her again. All she does is sleep and eat and poke her head in and out of her shell. She doesn't know how to play.' She paused for a breath, then continued. 'Will's cat's name is Scratch. I told him that's a brilliant name for a cat. It is, isn't it, Jan?'

'It is a good name.' I smiled. 'Cats scratch a lot.'

'Is that why Mummy says we can't have one?'

'Maybe.' Perhaps this would satisfy her.

'Cats can be naughty.' Sylvia exhaled dramatically. 'Scratch scratched a big hole in Will's school trousers. It was in the knee, so he didn't mind.'

'His mother didn't let him wear them with a hole in, did she?' I couldn't hide my horror.

'No, only till she mended them.'

'Our mum would never let us go to school with holes in our clothes.' My opinion of our neighbours was rapidly sinking as low as my mother's.

'But Mummy says it costs lots of money to buy our clothes, and there's only four of us. I bet it costs even more to buy clothes for eight of them,' Sylvia reasoned before dancing ahead into the house, where Mum, Dad, and the boys waited at the dinner table.

'Have you been on your adventures again?' Dad asked, opening his arms, then lifting Sylvia onto his lap.

I skittered into the kitchen behind my sister, automatically rushing to help our mother while Sylvia chattered. I steeled myself for trouble when Sylvia let it slip about the cat, but Dad just laughed, forcing Mum to bite her tongue.

'So now there's a cat and eight kids.' He sounded amused.

'Soon to be nine.' Mum let out a derisive snort.

'Why did you and Daddy only have four?' Sylvia asked.

'Because four is quite enough,' Mum dished up our meals while I held out the plates.

We worked seamlessly, like one person. My father often commented that it was like watching a well-oiled machine. We read each other's needs without explanation. Sometimes we cajoled Sylvia into helping, but it only worked if I turned it into a game. Even then, Sylvia soon tired and gave up in favour of her toys. If Mum became frustrated, I doubled my efforts to make up for the things my sister refused to do. It was no bother to me because I loved household tasks.

Sylvia was the family's golden girl, the firm favourite. Our teenage brothers mostly ignored me, but Sylvia's bounciness made her impossible to dismiss. Every day presented a new opportunity for adventure. Her zest for life was contagious, and she monopolised every family meal. Her chatter brought sunshine into our lives, and her unwavering love was a uniting force.

I had remained faithful to the vows I'd made five years earlier. As Sylvia's main protector, I was rewarded with the satisfaction of being the first person the little girl ran to for comfort. When Sylvia was ill, it was me she wanted, so I devoted hours to smoothing her forehead and spinning tales. We were opposites, both in looks and personality. Sylvia had inherited our mother's delicate features, coupled with our father's outgoing nature. She was the picture of innocence, yet our petite blonde was on the verge of becoming a tomboy.

Once the kitchen had been cleaned, 15-year-old Malcolm dashed off to play football in the park with his friends, and seventeen-year-old David escaped to his girlfriend's house.

I lay curled up on the sofa with a book while Sylvia ran back and forth, pretending she had a cat called Mittens with a naughty habit of unravelling balls of wool. Thankfully, her imagination was vivid enough to ensure no actual wool was necessary for the game. Sylvia rarely needed real props to enhance her play.

'Do you think it's serious?' Mum's voice drifted in through the open window. My parents were sitting outside, enjoying the late September sunshine.

'David and Sarah?' Dad asked. 'I suppose they have been dating for a while.'

'He's so young.'

'I knew I loved you when I was 17.'

'But I kept you waiting.' I heard the humour in my mother's voice. I suspected that if I was brave enough to peep out of the window, I would catch my parents either kissing or holding hands. I loved their displays of affection, assuring me that even after 18 years, they still loved one another.

I hoped for a happy marriage like theirs. When I had confided my yearnings to my mother, she'd dismissed them by insisting I was far too young for soppy romantic notions. Still, having a family of my own remained my secret goal. I couldn't picture a more fulfilling life than that of a wife and mother.

'I can't imagine David being very patient,' Dad chuckled.

'No. He's always lived life in a hurry. At least he's holding down a good job.'

David had left the secondary modern school at 15 to start an apprenticeship in the building trade. Two years on, he had earned a reputation as a hard worker. By comparison, Malcolm would remain at the local grammar school for another three years, aiming to gain a place at university. I hoped to get into the grammar school too. The results of my 11+ examinations would arrive any day. I had worked so hard, and my teachers were optimistic, praising my writing skills in particular. I loved making up stories, and I'd had plenty of practice because Sylvia was a willing audience.

There was a lull in the chatter. I supposed Mum and Dad were simply enjoying relaxing in one another's company. Finally, Dad broke the silence.

'I'm afraid I've got some bad news, Carol.' He sounded hesitant. 'I've been putting off telling you, but I can't keep doing that.'

'You seemed tense when you came home from work. I was waiting for you to tell me something.'

'I thought I'd hidden it well.'

'You put on a brave face for the children.' Mum lowered her voice, so I shuffled closer to listen. 'But your smile came from your mouth, not your eyes.'

Thinking back over our meal, I realised Mum was right. Dad's laughter had been hollow, and Sylvia's chatter had made up for his quietness.

'Thanks for not prying.' Dad's tone now matched Mum's.

'You always tell me when you're ready.'

I put my book down, giving my parents my full attention. What was my father about to say? I hoped Sylvia wouldn't come back in to distract me.

'I got laid off today.'

'Why?' Mum's voice faltered.

'They're blaming cutbacks, like always. I suppose it's an easy excuse.'

My eyebrows narrowed over the previously unheard words. What were cutbacks? And what was being laid off? The solemnity in my parents' voices told me something devastating had happened.

'I'm sorry, Bob.' Mum didn't sound angry. She was sad. 'Don't worry. You'll find another job soon. You always do.'

I sucked in my breath as understanding hit like a thunderbolt. If Dad didn't have a job, how would we manage? Would Malcolm have to leave school? Would Mum have to find work?

'It helps that I've got a wife who believes in me.' My father's voice broke into my worrying thoughts.

'We've never gone without.'

At that moment, Sylvia charged into the room, demanding my full attention. 'Mittens has gone to sleep now. I told him he's a naughty cat, so he had to get in his box.'

'I don't think cats listen like dogs,' I forced myself into her imaginary world. Thankfully, Sylvia was too young to sense my fear.

'Mittens will learn to listen, cos I'm gonna make him go in his box every time he's naughty.'

Ah, life was so simple when you were an innocent child.

'It's time for bed, Sylvie.' Mum appeared in the doorway, her expression giving nothing away. Sylvia ran over with her usual exuberance and wrapped her arms around her waist.

'Can Jan put me to bed?' she asked.

'Are you hoping for one of her stories?'

'Jan makes up the best stories!'

'She definitely does.' Mum's smile didn't reach her eyes.

I ushered Sylvia upstairs and supervised while she cleaned her teeth, knowing she would neglect this task if we let her, then helped with her pyjamas.

'You've gotta brush it a hundred times,' Sylvia said, thrusting her hairbrush into my hand.

'I don't think so.'

'Yes, you do, cos it makes it shiny. I know,' Sylvia was bursting with ideas tonight, 'you brush mine a hundred times, and I'll brush yours.'

'While I'm telling you a story?' I asked, already sure of the answer.

'No.' Sylvia frowned. 'I can't count while I'm listening.'

The hair brushing seemed to take an eternity, and Sylvia lost count when it was her turn. Finally, she let me put her to bed.

'What story do you want tonight?' I asked, knowing what the answer would be.

'One about my cat.'

'Your cat called Mittens.' I laughed, then began creating my tale.

Sometime later, following the story in which Mittens got into mischief whilst skulking around our neighbourhood by night, Sylvia was ready for sleep.

'Have Mr and Mrs Harris really got a window they leave open so a cat can sneak into their house and steal food from their kitchen?' she asked with a yawn.

'I hope not.' I tucked the covers more tightly around her, knowing they would be rumpled by morning because Sylvia was a restless sleeper. 'Stories are made up, remember?'

'I bet there are true ones.'

'Well, yes. One day, we'll be able to tell our children and grandchildren true stories about our lives.'

'Like about growing up in the same street as the Sloanes and their eight kids?' Sylvia asked.

'And David's job, and Malcolm getting into the posh school.'

'You're gonna go there too.' She had so much faith in me.

'I don't know.' I sighed. 'It's harder for girls to get into good schools. But if I manage it, perhaps you will too.'

'No.' My lazy little sister dismissed the suggestion with a toss of her hair. 'Malcolm said they make him work really hard, and I don't like hard work.'

'You definitely don't.' I giggled as I bent to give her a goodnight kiss. 'I'll see you in the morning. Goodnight, and sleep tight.'

'And watch the bedbugs don't bite!' Sylvia grinned.

I shuddered at the thought of the nasty creatures, convinced Sylvia wouldn't be so enthusiastic if she found one in her bed.

As Sylvia drifted into dreamland, I curled up on my bed, retrieving the book I had cast aside in my efforts to hear my parents' conversation. Books were my best friends, and I needed one that night more than ever. Losing myself in a story inspired me to make up my own. When I had asked my father if there were people who wrote for a living, he'd told me they were called authors. I hadn't divulged my secret ambition, but I felt sure that was what I wanted to be. I would write children's stories like the ones I told Sylvia, but I wouldn't do that until my own children left home. And I wanted four children, like my mother, so waiting for them to grow up might take a long time.

Reading helped me dismiss the worries about Daddy's job. I escaped into a fantasy world until it was time to close my book and settle down for the night. Mum was right. Dad would find another, because he was a hard-working man, and everyone loved and respected him. Plus, it would be okay because Jesus loved our family. He knew we needed money for food and clothes. We didn't expect to be rich. We just needed to get by. I reminded Jesus of this in my bedtime prayers as I turned out my nightlight and cuddled up under the heavy blanket, just in case He'd forgotten.

4

Three weeks passed, with my father looking for work every day, only to return home each evening with a heavy step. Had Jesus closed His ears to my prayers? Stony silences replaced Dad's cheerful humour. Even Sylvia's antics around the dinner table failed to lift his dark mood. Sometimes he snapped, telling her to be quiet and finish her meal. When he allowed his frustration to show, Mum averted her gaze, but I always noticed her tears.

One night when sleep refused to come, I snuck downstairs for a cup of warm milk. Mum had always given us warm drinks when we couldn't sleep. On my way to the kitchen, I overheard my parents arguing through the closed living room door. I knew it was wrong, but I couldn't resist sitting on the stairs to listen. Raised voices had been a rarity in our home, but now they were becoming more common.

'I'll take in washing, Bob.' Mum sounded desperate. 'It wouldn't earn much, but it'd be something.'

'Over my dead body!'

I sprinted upstairs on tiptoes as my father's voice moved closer. Moments later, the front door slammed with a force that shook the house.

I collapsed upon the landing, curling myself into a tight ball, all thoughts of comforting warm milk forgotten. I had never heard my father so consumed by anger. My heart pounded as my mind swirled with a reel of worst-case scenarios.

Eventually, I pulled myself together, uncurled, and returned to my room, where Sylvia sat in bed with the light on.

'What was the big bang, Jan?' My little sister held out her arms, and I hugged her tightly.

'It's okay,' I whispered. 'Go back to sleep.'

'It was Daddy, wasn't it? He's cross again.'

I nodded soberly.

'I don't like it when he's cross.' Sylvia clung even tighter.

'He'll be okay. Everyone gets cross sometimes.' But I didn't feel the confidence I was trying to convey.

My reassurances eventually settled my sister, but I prayed even harder that night, begging Jesus to please find work for our dad.

The following evening, I was working with Mum in the kitchen when Dad burst into the house. We snapped our heads up in unison but, although he closed the front door with a thud, I could tell Dad wasn't angry. He was whistling! Surely this was a sign of good news? I couldn't recall the last time I'd heard him whistle, and excited butterflies fluttered in my stomach.

'Who wants a surprise?' His voice boomed from the hallway as we heard him kicking off his outdoor shoes.

Sylvia ran in response to his call, and Dad swung her into his arms as he carried her into the kitchen.

'What's the surprise, Daddy?' Sylvia's blue eyes danced.

'What's going on, Bob?' Mum's rolling pin stilled, suspended in mid-air over a sheet of pastry, and I sucked in a breath of eager anticipation.

'I've got great news.' Dad smiled over Sylvia's head. 'Can't you tell?'

'Well, yes, you seem happy.' Abandoning the rolling pin with a clatter, Mum crossed to stand beside him. The butterflies tickled my bellybutton. Could I dare to hope Jesus had answered my prayers?

'I've found a job, and it's better than anything I've had before.' Dad planted a kiss on Mum's cheek.

'What job, Daddy?' Sylvia asked.

'Hugh Roberts said the blokes at the council need men to work in the pest control department, so I went to find out.'

'What's pest control?' I wondered aloud.

My father grinned. 'Getting rid of rats, mice and insects, like wasps in the summer.'

'What do you know about that?' Mum asked, chewing on her bottom lip. Why was she worried? Was it something Dad couldn't do? Were we going to be let down, again?

'They'll give me training.'

Mum's face finally relaxed into a genuine smile.

'It's good, steady work,' he continued. 'They say once you're in with the council, you've got a job for life.'

'I've heard that too. This is brilliant news. I'm so proud of you.' She wrapped her arms around him, kissing him on the lips in full view of me and Sylvia. 'When do you start?'

'On Monday.' The chatter continued as I made Dad's coffee and Mum returned to the rolling pin. However, Sylvia was unusually quiet, and I sensed more questions coming. Sure enough, it wasn't long before curiosity put paid to our parents' calm conversation.

'Daddy, what will you do with the animals?'

'What animals?' Our father seemed to be caught off guard.

'The ones you've gotta get rid of for the council.'

Considering Sylvia's passion for living things, I hoped he'd choose his answer carefully.

'The thing is, Sylvie,' Dad explained patiently, 'some animals spread disease, and if they get into places where there's food, they can make people ill. That's why they have to go.'

'Go where?'

'Well, I have to get rid of them.'

'How?' Sylvia persisted.

Our father sighed before choosing the honest approach. 'With poison or traps.'

'You're going to kill them?' Sylvia's blue eyes misted over. 'You can't do that. It's cruel!'

'They're rodents, love,' Mum reasoned. 'They're ten-a-penny, and if people didn't kill them, we'd be overrun with vermin.'

'But they're God's creatures, like us,' Sylvia insisted.

Sylvia's disappointment over our father's choice of career wasn't easily abated, even when he came home two weeks later with a brand-new work vehicle. Malcolm and David begged for a chance to drive, and even I couldn't wait to tell my classmates about our family's shiny new van.

'We can go on holiday,' Malcolm suggested one Saturday afternoon, having been coaxed into helping me with the washing up.

'How can we do that?' I asked. 'It's only got two seats.'

'Mum and Dad can ride in the front, and we'll pile into the back on blankets. We could go on a camping trip.'

'They might only let Dad use it for work,' I tossed a handful of knives and forks onto the draining board to be quickly gathered up by my brother.

'They told Dad we can use it as long as we're sensible.'

Our family soon settled into the convenience of having our own means of transport. Even Sylvia stopped referring to our father as a murderer.

'It's still bad, Jan,' she insisted in the privacy of our bedroom. 'If I found out where they were hiding, I'd help them get away before Daddy sets his traps or gives them the nasty poison.'

'I'm sure a lot of them still escape.' I methodically combed Sylvia's freshly washed hair.

'How do they know when Daddy's coming? They can't talk, so they can't tell each other to hide.' My comb caught on a tangle and Sylvia let out a squeal of protest.

'If God wants them to survive, I guess He makes sure they're in the right place at the right time.' My explanation seemed to mollify my sensitive sister, because Sylvia rarely mentioned the creatures after that.

Autumn soon turned into winter, with its short days and freezing nights. I surprised Sylvia with icy pictures hastily drawn on our bedroom window each morning, reminding her that Christmas was just around the corner. Everyone planned their special gifts, and David announced his engagement to Sarah, which came as no surprise. He was confident that by the following summer, they would be eligible for a council house.

Being ten years old, I no longer believed in the magic of Father Christmas, but Sylvia did, and we relished the chance to indulge our golden girl. I loved helping Mum organise her surprises. We wrote greeting cards and letters to distant friends and family, which Sylvia and I carried to the postbox on a particularly cold Saturday afternoon bundled up in coats, scarves and gloves.

After meticulously counting each envelope she posted, Sylvia skipped home, waving at friends and strangers alike as her scarf fringes flew. 'The postmen must have loads of cards and letters to sort out at Christmas time. I bet they get really tired and fed up,' she called to me between leaps.

'Maybe they get extra people to help.' I mused.

Sylvia stopped skipping and hung upon my arm. 'Will you have extra special nice things for Christmas cos you did so well in your big exam?' she asked.

I was proud to have passed my 11+ with flying colours. The prospect of joining Malcolm at the grammar school the following September was all the reward I needed. However, for Sylvia's sake, I pretended to mull over my answer to her question before saying, 'I doubt it.' I hoped my little sister would receive the bulk of the gifts because her excitement would bring us all joy.

Back at home, we found our father cleaning his van.

'Can we help?' Sylvia asked.

Dad brandished the dirty, dripping cloth. 'Your mum won't want you getting wet in this cold weather.'

'You're too little to carry water, anyway.' I nudged Sylvia towards the house. 'The buckets are heavy, so you'd spill it. I'll help Dad.'

I worked until the vehicle shone, beaming at my father's words of affirmation.

When Dad stood back with his arms folded over his chest, admiring his gleaming vehicle, he asked, 'Do you want to see something special?' His teasing tone told me an adventure was coming.

'Is it one of your Christmas surprises?' I asked.

'No. To tell the truth, I'm in a bit of a quandary, and I think you're the ideal person to help.'

I brimmed with pride. I liked the prospect of helping my father. It made me feel grown-up and important. My excitement grew as he led me towards the garden shed, only releasing me to unlock and prise open the door, which protested with loud, ear-jarring squeaks.

'I need to oil that.'

'You've been saying that since the summer,' I teased.

'And your mother's always lecturing me about putting important things off.'

It took my eyes a moment to adjust as he led me inside and pointed at an object tucked away in a far corner.

I squinted through the gloom. 'What is it?'

Dad nudged me forward, and I cautiously ventured further into his untidy domain. I rarely went into the shed because Mum insisted it wasn't safe.

Suddenly, I spotted a wicker basket on the ground with something moving inside. 'Kittens!'

'Three of them,' Dad said. 'And judging by their size, they're still very young.'

I knelt to inspect the contents of the basket. When I reached out a tentative finger, I was greeted with happy meows.

'I've never seen such tiny kittens,' I whispered as the new occupants of my father's shed scratched and played. 'Why have you got them?'

Dad knelt beside me, putting his arm around my shoulders. 'Mostly, I love my new job, Jan, but there are some things I'd rather not do.'

I waited patiently for him to continue, gazing in wonder at the squirming evidence of new life.

'I was called to a building that's being converted into a café. The new owners discovered they had some rather unwelcome guests.' He squeezed my shoulders.

'Where's the mother?'

'She wasn't there when they found them, and she hadn't come back when they sent for me.'

I gasped, unwilling to believe any mother would abandon her babies. 'She must've been feeding them.'

'Perhaps she was out hunting for food. There was a smashed window, so I expect she used that to get in and out.'

'She's going to be sad when she finds out they're gone.' My tender heart ached for the mother cat.

'She won't be able to get back in, because they've boarded up the window.'

'I don't understand. Why did they send for you?' My eyes were continually being drawn to the antics of the kittens. 'You're supposed to get rid of pests, not cats.'

Dad snorted. 'We're paid to clear out any animals, and I think we can both understand why kittens running around a place you're trying to turn into a café would be a nuisance. We're lucky the café owner didn't just dispose of them himself. I bet lots of people would.' He absentmindedly stroked a kitten's silky fur.

'How?' I regretted my question the moment it came out of my mouth.

Daddy hesitated before answering. 'People drown them.'

That did it. My mouth hung open in horror and tears pricked the back of my throat.

'I think that's what they were expecting me to do. Perhaps they couldn't bring themselves to do it, so they were hoping I would.'

'You can't!' I turned to him with pleading eyes.

'That's why I brought them here.' He smiled and kissed the tip of my nose. 'Your old dad's a softie, Jan. Surely you know that.'

'They can't stay in your shed.'

'I was hoping you'd help me.' He drew me closer. 'Do you suppose any of your school friends might want a kitten?'

'Maybe.' I sat back on my heels, watching the tiny animals at play, oblivious to the peril from which they had been saved. 'But we both know someone who does.' A plan was forming. 'She wants a kitten more than anything else in the world.'

'Sylvia.' Dad ran his fingers through his thinning hair. 'That's as maybe, but your mother's made her feelings clear.'

'We'll talk her round.' Enthusiasm made me confident. 'Once she's seen them, how could she not love them? They're so cute!'

'You think we can work on her?' he chuckled.

'We'll tell her about the benefits of having a cat. It would kill mice, and Mum hates them even more than she hates cats.'

'True.'

Was he warming to my idea? *Please, Jesus? Just imagine how excited Sylvie will be if she gets her kitten!*

'Did she ask for a cat in her letter to Father Christmas?' Dad asked.

'Of course.' We exchanged a conspiratorial wink. 'It was at the top of her list. Next was a dog. Mum definitely wouldn't go for that. Too much mess.'

'At least cats train themselves.'

'If there is any mess, I promise to clean it up.'

'You'll do anything for your little sister. You're a born mother, Janet Pew.' He patted my head.

I cared diligently for my tiny charges until I found homes for two of them with my classmates. We also worked on Mum until she finally relented. When Dad gave me the choice of which kitten to keep, I picked the smallest, an adorable black and white ball of fur, certain Sylvia would love him.

My brothers and I stayed up late on Christmas Eve, creeping around the house and helping to decorate as a special treat for our youngest sister. I made paper chains with Mum, while Malcolm and David blew up brightly coloured balloons and strung them in various places. Dad brought in a tree, and everyone chipped in to hang the tinsel, lights, and baubles. We ended the evening with mugs of steaming cocoa and mince pies, while the tree lights twinkled, and we admired our handiwork.

Sylvia shrieked with delight when she ran down in the morning and saw the decorations and presents. Then Dad made her sit by the tree and close her eyes as he gently placed the cat on her lap.

On opening her eyes, Sylvia sat still in disbelief. Then her excitement became infectious. 'He did it, Daddy! Father Christmas brought me a cat!'

'That he did.' Dad hugged her, cat and all.

A cloud crossed Sylvia's little face. 'Is Mummy going to be cross?'

'Not as long as you teach him how to behave.' Our mother smiled indulgently. 'What are you going to call him?'

Of course, I already knew the answer.

'Mittens!'

5

'Aren't you ready yet?'

Malcolm stood in the living room doorway, glaring as I struggled downstairs carrying two heavy holdalls. Of course, he wouldn't have considered offering to help. My tardiness was clearly testing what little restraint my brother could muster. School had broken up for Easter, Sylvia had celebrated her sixth birthday, and we were preparing to leave for our first proper family holiday.

'I can't find Sylvie.' I let the bags thump to the floor and glanced over my brother's shoulder, searching the living room with my eyes. 'Can you take these out to the van while I look for her?'

'She'll be fussing over her cat.' Malcolm snorted.

'She thinks he's her baby.' I dismissed his derision with a laugh. 'She's worried about leaving him, even though Mrs Harris has promised to feed him. Dad keeps telling her cats are independent, but Sylvie is sure Mittens will cry for her.'

'I sometimes wish Dad hadn't given her that stupid animal. It's all she ever talks about.' Malcolm bent to pick up the bags.

'You can't wish that.' I glared at him with my hands firmly planted on my hips. 'Sylvie adores Mittens. And she's been great about looking after him. Mum thought she'd get bored after a couple of weeks, but it's been nearly four months, and she's still doing everything we taught her.'

'I suppose.' Even Malcolm couldn't deny our sister's devotion to her pet.

'I bet she's in the back garden. I'll fetch her.'

I dashed through the kitchen and out into the garden, where my assumptions were confirmed. Sylvia sat on the patio wall talking soberly to Mittens, who purred contentedly on her lap.

'Remember, you've gotta be a good boy,' she crooned. 'Mrs Harris will look after you, so eat all your food, and don't cry for me. I'll be back in three days. And three days isn't long.'

'Time to go, Sylvie.' I positioned myself directly in front of her to ensure Sylvia couldn't ignore me. 'Dad and Malcolm are loading the van. We're only waiting for you.'

Sylvia released her pet and rose reluctantly.

'Aren't you excited?' I asked. My sister's lack of enthusiasm came as a surprise. Sylvia usually jumped at every chance for a new adventure.

'A bit.' She didn't take her eyes off Mittens. 'It'd be more fun if he came too.'

'Cats can't go camping.'

Sylvia narrowed her eyes, preparing for an argument. 'Why not?'

'They're not like dogs.' I pushed back a strand of fine blonde hair. 'He might wander away and get lost. You'd be really upset if that happened. It's safer for him to stay here.'

Sylvia huffed her acceptance of this logic and bent to kiss her cat goodbye, with one last plea for him to be good. I took her hand, leading her through the house and out the front door, where our parents and Malcolm waited beside the van.

'I'll lock up.' Dad jingled his keys and turned to Mum. 'Are you sure we've got everything?'

'Don't give Mum and Jan the chance to bring more stuff,' Malcolm complained. 'The van's full enough as it is.'

'I've never been camping before,' Mum said, 'so I don't know what we'll need. It's better to have too much than to end up wishing we'd brought more.'

I helped Sylvia into the back of the van while Dad secured our home. We soon made ourselves comfortable with blankets and sleeping bags amongst our belongings. I suspected the van's motion would lull Sylvia to sleep, allowing me to enjoy my latest library book.

'It's a shame David isn't here to see us off,' Mum said, adjusting her seat as Dad took his place behind the wheel.

'He's got more important things on his mind,' Dad replied, then called jovially through the wire mesh that separated the seats from the back. 'Everyone ready?'

'Let's go, Daddy!' Sylvia gripped my hand. She had found her excitement.

As the van wound its way along unfamiliar country lanes, we played guessing games until Sylvia grew tired. She laid her head on my lap, dozing peacefully while Malcolm and I read. Dad concentrated on the road, and Mum peered out of the window, occasionally passing comment on the scenery.

Two hours later, our van came to a halt in a large field dotted with old trees giving shade. Dad had stopped briefly to get directions from the woman in the little shop at the entrance to the site, and I had peered through the window at the display of camping goodies and tinned food.

We tumbled out of the vehicle and sprung into the activities necessary for setting up camp. Malcolm and Dad erected the tents while Mum gave orders, and I acted as a gofer. Sylvia ran around, getting in everyone's way, while exclaiming over the surroundings and the camp's other occupants. She soon found other children to play with, and we heaved a collective sigh of relief.

'Not missing her cat so much now, is she?' Dad laughed as he cast his eagle eye over our temporary accommodation.

That night, I lay awake listening to the canvas flapping and the occasional call of a nocturnal creature. Was that a hedgehog I could hear, scratching? Somewhere in the distance, a dog howled. Owls hooted, and I shuddered at their mournful sound. I cuddled closer to Sylvia, hoping the warmth and familiarity of her presence would lull me to sleep. As the night wore on and sleep failed to come, I longed for home and my cosy bed. Camping wasn't for me, but I'd make the best of it for my family's sake.

The daylight hours were more pleasant. I helped my mother cook on our makeshift stove. I played games with Dad, Malcolm, and Sylvia, and even learned to build a campfire under Malcolm's superior direction. He'd earned his campfire badge at Scouts and revelled in showing off his newly acquired skills.

'We'll sit around it tonight after dark, toast marshmallows, and tell stories,' Malcolm said, sitting back on his heels to admire his handiwork.

I liked the sound of that. Maybe camping wouldn't be so bad after all. I might even sleep tonight after a full day of running around in the fresh air.

'Tell us a funny story, Daddy.' Sylvia lay curled up on our father's lap, her eyes heavy with sleep. The marshmallows were gone, and we sat around the fire, toasting our hands and feet instead.

'You should go to bed.' Mum wrapped a shawl around her youngest child.

'I will after Daddy tells us a story. Please, Daddy?' Sylvia's shrill voice pierced the night air. 'Just a tiny one.'

Dad's stories were quickly becoming as popular as mine. It had all started because his job kept placing him in unusual situations.

'Don't you dare tell us about fleas again! Do you hear me, Bob Pew?' Even mentioning them had Mum scratching her arm.

The previous week, Dad had been called to a house where the occupants had little value for cleanliness. Upon opening the front door, he was greeted by an army of hopping fleas. This escapade was Sylvia's favourite story, and she hadn't even questioned his need to exterminate the pests. However, our mum had shuddered, and the following day, she roped me into giving the house a thorough spring clean, *just in case.*

'No fleas,' Dad promised. 'What if I tell you one about gravestones instead?'

'Gravestones?' Mum put a hand to her mouth.

'That sounds more like a horror story.' Malcolm leant forward keenly.

'Don't you go scaring the girls, or they'll have nightmares.' Mum wagged a finger.

'There's nothing scary about it.' Dad paused for impact. 'It happened last Friday, when my boss sent me to help my mate, Chris, with a special job.'

'Why was it special?' Sylvia's eyes widened with excitement.

'It wasn't something we normally do. They wanted us to spray the weeds at a cemetery.'

'Why did you have to spray them?' Sylvia asked. 'Mummy and Jan just pull them out with their hands.'

'The cemetery is much bigger, so there are a lot more weeds.' Dad adjusted Sylvia on his lap. 'We needed to spray around the gravestones to stop them from taking over.'

'Did you have to use big watering cans?'

Sylvia was full of questions, but my mind remained fixated on the cemetery. I had visited a graveyard once with my mother, to put flowers on my grandfather's grave. Hating the eerie silence and the ominous-looking gravestones, I hid behind Mum the whole time, even though she'd assured me dead people couldn't hurt us. Now, the mere mention of death or dying was enough to send me into a panic. I held my breath and ran past the gateway to the local churchyard every time I walked down a certain road, taking a detour when possible, even though it meant I had further to walk.

An owl hooting made me jump, and Malcolm laughed at my skittishness.

'What's the matter, Jan?' he teased. 'Not scared of owls, are you?'

'I hate them.' I fidgeted restlessly. 'They sound like they're crying or something.'

'They're talking to one another,' Dad said. 'Like we're talking now.'

'Well, I wish they wouldn't.'

Malcolm leaned towards me, doing his best owl impression, and I rewarded him with a sharp dig in the ribs.

'Tell us more about the spraying, Daddy.' Sylvia nudged his chest.

'Oh, yes.' He gave her a squeeze. 'We hired a Land Rover with a tank and a huge hose. I'd never seen so many yards of hose. I was sure we'd get it tangled. Chris said he knew what to do, so I let him take control and I drove the Land Rover.'

I kept one ear open for eerie sounds as our father talked on. For once, I didn't want to hear his story. But there was nowhere to escape. A shudder ran through my body, and it wasn't because of the evening breeze. I was well wrapped up, and the cheerful fire blazed in front of me. I couldn't understand my unease. Was it just the mention of the graveyard and the melancholy hooting of the owls? What was there to fear?

'It started off okay,' Dad continued. 'I kept letting out the hose, and Chris went along spraying the weeds. Then I spotted something. I tried yelling at Chris, but he couldn't hear me over the noise of the Land Rover. Eventually, I switched the engine off and jumped out. He got pretty mad because I'd interrupted his work, until I showed him the problem. His hose had knocked over some vases on the gravestones. There were bits and pieces everywhere.'

Sylvia and Malcolm chuckled, but I stayed tight-lipped. Why was this innocent story affecting me so badly?

'I hope you put them back,' Mum tutted.

'We did our best,' Dad said. 'Chris wanted to carry on regardless, but I told him to be more careful. You've got to have respect for the dead.'

Another shiver ran down my spine, accompanied by an overwhelming urge to run away from my family and the fire. 'I'm tired.' I couldn't hide the tremor in my voice.

'Are you all right, love?' Mum reached out a cool hand.

'I didn't sleep last night.'

'You never have coped well with disruption to your routine. You're our little homebird.'

I accepted a quick hug before retreating to the tent and climbing into my sleeping bag. The shadows cast by the flames through the canvas walls were mesmerising. Allowing my imagination to run wild, I transformed the shapes into pictures, seeing fairies, angels, and dancing pixies. Then suddenly, the images became more sinister. The flames reminded me of death and the souls buried underground who might have been disturbed by my father and Chris in the cemetery. I had been taught that once a person was dead and buried, they never came back, but what if that wasn't true?

'Please, Jesus?' I breathed into the darkness. 'Please make these scary thoughts go away. I can't tell my family because they'll think I'm being silly. What am I so afraid of? I feel like something scary is going to happen. Please, Jesus, let me be wrong. Mum's always saying I've got an over-active imagination. Is it just that?'

I pretended to be asleep when Mum carried Sylvia into the tent and settled her with a goodnight kiss. As soon as she closed the zip, I wrapped myself around my sister, holding her close while trying to shut out the owls, the flames, and everything else.

Eventually, I fell into a restless sleep punctuated by nightmares. Sylvia was calling for help, but my feet remained glued to the ground. Tall weeds sprung up around my precious sister, and Sylvia screamed as the strange foliage wound its way around her body. Then the weeds turned into flames, licking at her hair and her dress. An owl swooped overhead, hooting menacingly, and my throat was so dry I couldn't even scream Sylvia's name.

I woke in a cold sweat, relieved to see light through the canvas. Careful not to disturb Sylvia, I crept outside, gulping deep breaths of morning air.

Melodic birdsong echoed through the trees. My Sunday school teacher said the birds sang God's praises, and this morning, I believed it. I stood listening, my dark thoughts and fears slowly evaporating into peace.

Screwing up my eyes against the glare of the morning light, I recalled a Bible verse I had memorised. *Be still, and know that I am God.* On a morning like this, it felt as though God was everywhere, and I needed to be still to fully appreciate Him.

'I'm sorry I was a scaredy-cat last night, Jesus,' I whispered. 'I guess Mum's right. I have got an overactive imagination. I should have known You were looking after us. You always do.'

6

The summer term was well underway, and I had already celebrated my 11th birthday when I received an invitation from a classmate to stay at her house overnight. I resisted the new experience at first. I'd never spent a night away from my family, but my mother's gentle persuasion changed my mind.

'You're at home far too much.' Mum reached into the peg bag as we worked side by side, hanging out washing in the sunshine.

'I'm happy here.' Everything and everyone I needed was contained within those familiar four walls.

'I know.' Mum patted my shoulder. 'But you're growing up now, and with a change of school coming up in September, it's important for you to spend more time with your friends.'

'I see them all week.' Why couldn't she understand that an enforced night away from home felt more like a punishment than a reward?

'You'll be glad I pushed you into it as soon as you and Ruth find something to enjoy together. You probably won't want to come home.'

I chewed my lip in an effort not to argue. Mum was wrong. Home was my favourite place, cocooned in the safety and love of my family. I wasn't especially close to any of the girls at school, so why had Ruth picked me for a sleepover? Surely, someone more outgoing would be a better choice.

'Where are you going?' Sylvia asked as she sat on her bed on Thursday evening, watching me packing my overnight bag.

'I'm staying with my friend Ruth tomorrow night.'

'Why?' My younger sister's startled response clarified that she, too, was surprised by this irregular turn of events. 'Why won't you come home to sleep? That's what happens when I play with my friends.'

'Ruth asked me to stay.' I didn't want to confess my nervousness to Sylvia. 'It'll be okay.' I suspended my packing to hug her. 'I'll only be gone for one night. I'll be back on Saturday, so we'll still be able to go to Sunday school together.'

'What if you get ill again?'

'Oh, I'm sure I'll be alright.' It was true that I had been suffering from a cold for the past week and had missed two days of school, but Mum had cleared me to return the previous day.

'I think I'm getting your cold now.' Sylvia sniffed and rubbed her eyes dramatically.

'It wasn't a bad one.' My task completed, I zipped up my bag.

'But who's gonna look after me tomorrow night if you're not sleeping in our room?' Sylvia wailed.

'Mum and Dad will still be here, and you'll have Mittens.'

'He can't tell me stories.' Turning her back on me, Sylvia sulked, and I tried not to laugh.

'Mum will let you sleep in her bed if you're really ill.'

Sylvia turned back, her blue eyes pooling with sadness. 'I want to sleep with you.' She threw herself into my waiting arms, sobbing dramatically.

'You can do that on Saturday. I know, why don't we have some cocoa and chocolate biscuits? That'll take your mind off it.'

By the time I left for school on Friday morning, carrying my overnight bag, my sister had indeed caught my cold. Sylvia lay in bed complaining, with a high temperature and a runny nose, but our mother was confident she'd bounce back.

'Don't worry about her,' Mum said when I pleaded Sylvia's cold as an excuse to pull out of the sleepover. 'Concentrate on enjoying yourself. Sylvie can put up with me looking after her for a change.' She laughed and gave me a hug.

After school, my adventure commenced with a bus journey, accompanied by Ruth and her eight-year-old brother, Clive. I was glad to have my friend sitting beside me, because I was sure I wouldn't have known what to do.

'What if we get off at the wrong stop?' I had never been on a bus without my parents or one of my older brothers.

'Don't worry,' Ruth looped her arm through mine. 'We do this every day. We're used to it.'

'Even I know where we get off!' Clive puffed out his little chest.

Blonde-haired, hazel-eyed Ruth was nine months older than me, having celebrated her 11th birthday the previous September.

'Are you excited about going to the posh school?' Ruth asked.

'I'm not sure,' I admitted. 'I won't have many friends. Sometimes I wish I could go to the secondary modern with the rest of you. At least I'd know everyone.'

'You'll make new friends.' Ruth brushed back her fringe.

I shrugged. I didn't share Ruth's confidence because I'd never found it easy to talk to strangers.

'It's okay.' Ruth hugged my arm. 'We can still go to each other's houses. I don't care if you're at the posh school and I'm at the ordinary one.'

I hadn't realised Ruth wanted to spend time with me. I vowed then and there to make more of an effort with our friendship. Perhaps I did need more than just my family.

Ruth's home was larger than ours. It felt posh because there were two sitting rooms, one of which contained plush furniture with soft velvet cushions. A grandfather clock stood pride of place in the tiled hallway, and I jumped the first time I heard it booming the hour. I might have felt uncomfortable if Ruth's family weren't so warm and welcoming, putting me at ease in their beautiful home. Ruth was the eldest of four, with the youngest only 18 months old. My maternal instinct kicked in and I latched onto the baby and three-year-old, who responded by shadowing my every movement.

Ruth offered to relinquish her bed, but I insisted on sleeping on the floor, suspecting I would struggle to rest in unfamiliar surroundings. I longed for Sylvia, even while Ruth distracted me with fun and chatter. We giggled in the darkness over Ruth's muddled attempts at knitting, and I promised to help her try again the following morning. My mother had taught me to knit at the age of seven. As the grandfather clock in the hallway struck midnight and Ruth surrendered to sleep, I wondered if this was how it felt to have a close friend. Could she fill a longing I hadn't known I possessed?

The following morning, Ruth suggested a visit to the local shops would be more interesting than knitting. After looking around and admiring the window displays, we found a café, where we sat at a square table covered by a blue and white gingham cloth, sipping tea from a silver teapot, which we poured into gold-rimmed bone china cups. Our attempts at picking the cups up daintily had us poking our little fingers out at odd angles as we tried to balance them without spilling the tea. Peals of laughter soon forced us to take a firmer grip.

We ordered scones rather than the iced fairy cakes designed to appeal to children, lavishly applying cream and jam, then washing them down with yet more tea, whilst indulging in an earnest game of make believe. We were posh ladies who lunched, with all the time in the world to commiserate with one another over our husbands' laziness and our children's misdemeanours.

'I was called to the school the other day because Freddie set fire to a pair of curtains.' Ruth softened her voice to imitate her mother.

'Oh no!' I hoped I looked suitably horrified. 'Why did he do that?'

'He's such a naughty boy.' Ruth folded her arms over an imaginary bosom. 'I've told him he won't be having any birthday presents, because his headmaster is making me pay for the curtains.'

I let my face slip, and Ruth slipped out of character, as a fit of giggles overtook us. 'Clive's always getting into trouble,' she said. 'Last year, our parents cancelled his birthday party to teach him a lesson.'

'Did it work?' I added more milk to my tea. It was getting stronger as we emptied the pot.

'No. You've seen what he's like.' We laughed again.

'I'm glad my brothers aren't like that.' I finished my tea, replacing the cup carefully on its saucer. 'They're just annoying teenagers.'

'Your sister's sweet.' Ruth smiled. 'I've seen the way you look after her at school.'

'I've done that ever since she was born. I was so happy when Mum told me she was having another baby.' I folded my napkin into a neat square. 'She and Dad thought I'd be their last, but I'd always wanted a sister, so I love taking care of her.'

'I get fed up with looking after my brother and sisters,' Ruth admitted. 'I hate it because being the oldest means I have to.'

We lingered at the café until the last possible moment, then returned to Ruth's home, where I expected to be picked up.

'Is your dad gonna come in his van?' Clive had roped us into a game of Snakes and Ladders.

'He's excited that your dad drives.' Ruth's counter climbed a ladder, and her brother scowled. 'We've never had a car. Our dad goes to work on the train, and Mum's never wanted to learn to drive.'

'The van isn't ours.' I took my turn, held my breath as I passed over the mouth of a snake, and handed the dice to Clive. 'Dad's mostly got it for work.'

'Your holiday at Easter sounded like so much fun.' Ruth put out a hand to stop her brother from bypassing another snake. 'Stop cheating, or we won't play!'

'Will your dad take me for a ride?' Clive asked. 'I've never been in a van.'

'If he's got time.' My father was a soft touch with children, so he'd probably make time.

Hours passed with no word from my parents, and my mind started playing tricks on me. Was Sylvia's cold worse? Was one of my brothers in trouble? Or had they simply forgotten me?

As the grandfather clock struck another hour, I could stand it no longer. 'Should I go home on the bus?' I asked Ruth's mother.

'I'm sure your parents wouldn't want you doing that.' Mrs Gray put a comforting hand on my shoulder. 'It's a lovely day. Perhaps they took your little sister out for a treat? I expect they'll pick you up on the way home.'

'Sylvie's got a cold.' I glanced out of the living room window for the umpteenth time.

'Little ones bounce back overnight.'

Although I had enjoyed my overnight visit, all I wanted now was to go home. The family continued to treat me with warmth, yet as the hours wore on, my unease grew until I thought I might burst. I sensed a tremor in my hands. Something was definitely wrong.

At seven o'clock, there was a knock on the front door. I followed Mrs Gray into the hallway and stood frozen to the spot when I saw David on the doorstep. Why had he come?

'Did Mum and Dad send you?' I reached for my overnight bag, which sat waiting against a wall.

'I need to talk to Mr and Mrs Gray.' Something in David's tone ratcheted my anxiety up several notches.

'Can't we just go home?' Couldn't he understand? I needed that more than ever, although I didn't know why.

'Dad wants you to stay here for a few more days.'

'Days?' My question came out as a squeak and my head spun.

'They've taken Sylvie to the hospital.' David looked past me, fixing his eyes on the living room door.

'What's the matter? Is it her cold?'

'Sort of.' David's vague response failed to calm my fears.

'No one goes to the hospital because of a cold,' I argued.

'Stop asking so many questions, Jan!' He nodded apologetically at Mrs Gray, then barged past me into the lounge. Ruth's mother followed with a frown, shutting the door firmly behind them.

I crumpled upon the bottom step of the staircase, overwhelmed by anxiety for my beloved little sister. Ruth and her siblings attempted to cheer me up, but I put my head in my hands, crying like a baby.

When David and Ruth's parents came out of the lounge
sometime later, and I begged again for permission to go home,
my pleas were answered by more frustration from my brother.

'There's no one there to take care of you.'

'You and Malcolm will be there. I can look after myself and
cook for you.' I gripped his arm, but David pulled free of my
grasp.

'Don't be a baby, Jan.' He stomped towards the door. 'I don't
know why you're making such a fuss. Most kids enjoy staying at
their friends' houses. Just be glad the Grays want to keep you.'

David was gone, and I stared after him in bewilderment. As
I turned back to Ruth's parents, an unfathomable glance passed
between them.

Mrs Gray addressed her children in a tone that left no room
for argument. 'I think you should go to the kitchen with your dad
for a warm drink.' They filed out as Mrs Gray pulled me close.
'You like it here with us, don't you?' she asked gently.

I nodded. I wanted to be polite, but the sudden change of
plans was unnerving. I willed my flow of childish tears to stop as
Ruth's mother offered comfort. Why was the knot in the pit of
my stomach getting tighter? Surely, something terrible had
happened. Why were my family determined to keep me in the
dark?

Mrs Gray stroked my back. 'Don't worry. You'll go home
soon enough. Just you wait and see.'

I rubbed at my red eyes. I needed to pull myself together
instead of allowing my imagination to run wild. My mind was
awhirl with dark and scary thoughts. Was Sylvia afraid at the
hospital? Was she crying for me to come and cheer her up with
a story? Was she coughing and struggling to breathe because
the cold had gone to her chest?

'Would you like to join us for hot chocolate?' Mrs Gray held
out her hand, and I took it politely.

'Thanks for letting me stay here.'

'Anytime. We love having you.' A shadow crossed Mrs Gray's
face, but it was gone as quickly as it came, and she was back to

smiling. 'You could help us bake a cake,' she suggested. 'We love cake in this house.'

'So do my family. Especially Sylvia.' I needed to talk about her to reassure myself everything was okay, even though I sensed it wasn't. 'Can I keep a slice for her, please? I bet hospital food is horrible.'

'Of course.'

Mrs Gray drew me into her noisy kitchen, keeping me occupied with baking and games until well past my normal bedtime.

I should have been tired, yet as the night progressed, I heard every strike of the grandfather clock. Even my frantic prayers seemed to hit the ceiling, then bounce right back into my chest with a thud.

'Please make Sylvie better, Jesus,' I begged as my heartrate quickened. 'Please bring her home soon. I'll tell her stories when I'm not at school if she's got to stay in bed. Just please, let her come home.'

Sunday morning dawned bright and sunny, bringing no further news from home. I helped Mrs Gray in the garden, and Ruth's mother complimented me on my knowledge of plants and flowers.

'I help my mum in the garden,' I said, tugging at a stubborn weed.

'I can see that.' Mrs Gray bent to pull up one of the weed's long, straggly neighbours. 'My Ruth could learn some lessons from you. Especially with helping me out here or taking care of the children.'

I excused my friend by pointing out that Ruth had three younger siblings, whereas I only had Sylvia.

When Ruth invited me to the park, I opted for settling the baby for her afternoon nap. I drew both of Ruth's sisters to my side and told them the story of Noah's ark, realising that Sylvia and I were missing Sunday school. The Grays clearly didn't go to church, but I didn't have the courage to ask why not.

I spent another restless night listening to the ticks and chimes of the grandfather clock. Preparing to catch the bus to school with Ruth and Clive on Monday morning, I suggested taking my bag in readiness to go straight home.

'Your father will come for you when he's ready,' Mrs Gray insisted.

'I wish they'd let me visit Sylvie at the hospital.' I bit my lip so as not to cry.

'You'd better hurry, or you'll miss the bus.'

Mrs Gray urged me, Ruth, and Clive out of the house with a wave and a smile, but as I turned back to say bye to the baby, a tear was in the corner of Mrs Gray's eye. I shivered despite the sun's warmth.

7

I returned to the Grays' after school with Ruth and Clive to find their mother waiting on her doorstep. My palms became clammy. Had she been standing at her kitchen window watching for our arrival? If so, then something was wrong.

Mrs Gray didn't even paste on a smile. She dispatched her children into the kitchen for their after-school refreshments, then put an arm around my shoulders. 'Your father's waiting in the front room.' There was a tremor in her voice, and her eyes were red-rimmed.

'I didn't see his van.' I peered through the glass panel in the front door to confirm what I already knew.

'He came on the bus.'

'Why?' Mrs Gray's revelation added to the mystery. Dad never travelled by bus nowadays. He said the van was a luxury our family deserved to enjoy. 'And why isn't he still at work?' It was barely four o'clock. His workday didn't end until five-30.

'I don't think he went in today.' Mrs Gray gave me a gentle push towards the front room. 'He'll explain everything, I'm sure.'

She patted my back and left me alone to face my father. I usually looked forward to seeing him after work. In the past, I had been the first to welcome him home with hugs and kisses. Now that was Sylvia's privilege.

I hovered on the threshold of the Grays' front room, hesitant to approach the man who had always been my rock of safety. My father sat in a high-backed chair, his arms folded as his shoulders slumped into the velvet cushions, the sparkle of mischief in his eyes supplanted by something dark and foreboding. He seemed to have aged. Suddenly, I sensed the news he was about to share would change my life forever. I didn't want to hear it, but there was no escape.

'Hello, Jan.' His voice lacked its customary warmth as he dragged his eyes towards me with no accompanying smile. 'How was your day?'

'Not bad.' I wanted to freeze time, to hang on to what was left of the secure, happy life I'd always known.

I crept further into the room, perching on the edge of the sofa opposite my father. We sat in silence, suspended between the past and our new reality. If we stayed this way, I would never have to learn what had brought about this catastrophic change. Would we become like the wax models my teacher had described after a recent visit to London?

'I've got something to tell you, Jan.' Dad spoke in a whisper. 'It's something bad, and I don't honestly know how….' His voice trailed off.

My stomach dropped as my father's struggle, coupled with the sorrow in his eyes, confirmed my deepest fears. 'It's Sylvie, isn't it?'

Dad nodded almost imperceptibly.

'Is she gone?' I addressed my question to the plush blue carpet. There could be only one explanation for his brokenness.

'Yes.' He forced the word out.

I still couldn't bring myself to meet his gaze. 'What happened?' Did I really want to know? Would the truth shatter my heart too? 'David said you took her to the hospital.'

'That's right.' My father shuffled nervously in his seat. 'They did their best, but… I suppose it isn't always enough.'

'I don't understand! Did her cold turn into the flu or an infection?'

'Don't nag, Jan.' His tone was uncharacteristically sharp. 'Just accept what's happened and help me take care of your mother.' He looked away, then refocused on me. 'She needs you.'

'Where is Mum?' I swallowed down my tears. My father was asking me to be brave. I would do my best for his sake.

'At home in bed. She's in a bad way. We need to get back to her quickly.' He prised himself out of the chair and strode purposefully towards the door. 'Don't forget to thank the Grays for having you.'

I bade a hurried farewell to Ruth's family, thanking them politely for allowing me to stay for longer than planned.

Mrs Gray cried as she hugged me. 'We're always here. If you ever need to talk…' She released me with a kiss on my forehead.

I followed my father to the bus stop, automatically putting one foot in front of the other in a dreamlike state. How could Sylvia be gone when she'd been so alive on Friday morning, suffering from a common cold and vying for sympathy?

As we waited for the bus in awkward silence, I attempted to make sense of the little I understood. However, the harder I tried to connect the facts, the more my confusion grew. I wanted to ask why Dad hadn't brought the van, but the hard set of his jaw told me he wouldn't take kindly to my probing.

When the bus finally arrived, I watched the fields and houses rush by, forcing myself not to think about Sylvia, even though memories threatened to drown me. It was all a terrible mistake. Surely my sister would bounce out of the front door as soon as I got back, peppering me with questions, consumed by curiosity about my first sleepover. Then she'd request a story about two girls drinking tea out of dainty cups while playing at being mothers waiting to collect their children from school. She would pester until I promised to take her to the café with the lace curtains and the gingham tablecloths. If Mum said no, Sylvia would wear her down with nagging.

The house was eerily quiet when I followed my father inside. Could a building be in mourning? If so, then surely our home was grieving for the little girl who had filled its rooms with sunshine and infectious giggles. The curtains were drawn, plunging us into premature darkness despite the bright summer's day.

When I saw Dad's van parked in front of the house, I dared to ask whether it had broken down. Dad shook his head before marching into the living room, and I dragged myself up the stairs as the door snapped shut behind him. I hadn't asked about the boys, presuming they had gone out to escape our oppressive surroundings.

Tossing my bag onto my bedroom floor, I sucked in a breath and braved a glance at Sylvia's bed. Strewn with dolls and teddies, it waited for her to sink into its comforting warmth after another day of innocent fun. Sylvia would soon come bounding in to reclaim a forgotten toy. Perhaps she was at a neighbour's house or braving our mother's disapproval by playing hopscotch in the street with Will Sloane?

The distant echo of her sweet little voice tickled my ears, like a whisp of breeze on a sultry summer's day. 'Jan, where are you? I need you!'

The entreaty reverberated around my mind, growing in desperation as I longed to be reunited with my little sister. Sylvia had needed me, and I couldn't help her. From now on, no matter how hard I searched or how loudly I called, she wouldn't come. Aware of the futility of calling out my regular summons, I did it anyway.

'Sylvia Pew, where are you?' I croaked, then threw myself across my bed, overcome by a flood of anguished tears.

Time passed slowly as I lay choking on my gulping sobs, wondering if they would ever stop. Somehow, I found myself on Sylvia's bed, clutching Billy the bear and inhaling my sister's familiar scent. Sylvia always smelled of soap and fresh air, or the shampoo Mum used to wash her fine blonde hair. I would never use that brand again.

Despair turned to anger as my flow of tears dried up, and I cast Billy aside. If God had sent Sylvia in answer to my prayers, why had He taken her after only six years? Didn't He understand? We had looked forward to a lifetime of shared experiences and whispered confidences. Why had God taken Sylvia, leaving me alone?

Eventually, recalling my father's words about Mum needing me, I tiptoed onto the landing, peering with trepidation at my parents' closed bedroom door. The house had remained silent since our return. My father hadn't come to offer me comfort. I wondered what he was doing, and whether the boys were home. I knew I should be with my mother, but what could I say? Still, I had to try. I slowly pushed open the door, steeling myself for what lay beyond. I couldn't let Mum down when she needed me most.

I padded into my parents' room, allowing my eyes to adjust to the darkness. Mum lay motionless in the bed, her pale hair matted as it lay draped across her pillow, while she stared at the ceiling.

'Can I make you a cup of tea?'

'No, thank you.' Her tone was flat, and she didn't turn her head my way.

'When did you have one last?'

It occurred to me that our roles were being played out in reverse. I was the mother, and she was the child.

'It doesn't matter.'

Mum seemed confused. Had the doctor given her a sedative, like the one he'd prescribed for Mrs Jones across the street when her husband fell over and died from a heart attack? I had heard whispers about his poor wife clinging to his lifeless body, and how she didn't stop crying until Doctor Ross gave her something to help her sleep.

'You've got to drink.' I repeated the words my mother had often said to Sylvia.

I waited for an angry retort, but nothing came. A lump formed in my throat as I realised that I was now my parents' only daughter. Sylvia had gone as swiftly as she came. But would the shadow of her presence ever truly leave us?

Receiving no further acknowledgement from the figure on the bed, I ventured downstairs, going through the motions of making tea. I found Dad in the lounge, sitting in his favourite armchair. He wasn't reading his newspaper or doing any of the things that typically brought him pleasure. Instead, he sat perfectly still, dissociated from the world around him.

'I brought you some tea, Dad.' I placed the mug gingerly on the coffee table beside him.

Dad grunted his thanks without turning to look at me, and I backed out of the room, climbing the stairs with tea for my mother.

I coaxed her into having a few sips, but Mum only managed half a cup before grief overtook her. She fell back upon the bed, wailing Sylvia's name. When I offered comfort, she said she needed to be alone.

So I returned to my room to spend the rest of the long evening staring at Sylvia's empty bed. I heard the boys returning, but no one mentioned an evening meal. I was relieved, because I didn't have the energy to cook. I slept fitfully that night, occasionally moving from my own bed to Sylvia's, first desiring the comfort of my sister's toys, then casting them aside.

A new day dawned, and I gathered with Dad, Malcolm, and David in the kitchen for breakfast. We said little as we picked at our cereal, half of which ended up in the bin. My brothers' hefty appetites had shrunk overnight.

I was surprised when David left for work and Malcolm headed off to school, and I asked Dad what I should do.

'Can you stay with your mother?' he asked. 'I need to sort things out.'

My relief was palpable. I couldn't imagine going to school and pretending life hadn't changed. Once again, persuading Mum to take nourishment was a futile battle. Dad didn't come home until 2 pm, offering no reason for his long absence.

During the following days, our family crept around the house, each going silently about our individual tasks. There was no mention of me going back to school until my father broke the news that Sylvia's funeral would take place the following Tuesday.

'If you can stay at home till then, I think you should go back to normal after that.'

How could he speak of normality? Our lives would never be normal again. I simply nodded, not trusting myself to answer. Mum rarely rose from her bed. She ate little and took no interest in resuming her household tasks. It was all down to me, so I kept myself busy by cooking and cleaning. No one complimented my efforts, and I wondered what they'd do when I returned to school. My parents still resisted the most basic attempts at conversation.

I joined David in the garden as he diligently watered our mother's neglected plants on the eve of Sylvia's funeral. I needed answers to some of my most pressing concerns, and since Dad was unwilling to give them, I hoped David might offer the reassurance I craved.

'What will happen now?' I asked.

'I guess we'll just get on with things.' David shrugged. I couldn't imagine doing so. We were broken and bruised, and if we ever picked ourselves up, we would do so with heavy steps and fractured lives.

'Do you think Mum will cope with the funeral?'

'She'll have to.'

But how, considering Mum had barely left her room? 'Has Dad said when he'll go back to work?'

'He might look for a different job.' David moved to another row of plants.

'Why? He says his job with the council is the best he's ever had.'

'Maybe he needs a change.' My brother turned away, signalling his desire to end our awkward conversation, and once again my flimsy hopes were dashed.

The following morning, our family dressed in black to mark Sylvia's passing. A horse and cart carried her tiny coffin from the local funeral home to the little chapel we attended for Sunday school. The number of people who came to pay their respects was overwhelming. Almost everyone we knew squeezed into the small building, alongside a sea of less familiar faces.

The service passed in a blur as I bit my lip until it bled and fought not to cry. A fresh wave of grief hit every time my eyes strayed to Mum, whose keening wails punctuated every silence, and when it was time to leave, Malcolm and David practically carried her out of the church. Our father followed in a daze, content to leave his wife in the care of his teenage sons.

The final blow came when the coffin was lowered into the ground. My mother crumpled to her knees, screaming Sylvia's name as she clawed at the dirt and begged for her baby. Tears ran down my cheeks, but I might as well have been invisible, because my family failed to notice. Dad's expression remained detached, and David and Malcolm tended to our mother. The onlookers held back, uncertain how to help as the full weight of our loss crushed us.

As my mother's screams intensified, I plugged my ears and turned from the open grave, alone amidst a sea of mourners. When meaningful friends mumbled about time being a healer, I didn't believe them. There were also other whisperings I didn't understand. The neighbourhood women called it a tragedy, questioning how our family would survive.

'Can I do anything for you, love?'

I recognised Mrs Gray's voice, but I couldn't look at her. If I did, I would break. So I shook my head stoically.

'Remember what I said.' Mrs Gray put a gentle hand on my back. 'We're here for you whenever you need us.'

'Thank you.'

My resolve was crumbling, and I needed to get away. One more glimpse into Sylvia's grave would have me on the ground beside my mother. Had my lifelong fear of the cemetery been a foreshadowing of the fate that would befall my beloved sister?

Having reassured Mrs Gray with a confidence I didn't feel, I tiptoed around the edge of the crowd, trudged home alone and set about preparing for my family's return, grateful Dad had decided against the obligatory funeral tea.

Whilst tending to the various bunches of flowers sent as consolation, I pondered the minister's words at Sylvia's graveside. He had reminded us that even though we walked through the valley of the shadow of death, the Lord was still present as our shepherd, comforter and guide.

Yet I was no longer convinced of God's love. My faith crumbled at the graveside. I knew I would trudge through each day, doing my best and accepting whatever came my way, but the world was a cruel place that could snatch those you loved at any moment. Our sunshine girl had stolen all our hearts, and when she departed, she took a piece of each of us with her.

A memory surfaced, and I tried desperately to push it back down. I recalled my nightmare during our Easter camping holiday – of Sylvia being choked by weeds and consumed by fire. Was the dream a warning? If so, what could I have done to prevent my sister's death? Had I failed Sylvia? Was I to blame for not protecting her? Had she really died because she caught my cold? I would never know because my family were unwilling to answer direct questions.

After sorting the flowers, I wandered aimlessly around our desolate house. It was no longer a home because it echoed with emptiness. Satisfied that everything was in order, I sat at the kitchen table pining for Sylvia, for the happy family that was gone for good, and for my own destroyed future. Hope and joy were a thing of the past. I had tasted the bitterness of grief and loss, leaving me forever scarred.

8

'Everything changed after we lost Sylvia.' Janet reached for another tissue to dab at her streaming eyes. She glanced from Ola to Nettie, then focused on her cherished son.

Their reactions to her revelations were as different as their personalities. Nettie sat bolt upright on the edge of her seat, hanging on Janet's every word. By contrast, Ola's stoic facial features gave little away, and Benny seemed detached as he cuddled Beth. Was it an aftereffect of his seizure? Or had he switched off midway through her long and emotional tale? He struggled to concentrate at the best of times, rarely following an unabbreviated story.

Had it only been an hour since Janet rushed out of the kitchen at the sound of Beth's cries? It felt like an eternity. She had never planned to revisit the agony of her childhood. The words had simply tumbled out, leaving her unable to stop until the torrent dried up. Now, she was spent and exhausted.

'How did it change?' Nettie asked.

Janet fought not to resume her crying as she screwed her tissue into a ball, turning it round in her hand before adding it to the growing collection on her lap. 'Our light went out.'

'She did sound pretty bouncy.' Nettie passed her another tissue, and Janet blew her nose.

'Sylvie was the glue that held us together.' She sighed. 'She stole our joy, and without her, we only existed.'

'You were a family long before she came along.' Ola rose, picked up her bundle of soiled tissues, and tossed them into the wastepaper basket before standing in front of the gas fire with his arms folded over his chest. Ola wasn't great with words, but Janet knew that removing her tissues was an act of love.

'Losing a child…' Janet struggled to explain. On how many occasions had she helped Benny when he stumbled over his limited vocabulary? 'They say tragedy either makes or breaks you, and in our case, it broke us. David married Sarah, Malcolm threw himself into his studies, and my parents…'

'They're still married, aren't they?' Nettie asked.

'Yes, but they bicker more than they used to, and they sort of coexist as two lost souls surviving side by side. Dad got a job in a factory, and Mum looked after the house. Sort of.' Janet shivered and reached for the mohair cardigan hanging over the arm of her chair. 'They rarely laughed or talked, and we never shared another holiday. I suppose it would've been too painful because of the memories.' She draped the cardigan over her lap. 'Everything reminded us of Sylvia. It was easier not to talk about her, so we hardly talked at all.' Janet glanced at her Christmas tree with its twinkling lights and cheerful baubles as her family waited for her to continue. 'We didn't celebrate Christmas properly again. It became a non-event. We survived the first year, then the second, and we tried to leave our memories in the attic with the decorations.'

'That's so sad,' Nettie breathed. 'Didn't you have questions? I mean, didn't you want to find out how she died?'

'I suppose I didn't need to.' Janet fumbled nervously with her cardigan's large silver buttons. 'Dad said she was taken ill, and I already knew she'd caught my cold.'

'People don't die from colds.' Nettie reached over to smooth her own daughter's cheek. 'Not even little kids.'

'I suppose they can if it develops into an infection.' Janet's excuse sounded feeble, even to her own ears. 'I accepted my parents' unwillingness to explain because I'm a rule-follower, and although nothing had been stipulated, I sensed they couldn't talk about Sylvie's last few days.' Janet shivered again and slid her arms into the cardigan. 'I still don't know exactly when she died; only that it happened while I was at the Grays'.'

'What about you?' Nettie asked. 'Did you go to grammar school?'

'I had to because I'd already passed my 11+, but I lost interest in my work, and I didn't even try making new friends.'

'That's a shame.' Nettie wove her fingers through Benny's. 'At least you had Ruth and her family. Were the two of you still close, even though you were at different schools?'

'I avoided people as much as possible.' Janet picked up her half-drunk mug of tea, then put it down again when she realised it was stone cold. 'Ruth didn't take long to find another best friend at her new school. And the other girls I'd grown up with felt nervous around me because I'd lost my sister. They didn't know what to say.' She lapsed into a thoughtful silence, remembering the pain of loneliness. 'There was a lot of whispering behind my back, but I ignored it.'

'Why were they whispering?' Nettie asked, curious as ever.

Ola bent down to pick up Nettie's empty mug, signalling it was time for her to leave. 'That's enough for one night.'

'Sorry.' Nettie blushed. 'You're right. I should get Beth home to bed.' She lifted her daughter gently into her arms and turned to Benny. 'Will you see us out?'

Benny nodded, following Nettie and leaving his parents alone for the first time that evening.

'I expect you're tired.' Ola said as he gathered the rest of the mugs.

'I'm drained.' Janet closed her eyes, leaning back in her armchair. 'I didn't plan to tell all my childhood secrets.'

'Perhaps you needed to. They say it's good to talk.' Sharing his thoughts and feelings didn't come naturally to Ola, so Janet suspected he had no personal evidence on which to base his claim. His past was buried deeper than hers had been before she lifted the lid, exposing it for her family's scrutiny.

'Are you cross because I talked about private things in front of Nettie?' Janet worried this might lead to problems between them. Ola had strong opinions on what should stay within the confines of their family.

He shook his head. 'Benny would have told her soon enough.'

'I'm not even sure he was listening.' Janet rubbed at the back of her neck where a knot was forming.

'I think he was.'

A glum-looking Benny reappeared in the doorway. 'The snow's stopped.' His disappointment was palpable.

'It might start again.' Ola walked past him, carrying the mugs into the kitchen. 'It's cold enough.'

'I hope so.' Benny turned and trudged up the stairs.

As she heard Ola washing the mugs, Janet wondered whether she should follow her son. During his early years, she had tucked Benny in every night, lying beside him and holding his hand until he fell asleep. Those days were long gone. However, she sensed an insecurity in him that hadn't been there earlier, so she risked venturing upstairs.

'Are you okay, my love?' She hovered in his bedroom doorway, having the decency not to enter without an invitation.

'Yeah.'

Although Benny's response wasn't convincing, Janet had learned not to press him. At his age, he deserved some privacy. 'I'll say goodnight then.' She prepared to leave.

'You can come in if you want.'

Janet didn't need to be asked twice. Ignoring the schoolbooks and clothes strewn haphazardly around the room, she joined Benny on his bed, where they sat in silence while she waited patiently for her son to speak. His face went through a whole range of expressions, from embarrassment, to confusion, to sadness, before he finally reached for her hand.

Janet shut her eyes, remembering Benny as a much younger child in constant need of her reassurance. How many times had she held him on her lap? How often had he clung to her or fallen asleep in her arms? She was learning to enjoy a new relationship with the child who had captivated her heart from his first breath, forcing herself to remember he was no longer her baby.

'I'm sorry your sister died. I reckon that must've been hard.' He gave her hand a tender squeeze. 'I bet you cried loads, cos I'd cry if Emmie died. I don't reckon I'd ever stop.' Benny paused, and Janet guessed he was framing a question. 'Did you look after her cat?'

Trust Benny to remember Mittens. She shook her head, realising she'd never asked her parents about the cat. Her thoughts had been consumed by the loss of Sylvia. 'I never saw him again.'

'Do you think Grandma and Grandpa gave him to someone else?' Benny released her hand.

'I expect so. He meant so much to Sylvia. It would've hurt to keep him.'

'Yeah, but I reckon it would've been nice too.' Benny's thoughtfulness often caught Janet off guard. 'You didn't have no one to love. If they'd kept Mittens, you could've loved him.'

'Yes.' Janet fought against the pain of her memories. 'I suppose I would have taken care of him, for Sylvie's sake. Anyway, now I'm blessed with my own family. I have your dad, and Emma and my precious Benny.'

Janet caught her breath as her son leaned towards her. In the past, this simple gesture had signalled his desire for a hug, so she put her arms around him, and he melted into them willingly. Was he doing this for her? Did he understand how much she needed this closeness?

'Oh, I love you so much, Benny.'

Sixteen years of memories flooded back, starting with the first time she'd held him. That joyful moment was all too brief before a seizure tore her baby from her arms. She'd been inconsolable until they'd returned Benny to her, and she'd vowed she would never let him go. She barely did until he took his first steps.

'I love you too, Mum.'

Janet heard the distant echo of a tiny voice, barely able to form coherent words. Yet she had always understood every squeak and anguished cry. Now, her little boy was becoming a man. Benny pulled away and she stared into his blue eyes, gratified by the unflinching way he held her gaze. Eye contact wasn't a given with Benny, and he only gave it to those he loved and trusted. At first, it was only his mother and elder sister. Then he added Ola and now Nettie. Janet was still astounded by the intensity of his unbridled love for his girlfriend.

'See you in the morning.' She rose, then turned back to him from the doorway. 'Is there anything you need?'

'I forgot to make a drink.'

'I'll bring it.' Caring for him gave her a sense of normality. 'Warm milk?'

'Thanks.' He reached for the Bible lying on his bedside cabinet next to a framed photograph of Nettie and Beth.

'Aren't you too tired to read?' Janet still fretted after a seizure.

'Tim says it's good to read before I go to bed.' Benny's attention was on the Bible. 'He says it hasn't gotta be loads. And I can stick to the easy stuff. I only read the other stuff when I'm with him, cos I don't get it when I'm by myself.'

'What do you call the easy stuff?' Janet asked.

'The stuff about Jesus. Like when He healed people.' Benny smiled. 'Those bits are good.'

'Do you ever wish He'd heal you?' Janet didn't usually ask him those kinds of questions, but there was a special connection between them tonight.

'Maybe.' Benny tore his gaze away from his Bible and fixed it on her. 'I wish He'd make me better at my schoolwork. I reckon I would be if I didn't have to take so many tablets.'

'So you think the tablets affect your brain?'

'The tablets and the stupid seizures. If I don't have none for a few days, I can kind of think better. I remember stuff more until I have another one, and my brain goes weird again.'

'Your brain isn't weird, Benny. You're perfect, just as you are.'

'You say stuff like that cos you're my mum, and cos you don't reckon I ever do nothing wrong.' He laughed self-consciously. 'I know I'm weird. I'm not like no one else, but that's okay, cos that's how God made me. And Nettie loves me, so I'm happy.'

'Not just Nettie,' Janet insisted.

'Yeah. I know you and Dad do too. And Emmie. And Beth.' Benny turned a page in his Bible, signalling the end of their conversation.

Leaving him to study, Janet returned downstairs to find Ola in the kitchen, sipping black coffee.

'I can't believe you can drink it this late and still sleep.' She poured milk into a mug and put it in the microwave.

'Benny got you waiting on him again, has he?' Ola frowned.

'I offered.' Janet defended their son. 'He was going to do it himself.'

'You still enjoy fussing over him.'

'Don't we all deserve that sometimes?' Janet removed the mug from the microwave.

Ola gave her a wisp of a smile, accompanied by a brief nod. He took his coffee and mounted the stairs, where Janet joined him in their room after running her errand for Benny. Expecting to find her husband impatiently waiting for her to turn out the light, Janet was surprised to see him sitting with his back resting against the headboard.

As she undressed and climbed into bed, Ola reached over and took something out of the top drawer of his bedside cabinet. He held out a tatty-looking manilla envelope. Janet hesitated, uncertain of his intent.

'Go on.' He thrust it into her hand. 'You need to see what's inside.'

'Why?' Janet was bewildered by Ola's uncharacteristic behaviour.

'You've told your secrets tonight. So maybe I should share one of mine. You might say it's well overdue.'

Janet opened the envelope and stared at a sepia photograph. A pale-haired child stood on the steps of a small wooden house, clutching the hand of a striking woman with expressive eyes that seemed to stare right at her through the picture.

'Who is this?' Janet whispered. 'The boy... He looks like Benny.'

'I thought that too.' Ola adjusted the pillow behind his back. 'The last time I saw it, I was struck by our resemblance. I guess I'd never taken much notice before.'

'So, it's you.' Janet smiled at the child in the photograph. 'Is this the only photo you have?'

'Yes.' Ola pointed at the woman. 'She was my mother, Inga Wellander.'

'Was?' Janet hesitated to ask. 'Did she die?'

'I don't know. She might be dead by now. She disappeared when I was 16, and I never heard from her again.' He cleared his throat. 'I'm sure she had another man.'

'That's awful!'

'Some might argue she chose the best option.' Ola's tone was gruff. 'My father was a violent drunk.'

'Why didn't she take you with her?' Janet couldn't imagine leaving Benny.

'I suppose her new man didn't want a teenager as part of the deal.' Ola shrugged. 'And I wasn't an easy boy to love. I'm afraid I inherited too many of my father's character traits.'

'But you were only 16.' Janet pondered, adding, 'The same as Benny is now.'

'I hadn't thought of that.' Ola seemed startled by her revelation. 'Well, I might have been the same age, but I can assure you, I was nothing like our son. I was streetwise. I loved to fight, and I was already developing my own taste for alcohol.'

'You've never been a big drinker,' Janet protested.

'Only because I won't let myself.' A look of shame crossed Ola's face. 'When Benny was small and you slept in the spare room, I sometimes came home worse for wear.'

'I wish you'd told me this before.' Janet returned the envelope and reached for her husband's hand. Although Ola rarely encouraged intimacy, tonight he seemed to welcome it as his fingers curled around hers. 'I wish you hadn't felt the need to keep such painful secrets.'

'I might say the same to you.' Ola increased the pressure on her hand.

'My parents shut the door on Sylvia, so I had to do the same.'

'We both have our pasts and our secrets.' He surprised her with a tender embrace. 'Perhaps now we'll learn to appreciate one another more. It's never too late, is it, Jan? What you did tonight was very brave, and I thought I should be brave too.'

'Thank you.' Janet was gratified when Ola held her for longer than usual.

'It's time for us to get some sleep.' He released her, replaced the photograph in its drawer, and switched off the light.

As Ola settled down in their bed, Janet lay beside him, preparing for their nighttime ritual of sleeping with a gaping hole between them. However, her husband turned onto his side, wrapping himself snuggly around her in the darkness, enveloping her small body in his much larger frame.

'It's cold,' he offered as an explanation. 'Perhaps we will have more snow.'

'Benny will be disappointed if we don't.'

'He's hoping for a day off school.' Ola spoke with mirth rather than irritation. 'Any excuse with Benny.'

Janet knew now wasn't the right time to discuss their son's longing to leave school and work alongside his father. This precious and rare moment of intimacy was for them alone. She wondered whether it would lead to more, but the subtle changes in his breathing soon informed her that her tight-lipped, Danish husband had succumbed to sleep.

'Goodnight, my love,' she whispered into the darkness.

Janet lay wide awake. Her earlier weariness fled before her husband's revelations. The unmasking of her past had opened a window for Ola to draw closer. Could she dare hope tonight marked another milestone in their complex relationship, like when he'd realised the depths to which he had failed as Benny's father?

Whereas that incident had revolved around their son, this was their time. Emma was forging her own life, and even Benny was growing in his maturity. Perhaps one day, Janet's carefully feathered nest would be empty. She'd convinced herself that Benny would need her forever. Yet, if she and Ola were forming a new understanding, perhaps they could be happy growing old together. Would they spend more time overcoming barriers, with him giving her access to more of his world?

Such were the meandering thoughts that flitted through her mind as Janet finally surrendered to sleep, held securely in her husband's strong arms.

67

9

The shrill ringing of his alarm clock dragged Benny from a dreamless sleep. He turned over, reached out to silence the offensive noise, and scowled as something hit the floor with a resounding thud. Benny figured he would deal with it later, then groaned, remembering the cup of warm milk his mother had brought him the night before.

'Did I drink it? I can't remember.'

He shot out of bed, relieved to discover that although he had been correct about the mug, it was still intact and had already been empty. Even his overindulgent mum drew the line at spilt milk on his bedroom carpet.

Righting the mug, Benny gazed lingeringly at his bed, longing to return to its comforting warmth. He reached for his phone as a distraction, smiling when he saw a text from Nettie.

'So, your God definitely answers prayer.'

Her message baffled him. What did she mean? He responded with a question mark, almost dropping the phone when it vibrated in his hand. Nettie was calling him.

'Nettie?' He always answered the same way. His girlfriend said his use of her name as a question never failed to make her smile.

'Were you texting in your sleep?' she asked.

'I'm awake.' He glared at the phone. 'What're you on about?'

'Oh dear. Did someone get out on the wrong side of the bed?' she teased.

'I always get out the same side cos my bed is against the wall.' Why was she messing with his addled brain? Nettie knew he hated mornings, especially with the prospect of another gruelling day spent trying to learn things he struggled to understand.

'Oh, Benny!' She laughed.

'What?' He couldn't hide his irritation.

'I love you so much.'

'I guess I love you too?' His words lacked their customary warmth.

'You guess?' Her giggles echoed over the line. 'How come you're in such a grumpy strop?'

'I don't wanna wake up.' Benny threw himself back onto his bed. 'It's Wednesday. There's still another three days before it's the weekend. And you're not making no sense, Nettie.'

'I bet you'll cheer up when I tell you the schools are closed.'

He shot upright.

'So, are you coming out in the snow to play with me and Beth? Or are you gonna be a typical teenager and go back to bed?'

'Snow? What snow?' Benny bounded towards the window, pulled back the curtains, and gazed in awe at a world of pure white. 'It's snowed, Nettie!'

'You don't say,' she giggled. 'It must have started again during the night. So, now you'll understand what I meant about your God answering prayer. You said last night you'd been asking for a day off. Well, you've got one. And I can't go to work either, so...'

'So?' He was suddenly wide awake and eager to run across the road to be with her.

'Give me an hour to see to Beth and get ready to have fun.'

'I love you, Nettie.' This time, it sounded like he meant it.

'I love you more.' Her attitude sobered. 'I was worried about you last night. I wanted to stay longer, but I could tell your dad wasn't up for it.'

'It was only a seizure.' Benny wrinkled his brow. Nettie didn't normally fuss about his epilepsy.

'I wasn't worried about that. It was because of everything your mum told us.'

'Oh.' As usual, Benny was lost for words.

'It was a lot to take in, all that stuff from her past.'

'Yeah. It was sad about her sister.' He pressed his nose against the glass, wishing Nettie was standing beside him, holding his hand. 'It's weird that my mum had such a big secret. I mean, she's always just been Mum. I never thought about her life before she married Dad.'

'Poor Jan.' Nettie sighed. 'I mulled over it for ages after I got home, and there are still parts of her story that don't add up.'

'What do you mean?' Benny's confusion grew.

'For one thing, why did your grandparents disappear from her life after she married your father?'

'They didn't. Emma visited them sometimes. And I did a couple of times. Plus, Mum still phones them.' After dragging himself away from the window, he pulled on the jeans he'd discarded in a tangled heap beside his bed the previous night, lodging the phone between his shoulder and his ear.

'Your mother admitted they stopped being close.'

'Yeah. She said they didn't care about nothing after Sylvia died. I guess they were really sad.'

'Don't you think it was an extreme reaction?'

'I bet we'd be the same if Beth died.' Benny couldn't even imagine it, such was his devotion to his girlfriend's daughter.

'So if we were married, and we had other kids, you think we'd push them away because of our grief?' She paused. 'Wouldn't they mean even more to us because of the child we'd lost?'

'Dunno. We haven't got no other kids.' He shook his head in bewilderment. 'I guess if we did, we'd wanna be with them more. I don't reckon we'd stop wanting to see them, like my grandparents did with Mum.' Closing his eyes, he imagined the comfort of Nettie's hand in his. 'Why did they do that, Nettie?'

'I'm not sure. That's why I say there's more to it.'

'Should I ask her?' He stood in front of a mirror, dragging a comb through his wispy blonde hair. It always stood on end first thing in the morning.

'She might find it easier to talk to you because you're so close.'

'How do I get her to talk?' Benny started pacing in his agitation. 'I dunno how to do it, Nettie.'

'You'll know when the time comes.'

Nettie's confidence in his abilities caught him off guard. Feeling defeated, he flopped onto his bed with a shrug. 'You know I'm rubbish with words and stuff.'

'No, you're not.' She spoke tenderly as he stared helplessly at the ceiling. 'You're not rubbish at anything, Benny Wellander, and I'm hoping one day you might start believing it.'

They lapsed into a comfortable silence. Nettie understood his brain's need for time to catch up.

'I'll see if Mum's awake.' Benny yawned and stretched.

'That's a good idea. Remember, one hour. Then Beth and I will be round for some serious snow fun.'

She ended their conversation with another endearment, and Benny headed into the bathroom. The house was quiet, making him wonder whether his parents had seen the snow and chosen to stay in bed. Surely even his dad wouldn't go to work on such a wintery morning?

Benny glanced at his reflection in the bathroom mirror and poked his tongue out in disgust. People said he still looked young for his age, and he wondered for the umpteenth time what Nettie saw in him. He was pale-faced and painfully thin, his jeans hung loosely around his waist, and his faded blue t-shirt had seen better days. He should buy new clothes, but he didn't care about fashion. Shopping was a waste of time and energy. It stressed him out. He hated being jostled by crowds, especially at Christmas. He wondered if growing a beard would make him look older but dismissed that thought as quickly as it had come. His mother cut his hair, and he still only had to shave once a week, so it would take ages.

He ambled downstairs, finding Janet in the lounge, gazing thoughtfully at the falling snow.

'Isn't it beautiful?' She turned with a smile, and Benny thought Nettie must be wrong – his mother looked normal. As she held out her arms, he leaned in for their morning hug.

'Good morning, my love.' She held him for longer than usual, planting a tender kiss on his cheek. 'It looks as though your prayers for snow were answered.'

'That's what Nettie said.' Benny reached for her hand. Nettie used to tease him for being a compulsive hand holder, but these days, if their fingers weren't entwined, she presumed something was wrong.

'So you've already spoken to her?'

He nodded.

'No doubt Beth will be excited to see the snow.' Outside the window, a robin was pecking at the frozen ground. 'Poor thing,' his mum said. 'He won't find any worms today. Maybe I should throw him some bread.'

'We're gonna take Beth out to play.'

'Be careful.' Janet's eyebrows rose. 'Remember, sudden shocks or falls always bring on seizures.'

'Mum!' He rolled his eyes. 'It's only snow.'

'And how do you suppose you're going to stay warm, since you refuse to wear a coat?'

Benny's breath misted the window. 'Can I borrow one of Dad's?'

'It'd drown you!' Janet laughed.

'I don't care.' Benny released her hand and headed towards the kitchen.

'What do you want to eat?' His mother bustled after him.

'Nothing.' He filled a mug with milk, putting it in the microwave, aware of his mother watching anxiously. 'I left a cup upstairs. I'll bring it down later.'

'I'll fetch it.' She still loved taking care of him, and sometimes, it worked to his advantage. 'You can't go out in the cold with just warm milk inside you. Sit down, and I'll make you scrambled eggs on toast.'

Benny's refusal died on his tongue at the longing in his mum's eyes. Pastor Tim said he still needed to let her do things for him sometimes.

'I've gotta get my Bible anyway. I'm not gonna have time to read it later.'

'Can I read to you?' Janet asked as she set about beating butter and milk into the eggs.

'Yeah, all right. I get it more if I've only gotta listen, like I do when I'm with Tim.'

Before clattering out of the room, Benny gave her a brief hug. Remembering his father was still asleep, he slowed down halfway up the stairs. The last thing he needed this morning was Ola getting in a grumpy strop.

Moments later, Benny returned to the kitchen carrying his Bible and the empty mug. He washed the mug under the tap, then sat at the table, watching Janet scramble the eggs. 'Damo always puts loads of butter in it.'

'That's why I have to buy extra every time he stays here,' Janet said, dropping in an extra knob of butter as Benny laughed at the antics of his only schoolfriend.

'He reckons he's gonna live with his mum in London after he's finished his GCSEs.' A frown tugged on his lips as Benny played absentmindedly with a table mat.

'Oh, that's a shame, love. You'll miss him.'

'I'm glad Nettie's not gonna go away. Damo said I can go to see him in London, but I don't wanna go there. It'd be too busy and loud. I only wanna stay here. Perhaps I won't see him again.'

'He's bound to visit his gran, so he can stay with us while he's in the village.' Janet rushed across the kitchen to prevent the toast from burning.

'He might make more friends. He won't wanna hang round with me no more.' Benny reckoned his friendship with outgoing Damien Maubry was on borrowed time.

'Of course he will. You've been his closest friend.'

As Janet buttered the toast, Benny turned his attention to other things, soon becoming excited about how much Beth would enjoy the snow. When his mother brought their food to the table, she ate quickly, emptying her plate while Benny dawdled over yet another meal he wouldn't finish.

'What should I read?' Janet put her knife and fork down and reached for his Bible.

'I'm doing the Psalms in the morning cos there are short ones.' Benny grinned cheekily, and she smiled back at him.

'I used to like those too,' his mum said, flicking through the pages.

Benny's head shot up. 'I didn't know you read the Bible.'

'I told you I went to Sunday school when I was a child.'

'I guess I forgot.' He reached across the table to cover her hand. 'Sorry, Mum. I don't remember stuff if it isn't about me. I'm trying to learn, so will you tell me again?' He hoped she would see his sincerity.

'I loved it.' Janet's face took on a faraway expression. 'Especially the Bible stories and songs. I used to go home afterwards and tell my family of dolls what I'd learned, so I guess they had their lesson too.'

'I reckon Beth's gonna be like that.' Benny laughed.

'Oh, she already tries.' There was a twinkle in his mother's eye. 'I've heard her telling her toys off when they're not doing what she wants.'

'She's gonna be bossy, like Nettie.' He wasn't really criticising, for his heart warmed when he thought of Nettie, and an indulgent smile spread across his face. 'She's gotta be bossy with me, or I won't do nothing.' He took another mouthful of his breakfast before looking back at his mum. 'How come you stopped going to church if you loved it so much?'

'When we talked about it a long time ago, I said it was because I grew up and married your father, and he's never been a churchgoer. But the truth is, I stopped going after Sylvie died.'

'Were you mad at God?'

Janet's eyes widened in surprise.

'Tim told us at youth group,' Benny continued, 'that sometimes people get like that if God doesn't do stuff the way they want Him to.'

'I'm not sure I was angry.' She played with her wedding ring. 'Just very sad. And the sadness took over until it was easier to hide in my room and read. Perhaps I was disappointed in God. If I was, I never dared to say it out loud. It was hard because I'd prayed for a sister, and God took her away. That didn't seem fair.'

'It's not.' Benny pushed his plate away, discarding his second piece of toast. 'I'm full.'

'How can you be when you've hardly eaten?'

'I don't need to eat much.' Benny gave his standard reply, wishing she didn't always nag him about food. He ate when he was hungry.

His mum sighed, leafing through the pages of his Bible until she found the Psalms. 'Do you have a favourite?'

'I like the one about the shepherd and the sheep.' After rising to stand behind her, he flicked through until he found a section highlighted messily with a green marker. 'That one.' He pointed to the passage before returning to his seat.

'Psalm twenty-three.' Janet averted her gaze, but Benny noticed the catch in her voice.

'Do you remember it?'

'I had to memorise it when I was eight years old.' She still couldn't look at him. 'Our Sunday school teacher promised us a New Testament with pictures. I spent hours poring over that psalm until I could recite it from memory.'

'I couldn't do that.' He shrugged. 'I'm rubbish at remembering stuff. Do you still remember it?' Benny wondered whether his mother would change the subject, yet the intensity of her stare told him she might not.

'The last time I heard it was at Sylvia's funeral.' Her voice was raw with emotion. 'They always read it at funerals. I suppose it's because it gives people hope.'

'I'm sorry.' Benny was behind her again in an instant, his arms around her neck and his cheek touching hers. 'You can read something else. Or you haven't gotta read to me if you don't want to. I should do it. I was just being lazy.'

However, Janet was already closing her eyes, speaking the long-forgotten words from memory.

The Lord is my shepherd; I shall not want.

He maketh me to lie down in green pastures: he leadeth me beside the still waters.

He restoreth my soul: he leadeth me in the paths of righteousness for his name's sake.

Yea, though I walk through the valley of the shadow of death, I will fear no evil: for thou art with me; thy rod and thy staff they comfort me.

Thou preparest a table before me in the presence of mine enemies: thou anointest my head with oil; my cup runneth over.

Surely goodness and mercy shall follow me all the days of my life: and I will dwell in the house of the Lord for ever.

Janet completed the psalm with tears rolling down her cheeks while Benny held her, feeling her agony and silently entreating his Saviour for help. All his life, his mother had cared for and nurtured him. Now she was the one in need, and Benny would rise to the challenge however he could.

During the silence that followed, Janet composed herself and opened her eyes. Benny slowly released her, picked up his plate, and crossed the kitchen to scrape his unfinished meal into the bin.

'Those are different words to what's in my Bible,' he said. 'But I liked how you said them.'

'We only had the King James Version when I was growing up.' She rested her chin against her hand. 'Those were the words the vicar read at Sylvia's graveside. I can still hear his monotonous voice going through the motions. I suppose he shared the psalm to encourage us, but I felt as though he was acting. I thought that if a vicar was only pretending to care about our family's pain, then maybe God was too.'

'I don't reckon that's right.' Benny spoke over his shoulder as he rinsed his plate. 'Tim's teaching me that God always cares when we're scared or upset.'

'Your confidence is growing with your faith.'

'I'm still rubbish at understanding the Bible. I give up too quickly, even though Tim found me one that's meant to have easier words.' Glancing at the clock on the wall, Benny realised his hour was up. He picked up his Bible and headed for the door. 'I've gotta go now.'

While Benny left without a backward glance, his thoughts remained fixated on his mum's ability to recount words she hadn't heard since her sister's funeral. The only verse he had memorised was John 3:16. *For God so loved the world, that he gave his one and only son, that whoever believes in him shall not perish but have eternal life.* Returning the Bible to its place beside his bed, Benny asked Jesus to help.

'I know You want me to help her too, cos she's always helped me,' he prayed silently. 'But I don't know how, so if I need to say something, can You tell me?'

Satisfied that for now, he had done all he could, Benny's thoughts turned to the fun he would have with Nettie and Beth on this unexpected snow day. A slow smile crossed his face as he imagined snowball fights, building snowmen, and making snow angels with Beth, interspersed with the joy of stealing kisses from Nettie. Nettie, Beth and Jesus. They'd all turned his world upside down. It was fuller, with meaning and purpose, and he didn't want it to change. He was experiencing the freeing effects of love in all its fullness, and the more he received, the more he wanted to give.

10

By the time Benny arrived at the Thompson house, the snow had stopped falling. Beth stood in the hallway, her warm breath frosting her grandparents' front door as she pressed her button nose against the glass.

'Benny!' Her cries of delight reached his ears long before Nettie appeared to open the door with the smile she reserved especially for him, accompanied by a welcoming kiss.

'She's been like this all morning.' Nettie jabbed a finger at her bouncing toddler and scowled. 'I can't even get her to eat breakfast. She won't keep still.'

Benny made a grab for Beth as she tried to push past him through the open front door.

'You can't go out with no shoes on.' He held her firmly as Beth attempted to wriggle free, and Nettie closed the door with a thud.

'Wanna play.' Beth looked up with doleful eyes that melted Benny's heart.

'We will. But you've gotta eat your breakfast first.'

He swept her up in his arms, carrying her into the kitchen with Nettie trailing behind them. Sitting at the table with Beth on his lap, Benny playfully coaxed her into eating a slice of toast.

Nettie was watching him with an indulgent smile. 'She'll figure you out one day.' She reached for a cloth to wipe Beth's sticky hands and face.

'About what?' Benny looked at her in confusion while licking a blob of jam off his finger.

'You're always trying to make her eat, but you eat less than she does.'

'I eat the stuff she doesn't want.' He munched on Beth's discarded crust.

As she picked up her daughter's empty plate and washed it, Nettie laughed.

Half an hour later, they were walking hand in hand through the snow-covered streets. Beth rode on Benny's shoulders, exclaiming over everything she saw from her elevated position. Children built snowmen in their front gardens, while others rolled huge snowballs or slid around on anything slippery they could find.

A nearby hill provided excellent opportunities for sledging, and Benny laughed with Nettie at the antics of adults and children alike. Beth soon demanded to be on her feet, where she danced around, pelting anyone who dared to approach her with snowballs, and expertly dodging those that were aimed at her in return.

Their neighbour, Karen Moss, had brought her young son, Marcus, to join the fun, and he and Beth played happily together under Karen's watchful eye. Benny spotted Karen's 18-year-old son, Dale, and prayed the older boy would leave him alone.

'You're still afraid of him, aren't you?' Nettie squeezed his hand whilst subtly indicating Dale.

'How come you can tell?' Benny scowled.

'Because I love you.' When she snuggled closer, he revelled in her nearness. With Nettie at his side giving him strength, perhaps he could face Dale Moss without turning into a mumbling wreck.

'All right, Weed?' Dale sneered as he towered over Benny. He was almost six feet tall, with broad shoulders and a swaggering gait. Benny stood six inches shorter, and his shoulders were as narrow as the rest of him.

'Yeah.' Tightening his grip on Nettie's hand, he met Dale's glare head-on. 'I reckon Marcus likes the snow as much as Beth does.'

Dale's face registered shock at Benny's show of confidence, and he only managed a grunt.

Benny let out a sigh of relief when his nemesis backed away and he released his vice-like grip on Nettie, hoping Dale hadn't noticed the tremor in his hand.

'Hi Benny!' An unfamiliar female voice caused Benny to spin. Recognising Heather from the youth group, he acknowledged her with a self-conscious wave.

'Who was that?' Nettie asked.

'Heather.' He dismissed her question with a shrug.

'How do you know her?' Green eyes bore into blue, and Benny experienced a familiar confusion. Why was Nettie mad with him for waving at a girl?

'She goes to my youth group.'

At his faltering explanation, Nettie rewarded him with a kiss, which only baffled Benny further. 'How come you were mad at me?' The pitch of his voice rose with his growing agitation, and his face reddened in embarrassment.

'I'm sorry.' Nettie gave him a reassuring smile. 'It was my fault.'

'What did you do? I don't get it, Nettie.' He walked several paces away from her. She followed, and he soon felt a comforting hand on his back. 'I hate it when I don't know stuff and I act stupid.' He fought not to cry. Why did confusion lead to tears? Why couldn't he control his emotions like normal boys his age?

'You're not stupid.' Nettie's gentle touch acted as a soothing balm.

Benny inhaled deeply and they stood in silence while she gave him time for his confusion to subside.

Soon, his facial features softened. 'Do you mean that? Do you really think I'm not stupid?'

'Of course you're not.' She enfolded him in her arms, and he rested his cheek against hers. He didn't care whether Dale was waiting for an opportunity to make fun of his neediness, because Benny craved all the love Nettie offered.

'All right?'

He nodded, and she pulled away, turning her attention to Beth playing in the snow alongside Karen and Marcus.

'I guess I'm not used to you being noticed by other girls,' she said. 'I think I was jealous.'

'You haven't got nothing to be jealous about. None of them talk to me much.'

'Probably because you're still too shy to talk back.' She winked at him, and he nodded. 'I was surprised you kept going to church after Brian left for uni.'

Brian Brooks had encouraged Benny so much with his schoolwork that when he asked him to attend the youth group, Benny had given in. Shortly afterwards, Benny had made his own commitment to Jesus.

'I like it if I don't have to say nothing,' he confessed. 'And Pastor Tim helps me understand stuff.'

The morning wore on, and Beth's excitement gave way to weariness. Still, she refused to give in, even when Karen said she was taking Marcus home for a nap.

'Why don't you let me take her too?' Karen addressed Nettie, who stood rocking her fretful toddler. 'I bet she'll sleep when Marcus does.'

'I wish she was more like him.' Nettie glanced down at the two-year-old standing obediently, holding his mother's hand. Unlike Beth, Marcus had no problem admitting he was tired.

'Give her to me.' Karen held out her arms, and Nettie gladly handed Beth over.

'See you later, Bethy.' Benny waved as Karen carried Beth away with Marcus trotting along at her side.

Enjoying some rare alone time, they climbed the hill for a better view of the fun below. The wind whistled around them, carrying the excited squeals of children and the voices of chattering parents huddled in small groups as the kids played. Benny had never felt so bitterly cold. His ears and nose burned, and he could barely feel his fingers or toes. For once, he was glad of the extra layer of warmth provided by his father's oversized coat. He yanked the zip up as high as possible and raised the collar.

'Do you want a go on my sledge?' A breathless Heather stopped beside them. Her face glowed from the exertion of dragging the sledge up the slippery mound, with minimal help from her bright-eyed younger sister.

'I dunno…' Benny was dubious, but Nettie's eyes lit up.

'I haven't been sledging for years!'

'I've never done it.' He turned to Heather with a shy smile. 'My mum never let me. She was scared I'd have a seizure.' He didn't want to admit that the intense glare of the snow was already bringing on a headache. He was having too much fun being with Nettie, watching their neighbours sliding on sledges, plastic bags, and tin trays.

'You've got to try it at least once!' Heather urged.

He shouldn't do it. He wasn't well. But he didn't want to disappoint Nettie. 'Okay.'

Benny immediately sensed his girlfriend's pleasure. Soon, he was hurtling down the hill, hanging onto the sledge for all he was worth. Nettie gave a whoop of glee behind him as her red hair flew in the breeze.

When they landed at the bottom, tumbling off the sledge in a heap of arms and legs, Nettie giggled and pulled him to his feet, brushing snow off his back as she hugged him. 'That was amazing! I've got to do it again!'

'Yeah, well…' Benny couldn't share her enthusiasm. 'Can you go down with Heather next time? I reckon I'd rather watch.'

'All right.' She kissed him before taking hold of Heather's sledge to drag it back up the hill.

An hour later, Benny knew he had to go home. The pain that had started as a dull ache was now a nail being hammered right into the centre of his forehead. He hated letting Nettie down, but when he told her, she only offered understanding and warmth. They walked silently back through the streets still thronging with excited children, and she kissed him tenderly when they stopped at his front door.

'I had so much fun today.' She placed a cooling hand on his thundering forehead.

'Me too, but I've gotta go home now.' Even forming the words was too much of an effort.

'It's okay.' Nettie stroked his cheek. 'Do you want me to come in with you?'

He shook his head. 'I'll be okay after I take a tablet. I just can't look at the snow no more. It's too bright.'

Nettie released him with the reassurance that she was only a phone call away.

'Will you come over later?' Benny hated having to waste even a minute of their unexpected day together.

'Phone me when you're better, and Beth and I will come and cheer you up. Maybe we can go for another walk after she's in bed. It'll be dark by then, so the snow won't seem so bright.'

Benny nodded, and a familiar wave of nausea swept over him as he fumbled for his house key. Once he was inside, he darted for the downstairs cloakroom, reaching it just in time to empty his stomach into the toilet bowl.

'Benny?' His sister, Emma, appeared in the doorway as he leant over the sink to wash his face. The pain in his head had eased, as it often did after he vomited.

'Was it a seizure?' Emma asked, giving him her arm.

'No.' Benny was shaking. He leaned gratefully against her. 'I threw up cos I had a headache from the snow.'

Emma helped him into the lounge, and he flopped onto the sofa. 'How come you're here?' His speech was slurred.

'I walked over because I didn't have to go to college.'

Emma shared a flat nearby with Erin Moss, Dale and Marcus's elder sister. The two friends had claimed their independence shortly before Emma began training as a social worker.

'Where's Mum?' Benny had expected Janet to come running as soon as he stumbled through the door and rushed for the cloakroom. She always hovered over him when he was sick.

'In bed. I went up to see her, and she said she's got a headache too. Can I get you anything?'

'A cup of tea.' The cushion next to him looked like a good place to bury his head. In his weakness and exhaustion, Benny felt much younger than his 16 years. He was glad his sister was there to take care of him.

'All right, Pestie.' Emma bent to kiss his cheek, then left him, returning five minutes later with a mug of milky tea, prepared just the way he liked it.

She took the chair opposite as Benny sat up and sipped his drink.

'Where's Dad?' he asked.

'He told Mum he had loads to catch up on at the garage, so he walked to work.'

'That's typical.' Their father's work ethic was legendary in the Wellander household. Ola rarely took a day off, even when he struggled with the usual coughs or colds. He wouldn't give in to weakness. Snow meant nothing to a man raised in Denmark.

'Mum seemed upset.' Emma glanced at him questioningly. 'She had a load of screwed up tissues on the cabinet by her bed, so I could tell she'd been crying. Do you know what's wrong? Has Dad been having a go at her again?'

'Her sister died.' Benny spoke with no trace of emotion.

'What are you on about?' Emma gaped at him in bewilderment. 'Mum hasn't got a sister. Do you mean Uncle David's wife? It can't be Malcolm's. I think they got divorced, so I doubt whether anyone would bother to tell us if she died.'

'No. Sylvia.'

'Who's Sylvia?' Emma sounded exasperated.

'I told you. She was Mum's sister, and she died.'

'When?'

'When she was six.'

'Who? Mum or Sylvia?' Emma was clearly flummoxed by her brother's unsatisfactory explanations.

'I've gotta go to bed, Emmie.' Benny rose unsteadily.

'No, you don't.' She held up a hand to stop him. 'Not until you've explained this nonsense about Mum having a sister.'

'She told us last night.' He fumbled over his words. 'Sylvia was six, and Mum was 11, and Mum went to stay with her friend, but when she got back, Sylvia was dead. They had a funeral and stuff. She was crying loads, so I reckon that's why she's feeling rubbish today. I always get headaches after I cry. It can't be the snow cos she hasn't been out in it.'

'Mum had a sister, and she never told us?' Emma followed Benny to the door.

'Dad will tell you about it when he gets back. You know I'm rubbish at explaining stuff.'

Emma nodded, and Benny was grateful when she let him go.

11

Benny woke a couple of hours later, relieved to discover his head was clearer. His room was dark. He switched on a lamp and glanced at his bedside clock as his stomach rumbled with an unfamiliar hunger pang. It was almost time for tea. He'd slept most of the afternoon away, wasting an opportunity to be with Nettie.

Reaching for his phone, he dashed off a text peppered with spelling mistakes, telling his girlfriend he was better and begging her to come over. Nettie responded quickly, saying that taking Beth out again and over-exciting her would delay her bedtime. They needed to wait until the toddler was fed, bathed, and tucked up for the night before indulging in one of their evening walks.

Benny ambled downstairs, expecting to find his mother preparing their evening meal, but the kitchen was empty. Hearing voices from the dining room, he joined his father and sister, who sat with a chessboard on the table between them. His dad must have cut his working day short because of the snow.

'Are you better?' Emma asked as Benny sat down beside her.

'Yeah.' He yawned and stretched, still attempting to conquer the aftereffects of a headache-induced sleep. 'Is Mum still in bed?'

'When Emma took her up a cup of tea about half an hour ago, she was still crying.' Ola sighed and focused on his next move. 'I don't know what's wrong with her today. She was tearful when I left for work, and she's even worse now.'

'Did you tell Em about Sylvia?' Benny asked.

'Yes. I explained everything since you only confused her.' Ola used his knight to take one of Emma's pawns and gave his daughter a challenging look.

'I can't say stuff right when I'm okay. It's even harder when I've got a headache and I've thrown up.' Benny sensed his father's frustration, so felt the need to explain.

'All right.' Ola silenced him with a subtle hand gesture. 'It doesn't matter now because Emma knows as much as we do.'

'Do you reckon that's why Mum's crying and staying in bed?' Benny hoped they would help him understand his mother's uncharacteristic behaviour, but they seemed as clueless as he was.

'I don't see why.' Ola waited for Emma to take her move, then appraised the board with a satisfied nod. He glanced at Benny and back to the board. 'It happened a long time ago, so why should it affect her now?'

'She cried loads when she told us.' Why was his father dismissing Mum's pain so easily? Why was he more interested in a chess match than in the person who lay suffering alone in her bed?

'Your mother's an emotional person.' Ola didn't even lift his eyes from the board this time. 'You should understand because you take after her.'

Benny tried not to show how much his father's words stung his tender heart. 'Is she gonna cook our tea?' There was no point talking about it any longer. His dad would only become angrier.

'Since when have you cared about food?' Ola's tone was cutting. 'If you're hungry, you're more than capable of making a sandwich.'

Benny rose and headed for the door.

'Can I make you something?' Emma asked.

Benny was sure his sister knew he was upset. She had the same instincts as Nettie for sensing his struggles. 'It's okay. I can do it.'

Ola and Emma continued their game while Benny ate. They were still engrossed when Nettie arrived. Benny was relieved to see her, and grateful for an opportunity to escape from his father's dark mood.

They walked hand in hand, crunching through thick snow under a starlit sky, until Nettie pulled him to a halt under a streetlamp. 'Something's wrong.' The orange glow gave her face a pale and ghost-like appearance.

'Everything's weird at home.' Benny shuffled nervously.

'How do you mean?'

It took him a while to form his reply, but Nettie's patience gave him the courage to speak. 'Mum's been in bed all afternoon, and Emmie and Dad reckon she's up there crying.'

'Have you talked to her?'

Nettie's question hit him like a gut punch. 'Do you think I should?'

'I can't imagine your dad or Emma giving her much sympathy. They're not the type.' Nettie spoke in her matter-of-fact, no-nonsense way. It was one of the things he loved most about her. She didn't use clever words to confuse or catch him out.

'Dad's cross because he doesn't get her.' But Nettie understood him. If she pushed, it was because she cared. 'I don't reckon I get it either.' He drew her in for a hug.

Nettie leaned down, tucking her head under his chin, even though she stood a couple of inches taller. 'Like I said this morning, you're the one who's closest to Janet.' She stroked his cheek, and Benny kissed her fingertips. 'If she's gonna talk to anyone, it'll be you.'

'I won't know what to say.' He gazed helplessly at her.

'Maybe listening will be enough.' Straightening up, she reached for his hand and urged him forward. 'When I'm stressed because Beth's winding me up, I offload onto you, and you listen.'

'But I can help with Beth.' An unexpected patch of ice caused Benny to slip, and Nettie tightened her grip to steady him. 'I can take her out to give you a break.'

'I don't always need practical help. Some days, I just need to moan, and to know you're listening.' They stopped walking, and Nettie turned to him with an adoring smile. 'And you always do.'

'I listen cos I love you.' Benny ran his fingers down the length of her hair, and Nettie closed her eyes with an appreciative smile.

'And you love your mum too, so it won't hurt you to listen if she wants to talk about Sylvia.'

'Dad said the Sylvia stuff happened ages ago, so she shouldn't still be upset.'

'Sylvia was her sister.' Nettie spoke gently as she leaned against him. 'And your mum couldn't talk about her for over 30 years.' She sighed. 'That must have been so hard. I still think there's more. I mean, she's bound to have questions about why Sylvia died. No one dies from a cold, and I think Janet knows that too.'

Benny was more than ready to change the subject. They walked on, laughing over Beth's antics in the snow and the fun she'd had with Karen and Marcus, until they returned to his house, where they indulged in goodnight kisses on the doorstep.

'See you tomorrow.' Benny reluctantly let Nettie go, hoping one day he wouldn't have to.

He entered the house, and was surprised to discover Emma hadn't left. She said she was staying the night because she didn't want to walk home in the snow. Benny had presumed she would never sleep in their parents' house again, so he planned on making the most of this unexpected treat.

He snuck into her old room and when Emma walked in, he was there waiting.

'Did I say you could come in here?' His sister dug him in the ribs with her elbow, and he let out an exaggerated yelp of pain. 'That didn't hurt! You're such a baby.' She flopped down beside him on the bed. 'Budge up.'

'Do you remember how I always slept with you when I was little?' Benny rolled onto his side, burying his face in her pillow.

'But now you're 16, and you keep trying to tell us you're growing up,' Emma teased.

'I am!' He glared at her out of the corner of his eye. 'I've got a girlfriend and a part-time job.'

'No matter what, you'll always be my little pest.'

Benny uncovered his face, slid closer to Emma, and looped his arm through hers.

'Emmie?' He spoke her name in barely more than a whisper. 'Should I talk to Mum? Nettie reckons I should.'

'What about?' Emma sounded baffled.

'The Sylvia stuff.'

'You definitely can't go marching in there now.' Emma shivered and reached for a blanket off the bottom of the bed. 'Mum and Dad will be asleep. He'll go mad if you wake them up.'

'I might do it at the weekend.' Benny yawned.

'What do you want to talk to her about?' Emma tugged on the pillow. 'Learn to share, Pestie!'

'I told you. All the stuff with Sylvia.' Benny allowed her to slide the pillow her way.

'Let it go, Benny.' She paused before continuing. 'I still think it's weird how Mum brought it up after all these years.'

'It was the photos.'

'What photos?' Emma's head shot up. 'Dad didn't mention those.'

'They're from when Mum was little.' Benny tugged the blanket off her, stealing it for himself. 'They're in one of those books. There are pictures of her with Grandma and Grandpa and her brothers, but there aren't any of Sylvia.'

'Why did the photo album make her talk?'

'Nettie asked if she wished she had a sister, and Mum started crying. That was when she started talking about Sylvia.'

'It is strange that Sylvia wasn't in any of the photographs.' Emma's tone was contemplative.

'Did Grandma and Grandpa get rid of some of them?' Benny asked.

'I suppose people sometimes throw things away when the memories are too painful…'

'I bet Mum wishes she still had pictures so she could remember what Sylvia looked like.' Benny was enjoying having his sister close again. They hadn't chatted like this for ages. 'Perhaps that's why she's been crying all day.'

'Or the crying is her way of letting the sadness out,' Emma said. 'Whatever it is, there's nothing any of us can do to change the past. Dad's right. Mum will have to move on.'

Benny chose not to answer, hoping Emma would presume he'd fallen asleep.

'Just like old times, Pestie,' she chuckled, giving him a gentle punch. Then she wriggled under the duvet, leaving Benny on top with the blanket. He was relieved she hadn't sent him away. With Emma next to him, he would sleep, just as he always had.

When Benny awoke in the pre-dawn darkness of the following day, he turned over to greet Emma with an impish grin.

'You're still here then.' She yawned. 'I bet you pretended to be asleep just so I'd let you stay.'

Benny shook his head emphatically. 'I was gonna talk and then go back in my own room to sleep. But it was too nice having you here, so I didn't wanna go.'

When Emma offered to prolong their nostalgia by making pancakes, they snuck downstairs like children planning a midnight feast while their parents slept on in oblivion.

'Do you reckon I'll get another day off?' Benny peered out of the kitchen window at the snow still blanketing the ground.

'It's turned icy, so yes.' Emma sat opposite him and watched as he devoured his pancakes and washed them down with a mug of hot chocolate. Although Benny was usually a fussy eater, he'd never refuse this special treat.

Ola joined them shortly after sunrise, followed by a bleary-eyed Janet.

'What are you doing here?' their mum asked, gazing in confusion at her daughter.

'I stayed the night.' Emma smiled. 'And I ended up with a pest for company.'

Benny expected his mother to laugh, but Janet moved around the kitchen in a daze, not even remembering to give him his morning hug. He watched her anxiously as his unease grew.

He resolved to stay at home, even though Nettie would be free to spend time with him. She didn't complain when he confessed his concerns for his mother by text.

When Emma left with their father, Janet complained of another headache and returned to her bedroom. Benny made to follow, but she surprised him by closing the door. He stared at the barrier in bewilderment. His mother had never refused him entry to her room. She usually relished their time together, allowing him to monopolise her as he had during his early years as her constant shadow.

Benny lay on the sofa and texted Nettie. 'Mum doesn't wanna talk to me. It's weird and scary.'

'I'll be right over.' Nettie was as good as her word, arriving with her sleeping daughter bundled up in a fleece. They settled Beth on the sofa, sitting beside her with warm drinks and a packet of chocolate biscuits.

'Perhaps your mum needs time.' Nettie sipped her coffee.

'Time for what?' Benny asked.

'To sort her head out.'

'I don't get it, Nettie. She was acting normal yesterday before I went out. She made breakfast, and she even read my Bible.' He thought for a moment, then clarified. 'Well, no, she didn't read it. She… kind of said a psalm. She remembered it. And she got upset because it was the one the vicar read at Sylvia's funeral.'

Beth stirred and whimpered. Nettie put her mug down and lifted her daughter onto her lap, rocking her tenderly while mumbling soothing words. 'It isn't time to wake up yet, Bethy. You need a bit more sleep.' She turned back to Benny when Beth stubbornly ignored her suggestion. 'So, the psalm brought back more memories.'

'Yeah. And Mum must've gone funny afterwards.' Benny reached for a chocolate biscuit and dipped it in his tea.

'And me, Benny!' Beth tried to make a grab for his biscuit.

'Hang on.' He dipped it again, and Beth smacked her lips in appreciation.

They spent the next hour building a snowman in the back garden until it rained. As the shower grew heavier and forced them indoors, Beth cried as she watched the snow turning into slushy puddles. 'Come back, snow. Back, back.'

Benny held her lovingly, sharing her sadness. Janet had reappeared, but she still seemed quiet and distant.

By the time his dad came home, Nettie and Beth had left, and Janet had served a hot meal. The family ate in silence, reminding Benny of the past, when their strained relationships had almost destroyed them. The atmosphere in their home was eerily familiar, and he hated it.

Once the dishes were cleared away, Ola buried his head in his newspaper, and Janet went back upstairs. Since Benny was the last to go to bed, it was up to him to turn out the lights on the Christmas tree. It had brought happiness the previous Saturday, when his mother had insisted on decorating early to please Beth. They usually waited until the middle of December, but Janet had broken with tradition for a little girl who wasn't even her grandchild. Both Nettie and her daughter had been accepted as part of their family, and even Ola hadn't questioned the change in their routine.

The glittering tree no longer seemed to belong in a house filled with mourning. Why had his mother's revelation changed everything? A fog had descended, and Benny could do nothing about it.

He climbed the stairs and sank onto his bed, feeling the sting of bitter tears as he prepared to turn over and surrender to sleep. At least if he slept, he couldn't think about things he struggled to understand.

A stab of guilt pricked at the edges of Benny's conscience as he realised two days had passed since he'd read his Bible himself. Last night, he'd fallen asleep on Emma's bed, and he hadn't even thought about reading this morning because of his worry over Janet. After that, he'd allowed Nettie and Beth to distract him.

Benny's thoughts turned to a verse Pastor Tim had read at last week's youth group, and he reached for his Bible to look it up. He'd placed a bookmark on the page, because something had jumped out at him. Benny was striving to listen to God, yet all too often, he failed. Tim assured him that Jesus saw his heart and appreciated his efforts, but Benny worried about whether they were enough.

Benny found the verse and waited for the letters to stop dancing on the page. Tim had taught him to pray before reading, so he asked for help, allowing his swirling thoughts to focus. His mind was like his mother's spinning washing machine. It sometimes got faster and faster until it ended in a seizure. Then he found himself flat out on the floor as his body did what it would do, while his mind floated away to a detached, unreachable place. When the seizure ended, he came back with a jolt, and he always vomited.

He'd tried explaining this to his friend pastor Tim, and Tim had offered to pray for him. Benny knew the seizures affected his brain, and he worried he'd never understand something as hard as the Bible. Tim encouraged him to work at his own pace, tackling one verse at a time.

'Just take it slowly.' Benny heard Tim's reassuring voice in his head. 'Build it up, like the pieces of a jigsaw, and pray for understanding. God's not one of your teachers. He's not waiting to mark you down because of your struggles. He's your father. He wants to help you.'

Benny read slowly, forcing his mind to consider each word. *Give all your worries and cares to God, for he cares about you. Stay alert! Watch out for your great enemy, the devil. He prowls around like a roaring lion, looking for someone to devour.*

A shiver ran down Benny's spine every time he thought about the Devil. Was the Devil trying to attack his family, messing with his mother's mind and making her depressed because of her childhood? Was she feeling rubbish, as Benny often did? And what could he do to help her? He sensed the verses would tell him, so he read them again, his eyes lingering on the first part. He needed to leave his worries with Jesus because Jesus cared for him. If that were true, then Jesus cared about his mother too.

Benny closed the Bible and shut his eyes, experiencing the comforting presence of his heavenly companion right there in his bedroom.

'I dunno how to help my mum,' he confessed, 'but I reckon You do. You know everything. So, I'm gonna try to do what You said. I'm gonna give my worries to You, and I'll try not to get stressed while I wait to see what You'll do. Thank You, Jesus. Amen.'

He switched off the lamp, slid under the covers, and drifted into a peaceful sleep.

12

Friday was Benny's most challenging day, and this week seemed even worse, despite his efforts to give all his worries to Jesus. He ran home, after trying not to throw up on the overcrowded school bus, slammed the front door and rushed straight upstairs to swap his school uniform for jeans and a sweatshirt. If he hurried, he'd get in an hour's work with his dad. Time was precious if he wanted to prove his worth as a trainee mechanic. His father was a tough employer who didn't make allowances, even for Benny.

'Don't you want a cup of tea before you go back out?' His mum was waiting in the hallway as Benny clattered downstairs.

'No time.' His hand was already on the doorknob.

'Your dad wouldn't mind if you gave it a miss sometimes, love. Especially on these wintery nights.' She put a restraining hand on his shoulder.

'The snow's gone, and I don't care about walking in the rain.'

Benny was out the door before his mother could voice more protests. She was over-fussing again, and he'd thought they were past that. It only occurred to him as he was running to the garage that it was good she was finally out of bed.

The weekends allowed Benny breathing space from the pressure of school. Once he'd pushed through the most chaotic night of his week, there were two whole days when he didn't have to focus on the things he was rubbish at.

After his time at the garage, he would return home, rapidly consume as little as possible of his dinner, then dash off to the Friday night youth group. By bedtime, he would be mentally and physically exhausted. However, he had no desire to change things. He rarely saw Nettie on Fridays unless she came round for a hot chocolate when he texted to say he was home. He always hoped she would, even though it was late.

'I'm glad you're on time.' Ola didn't look up from fitting a new oil filter into a green Honda. 'I need your help.'

His father usually preferred to work alone, leaving Benny in the gentler hands of Peter Moss. Benny experienced a momentary panic. This was the opportunity he'd been waiting for. What if he blew it by making mistakes? He made a silent request for heavenly help. *'Don't let me mess it up, Jesus. I want him to know he can trust me.'*

Benny took his time, following instructions and asking for clarification, and his dad relaxed as they settled into their task.

'You did well today,' Ola said later, as he steered their car home through the pouring rain. 'You learn quickly when you listen.'

'I enjoyed working with you.' Benny turned to face him. 'I like Peter too, but…' He inhaled deeply and took the plunge. 'Can we do it again, Dad?'

'I suppose I've always put you with Peter because he's more patient.' Ola checked for oncoming traffic, then swung round a corner. 'I prefer working alone. I like things to be done my way, or not at all. You might say I'm a creature of habit.'

'I always do stuff the same too,' Benny said. 'I don't reckon I could do it if it had to be different every time. Even though I'm rubbish at learning, when I get something, I reckon I'm like you.'

Ola smiled as he turned onto their street. 'Perhaps we're more alike than I realised.' He cut the engine and gave Benny his full attention. 'We can work together more regularly as long as you promise not to get upset and tell tales to your mother when I shout. I get irritable when things don't go my way, and if you're in the firing line, you'll have to put up with it.'

'I will,' Benny promised. 'And I won't say nothing to Mum.'

'If I have a go at you, it's not personal. When we're at work, we're colleagues, not father and son.'

'You'll always be my dad.' Benny grinned, and Ola patted his hand. It was still hard to believe they were having conversations like this, given what their relationship had been like a short while ago.

'I'm pleased we're learning to work together.' Ola gave him a quick hug. 'I never thought we would.'

Benny wanted to say more, yet he needed to prove himself to his father before bringing up the subject of making it permanent. He was desperate to leave school, but he had to persuade Ola to see it his way. What was the point in studying for exams he was bound to fail? Even imagining them made his stomach churn. He wouldn't be able to make it through a single one without having a seizure and throwing up.

When they entered their home, his mum was waiting to put tea on the table. As usual, Benny played with his food. He noticed his mum doing the same and wondered if she had an upset tummy.

'Do you feel sick?' Food turned his stomach most days, except for ice cream or chocolate biscuits.

'No, I'm fine.' Janet gathered up their plates.

'I can't help with the washing up tonight.' Benny rose and slid his chair back under the table.

'Of course not. It's Friday.' Janet rewarded him with a smile. She never asked for help, but he offered it willingly these days. It gave them an excuse to spend time together and he knew she needed that.

'The rain's getting worse.' Ola pulled back the curtains to peer out. 'Do you want me to drive you to the church? You'll get soaked if you go on your bike.'

Benny considered his father's tempting offer but shook his head reluctantly. 'It's okay. Brian's home for Christmas. He's got a car now, so I guess I should go with him cos he asked.'

Despite their differences, Benny and his old tutor, Brian, had formed a tentative friendship that matured when Benny found faith in Jesus.

'It'll be nice for you to see him,' Janet said.

Benny was unwilling to acknowledge his reluctance to see Brian. He was convinced his time at university would have changed him. Surely they'd have even less in common now?

Benny had considered leaving the youth group when Brian left home, but Tim had persuaded him to stay, and although he still sat at the back, barely exchanging more than a hello with the others, Benny enjoyed listening to Tim's teaching. The pastor explained whatever he didn't understand during their study sessions on Saturday mornings, and Benny looked forward to those because Tim had a gift for simplifying the Bible. It wasn't the same as being at school. Benny relaxed with Tim, and he truly wanted to learn.

'How's school?' Brian drove, with Benny seated beside him. His parents had gifted him the car for his 18th birthday.

'Rubbish.' Benny laughed self-consciously. 'How's uni?'

'Great!' Brian beamed. 'I'm loving my course, and we've got a brilliant Christian Union.'

'What's that?' Benny thought he should know but had to admit he didn't.

'It's where the Christian students get together to pray and study.' Brian seemed happy to explain. 'It's like our youth group. We take it in turns to lead it.'

'I bet you're good at that. You like teaching.' Brian's goal was to become a physics teacher.

'Teaching the Bible is different. I've been going to church all my life, but it's amazing how much I still don't understand.'

'But you're a helper at youth now,' Benny said.

'Doesn't mean I know everything.'

'Tim reckons he doesn't know everything, even though he's a pastor, but you both get way more than me.'

'You've only been a Christian for a few months.' Brian smiled. 'Of course you won't understand the Bible the way we do. I bet you're learning.'

'I'm learning it better than I learn my schoolwork.' Benny grinned. 'And Dad reckons I'm doing okay at the garage.'

'Do you think you'll persuade him to take you on full-time now you're 16?'

'I thought you'd say I should stay at school and finish my GCSEs!'

'Why did you think that?' his friend asked.

'You liked school.'

'It's not for everyone.' Brian parked in front of the church. 'God made us different. He created me to be a physics teacher and you to be a mechanic.'

'Do you reckon?' Benny relaxed. Now he was sure of their continued friendship.

'You'll be a great mechanic. So, I'll teach your kids physics and send mine to you when they wreck their cars.' Laughter filled the car. They were enjoying one another's company despite their differences.

When the youth group was over and the youngsters gathered at the back of the hall for refreshments, Benny was surprised to see Heather making a beeline for him. She carried a cup of coffee and a plate of biscuits.

'Your girlfriend's daughter is really sweet.' Heather held out the plate.

Benny took a biscuit and dunked it in his tea. He had never talked to a girl apart from Nettie. This one was being friendly, so he needed to try. 'Thanks for lending us your sledge.' It was the only response he could think of, and it earned him a beaming smile.

'I reckon Nettie liked it more than you did.'

'Yeah.' His blush must have given him away.

Throwing back her head, Heather laughed. 'It's a pity she hasn't come here before. I guess she can't because of Beth.'

'Nettie doesn't go to church. I hope she will one day. I mean, I want her to and stuff.'

Though he fumbled over his words, Heather displayed none of the impatience he'd experienced from most of his peers. 'I'll pray for her.' The sincerity in her eyes assured him she meant it. 'The two of you are pretty serious, aren't you?'

'How come you know?'

'It's obvious by the way you act when you're together.' Heather sighed plaintively. 'I wish I had a boyfriend.'

'I bet you will one day.' Benny was amazed at how much he was enjoying this unexpected conversation.

'Most of my friends are seeing someone,' Heather said. 'I want to wait for a boy who won't want things I'm not ready to give him. Do you know what I mean?'

Benny felt his face turn crimson.

'I guess you can understand,' Heather continued, 'because you're seeing a girl with a baby.'

'I reckon Nettie wishes she'd done stuff different.' Benny cleared his throat, wondering how to explain. 'We're glad we've got Beth. I mean, I love her, even though she's not mine.' Was he saying too much? This was so out of character that he barely recognised himself.

'Most guys your age wouldn't choose someone with a baby. What you're doing… It's amazing.'

Heather was called away, and Benny sighed with relief. It took so much energy for him to talk to anyone except the few people he was close to.

'Are we still on for tomorrow?' Tim called out as Benny prepared to follow Brian to the door.

'Yeah.' Benny backtracked to the pastor's side. 'Will it be okay if...' he looked away, then back at Tim. 'My mum told us stuff about when she was a kid, and now she's acting weird, so I dunno what to do.'

'It might help if we talked it through. And it won't go any further.'

Benny smiled. He trusted Tim implicitly. 'Is it okay if we do that instead of studying?' He was still trying to come to grips with the rules that governed his new life as a Christian.

'Of course,' his pastor said, giving him a friendly pat on the back. 'We all need to talk sometimes. It's how we transfer what we're learning into everyday life. Biblical knowledge is great, but we've got to work out how to live it.'

Benny nodded. That was exactly what he needed, especially following his revelation the previous night. He knew what Jesus wanted. He just wasn't sure how to apply it to helping his mother. He still felt uneasy. He had been talking to his Saviour on and off all day instead of focusing on his studies. Would Jesus be mad about that? Tim had told him he could pray any time, but was praying when he was supposed to be listening to his teachers even allowed? Benny hoped Tim would provide answers to his many questions.

When he returned home, Benny was thrilled to hear Nettie's voice coming from the kitchen.

'Surprise!' She met him in the doorway for a hug.

Benny marvelled at how beautiful she was, even in her everyday clothes with no makeup. 'How come you're here?' He hoped she wouldn't misinterpret his words as disappointment.

'I needed to see you.' There was no hiding the love in her eyes.

'I wanna see you all the time.' He squeezed her hand and kissed her.

He'd been looking forward to seeing his mum too - perhaps she'd got better? But Janet soon put paid to that hope by retiring to her bed. Despite the rules they had to follow about being alone together, they soon heard Ola switching off the television and mounting the stairs.

'I'd better go soon,' Nettie said. 'I don't want to disrespect your parents.'

'One more cuddle,' Benny replied, releasing his hot chocolate to pull her closer.

While they finished their drinks, Benny talked about his work with Ola, and Nettie said she was pleased he'd had another breakthrough with his father. He also revealed his struggles during the conversation with Heather at the youth group. 'It's nice she wanted to talk to me. I'm just rubbish at working out what to say.'

'You struggle more when you get uptight.' Nettie's tone turned teasing as she batted her eyelashes. 'Just don't relax too much.'

'Why?' He knew the answer. He just wanted to hear her say it.

'I might get jealous.' Nettie slid onto his lap, and Benny wrapped his arms around her. 'Call me selfish,' she whispered, 'but I don't want you to be as relaxed with any other girl as you are with me.'

'That's never gonna happen.'

Their relationship had matured to the point where Benny was more confident in Nettie's teasing. She loved him, and he loved her with every fibre of his being. As she sat on his lap though, Benny tensed. It was easy to understand why couples went from handholding, to kissing, to more. Taking their relationship to the next level was harder to resist as their love grew.

However, several conversations with Tim had helped him understand the pitfalls and made him grateful for the rules his parents had put in place to protect them. Nettie had already been hurt by one man. Much as he desired Nettie, Benny would only add to that if he took what he wanted without marrying her first. When he was mature enough, he would marry her. He would willingly commit to being Nettie's husband and Beth's father if they still wanted him.

'I love you, Benny Wellander...' Nettie kissed him, then climbed off his lap. Where Benny was bashful with strangers, he was an open book with Nettie. They had both owned up to what they wanted and mutually agreed to wait. '...but I better go.' She rose and walked towards the doorway. 'I'm so glad I came here tonight.'

As Benny joined her for a final cuddle, he thought how much Nettie belonged in his arms. Holding her made him braver. Benny vowed to become a decent mechanic like his dad in order to provide for their future. His girlfriend brought out the best in him, and his self-belief grew every time he was with her.

'See you after your meeting with Pastor Tim.' She extracted herself from his arms, and Benny reluctantly kissed her goodnight before opening the front door.

'We'll take Beth for ice cream and play with her at the park,' he promised.

'Will the ice cream be a treat for her or you?' Nettie walked away with a tinkling laugh, a wave, and a beaming smile, turning back to blow him a kiss when she reached her parents' driveway.

Benny locked up and mounted the stairs to his room, more thankful than he could express. Tonight, he definitely wouldn't forget to pick up his Bible.

13

Benny woke the following morning to a message from Nettie. Beth had come down with a heavy cold.

'It looks like I'll be stuck at home with her today.' Their plans would have to be cancelled.

'It's okay.' Benny dashed off his reply. 'I'll come over later.'

'Are you sure?' Nettie's response came straight back. 'You're bound to catch Beth's cold.'

The answer would take too long to type, so he called her.

'Hi.' Nettie sounded pleased to hear from him and Benny was glad he hadn't stuck to texting.

'Poor Bethy. Is she really ill?'

'She's being a little drama queen.' Nettie's weary voice was accompanied by the distant sounds of Beth's grizzles. 'She'll be fine again tomorrow. The trouble is, she cries every time I put her down.'

'I still wanna see you both.' Benny wished there was more he could do. 'I don't care if I catch it. I can give you a break.'

'You're probably the only other person she'll go to, so thanks.'

There weren't words enough to share his love for her and Beth, but Benny ended the call with what words he had before ambling downstairs for his morning cup of warm milk.

The smell of burnt toast filled the kitchen, where Ola stood, buttering two overdone slices. 'Do you want some?' he asked, looking up.

'No thanks. I've gotta go.' Benny put his drink in the microwave, then turned back to his father. 'Where's Mum?' Janet was usually the first to rise.

'She didn't sleep, and she's got another of her headaches.'

'She's had one every day since Wednesday. Is she still upset about her sister?' Benny's eyes were drawn to the mug, slowly rotating in the microwave. He wondered how many times it would turn during the 30 seconds remaining until it pinged, and the light went off.

'I don't see why she would be.' Ola dismissed his words by exiting the kitchen with his breakfast.

Benny had learned not to push when his dad wasn't in the mood for conversation. After rapidly consuming his drink, he fetched his Bible from his room and raced out of the house.

Less than a quarter of an hour later, Benny entered Pastor Tim's small upstairs office at the church, carrying his Bible under his arm. He'd cycled the short distance from home, barely noticing the biting wind or the spattering of icy rain.

'Help yourself to biscuits.' Tim put two mugs of tea on his paper-strewn desk, sat down, and waved towards a second chair.

As he walked around the desk, Benny knocked Tim's paperwork. It fanned out messily as it fluttered to the floor.

'Sorry.' He picked up the scattered pages, painfully aware how warm his cheeks had got. 'I hope I didn't mess it up.'

'It's fine.' Tim sat back in his chair, letting it spin a little while Benny sorted himself out. 'I saw you talking to Heather last night. I'm glad you're making more friends.'

'I don't reckon we're friends just cos she talks to me.' Benny eyed Tim's collection of biscuits with disdain. 'How come you like those pink wafers?'

'I don't.' Tim smiled. 'Unfortunately, one of the cleaners keeps buying them, so I'm obliged to eat them.'

'I won't eat nothing I don't like.' Benny scowled at the offensive biscuits.

'That's hardly surprising, considering your low opinion of food.' There was a twinkle in the pastor's eyes.

Casual conversation helped Benny unwind. He knew that was why Tim played along, and he appreciated the effort.

'Going back to Heather…' Tim slid a mug closer to Benny.

'What about her?' Benny picked up the mug, blushing again as his hand shook and tea dripped onto the desk. 'I'm messing everything up today.'

'These things never come in ones or twos.' Tim offered him a tissue. 'If I knock one thing over, you can guarantee there'll be a second and possibly a third.' They shared a smile. 'You're not the only person who spills things and you'd do it less if you weren't so stressed.'

'Yeah.' Benny wiped his spilt tea, screwed the tissue into a ball, and inhaled deeply. Tim was right. He was stressed. It had been a stressful week. So many things weighed on his mind. He didn't have a clue where to begin, so he waited for Tim's help.

'You said you don't see Heather as a friend just because she talked to you.'

Why was Tim still going on about Heather? Benny had more important things to think about. He frowned back, but Tim didn't seem to get the hint.

'Isn't that what friends do, talk? All relationships start with conversation. I expect that's how it was for you with Nettie, Damo, or Brian. And it's how we got to know one another.'

'I guess.' Benny's frustration turned to thoughtfulness. Maybe Tim had a point. He trusted him, so he'd go with it. 'I've never had loads of friends. I don't need them.'

'Don't ignore the gifts God's giving you,' Tim warned. 'He's broadening your horizons. Opening yourself up to more friendships is an important part of that.'

'But Heather's a girl.' The room felt hot and airless. Benny wanted to ask if he could open a window.

'So?' Tim wasn't letting him off the hook. He never did.

'It'd be bad if we were friends, because of Nettie.' The screwed-up tissue made a surprisingly good distraction as he rubbed it between his fingers.

'You don't think two Christians of the opposite sex can have a friendship without becoming romantically involved?' Tim's gentle brown eyes bore into Benny's.

'I never thought about it before.' Benny aimed the tissue at the wastepaper basket. It fell a few inches short. 'We saw her on

Wednesday. She let us borrow her sledge, and Nettie got in a grumpy strop when Heather talked to me. Maybe Nettie doesn't want me talking to no other girls.'

'Was she jealous?'

'I guess, till I told her Heather was only someone from youth group.' Benny rose, picked up the poorly aimed tissue, and dropped it into the bin.

'Nettie has to learn she can trust you.' Tim slid his glasses out of their case on his desk and polished them on his trousers. 'Trust is one of the biggest ingredients in a relationship. It's like the foundation of a building. It's what keeps the whole thing from collapsing.'

'How do you get it?' Benny wanted to learn.

'By proving to Nettie that you'd never cheat on her with Heather or any other girl, no matter what.'

'I won't, Tim.' Benny was certain of it. 'I love Nettie, and I'm gonna marry her when I'm old enough.'

'I can tell you're serious.' Tim took a long sip of his tea.

'Lots of boys my age mess around.' Benny crossed to the window, gazing down into the car park where his bike leaned against a wall. The rain had stopped, and the sun glistened on the wet tarmac. 'They go out with a girl for a few weeks, then they dump her for someone else.' He turned to face Tim. 'My mate Damo does that. He even dated two girls at the same time once. He said they'd never find out. I told him they would, and they did, so they both dumped him.'

'Even if they hadn't, Damo was disrespecting both of them.' Now Tim was leafing carefully through his Bible's thin pages. He shook his head distractedly, then closed his eyes. Benny wondered whether he was praying.

'You talk about respect a lot.' Benny returned to his seat opposite the pastor.

'I believe it's central to our faith, along with truthfulness and love.' Tim looked him squarely in the eye, and Benny held his gaze unflinchingly for at least ten seconds before he had to look away.

'I wanna respect Nettie. I try to, but... It's hard sometimes. Before we got together, my life was all about me.' His face warmed again at the admission. 'My mum kind of spoiled me, I guess. If stuff was wrong, or if people were mean, I went crying to her. I knew she'd make it okay. But sometimes, I reckon it was my fault. I didn't always treat other people with respect.'

'That's a brave thing to admit.'

'I don't wanna do that to Nettie.' Benny was on his feet, pacing the box-like room. He wished it was bigger so he could go further: five paces to the window, and five paces back to the door. Even though he probably looked stupid, he had to be on the move.

'You treat her and Beth well, from what I've seen.' Tim swung on his chair again. He had never been bothered by Benny's pacing.

This time, Benny stopped when he reached the door. He didn't want to be close to the desk when he made his confession. He could walk out whenever he wanted. If he did, Tim wouldn't force him to come back because he'd always allowed him the freedom to choose.

Benny gripped the door handle for support. Something inside urged him to speak. Hadn't he come here seeking his pastor's advice? 'Nettie was at my house last night. Mum and Dad were in bed, and... and...' He was suddenly lost for words.

'Did anything happen?' Tim asked gently.

'No.' Benny studied his trainers. They were old and shabby. He needed new ones, just like he needed new everything else. Nettie was always smartly dressed, but she never criticised his appearance. 'I reckon I wanted it to. Only I didn't too, cos of the stuff you've been teaching me.'

'You didn't fail God or Nettie.' Tim's reassurance gave Benny the courage to retake his seat. 'Those feelings you're having – they're normal. It's what you do with them that counts.'

'So God won't be mad cos I wanted to...' Benny fumbled over his words.

'Absolutely not.'

Relief washed over Benny like a weight lifted off his shoulders, and the room no longer seemed small and stifling. 'I'm trying to listen to God. I didn't read my Bible properly for a couple of days cos there was loads of stuff going on at home. Then God told me to, and I listened.'

'Tell me about that.' Despite the annoying glare from the sunlight reflecting off his glasses, Tim's gaze was reassuring.

'I'm rubbish at explaining. You won't get it.'

'I usually do. And if I don't, I ask. That's how we've always worked, isn't it?'

Benny nodded and allowed his story to tumble out, hopping from one subject to another. It probably wasn't in logical order. One moment, he was talking about his mum and Sylvia. The next, he switched to playing with Beth in the snow. When he realised he'd missed some vital details from his mum's past, he circled back.

Tim's face took on a look of concentration as he tried to join the dots. 'So your mother had a sister, and she died.'

'Yeah, but she didn't say nothing till Tuesday night. And then she said it all.' Benny's waterfall of words had dried up, and he was exhausted by the effort of speaking.

'And you say she's been acting differently?' Rising from his seat, Tim half-closed the blinds to block out the sun's dazzling glare.

'She's stressing over me again and stuff. Or she stays in bed cos she reckons she's got a headache.'

'I imagine it was draining to share something that was so deeply buried.'

'Now she's told us, Dad reckons she should forget it.' Benny felt the pressure of more words forcing their way out. 'But I dunno if Mum can. Nettie says Mum needs to understand why Sylvia died, but Dad and Emma keep telling her to let it go.'

'What about you? What do you think?' Tim bit into a pink wafer, screwing up his face in disgust.

'I don't think much about nothing, do I?' Benny swallowed back tears. He wouldn't cry now. He couldn't.

'That's not true.' Tim slid the box of tissues closer to him. 'You've already proved that in your efforts to respect Nettie.'

The tears fell, and there was nothing Benny could do to stop them. 'My brain isn't normal, is it, Tim? When I try to sort loads of stuff out, I get muddled. And I end up like this.'

'It's okay.' While Benny blew his nose, Tim waited patiently. 'Shall we do this bit by bit?'

Benny nodded weakly as Tim summarized everything they'd discussed, allowing time for reflection.

'You tried to go back to some of your old habits,' the pastor concluded.

Benny's eyes opened wide in astonishment. 'What do you mean?'

'You spent Wednesday night lying on your sister's bed. Wasn't that what you used to do?' Tim paused as Benny nodded. 'And on Thursday, you were uneasy, so you spent time with Nettie and Beth as a distraction. You worried over the way your parents were acting out of character. You did everything except pick up your Bible and hand your worries over to Jesus.'

'I did that in the end.' A motorbike whizzed past the church, making Benny jump. Why did sudden noises make him jumpy?

'That was your moment of victory.' Tim's smile was triumphant.

'I dunno.' Benny sighed. 'I only read a few verses.'

'You listened to the Holy Spirit, leading you to the right verses for just the right time. After that, you gave over your worries and slept.'

'I wish Mum could do that,' Benny mused. 'If she's still upset about Sylvia, I guess that's what she needs to do. But I'm still mad at myself cos I messed up. I shouldn't have done that, should I? I let God down.'

Tim opened his Bible to the last chapter of John and waited for Benny to do the same. He explained how the disciples wanted to return to the familiarity of fishing after Jesus' death and resurrection. 'They were scared and uncertain. Although Jesus had risen, they didn't understand what that meant, or how they should respond. So they reverted to what they knew.'

'Till Jesus sorted them out.' Benny's response was straight to the point.

'Like He sorted you out when He told you to read your Bible.' Tim took off his glasses, signalling that their brief study was complete. 'You're still learning, Benny. You listened, so give yourself grace. You won't get everything right all the time. No one does. Remember, Jesus looks at your heart, and your heart is seeking after Him.'

'Yeah, it is.' Benny scribbled in the margin of his Bible. *Jesus*, followed by a doodle of glasses and a heart. 'So is that what's happened to my mum?' he asked. 'Is she going back to old stuff, like I did? Is that why she's fussing over me, lying in bed and getting stressed?'

'It might be.' Tim picked up their half-empty mugs of cold tea. 'We've earned a refill.'

Benny followed his pastor downstairs. 'I wish I could help Mum like you're helping me.'

'Pray about it.' In the kitchen, Tim filled the kettle and switched it on.

'I'm not like you, Tim.' Benny hovered in the doorway. 'If I say stuff, I mess it up.'

'You said your mum has always understood you.'

Benny's attention was caught by a set of brightly coloured posters depicting Noah's ark and Daniel in the lion's den. Why hadn't he noticed them before? He moved closer while talking to Tim through the open kitchen door. 'When I was little, Mum always knew what I wanted. I didn't talk much. I was scared, and I thought I'd get it wrong. Dad had a go at me cos I pointed and squeaked. Beth does that when she doesn't know how to say stuff, but I get what she wants.'

'That's because you spend so much time with her.' Tim joined Benny in the hall as the kettle grew louder. 'You're in tune. I bet you still have that bond with your mother too.'

Benny wasn't sure. He didn't doubt his mother's love, but their relationship easily became strained because of his frustrations over her fussing. And she shut the door on him the other night. What was that about?

'Jesus will show you what to say, and when to say it,' Tim encouraged.

Benny enjoyed his second cup of tea, along with two chocolate biscuits from a packet Tim found hidden away in the back of a cupboard. He left the church with plenty to mull over, heading straight for Nettie's. Beth monopolised him from the moment he arrived. Her cold had progressed into a chesty cough, and she slept the afternoon away fitfully on his lap.

When Benny tried talking to Nettie about his chat with Tim, he fumbled over the details.

'What's any of this stuff with you and your mum got to do with the disciples going fishing?' she asked with a frown.

Benny looked away, gathered his scattered thoughts, and wondered whether Jesus could give him the words he lacked. Nettie was now knelt on the floor changing Beth, so there was no rush for him to answer.

'Tim's been teaching me that when you're a Christian, you've gotta learn new ways of doing stuff. So I've gotta learn not to copy Damo when he swears, and how to make reading the Bible every day as normal as…' He couldn't say eating, because that was more of an effort than reading his Bible. He smiled as he came up with the perfect analogy, and he wondered whether it had come from God. 'It's gotta be as normal as drinking milky tea, dipping chocolate biscuits, and eating ice cream.'

Nettie's eyes sparkled with mischief. 'If you gave those up, I'd presume you were dying.'

'Reading the Bible has gotta be like that too.' Anticipating her next move, Benny rose to fetch the baby wipes and handed them over. 'When I was stressed about stuff at home, I did what I used to. I acted like a little kid with Emmie, and I got scared cos Mum didn't want me around.' He shrugged. 'That was stupid. I'm saying I want her to let me grow up, and I still get scared when she does. That's like what the disciples did when they went fishing again after Jesus died. They couldn't cope, and they didn't know what else to do.'

Nettie focused on her task, and Benny sensed she was thinking.

'I suppose when I'm stressed, I go back to the things I enjoyed before I had Beth. I spend too much money, or I have a couple of glasses of wine.' She rose and tidied away the changing equipment while Beth clambered up onto Benny's lap again. He didn't mind; he was always more than willing to give cuddles.

'Then I feel guilty and ashamed,' Nettie continued. 'If Beth got ill during the night, I'd be over the limit, and I wouldn't be able to drive to the hospital. So yeah, I guess I know what you mean.'

Benny experienced a thrill of victory because Nettie had understood, and he resolved to pray more before speaking.

'I still wanna help my mum.' He patted Beth's back as she snuggled into his chest. 'I just need to work out how.'

'If what you believe is true, Jesus will tell you.' Nettie's words were sincere, with no trace of sarcasm.

Time passed quickly, and Benny soon had to go home for tea, even though he hated leaving Nettie to struggle with Beth alone.

'You'll be okay, Bethy.' He kissed her as he prepared to leave, and the little girl howled her displeasure.

'Benny's got to go home.' Nettie prized her daughter out of his arms. 'We'll see him again tomorrow.'

At the door, Benny leaned over to kiss Nettie with Beth between them. As he hugged them both, he was overwhelmed by love. They belonged to him, and his heart was theirs. They were already a family.

14

Benny was exhausted when he flopped into bed on Saturday night. He fell asleep with the light on, forgot to set his alarm, and woke up late on Sunday morning with a jolt. There was no way he'd make it to church on time.

'Why didn't you call me?' He catapulted into the kitchen, where his mother fried sausage and bacon while his father gazed into the cupboard under the sink, an open toolbox on the floor beside him.

'Why should she?' Ola looked up from examining a leaky pipe. 'You've got an alarm clock.'

'I forgot to set it.' The smell of bacon made Benny's mouth water, tempting him to skip church in favour of a hearty breakfast.

'I thought you deserved a lie-in.' The sausages popped and sizzled tantalizingly as Janet turned them. 'You hardly ever call me these days when you're ill. I was afraid you'd had a seizure, cleaned up after yourself, and gone back to sleep.'

Benny did that more now, following his milder seizures. He was seeking to take responsibility for his illness and its embarrassing after-effects. If his body gave him enough warning, he lay on the bathroom floor with a bowl at the ready, sometimes managing not to vomit over the lino. If he did, and he was able to stand, he cleaned it up. If not, he called for help.

His dad was often the first to respond, marking a dramatic change from Benny's childhood. On the rare occasions when he struggled to walk, his strong, capable dad carried him back to his room, his calmness quenching Benny's impulse to panic.

'Why don't you stay at home rather than rushing in late?' Janet switched off the gas ring and carried her frying pan over to a worktop, where empty plates waited to be filled. 'Have breakfast with us. I've made plenty.'

'It's okay. Tim doesn't care if we're late.' Benny put his arms around his mother's waist, swiped a sausage to nibble during the walk to church, and ran out of the house.

The service had started by the time he arrived at the modern, red-bricked building. His eyes swept frantically over the back rows on either side of the aisle, searching for a vacant space while the congregation sang the opening hymn.

Brian beckoned, pointing at an empty seat in the second row, where he sat with his family.

Benny had never sat so close to the front. Getting there would be embarrassing. He'd prefer to stay at the back, even if that meant standing through the whole service.

'Come on,' Brian mouthed as the congregation moved into the second verse.

Although Benny shook his head emphatically, his friend soon joined him in the doorway, and Benny felt like everyone watched him as Brian urged him down the aisle.

It took longer than usual for him to settle into the service from his new vantage point near the front, but as Tim led the congregation through a moment of silent prayer, Benny's body and mind relaxed. He was here to meet with Jesus, so he closed his eyes and prayed for his mum, for Nettie, and Beth, and for the courage to speak up to his dad about his longing to leave school.

Tim's sermon was about the shame Mary endured over being pregnant out of wedlock. Benny thought of how brave Nettie had been to carry Beth to term. He wondered whether Mary's story might give him another opening to talk about his faith, and he asked God for more words. There had been a shift in his and Nettie's relationship following their breakup the previous summer and her subsequent choice of him over Beth's father. They had made a commitment from which neither of them would retreat.

Benny's ears pricked up at the mention of Joseph's willingness to stand by his fiancée, fathering a child who wasn't his own. His eyes strayed to the nativity scene beside the pulpit, resting on the figure standing next to Mary.

'Did you love Him like I love Beth?' he mused. 'Did you wanna take care of them, even though people said you shouldn't?' He considered all he'd learned about Jesus' earthly father. 'You had a job. You were a carpenter, so you could look after them. I bet no one made you stay at school to sit a load of exams you couldn't pass. If you were alive today, I reckon you would've passed them. You've gotta be brainy to do woodwork. I tried it once. My whole class did. We made fruit bowls, and mine was rubbish.'

'I'd be rubbish at fixing cars.'

Benny shook his head. Was he really having an imaginary conversation with a piece of plastic? How stupid was that? Perhaps he'd buy a nativity set for Beth. She liked stories, so she'd probably enjoy learning about Mary, Joseph, baby Jesus and their strange visitors. He understood enough now to tell her, as long as no one else heard his fumbling explanations.

Brian's parents offered Benny a lift home, and he realised it would be rude not to accept. While the Brooks family chatted in the car, Benny formed a plan to ask his mum to take him shopping. She could find a child's nativity set for Beth and advise him about a present for Nettie. It needed to be something special. Benny was still clueless about that sort of thing, but his mum would know.

Janet had prepared a traditional Sunday roast, and although Benny only picked at the food, he enjoyed sitting around the table with his family. Emma mostly joined them on Sundays. Sometimes Nettie did, too, but that wouldn't be happening today because of Beth's cold. Benny sent her a text, offering to spend the afternoon with her and Beth. If Bethy was still being clingy, Nettie would be desperate for a break.

After lunch, Benny offered to help with the washing up.

'We should play a few rounds of Uno again soon, for old time's sake.' Emma smiled. 'Remember our Friday night tradition, Pestie?'

Benny picked up the tea towel as Janet slotted the first plate into the drainer. 'Not today. Beth's got a cold. I need to help Nettie.'

'You'll end up catching it,' his mum fretted.

'He probably already has, so he might as well make himself useful.' Ola picked up two mugs of coffee and headed out of the room with Emma.

Working alongside his mother, Benny mentioned Christmas gifts.

'You want me to take you shopping?' Janet stared at him, open-mouthed. 'You hate shopping!'

'I hate it when it's for me,' he said. 'I don't mind if it's for Nettie or Beth.'

'I suppose it would make sense for us to go soon.' After reaching for another saucepan, she plunged it into the soapy water. 'The shops will only get busier.' She paused, then asked, 'Do you know what you want?'

'Maybe a necklace for Nettie.' Benny stacked plates and carried them over to a cupboard. 'And a nativity set for Beth, like the one at church. Something she can't break.'

'I might be able to help with that without taking you shopping.' Janet's face broke into a thoughtful smile, and Benny looked at her questioningly. 'Can you come upstairs after we've finished? I know you're in a rush, but there's something I'd like to show you.'

Benny nodded as Emma returned to the kitchen to tell them she was leaving. What was his mum up to now?

Janet was on a mission as she searched the top shelf of her wardrobe, convinced the item she sought was up there somewhere. She cast aside dusty boxes, her arms straining to reach the back.

'Can I help?' Benny watched from the safety of the double bed.

'You're shorter than me.' Janet laughed for the first time since Tuesday evening. Did this mean the clouds of grief were finally lifting?

Several items tumbled onto the carpet amid a shower of dust, making them both cough.

'I need to sort this lot out.' Janet stepped back, gazing in bewilderment at the mess in her wardrobe.

'Dad reckons you keep too much junk.' Benny moved to stand beside her, reaching up to prevent another avalanche.

'I hate throwing anything away. But I suppose they'll have to come out if I want to find what I'm looking for.' Janet lifted things down one by one, handing them to Benny, who made a neat stack against a wall.

'I'm sentimental.' Janet slid a rectangular box towards her with an accompanying whoop of triumph. 'Ah! Here it is!' She was positively elated. Benny would love her surprise. Once again, her greatest pleasure came from making him happy. This was normal, more normal than anything in her world since Tuesday night.

'I told you I'd find it.' She held the unmarked box out for her son's inspection.

'What's in there?'

Janet sat down, patting the space beside her. 'Come and see.'

She put her arm around Benny as he joined her on the bed and took the box, opening it to discover a brightly painted set of nativity figures made of solid and durable plastic.

'Is that the sort of thing you had in mind for Beth?' Janet asked.

'Yeah, I reckon.' Benny inspected the figures, then turned to smile at his mother. 'This is great. Was it yours?'

'A lovely friend bought it for your sister's first Christmas.' Janet closed her eyes, overwhelmed by memories. Hadn't she suffered enough because of the past? It was relentless. This was supposed to be a special time with her treasured son. She wouldn't let shadows creep in and spoil it. 'Your father thought it was silly, because we were only living in a tiny flat. I just wanted to make Emma's first Christmas special.'

'Did she play with it?'

'When she was old enough.' Janet lifted out each figure in turn, starting with baby Jesus. 'We played for hours, especially with the shepherds and the sheep. Emma loved those.' She pointed at a headless shepherd. 'He was her favourite. She called him Ed.'

'Ed the shepherd?' Benny laughed.

'She was such a funny little girl, always making up games and songs. Her toys were her friends. They had personalities, likes, and dislikes. She asked me to make up stories about their adventures.'

'I didn't do stuff like that.' Benny frowned.

'You were sweet in other ways.' Janet smoothed his hand lovingly. 'You always wanted cuddles. Your happiest place was on my lap.'

'Did Emmie lose Ed's head, or is it still here?' Benny searched the contents of the box.

'It's bound to be in here somewhere because she insisted on keeping it safe.' Janet moved aside some tissue paper and found the shepherd's head. 'There it is.'

'Do you reckon Dad could glue it back on?' Benny held it up to the light.

'I expect so.' Janet placed the headless shepherd on her bedside cabinet, took the missing piece from Benny, and reunited it with its body. 'Your sister seemed to love Ed as he was.' Janet gathered up the nativity figures, returning them to the box as she spoke. 'Emma kept him under her pillow every night for almost a year because she wanted to keep him safe.'

Benny stretched out along the bed and nestled his head on her lap. Janet couldn't resist stroking his wispy blonde hair as her tender heart brimmed with nostalgia for her little boy, who had only felt safe when she held him.

'Do you remember loads of stuff about when me and Emmie were little?' he asked with a wistful smile.

'Of course.' Janet closed her eyes, revelling in the moment. 'I remember it all.'

'I hope me and Nettie do that with Beth.' Benny sighed. 'I know she will, but I hope I do too. I forget stuff.'

'I'll help you remember.' Janet bent to kiss his forehead.

'Like my times tables?' He grinned up at her. 'You never yelled at me when I forgot them.'

'Of course I didn't. I loved helping you.'

'Did you help Sylvia?' Benny's words caught Janet off guard. 'Did you teach her to read and write, to tie her shoelaces and clean her teeth? Or did your mum do it?'

'It was mostly me.' Once again, the pain of loss fought its way to the surface.

'I thought so.' Benny sat up, breaking her unexpected moment of pleasure. 'When you talked about her on Tuesday, it sounded like you were the one who did all that.' He picked up the headless shepherd, turned its body around in his hand, and put it back down. 'I reckon Beth's gonna be funny like Emma was.'

The change of subject gave Janet some much needed breathing space. 'She already is.'

Janet rose and walked to the window, where she peered down into her beloved garden. During the summer, it would be awash with the vibrant colour emanating from her roses, carnations and other blooms. Right now, everything appeared to be dead. Janet was accustomed to nature's cycle of life and death, but she longed for the new growth of spring. The bleakness of winter reminded her too much of the state of her family after Sylvia's death, although she hadn't acknowledged that fact until now.

Had sharing the truth about Sylvia improved things or made them worse? At first, there was relief over the unearthing of a long-buried secret, but that was short lived. While Benny was out enjoying himself in the snow with Nettie and Beth, Janet had plummeted down a tunnel of pain and despair with no end in sight. She had tried talking to Ola, longing for comfort after their rare moment of intimacy when he'd shown her the picture of his mother, but his walls were back up. Her tight-lipped husband had returned with the cold light of a snowy Wednesday morning. He'd insisted on going to work, leaving Janet alone with her painful memories instead of staying to support her.

For two days, she had lain in her bed sobbing over a past she still didn't accept or understand. Ola came and went, growing more distant by the hour because he couldn't handle her emotional outbursts. Janet had relived every moment of her final days with her sister, searching for clues. Nettie was right. Healthy children didn't die from simple colds. There must be another explanation. However, Janet had accepted she would never receive it, so for the second time in her life, she'd forced herself to let Sylvia go.

Now she needed to turn her attention to rebuilding her shaky relationship with her husband. Janet was a wife and mother. Her family needed her, and she couldn't afford to let things slide back to how they were during Benny's difficult early years. She and Ola had come too far to let that happen. Their marriage might not have had the most romantic of starts, followed by a rocky middle, but during the past couple of years, they had found level ground, and their appreciation for one another was growing.

Janet thought back to their brief courtship. Her man of few words had offered her an escape from the shroud of sadness that hung over her parents and their loveless home. Their first year of marriage was fraught with two house moves and an unexpected pregnancy. Janet and Ola barely knew one another, and it showed. Then Emma came along, uniting them and giving them a common sense of purpose. What a gift their precious daughter had been. Caring for her had given Janet the same pleasure she'd experienced as a five-year-old, vowing to care for her sister. Emma's arrival had restored her hope for a happy future despite their less than ideal living conditions. Yet her love for her daughter was clouded by worry. What if she failed Emma like she'd failed Sylvia? How would she bear it if she lost another little girl? Would Ola forgive her? Would she be able to forgive herself?

'Mum,' Benny said, pulling Janet from her musings. 'Can you tell me more about the person who gave you the nativity set?'

Janet returned to the bed and threaded her fingers through her son's. Perhaps returning to this memory wouldn't be so painful. Breaking into a cold winter's day, when her fears were at their worst, had come the kindness of a stranger offering hope, friendship and a fresh perspective.

15

My fretful baby's wails echoed around the narrow passageway as I struggled breathlessly up the three flights of stairs leading to our one-room bedsit.

I clutched tiny Emma protectively against my chest. 'Nearly there now,' I soothed. I hoped Emma couldn't feel my pounding heart as I fought not to cry with her.

'Do you need a hand?' An older woman, bundled up in a coat with greying hair partly hidden under a scarf, met me on the second-floor landing. 'Your baby doesn't sound happy.' She smiled gently.

'I'm sorry. She's hungry and wet, and she's got a cold.' I was so shy and embarrassed that I couldn't meet the older woman's gaze. No doubt Emma's crying was disturbing the entire building. If I didn't settle her soon, I'd have angry neighbours knocking on my door. That had happened the previous week, because the man in the flat below us worked night shifts as a security guard. We had only been living there a fortnight. The last thing we needed was to make enemies.

'I remember the challenges of a newborn from when my two were her age.' The stranger's smile grew wider. She wasn't put off by Emma's cries. 'Did you leave your bags by the front door? I hope you don't mind me asking. I saw you getting off the bus through my window, and you seemed to have a lot of them.'

'They're under the pram,' I adjusted Emma in my arms. 'I've got to leave it parked in the entrance hall because there's no space in our room. I'll put the baby down, then fetch my things.'

'There's no need.' The friendly woman reached out to pat my arm. I couldn't remember the last time I'd received such a motherly gesture. 'You tend to your little one, and I'll fetch your bags.'

'You don't have to do that.' I wasn't accustomed to receiving help from strangers.

'I want to. Call it a little gesture from one mother to another.'

The woman was gone before I had time to protest. I climbed the last flight of stairs, balancing Emma in the crook of my arm whilst fumbling in my bag for my keys.

'We're nearly home, sweetheart,' I soothed. 'As soon as we're inside, Mummy will make you better.'

Should feeding or changing come first? I was never quite sure. I wished my mother was on hand to offer advice, but my parents lived seventy miles away and they still didn't own a car. Phoning them meant trudging to the closest phone box, and the coins I saved for that purpose ran out too quickly.

I was torn between a longing to introduce Mum and Dad to brown-haired, hazel-eyed Emma and the sad knowledge that when I did, they would greet their latest grandchild with little enthusiasm. They barely commented on my brothers' children, even though David's family lived close by them. Whereas Malcolm had chosen not to return after three years at university in Birmingham. When I asked why, he'd said the sadness at home was too oppressive. He no longer wanted to be sucked down by its vice-like grip. That was the closest we ever came to mentioning Sylvia. Our parents and David didn't speak of her at all.

Entering our tiny one-roomed flat, I reached for the light switch, only to scowl as the dim bulb illuminated the dirty breakfast dishes piled up on our square Formica table. I had planned to take them to the shared kitchen for washing after Ola left for work, but Emma had demanded feeding. By the time she was fed, burped and changed, I had to run to catch the bus. I couldn't afford to miss it. I'd been low on cotton wool, washing-up liquid, and other essentials.

'Knock-knock.'

I turned to see my neighbour in the doorway, struggling with my shopping.

'Oh, thank you.' My face flushed as I lowered Emma onto the neatly made bed, crossed to the door, and reached for the plastic bags. I didn't want her to come in and see all the mess. The dirty dishes and my wailing baby would reveal my inadequacy as a wife and mother. My overwhelming inadequacy.

'It must be a struggle living here with your husband and a tiny baby.' The kindly neighbour remained in the doorway. Would she think me rude if I didn't invite her in?

I put the bags in front of the table. Emma's screams made it hard to think of anything else. 'It's all we can afford.' I lowered my gaze. Anxiety was making my mouth run ahead of my brain. Ola wouldn't approve of so much openness. We'd only been married just over a year, but I already knew my husband was a fiercely private man who kept his cards close to his chest. He rarely discussed our finances with me, let alone with strangers.

'I understand,' my neighbour said. 'I might not have a husband and baby, but I know how it feels to long for more space.'

'Would you like to come in?' I decided the least I could do was offer refreshments in return for her kindness.

'Thank you.' Having closed the door, the woman crossed the room to peer down at Emma lying on the bed. My baby's face was flushed with the exertion of crying; her tiny fists scrunched into two tight balls. 'Poor little thing,' she said, cooing over Emma, her hand hovering as if she longed to pick her up.

'Do you think she's too hot?' I joined my visitor by the bed, placing a hand on Emma's forehead. 'She's burning up.'

'That's because she's winding herself up with all this crying.' My neighbour placed her hand next to mine. 'She'll cool off if you let some air get to her. You've got her well wrapped up.'

'I didn't want her cold getting any worse.' My fingers trembled as I removed Emma's shawl and fumbled to unbutton her tiny cardigan. 'I took her to the doctor this morning because her chest seemed tight, but he wouldn't give her anything.'

'She looks like a strong little girl.' The woman smiled down at Emma, whose cries had now reduced to a whimper.

'My husband says I worry too much.' I smoothed the cheek of my cherished miracle.

'Tell him all new mothers do until they get used to it.' The neighbour picked up Emma's discarded shawl, folded it neatly, and placed it on the bottom of the bed. 'She's such a little sweetheart. You're blessed to have her.'

'She's sweet when she's not crying.' I laughed nervously.

'Her name's Emma, isn't it?'

I nodded. 'How did you know?'

'I've heard you talking to her on your way past my door. How old is young Emma?'

'Ten weeks.' I swallowed down a lump in my throat. I was beyond exhausted. Motherhood took every ounce of energy I possessed. I had spent most of the previous night jiggling Emma, who cried every time I put her down.

'She's a good size, with a healthy set of lungs.'

'I worry about those lungs.' I picked Emma up as she made sucking motions with her rosebud lips. 'I can't always keep her quiet at night. I'm sure all our neighbours must hate us. And my husband has to get up at the crack of dawn, so he needs his sleep.' I paced the small room with Emma. Only milk would satisfy her now, but I couldn't feed her in front of a stranger.

'What does your husband do?' The woman's questions didn't come across as nosy. She seemed kind and compassionate, as though she genuinely wanted to understand my plight.

'He's training to be a mechanic.' I suddenly remembered my manners. 'I'm sorry. Would you like a cup of tea?' I pointed at a battered armchair. It was Ola's seat, but he wouldn't be home yet. My visitor could use it while I sat with Emma on the bed.

'Only if you'll let me make it while you feed your baby.' The woman was already up on her feet.

'I can't expect you to make the tea while I just sit here!' The combination of Emma's crying coupled with my own embarrassment was almost my undoing. But I held it together. I mustn't cry in front of a stranger.

The neighbour put up a hand to quell my protests. 'I'll fetch some mugs from my room, make the tea, and be back in a jiffy.'

She was gone in an instant, leaving me to sink onto the bed holding Emma, while shedding tears of gratitude that, for once, someone had offered to bring me tea. I longed to close my eyes and sleep. Instead, I unbuttoned my blouse and put my hungry baby to my breast. Emma latched on immediately, sucking for all she was worth.

'Not so hard, little one.' I winced.

Emma was still feeding contentedly when our neighbour returned ten minutes later, devoid of her coat and scarf. She carried a tray containing tea-things and a packet of digestive biscuits.

'Sorry they aren't chocolate.' She put her burden on the table and perched on the edge of Ola's armchair, not batting an eyelid at my unbuttoned blouse. 'I finished those off last night.'

'I'm still trying to get rid of the baby weight,' I replied, trying to force myself to relax. Emma was content and the kettle was boiling. Besides, I should be too exhausted to care. 'I can't eat too many sweet things.'

'I wouldn't worry about that just yet. You need to keep your strength up for Emma.' My new friend swept her eyes around the room, then refocused her attention on me. 'I've just realised. I haven't even told you my name, so let me put that right. I'm Maureen Grantham. Most people call me Mo.'

'I'm Janet Wellander.' I smiled. 'And they call me Jan.'

'Do you mind me asking how old you are?' Mo busied herself with the tea.

'I'm twenty-two.'

'I wasn't much older than you when I had my first baby.'

Talking came easily to Mo, so I settled comfortably into the rhythm of her voice, accompanied by the familiar sounds of Emma suckling. Mo spoke warmly about her late husband, her two grown children and six grandchildren.

'If you're so close to them, why are you living here?' I immediately chided myself for being nosy.

'My children have busy lives of their own.' Rather than being annoyed, Mo seemed to welcome my questions as she carried the tea over. 'I wouldn't expect them to look after me. They both wanted to when their father died, but I insisted that wasn't their responsibility. I'm only a short bus journey away, so I see them regularly.'

'Will you be spending Christmas with them?' I asked.

'Absolutely,' Mo enthused. 'Just you try stopping me. There's nothing quite like watching my grandchildren tearing into their gifts. And my girls still say no one cooks a Christmas dinner like their mother, so I guess I'll get roped into that.'

'How will you get there? There are no buses on Christmas Day.' I lifted a resistant Emma to my shoulder for winding.

'One of their husbands will pick me up. I think of them as my sons, and they tease me like they tease their own mothers.'

'You're lucky to have such a close family.' My tone was wistful as I sipped at my tea.

'Will you be visiting yours for Christmas?' Mo proffered the biscuits, but I shook my head.

'I'm hoping we'll visit them soon.' I patted Emma's back. 'They haven't met Emma yet.'

'I bet your mother can't wait to cuddle her.'

Unsure how to respond, I turned the conversation back to Mo, asking about her husband and how long she'd been widowed.

'What have you been doing today?' Ola addressed Emma as he balanced his cup of coffee while she lay on his knees. 'Have you been shopping with Mummy?'

'We were running out of a few essentials.' I tried not to waste money because Ola worked hard for every penny.

'Did you struggle with Emma and the pram?' Ola sipped his coffee, and Emma gurgled up at him. She seemed happier this evening. Perhaps she was over the worst of her cold.

'The local bus drivers are really kind and helpful.' I was touched by my husband's show of concern. I had observed that Ola often revealed his softer side when he held Emma. His love for our daughter was obvious, even if he sometimes struggled to show affection to me.

Emma's gurgles transformed into cries, and I instinctively reached for her. 'I expect she's hungry again. I was hoping to get our tea on the table first.' I hated making Ola wait for his evening meal. No doubt he'd worked through his lunch break without stopping to eat.

'It's Friday night. We should have a treat.' He surprised me by rising and draping an arm around my shoulders. 'You're looking tired, Jan. It's been hard on you, moving to another strange place so soon after having Emma.'

So much thoughtfulness in one night. I felt spoiled. I rested my head on his broad shoulder as I tucked Emma's under my chin. 'It's okay, Ola. I understand. You had to take work when you found it.'

'Things won't be so tight once I'm fully trained.' Ola's voice was uncharacteristically gentle. 'We might even be able to afford our own house. Won't that be better than living squashed together like this in one room?'

'Emma and I don't mind waiting.' I lifted my head to meet his gaze with tenderness, and Ola bent to kiss me. That was as close as he would come to admitting the depth of his feelings. It had to be enough. My husband could be difficult and exacting, but he always provided for me and Emma.

Of course, there were evenings when he came home from work and said little. On those occasions, he wore a dark, brooding expression, and I knew better than to bother him. However, his mood had been thawing since Emma's birth. Our little girl had her ways of making her daddy smile and even laugh on rare occasions. She was the glue, bonding us in our fledgling marriage.

I wasn't totally convinced of our love the previous spring when I accepted Ola's marriage proposal, after having only known him for a few months. It certainly wasn't the bond I'd witnessed between David and Sarah, or my parents before Sylvia's death.

But by the time I met Ola, laughter was a distant memory in the Pew household. I could barely recall the faint echo of my parents' chatter whilst sharing a pot of tea together in the garden on warm summer evenings. Instead, Mum wandered mechanically around the house, doing her duty, while Dad worked his job at a local factory. We spoke only when necessary, using words sparingly, as if the very act of speaking cost too much effort.

Family milestones had passed with little fanfare. David's wedding to Sarah had been low-key, as had Malcolm's to his wife. I had itched for an opportunity to escape, and Ola had come into my life at just the right time. There was no way I would refuse him.

'I'll fetch us fish and chips.' Ola strode purposefully towards the door. 'You feed Emma and get everything ready.'

He returned half an hour later with our evening meal wrapped in newspaper. We enjoyed the rare treat while Emma slept, having been fed in her father's absence. Ola was unusually talkative, regaling me with anecdotes about his work and the people he'd met. He asked about my day, and I wondered how much to divulge.

'I spent time with one of our neighbours,' I revealed, chewing on my fingernails.

'How did you meet her?' Ola's eyebrows narrowed.

I gave him a brief explanation, and he relaxed and nodded his understanding.

'She's an older lady, with two children and six grandchildren.' I scraped the batter away from my fish.

'So many!' My husband's look of horror made me laugh out loud. 'That would be too noisy.'

'I liked her. She seems kind.' I waited with bated breath for Ola's approval. I longed to pursue this new friendship with Mo Grantham, and I hoped he wouldn't stand in my way.

'It'll do you good to have some company. And if she's used to children, she'll help with Emma. You worry about her far too much.'

'There's a lot to learn with your first baby.' I wouldn't tell Ola about my trip to the doctors with Emma. He would only accuse me of fussing. Yet with my family history, how could I not? I worried constantly, even over a cold. No, especially over a cold. A shiver ran down my spine. If Ola knew… He didn't, however, because I hadn't told him about Sylvia. That would feel like a betrayal of my parents. If they couldn't talk about her, what right did I have to do so?

Ola rose, crossed the room and picked up his newspaper, signalling our conversation was over.

'Will you keep an ear out for Emma while I do the washing up?' He nodded, and I gathered our plates and cutlery.

I rushed down to the communal kitchen, pleased to have it to myself so I could attend to the dishes quickly and return to my family before Emma demanded another feed.

I hummed quietly as I worked, feeling more positive than I had in a long time. Earlier in the day, my mind had been consumed by worries over Emma's health. Now my baby rested contentedly, under the watchful eye of her father. The doctor was probably right in urging me not to worry. Emma's cold was improving. There was no cause for panic. Surely whatever happened to Sylvia must have been rare.

16

Mo sought me out several times during the following week, always with kind words and cuddles for Emma. When I asked for advice, my new friend had plenty to give. She invited me to lunch in her room and even suggested some Christmas shopping.

'Shall we go in there for a cuppa?'

I was admiring a toy shop's seasonal window display of cotton wool snowmen and red velvety Father Christmases when Mo turned my attention to the café across the road.

'I'll treat us both. I need to take the weight off my feet,' she said.

'Me too.' I had been fighting exhaustion all morning after another sleepless night with Emma.

I guided the pram across the road, and Mo opened the door to the café. I froze.

'Looks warm and inviting, doesn't it?' Mo smiled, oblivious to my discomfort. 'And very quaint. I love traditional cafés.'

As I stood in the doorway, unbidden memories bombarded me without permission. I was 11 years old again, drinking tea and eating scones with Ruth Gray, playing pretend in a café just like this one. There were the net curtains, the blue and white gingham tablecloths, the silver teapots and the bone china cups with tiny handles. I squeezed my eyes shut against the recollections of my last day of childlike innocence.

'Are you okay?' Mo's voice jolted me back to the present, and I shook myself free of the memories.

This wasn't the same café I'd visited with Ruth, so why was it affecting me so deeply? There were so many differences, and I forced myself to see them. It was winter, not summer. The room was strung with tinsel and fairy lights, and I was a grown woman with a child of my own. I no longer needed to play pretend. I could do this. I had to.

'Yes, I'm fine.' I pasted on a smile. 'Sorry. I think the crowds overwhelmed me.'

'I can see a space.'

Mo pointed, and I followed her gratefully to a table near the back of the bustling room. I parked the pram, relieved that Emma was sleeping.

Mo ordered tea and scones, while I opted for a toasted teacake. A different treat would distance me from comparisons with the past.

'Have you arranged your visit to your parents?' Mo pulled her arms out of her coat and sat back with a contented sigh.

'It'll have to wait until the new year.' I fiddled with my handbag's metal clasp. 'Ola can't take time off, and I'm worried about going by myself on the bus with Emma. It would be my first time travelling alone with a baby.' I paused while the waitress set the tray down, and Mo thanked her politely, commenting on the busyness of the café due to the Christmas rush.

'I suppose I could do it...' I buttered my teacake as I spoke. 'I just get worried about missing my connections and ending up stranded in the middle of nowhere.'

'Can't Ola take you on a Saturday?' Mo asked.

'He doesn't get on with my parents.' There I went again, saying too much, but this woman had an uncanny ability to draw me out. I had given Mo an opening to ask more questions, but how would I explain without betraying at least one family member?

'That's a shame.' Mo stirred the tea in the pot. 'It still looks like dishwater, so let's eat first.'

I nodded. 'Ola doesn't say a lot. And neither do my parents, so it's awkward when they're together.'

'I can imagine.' Mo covered her scone in delicious cream and jam, and I chided myself for overreacting. Mo's treat was making my mouth water. My teacake appeared bland by comparison.

'If you want to see your mum and dad before Christmas, I'd be more than happy to travel with you.'

I gaped at my new friend. 'You hardly know me! And it's seventy miles! We'd have to go one day and come back the next.'

'I enjoy discovering new places.' Mo seemed unperturbed. 'I'm sure I'll find somewhere to stay overnight while you spend time with your family.' She turned her attention to pouring the tea. 'Think about it. Talk it over with your husband.'

I appreciated the way Mo didn't force the issue. My shoulders untensed as I bit into my teacake, which turned out to be much nicer than it looked.

'Oh, just look at that!'

The lure of the toy shop opposite the café had been too much for Mo to resist. Now she stood admiring a colourful child's nativity set while I carried Emma in my arms because the shop was too narrow for the pram.

'Isn't it lovely?' Mo picked up a sheep, turning it around in her hand. 'This would be perfect for my little Rebecca. The figures are chunky, so she won't swallow them.' She laughed as she held the plastic sheep out to show me. 'You know what little ones are like for putting everything in their mouths.'

'They're beautiful.' I bent to look more closely. 'I love those cheerful colours.'

As Mo lingered beside the nativity set, I cast my eyes longingly over the various toys and games. Emma was too young to play, so Ola and I had agreed not to buy gifts for her first Christmas.

'There'll be plenty of time for that when she's old enough to understand,' Ola had said. 'We don't need to put ourselves under extra financial pressure so soon after the move.'

I saw the sense in his words. Still, I longed to mark the occasion with a special gift. I had hung silver paper chains in our room in an effort to bring some festivity, and Emma loved babbling up at them as they swung and caught the light. I was already seeing marked changes in my baby. She relished exploring the limits of her world, delighting me with her coos and funny little facial expressions.

'I'm definitely going to get this.' Mo selected a box containing one of the nativity sets. 'Rebecca has a good imagination. I'll be able to use it to help her recreate the Christmas story.'

'I remember doing that with my dolls when I was little,' I confessed as my cheeks warmed. 'I got the idea from our Sunday school Christmas play.'

'So you went to Sunday school?' Mo headed for the cash desk with me and Emma in tow.

'Until I was about 11.' Three women with bulging baskets stood ahead of us in the queue. We were in for a long wait. I just hoped Emma wouldn't start fussing because if she did, she'd soon empty the shop with her noise. I suppose that would lessen our wait…

'What made you stop going?'

Mo's enquiry was innocent. Even so, I had to hide my eyes. I instinctively knew Mo was trustworthy, yet something indeterminable held me back. Was it loyalty to Ola and my parents, or guilt because I still fretted over my own contribution to Sylvia's death?

'I moved on to other things.' I hoped that would satisfy Mo, and was relieved when she didn't ask further questions.

'Emma should have a nativity set too.' Mo prepared to relinquish her place in the queue. 'I'll fetch another one.'

'Oh, no.' I gripped her arm with alarm in my eyes. 'Ola and I decided not to buy presents this year. We're concentrating on saving to move again, so Emma will have more room to play by the time she's walking.'

'That may be, but you can't stop other people from buying her gifts.' There was a twinkle of mischief in my new friend's eye.

'You've got enough to buy for your own grandchildren.' I didn't want to take advantage of Mo's kindness.

'Well, now I have the blessing of an extra little girl to love.' Mo reached out to cover one of Emma's tiny hands. My daughter grasped her finger, lifting it to her lips to examine it with her tongue. 'All little girls need a nativity set.'

The decision made, I waited while Mo fetched the second box.

'What's this?' Ola noticed the nativity set the moment he walked into our room later that evening, just as I'd feared. I had set it up on the table, under the paper chains, indulging in a moment of childlike pleasure as I introduced Emma to each figure whilst chattering about Mary, Joseph, and the baby in a manger. There was no denying it. The set brought a touch of festivity into our darkened room, increasing my gratitude for the kindness of my friend.

'Mo bought it for Emma.' I attempted to inject a note of enthusiasm into my voice, hoping the mention of his daughter would mollify Ola. 'Isn't it pretty?'

'She's too young.' Ola grunted his disapproval. 'It was a waste of money.'

'She'll enjoy it more next year.' I felt instantly deflated. 'She babbles at the figures when I hold her near them.'

'How do you know what she likes? She's a baby.'

His dark mood told me Ola had endured a long, gruelling day.

'There's not much room in here as it is, and now you're cluttering it up with nonsense.' He turned his back on me and my heart ached.

'It would've been rude not to accept a gift.' I dropped my gaze, hoping he wouldn't insist on giving back the gift. That would hurt Mo.

'I suppose so.' Ola sank into his armchair, ignoring Emma, who lay happily cooing on the floor, her tiny fingers exploring the holes in a knitted blanket.

We ate in silence, after I pushed the nativity set to one side to create more space on the table. Ola didn't mention it again, barely giving it a second glance. As usual, I left him in charge of Emma while I went downstairs to wash the dishes.

When I returned to our room sometime later, I stopped short in the doorway. Ola was standing next to the table, holding Emma against his chest. My breath caught as my husband's stony expression softened into a proud, fatherly smile. Our beautiful Emma had once again worked her magic.

'You're right. She is noticing things.' Ola looked up as I padded into the room. 'She's talking to the paper chains.' He looked amused and slightly baffled.

'That's what babies do.' I indulged in a girlish giggle. 'Haven't you noticed the way she talks to her fingers and toes?'

'I'm not used to babies,' Ola admitted. 'I presumed it would be months before she started taking notice of things.'

'She knows who we are.' I still felt cautious as I moved closer to him. Ola's mood could change in an instant.

'Do you think?' He seemed genuinely interested in my explanation.

'She gets excited every evening when I tell her Daddy's coming home.'

'That's good.' Ola closed his eyes. I couldn't read his expression as he stood rocking our daughter, then bent to kiss Emma's cheek. 'So you like shiny things, do you?' He paused as though expecting an answer. 'Well, perhaps Daddy should buy you some.'

The following evening, Ola presented me with several strands of red, gold and green tinsel, and a selection of flat-packed foil decorations. 'I think you unfold them and hang them from the ceiling.'

I nodded my understanding. I had seen them before. 'They're really pretty,' I said, rubbing the packaging between my fingers as my heart filled with joy.

'I thought we'd hang them over Emma's cot.' Ola handed me a pot of drawing pins, then picked up his newspaper.

Emma thanked her father with a hearty burp, and he laughed out loud. I loved hearing him laugh – it was so rare.

Our room looked surprisingly festive once the tinsel and decorations were hung. We stood back to admire our handiwork, our fingertips touching until Ola took my hand and applied gentle pressure.

'It looks like Christmas,' he admitted, with the trace of a smile.

'Thank you.' I experienced an overwhelming surge of love as I drew him towards our bed.

Emma was already sleeping, so we turned out the light and lay in the semi-darkness. The orange streetlights cast a warm glow through the thin curtains, and our foil decorations glistened as they swung in the draft from the poorly fitted single-glazed window.

'Are you still planning on taking Emma to visit your parents?' Ola asked.

'I want to.' I replied through chattering teeth.

'You're cold.' Ola wrapped himself around me. 'Should I check on Emma?'

'I made sure she's got plenty of blankets. But we definitely need thicker ones.'

Ola agreed and I snuggled into his arms before he turned the conversation back to my parents. 'I'm sorry I can't go with you.' He sounded genuine.

I hated to spoil the mood. Moments like these were precious. I paused, then tentatively offered my solution. 'Mo Grantham offered. I told her I'm worried about traveling alone.'

'Were you complaining about me?' The edge of annoyance was back in his voice.

'Of course not.' I was quick to put his mind at rest. 'I explained about your work. She said she enjoys visiting new places, so it'll work for both of us.'

'Your parents won't want a stranger in their house.' Ola rolled onto his back. 'They barely tolerate me.'

I could have countered that this was partly due to Ola's frostiness towards them, but that would only cause an argument. I didn't want to spoil our evening by raising petty issues that neither of us had the power to change.

'She said she'll find a B&B and travel back with me the following day.' I felt the cold again now Ola had released me.

'Fine, if you're happy with that.'

I was startled by how easily he had accepted my suggestion, and even more so when he pulled me back into his arms. 'I didn't like to think of you traveling alone with Emma.'

Ola's agreement left me free to accept Mo's offer when we met in the hallway the following morning.

'I'm glad.' Mo flashed one of her gentle smiles. 'Your mother needs to meet her granddaughter.'

'It's been over a year since I last saw them.' I settled Emma in her pram, ready for another outing with our new friend. 'We've moved twice since we got married.'

'It's a shame your mother couldn't come to help after you gave birth.' Mo held the front door open while I manoeuvred the pram.

'She doesn't like leaving home.'

I wasn't sure what the visit to my parents would achieve and reminded myself not to set my goals too high. If Mum gave little attention to her older grandchildren, why should things be any different with Emma? Yet I was her only daughter, so surely that had to mean something. Or was my mother still blaming me for Sylvia's death?

I had often stewed over that question during the long years without my sister. I remembered how close my mother and I had been, how well we had worked together and how instinctively we understood one another's moods and requirements. Why had she shut me out? If Sylvia had died because she'd caught my cold, surely that wasn't my fault. I had loved Sylvia as much as anyone. Possibly even more. It was wrong for Mum to lay blame at my door, if that was what she was doing. Yet, as the years passed, the distance between us had only grown.

As I walked alongside Mo, I thought back to the day I'd told my parents about Ola's marriage proposal. Even though I hadn't been secretive about our budding relationship, they showed no desire to become better acquainted with my first real boyfriend.

'Are you sure?' Mum was chopping carrots when I shared my news.

'Yes. It feels right.' Despite her cold shoulder, I picked up a knife to start on the potatoes.

'Well, you're old enough to know your own mind.' Mum focused on her work, dismissing my impending marriage as something of little importance.

My father had reacted much the same way. 'You're an adult now, so it's your choice,' was all he'd said.

So, I'd married Ola in a simple registry office ceremony, with my parents present in body only. They were eager to walk away, handing me into his care.

'When would you like to go?' Mo's question was a welcome interruption into my unpleasant thoughts.

'What about next Wednesday?' I needed to confirm the date before surrendering to fear and changing my mind. 'I'll ring my mother to make sure.'

'That's fine by me.' Mo put a hand on my shoulder as we walked. 'We'll have a lovely time.'

I nodded mechanically, unwilling to quench Mo's enthusiasm with reality.

17

My mother barely reacted when I called to ask if I could bring Emma for an overnight visit. However, when I explained Mo's offer of companionship, Mum was adamant that Mo should spend the night in the spare room. If she was kind enough to travel with me and Emma, the least she and Dad could do was offer her a place to stay.

I was relieved when Emma slept for the bulk of our journey. Feeding her on the bus felt awkward at first, but Mo's reassurances soon put me at ease.

As we drew closer to my childhood home, my body tensed. Emma must have sensed the change in me because she became fretful. By the time I was able to step outside and breathe the crisp December air, I felt sick with a thundering headache.

'Let me carry Emma.' Mo must have noticed my pallor.

'You're so good to me.' I handed my baby over, turning away to hide brimming tears.

Mo smiled as she balanced Emma in the crook of one arm whilst pulling me close for a hug. 'You and your little one have become two of my greatest blessings.'

I turned at the sound of a beeping horn and spotted my eldest brother across the busy road, waving through an open car window. My breath caught as David climbed confidently out of his vehicle. He strode towards us dodging traffic, a cautious smile on his face.

'Sarah was sure you'd be tired after your journey.' He towered over me, as imposing as ever.

'We are.' My shoulders relaxed with relief. 'This is my friend, Mo Grantham.'

'Nice to meet you.' David smiled at Mo, then focused on his niece. 'There's no mistaking whose daughter she is. She's the spitting image of you, Jan.'

'That's what Ola said the first time he saw her.' I blushed.

'It's a shame he didn't come with you.' David's words lacked conviction, another reminder of my family's coldness towards my husband.

'He's working non-stop.' Even to my own ears, it sounded like a flimsy excuse.

Fifteen minutes later, Mo and I stood in my mother's kitchen, David having excused himself to return to his family. He'd answered my questions about Sarah and the children by promising to bring them to share the evening meal. David, at least, had seemed pleased to see me, although there were no outward displays of affection.

My misgivings over seeing my mother were eased by Mo's easy-going nature. Mum offered polite hospitality to the stranger in their midst.

'It was so kind of you to let me stay, Mrs Pew.'

Mum had no time to respond before Mo thrust Emma into her arms. 'I'm sure you're dying for a cuddle. Whenever I see one of my grandchildren, I can't wait to hug them and cover their little faces in kisses. They are miracles from heaven.'

Mum nodded, gazing down at Emma, who chose that moment to open her eyes, gape at her grandmother in confusion, then let out a hearty wail.

'I expect she's hungry.' I offered the perfect excuse for Mum to relinquish Emma. However, she did not immediately do so.

'You used to look like that when you were unsure about meeting new people.' Mum's tone was wistful as she studied her granddaughter more intently. 'You were always a nervous little thing.'

Emma puckered her lips into a sucking motion, and my mother held her out to me, followed by an offer of tea and cake.

My mother made small talk with Mo while I saw to Emma, relieving me of the stress of stilted conversation. Mum didn't ask after Ola, and when Dad returned from work an hour later, he didn't either.

'She's a healthy-looking little thing.' He didn't show the slightest desire to hold his granddaughter, who lay on the sofa beside me, cooing and blowing bubbles.

'She eats well.' I kept a watchful eye on my bright-eyed baby. 'The midwife says she's gaining the right amount of weight.'

It was Mo who kept the conversation going until David and Sarah joined us for dinner, with their two daughters.

'Can I hold baby Emma?' Six-year-old Lucy pounced on me as soon as she walked through the front door.

Lucy overflowed with the same openness and zest for life Sylvia had possessed, and I wondered whether my mother also saw the similarities between black-haired Lucy and the little blonde who had filled our lives with love and laughter. If so, she hid it well. She chided Lucy for throwing her coat over a chair instead of hanging it up properly, while Sarah endeavoured to prise herself away from her clingy toddler.

'Hannah's the shy one,' Sarah said, giving in and lifting her grizzling infant into her arms. 'She won't go to anyone.'

As the evening progressed, Hannah remained glued to her mother's side, while Lucy's chatter was a welcome distraction. She flitted around the house, annoying her father and grandmother with a never-ending supply of imaginary games. The stairs became a bus to take her family of toys to the seaside, and a bowl filled with clothes pegs was a delicious meal of fish and chips.

Mo was enchanted, and Lucy's devotion to baby Emma melted my heart. She picked her up for a cuddle between each new game, telling Emma she would soon be big enough to join in. When it was time for David and his family to leave, I had to prise my sleeping daughter from her lap. The little girl kissed Emma's forehead, murmuring goodnights before slowly following her parents to the front door, with backwards glances.

'It's always a relief when they go home.' My mother gathered up her grandchildren's discarded toys, tossing them into a wooden box at the far end of the lounge.

'Isn't it fascinating how different they all are, even at such young ages?' Mo loaded dirty crockery onto a tray and carried it into the kitchen.

Her ability to find something positive in every situation was baffling. I wished I was more like my friend, but the truth was, I was plagued by too many fears and insecurities. I wondered if Sylvia would have been like Mo. Would our roles have reversed in later years, with Sylvia encouraging me, her withdrawn older sister?

My headache had returned with a vengeance, so I was relieved when my mother suggested an early night.

'You've got a long day ahead of you tomorrow.' She bade me a cool goodnight before climbing the stairs. Mo had also retired to her room, leaving me alone with Emma in the kitchen.

Lifting my baby to my shoulder, I wandered into the lounge, where my father sat in front of the television watching the evening news.

'Off up to bed, are you?' He barely looked away from the screen.

Melancholy overwhelmed me as I mounted the stairs, and Emma let out an agonised cry. Her little face contorted as she drew her knees up to her chest.

'Is it colic?' A dressing-gown clad Mo appeared in the guest bedroom doorway, beckoning for me to join her.

I pulled the door closed, then glanced around the room that had once belonged to my two brothers. All traces of their presence had been removed except for a battered chest of drawers and a wardrobe that had seen better days. Mo pointed me towards a double bed covered in a flowery bedspread, and I sank onto it gratefully.

'Are you okay?' she asked.

The compassion in her voice instantly brought me to tears. 'I shouldn't have come.' My feeble attempts to soothe Emma were failing.

Mo leaned down to pluck my baby out of my arms. She paced the tiny room, rhythmically patting Emma's back and muttering lovingly. 'Oh dear, little one. Have you got that nasty wind again?'

I closed my eyes and lay back on the bed, allowing Mo's voice to settle my frayed nerves. She sang softly to Emma. *'Jesus loves me, this I know. For the Bible tells me so.'*

Long-buried memories carried me back to Sunday afternoons attending Sunday school at the local chapel with Sylvia as I sang along in my mind. I heard the faint echo of my sister's piping voice, singing tunelessly, with great gusto. *'Yes, Jesus loves me! The Bible tells me so.'*

It came as a relief when Mo's song ended. I couldn't think about Sylvia, though I was moments away from spending the night in the room we had once shared. Even though Sylvia's belongings had been removed shortly after her death, the memories lingered.

'She's dropping off.' Mo continued her pacing. Emma's cries had reduced to the occasional whimper.

'Do you think I should ask the doctor about her colic?' I asked.

'It's perfectly normal in a little one her age.' Mo never chided or dismissed my worries as Ola did but gave gentle reassurances.

Tell her about Sylvia.

Where had that thought come from? I hadn't spoken my sister's name since the funeral, and that was how it had to stay. Conjuring up old ghosts would only make things worse. I was just emotional because of my surroundings and because of my headache.

'I need to get Emma settled.' I rose reluctantly, reaching for my baby. 'We've got an early start in the morning.'

'I'm surprised you've chosen the ten o'clock bus,' Mo said. 'I thought you'd want to spend the morning with your mother.'

'I need to be home before Ola gets in from work.' I stood with my back against the door. 'I can't expect him to make his own meals two nights on the trot.'

'I'm sure he'd cope.' Mo's eyes twinkled with amusement.

'I've been here long enough.' I hung my aching head.

Mo crossed the room to put a hand on my arm, preventing me from turning and opening the door. 'I've seen how difficult this visit has been.' She paused, and I wondered what she was building up to. I hoped her words wouldn't be the final blow that caused me to melt into a puddle of ugly crying. I couldn't face that in this house where memories of my sister threatened to pounce from every dark corner. With her hand still on my arm, Mo continued. 'I'm getting the sense there's more going on here than meets the eye. There's a deep sadness here, and especially in your parents.'

I could only nod.

'It's okay,' Mo reassured me. 'I won't poke my nose in where it doesn't belong. I just want you to know that I care.'

'Thank you.' I cleared my throat.

'It's a good thing you brought Emma here.' Mo put her arms around me, and I indulged in resting my head on her shoulder, envying Mo's daughters who had experienced their mother's comfort and understanding since childhood. Did they realise how lucky they were?

'Do you think so?' My voice threatened to crack. 'I'm not so sure.' I gently freed myself from her embrace.

'I know it's painful.' Mo closed her eyes, as if she were praying. 'But you mustn't give up on your parents, Jan. They love you.'

'They've given up on me.' Bitterness replaced the compulsion to cry. 'They don't care.'

'You're still their daughter.' Mo's intense gaze pierced my soul. 'One day, they're going to realise how much they need you. So even if they seem to push you away, you keep coming. Bring Emma here as often as you can, because she's a special little girl sent to bring light into your lives. She's the glue that will keep you together.'

'My parents have hardly taken any notice of her.'

'That's what you think.' Mo smiled. 'I've caught a few glances out of the corner of my eye. And I noticed the way your mother held her.' Mo placed a hand on the back of Emma's head. 'Your parents are like hedgehogs. They've curled themselves up into tight little balls to hide away from feelings they can't handle. That makes them prickly, and you get caught on their spikes, but the truth is that they're two unhappy people, desperate to survive.'

She was right. Our whole family had locked up our emotions after losing Sylvia. It was the only way to survive. But Ola and I couldn't let that continue with Emma. Despite the secrets we carried from our pasts, our daughter needed the security of her parents' love.

I knew very little about Ola's childhood except that he had grown up in Denmark. I resisted asking him about it because too many questions made him angry.

'I'll keep trying with my parents.' That was all I could promise, but it seemed to be enough for Mo, as she nodded and bade me goodnight.

'I'll pray for you.'

Despite the emotional and physical exhaustion of the day, I hardly slept a wink. I tossed and turned in the room I'd once shared with my sister, and when Emma woke for her two o'clock feed, I decided to carry her downstairs. Once she was fed and changed, I spent the rest of the night cradling my baby in my father's armchair. Why had sleeping in my old room affected me so deeply? I had slept in there until I left home to marry Ola, Sylvia's bed having been replaced by a battered old sofa on which I spent endless hours escaping into happier worlds through a good book. During my lonely teens, my bedroom had been my haven from the melancholy that hung over our home like a heavy wool blanket. Yet tonight, everything felt wrong and unsettling.

I must have dozed somewhere in the early hours because I woke with a start when my mother entered the room and drew back the curtains, revealing the post-dawn gloom of another dreary December morning.

'Kept you up, did she?' Mum pointed at Emma, and I nodded. 'You'd best have something to eat before you travel.'

I lowered Emma upon the sofa, surrounding her with cushions before helping with the morning routines. Mum and I worked in silence, united in our tasks, if not in the companionship we had once enjoyed.

By nine o'clock, Mo and I were ready to go. Sarah had offered us a lift to the bus stop, but I had assured her there was no need. We would enjoy the chance to stretch our legs before another arduous journey.

'There's something I wanted to give you.' My mother thrust a plastic bag at me as I stood in the hallway holding a swaddled Emma against my chest. 'A Christmas present for the baby. It's a pack of babygrows and a few other things I'm sure you need. And...' She shuffled awkwardly. 'I was cleaning out the top of your wardrobe, and I found your book of Children's Bible stories. The one you used to read to your dolls and teddies. I wondered if you might want that for Emma, so I put it in the bag as well.'

I could have pointed out that it was Sylvia I'd read to. I'd mastered the art of reading with the sole aim of telling Sylvia those Bible stories. The first time I'd fumbled through the account of Jesus' birth with my one-year-old sister snuggled in a blanket on my lap had been one of my proudest moments. Surely Mum remembered because she was there, sitting close by to help me with the long words. Had she really forgotten, or was she just pretending? Of all the things she could have given me, why had Mum chosen the Children's Bible? I had hidden it shortly after Sylvia's death to avoid painful memories.

'It's good for little ones to hear those Bible stories.' Mum turned away, leaving me to gape at her back.

'Yes, definitely.' Mo walked down the stairs towards us, carrying her overnight bag. 'I read them to my granddaughters. Along with Sleeping Beauty, Alice in Wonderland, and the other fairytales little girls love. Of course, with the boys, it's different. They prefer rowdy games,' she laughed.

'Yes, I remember how Malcolm and David drove me crazy with their races around the house and garden.' Mum had turned to address Mo.

I couldn't bring myself to open the bag. I was tempted to take out the gifts for Emma and leave the book at one of the bus stations we'd visit on our way home. No one would ever know, and Emma was too young to appreciate Bible stories. Yet when the opportunity came, I failed to take it. Although I would never be able to share the stories Sylvia had loved, I might let Emma have the book when she was old enough to read.

The flat was cold and empty when I carried Emma through the front door. I settled her in her cot in readiness for Ola's homecoming and set about preparing dinner.

When Ola arrived home, he walked past me, making a beeline for Emma. He lifted her into his arms and hugged her protectively. 'Were your parents pleased to meet her?' he asked.

'They both said she looks like me.' It was the safest answer. I continued cooking, fighting against resentment at his lack of affection for me.

'Well, she does.' Ola proffered one of his rare smiles, then gave me a peck on the cheek, as though he'd read my thoughts. Or had my expression given me away? 'It's good to have you both home.'

My world settled back into place. That was the best I could hope for from my stoic husband, so it had to be enough.

The following morning, I felt strong enough to open the bag from my mother. I tidied away the gifts for Emma. There was no point saving them for Christmas, but I was grateful. The items were exactly what I needed in the relentless battle to keep Emma in clean clothes. When my fingers curled around the book of Bible stories, I lifted it out of the bag without giving it a second glance, then hid it in an old suitcase under the bed.

'Why don't you and Emma come to the midnight service tonight?' Mo posed the suggestion on Christmas Eve as we sat in one of our favourite cafés drinking hot chocolate.

'I don't usually go to church.' I drank slowly, savouring the treat.

'Lots of people turn up as a one-off.' Mo put her empty mug down on the table. 'The service is candlelit. You and Emma will love it.'

I glanced at Emma, sleeping in her pram, and realised I couldn't refuse Mo's kindness, nor deprive my daughter of the experience.

Ola made no comment when I announced my intention to attend the midnight service, using Mo's excuse that Emma would enjoy the lights and music. He simply nodded, urging me to be careful at such a late hour.

A heavy frost hung in the air as I bundled baby Emma into a shawl later that night, preparing to meet Mo in the shared hallway. When we arrived at the church, Mo chose seats near the back, making it easy for me to sneak out with Emma if necessary. Once again, I was touched by her thoughtfulness.

I felt uneasy at first. I hadn't set foot inside a church since Sylvia's funeral. Then gradually, as the candles glimmered and the singing began, a calmness washed over me, a sense of coming home. Holding my daughter close, I sang the familiar words of the well-loved carols, reminding us of the infant who slept in heavenly rest, as content in His mother's arms as Emma was in mine.

Had Mary felt the same pride and longing for her child to grow up secure in the knowledge of His parents' love? Surely these were the desires of every mother. Yet, if the stories were true, Mary's son was torn away from her at an early age. Not as a child like Sylvia, but as a young man in the prime of His life. How did Mary cope? How would I bear it if I lost Emma? No wonder my mother was permanently scarred. I blinked back tears as the congregation stood to sing yet another carol.

This time, it was Sylvia's favourite. *'Away in a manger, no crib for a bed...'*

Once again, I heard the echo of a little girl standing next to me, felt the phantom sensation of fingers threaded through mine.

'Be near me, Lord Jesus. I ask Thee to stay…'

Where had He been on the day Sylvia died? Why hadn't He saved her? Why had He allowed her to catch my cold? And why had it changed everything?

'Bless all the dear children in Thy tender care. And fit us for heaven to live with Thee there.'

The song ended, and I sat back on the hard wooden pew, weeping silently into Emma's lacy shawl. Was Sylvia in heaven with Jesus? I yearned to believe it. I ached to reach out and grasp the things I'd clung to as a child, but an unrelenting barrier had formed around my heart. I'd needed it to care for my mother following Sylvia's funeral when she'd wandered around the house like a ghost. I'd needed it to go back to school and do the things my family expected.

The service ended, and I walked home with Mo in the moonlight. My friend was unusually quiet, and I was grateful for the space her silence allowed.

'Thanks for inviting us tonight.' I hugged her as we prepared to part outside her flat. 'Have a lovely time with your family tomorrow.'

'I always do.' Mo kissed my cheek. 'And you make sure to enjoy your first Christmas with your little one.'

I nodded. As I mounted the stairs, my mind rang with the melodies of the carols and the flicker of candlelight. Perhaps I would summon up the courage to read Bible stories to Emma. If Sylvia was in heaven with Jesus, she'd want her niece to enjoy the same stories she'd loved. It would create a bond between Emma and the aunt she would never know. And perhaps I might find healing in telling them.

18

The shrill ringing of her son's mobile phone jolted Janet back to the present. Predictably, it was Nettie. Benny had listened the whole time Janet recounted her history with Mo, but he hadn't stayed still the whole time. He'd fiddled a little with the pillows on the bed, got up and paced a bit, and looked out of the window. But he hadn't once asked her to stop, so, with her tongue loosened, Janet had just kept going. Then, when she'd mentioned attending church, Benny had sat back down and retaken her hand. But now, he dropped it again and walked out onto the landing to talk to his girlfriend.

Ola was right. No good came from raking up the past. Things that couldn't be changed should be buried and forgotten. That first Christmas with Emma had its treasured moments, counteracted by their cramped living conditions and Ola's constant mood swings. Janet hadn't been able to predict his reactions from one day to the next. Sometimes, he'd suggested a walk with Emma in her pram, claiming the fresh air would do their baby good, while at other times, he'd ignored Emma and answered Janet's questions with barely more than a grunt. His irritability was a constant cause of tension, only lifting when Emma broke through his barriers.

'She'll be okay, won't she?' Benny paced the landing, and Janet heard the anxiety in his voice.

She beckoned him back into her room, where he stood in the doorway, still holding his phone against his ear.

'What's wrong?' Janet mouthed her question to ensure Nettie would remain unaware of her presence.

'I'll come if you need me.' Benny was completely absorbed in listening to Nettie. 'There are no buses today. I'll have to ask my dad to bring me. I bet he will, for Beth.'

The conversation ended, and Benny turned to her with terror-filled eyes and a tremor in the hand that still gripped his phone. 'Beth's in hospital.'

Hearing the catch in his voice, Janet was immediately ready to comfort him. 'Did she have an accident?'

'Her cough got worse, and her temperature's really high.' Benny fidgeted restlessly. 'Nettie was worried cos she was breathing funny.'

'Did Nettie's parents go with them?' A clearer understanding of the facts was enough for Janet to share her son's fears.

'They aren't home. Nettie drove Beth to the hospital.' Benny lowered tear-filled eyes. 'I said she should've phoned me.'

'What have the doctors said?' Janet's mind conjured up terrifying scenarios for the child they loved.

'They reckon she'll be okay.' Benny sniffed. 'It's not fair that Nettie's on her own.' He scaled the room in his agitation and stared out of the window. 'I've gotta go to her. Dad will take me, won't he? I can't go by myself.'

'Of course he will.' Janet hoped Ola would exercise patience and understanding, even though he wouldn't appreciate the interruption to his plans for a quiet Sunday afternoon watching sport on the television.

Benny strode out of the room and ran down the stairs with Janet close behind. She waited in the lounge doorway as Benny approached his father, biting her lip and praying Ola would comply.

'Beth's in hospital. Nettie's by herself. And I can't go cos it's Sunday.'

His words tumbled out, reminding Janet of the little boy who'd struggled to make himself understood by anyone except her. She recalled his tears of frustration, followed by the temper tantrums that ended with him throwing himself on the ground and pounding the floor until she scooped him up in her arms with the reassurance that she understood. Although he usually spoke more carefully now, his fears had him reverting backwards. Janet could fill in the blanks, but Ola didn't have the patience to try.

'If you want to tell me something, say it properly,' Ola snapped.

Janet was instantly at Benny's side. The atmosphere between father and son would deteriorate if she didn't help. However, Benny surprised her by nodding, taking a deep breath, turning away to compose himself, then looking back at Ola with a steadier gaze.

'Sorry, Dad.'

Ola's expression softened, and Janet let out the breath she'd been holding.

'Good. Now tell me what's wrong.' He switched off the television and rose to put an arm around his pale-faced son.

'Beth's cough got worse.' Benny held his father's gaze unflinchingly. 'She couldn't breathe, and she had a temperature. Nettie had to drive her to the hospital.' He gripped Ola's arm. 'Her parents aren't there, so I wanna be with her. Please, Dad, will you take me?'

'Of course.' Ola headed for the door, followed by a relieved-looking Benny.

'Should I come too?' Janet asked.

'Yeah.' Benny answered without turning back. 'Beth likes you, and you can help Nettie. I dunno what to do. If the doctors say stuff about what's wrong with Beth, I'm not gonna get it. You'll help her understand.'

As Ola drove with Benny in the passenger seat, Janet fought to bring her own fears under control. Beth was only two years old, her temperature had skyrocketed, and she was struggling to breathe. Sylvia had been older. She'd only had a simple cold, yet they'd still lost her. If anything happened to Beth, would Benny carry the same guilt that had weighed on her for over 30 years? He was at church when Nettie needed him. Janet had been at her friend's house. They had both put their own desires ahead of the people they loved, and in Janet's case, she had never seen Sylvia again.

'Don't let it be too late!' Janet prayed for the first time in many years. *'Please, help her. Help my son. Don't let him suffer like I did. And don't let Nettie lose her little girl.'*

As he walked alongside his mum through the hospital's main entrance, Benny's mind fixated on finding Nettie, just as it had when he'd come here on the day of Beth's birth. His heart pounded, and his brain whirled with disjointed questions and fears. Where were they? Would Beth be okay? If he didn't calm down, he'd end up having a seizure. He'd be no use to Nettie if he threw up. The nurses would make him go home, and Nettie would be alone.

'Help me, Jesus. Don't let me have a seizure. Don't let me be stupid. Please, help me find Nettie and Beth.' Silent prayers pounded through Benny's head as he gripped his mother's hand.

Janet drew his attention to a map of the hospital's interior hanging on the wall of the lobby. Benny waited amid a sea of bustling patients and staff, trying not to let the crowds and the noise overwhelm him. The colours and lines on the map meant nothing, but they seemed to make sense to his mother.

'She'll be on the children's ward.' Janet pointed, and her son nodded his agreement.

He hated even thinking about the place where he'd spent too many weeks begging his mum to take him home after multiple rounds of needles, tests and scans.

'It's not fair, Mummy. They're mean!' Benny remembered his cries of protest as he followed his mother onto the familiar ward. The sounds of hissing oxygen masks and beeping machinery, coupled with the smells of illness and disinfectant, still terrified him. Past and present threatened to merge as he teetered on the edge of panic.

Then a well-loved voice dragged him from the brink. 'There you are!' Nettie flung herself into his arms. She must have been watching for their arrival.

Benny hoped she wouldn't notice he was shaking. 'How's Beth?' His girlfriend needed him. He had to get a grip.

As they pulled apart and their gazes locked, Benny knew at least some of his prayers had been answered. His heart rate slowed, his thoughts stopped spinning, and he gave Nettie his full attention.

'She's sleeping, for now.' Nettie reached for his hand. 'They're giving her antibiotics through a drip. They said it's an infection, so I did the right thing. I was worried they'd accuse me of being a fussy mother. I'm not used to any of this, so I don't always know what's normal.'

'You're a great mum.'

Nettie curled her fingers around his. 'I feel better now you're here.'

If she needed to draw strength from him, that meant he'd have to be strong. 'Me and my mum can stay as long as you want. Dad said he'd pick us up later.' Benny pulled back his shoulders and stood straighter. He was no longer the scared little boy being poked and prodded by strange doctors and nurses. He was Nettie's boyfriend, and the closest thing Beth had to a father.

'We'd better get back to her.' Nettie tugged on his hand.

Benny nodded, allowing her to guide him to the bed in which Beth lay, her left arm exposed on top of the covers as a needle dripped medication into her bloodstream. The toddler whimpered, and Benny leaned over the bed to plant a tender kiss on her forehead.

'Hi, Bethy.' Benny longed to gather her up in his arms.

'Benny?' Huge tears rolled down Beth's cheeks. She attempted to sit up, and he gently restrained her.

'You've gotta lie still while the doctors and nurses make you better.' He'd never been able to keep still, but he might be able to help Beth.

'Hurts!' Beth used her right hand to point at the needle in her left, and Benny held on to make sure she didn't pull it out.

'It's making you better.' He rubbed circles around the back of her free hand, soothing her with his touch. 'They'll take it out soon. You'll come home, and we'll feed the ducks in the park.'

'Duckies!' Beth's eyes closed like she'd surrendered to sleep, then shot open again. 'Benny stay?'

'Yes, Benny's going to stay.' Nettie covered both their hands with one of hers. 'Mummy and Benny will stay, and Bethy will go to sleep like a good girl, so she'll get better.'

Janet dabbed at her watery eyes with a tissue as she watched the tender exchange between Benny, Nettie and Beth. They were a family, a mother and father offering reassurance to one another and their child. Despite his youth, and the fact he hadn't been responsible for Beth's conception, Benny's heart belonged to Nettie and her daughter. All too soon, he would leave home and make a new life with the girl he loved.

Janet saw the man her treasured son would become. He would always have his struggles and limitations, but Benny's destiny was sealed.

'Thanks for coming, Jan.' Nettie caught her gaze as Beth drifted back to sleep.

Janet ventured closer to the bed. 'Are they positive there's nothing else going on?' Her thoughts were consumed by Sylvia. 'Shouldn't they do more tests?'

'They won't need to if she keeps improving.' Nettie tucked Beth's favourite teddy in next to her. 'They said things change quickly with toddlers.'

'I don't like the look of her,' Janet fretted.

'She was worse than this earlier.' Nettie smiled reassuringly as she kissed Beth's flushed cheek. 'She isn't coughing so much now.'

'Have you had anything to eat or drink?' Janet put a hand on Nettie's back.

Nettie shook her head. 'She wouldn't let me put her down. I haven't eaten since this morning.'

'You and Benny should go to the cafeteria.' Janet pointed at the chair beside the bed. 'I'll sit here with Beth.'

'I promised I'd stay with her.' Benny tucked the blanket more tightly around Beth and her teddy. 'Can you take Nettie for a drink?'

Janet was astounded by her son's forcefulness. 'What if you have a seizure?' She saw potential pitfalls around every corner.

'I'm okay.' Benny squeezed her hand. 'Please, Mum?'

The hospital cafeteria seemed unusually busy for a Sunday. Nettie offered to wait in line, so Janet pointed out a table near the back before handing over her purse. 'Get whatever you want, love,' she said.

As Janet sat down, she studied Nettie taking her place in the queue. The teenager was usually fashionably dressed and made up, with her long red hair neatly combed. Today, she wore an old pair of jeans, and her sweatshirt sported a stain. Her hair was pulled back into a scraggly ponytail, and her face was devoid of makeup. She had the look of a tired and worried mother; something Janet understood too well.

Nettie returned with a tray containing two polystyrene cups and a plastic-wrapped sandwich. 'I got myself something to eat. I hope you don't mind.' She sat opposite Janet and tore open the packaging. 'I'll pay you back. I was in such a hurry to get Beth here that I came without my purse.'

'It's fine.' Janet's smile was returned by Nettie. 'You don't need to pay me back.'

They sat in silence while Nettie chewed daintily on her sandwich. She seemed in no rush to get back.

'Benny's great with Beth.' Nettie broke the silence. 'I wouldn't cope without him. I get stressed, and sometimes I yell at her because she doesn't do what I want.'

'That's typical toddler behaviour.' Janet was touched by the tenderness in Nettie's eyes when she mentioned her son.

'Benny gets her to do whatever he wants.' Nettie looked down at her sandwich, then back at Janet. 'I reckon she thinks he's the most amazing person in the world.'

'He is.' The words slipped out before Janet could stop them.

'I should've known you'd say that.' Nettie laughed, then blushed. 'I guess I agree.'

'You really love him, don't you?' Janet had never been alone with Benny's girlfriend for more than a couple of minutes. This was their first opportunity for a serious conversation. Although she knew Nettie as Beth's mother and the girl who'd turned Benny's head, she understood very little about her as a person.

'Yes.' Nettie's simple answer and the sincerity in her eyes spoke volumes. 'But the way I love him is totally different from how you do.'

'What do you mean?' Was Nettie trying to say she loved him more? How could anyone possibly love Benny more than his mother?

'There are always going to be things he'll need help with, but I know when he's using his struggles as a reason not to try.' Nettie's green eyes pierced Janet's soul. 'I don't let him get away with that like you do.'

'You think I've spoiled him?' Janet tried not to look offended.

'You still do.' The corners of Nettie's mouth curled up into a grin. 'He plays on it when he wants his own way, then feels guilty and comes running to me with his tail between his legs. When he's ready to listen, we sort things out. He's learning he can do a lot if he tries, and he wants to. So we're good for one another. He calms me down when I'm in a grumpy strop with Beth, and I help him not to chicken out of life. We're a good team.'

'This isn't what I pictured for Benny.' Janet closed her eyes. 'I presumed I'd have to take care of him for the rest of his life. I thought he'd always need me.' She swallowed the lump rising in her throat. Now wasn't the time to cry.

'He will.' To Janet's surprise, Nettie reached across the table and patted her hand. 'Just not the way he used to.'

Janet pondered Nettie's words as she sipped her tea. For the past 16 years, her whole identity had been wrapped up in caring for Benny. Was it time for her to consider other options? Could Janet Wellander dare to imagine being more than Benny's mother?

'I know why you were so worried about Beth.' Nettie's words cut across Janet's musings. 'It's because of Sylvia. You were scared because they told you she only had a cold.'

'I doubt if I'll ever understand what happened.' Janet put her cup down and folded her arms.

'You will if you're brave enough to ask the right questions.' Nettie took the last bite of her sandwich and reached for a napkin. 'Kids don't die from colds.'

'Maybe they can if colds turn into infections. Look at what's happened with Beth.' Janet screwed up her own napkin, realising her words might worry Nettie. 'They weren't as medically advanced back then,' she qualified.

'They knew about colds.' Nettie's tone showed no offense and left no room for argument. 'Why don't you ask one of your brothers for the truth?'

'I'm sure they would have told me if there was more to say.' Was she trying to convince Nettie or herself?

'Benny told me Emma sometimes visited your parents during the summer holidays.' Nettie had changed tactics.

'She enjoyed visiting her cousins. My brother David and his family stayed close to where we grew up.' Janet smiled ruefully. 'I wondered whether she put up with her grandparents for the sake of having other children to play with. It wasn't always possible for her to have friends at home.'

'Why not?' Nettie opened her handbag, took out a compact mirror and a lipstick.

'Benny was wary of strangers,' Janet explained. 'He hated noise, and… Well, Emma was his only playmate. He became jealous if he had to share her.'

'So Emma suffered because of his problems.' Nettie focused on applying her lipstick.

'I didn't make her. They played well together most of the time. Emma loved her little brother, and Benny idolised her. We were all he had. I'm sure he's told you how things were with Ola.'

'No wonder Emma loved seeing her cousins.' Nettie returned the lipstick and mirror to her bag.

'Benny cried his eyes out whenever she went away.' Janet recalled her son's tantrums over the temporary absence of his sister, and Ola storming out of the house to spend the evenings at the pub.

'Why couldn't he go with her?' Nettie asked.

'He wouldn't have wanted to.' Janet laughed nervously. 'He cried whenever I left him. He could barely handle being away from me during a school day, and he's never spent a night away from home. When Emma persuaded him to try it for a school camp, the stress brought on a seizure. We had to pick him up in the middle of the night.' Janet paused, shuffling to the left to make room for a pyjama-clad man squeezing past in a wheelchair. 'Even when he visits Damien at his gran's, he always comes home to sleep.'

'He'll do it one day.' Nettie's eyes swept over the queue of hungry customers snaking their way towards the counter. When she looked back at Janet, her expression was sober. 'Did you realise how rubbish he felt because his grandparents didn't want him?'

'I presumed he was relieved.' Confusion caused Janet to shake her head. What was Nettie getting at?

'Maybe he was… a bit.' Nettie squashed her napkin into the empty sandwich packet. 'But I think he struggled too. Benny doesn't understand his emotions unless someone helps him sort them out.'

About this, she could agree. 'I'm afraid my parents wouldn't have coped with Benny. I tried to shield him from their coldness by cuddling him to sleep on my lap. He was always clingy because long car journeys made him sick. And our visits had to be brief because Ola didn't get on with my family. It made more sense to stay at home. That's why I sent Emma by bus as soon as she was ready to travel alone.'

'Was that when you stopped going?' Nettie asked.

Janet sighed. 'I saw the disdain in my mother's eyes every time Benny was sick or cried, and I couldn't console him. When Emma was born, I made friends with an older woman called Mo. We lived in the same block of flats. She travelled with me the first time I took Emma to meet my parents. Mo sensed the tension between us, but she made me promise to keep trying, so I did, even though I received nothing in return.' Janet's shoulders slumped. 'It was too hard after I had Benny. Our visits were less frequent. Then they stopped.'

'What happened to your friend?' Nettie enquired.

'Ola and I moved around a lot when Emma was little. We barely stayed in the same place for more than a year. Mo and I kept in touch, but I didn't have the energy for long letters when Benny was a baby. I really missed her. Especially the first Christmas when I took both children to visit my parents.'

As Nettie lifted her polystyrene cup and sipped her tea, relief washed over her face. 'Would you tell me the story?' Nettie asked, not opening her eyes.

'Oh… I'm not sure…'

'Please, Jan. I'd love to understand more, and this tea's too hot to drink quickly.'

Janet turned her own cup round, wondering if she should give in. Then she recalled what Nettie said about Benny needing help to understand his emotions. Maybe if she knew the story, Nettie could help Benny.

'Alright. I'll tell you.'

19

'I'll miss you, Daddy!' Six-year-old Emma threw her arms around Ola's waist as he helped her out of the car on a grey, damp morning in early December, leaving me to struggle with Benny. My baby was already fussing, even though we had only travelled the short distance from home to the bus station.

'You'll have so much fun playing with your cousins that you won't even think about me.' Ola lifted a holdall out of the boot, setting it on the ground at my feet.

I had packed the bare minimum for our weekend visit to my parents, knowing I would struggle to handle a case, Benny's changing bag and my two children without Ola's help. I had made this trip several times with Emma during the past six years, but this would be the first time with Benny.

'Mummy's here, sweetheart.' I lifted him into my arms, anxious to settle him with my nearness before his crying brought on a seizure. 'It's okay, my love.' I wrapped the blanket more tightly around him, both for warmth and to add to his sense of security. Benny loved being bundled up.

My precious boy opened his eyes to stare up at me in bewilderment. He let out a cry, coughed, and spat up milk.

'Oh, no!' There was no time to change him before the bus came, so I did my best with a muslin cloth.

'I'm sure that will be the first of many, so there's no point worrying about it.' Ola kissed Emma. 'I'll be here to collect you on Monday evening. Let me know what time.'

I had planned on a three-day trip to make the transition easier for Benny. Now I dreaded it. It was a crazy idea. We should have stayed at home. Benny wouldn't cope in a strange environment. Would my parents tolerate his seizures and his constant need for attention? Mo's words about maintaining contact with my family rang in my ears, but they were slowly being drowned out by my baby's needy cries and my parents' lack of interest in me and my children. I missed my friend now more than ever. Mo was a hundred miles away, recovering from a fall that had resulted in an injury to her hip. I hadn't seen her for three years, although we'd kept in touch regularly until Benny's birth nine months earlier.

My mother had given a half-hearted offer of help following our most recent house move and the arrival of our son. Yet she'd seemed relieved when I put her off, confirming my suspicion that she hadn't wanted to come. Since then, I'd rarely had time for phone calls because Benny consumed my every waking moment.

'I wish Benny was like him.' Emma was captivated by the baby belonging to a young couple sitting near us on the crowded bus, who blew bubbles, gurgled, and waved his chubby little arms in the air.

Before I could restrain her, Emma had risen from her seat and crossed the aisle, where the other mother welcomed her.

'What's his name?' Emma asked.

My face turned crimson. 'I'm sorry.'

'He's Tommy,' the woman told Emma, smiling away my apology.

'My baby brother's called Benny.' Emma pointed over her shoulder. 'He's a naughty boy cos he cries all the time. He has funny fits, and he's always being sick.'

'You get back here now, Emma Wellander.' My tone was uncharacteristically sharp. I was tired, my head ached, and Benny had just vomited for the third time since we left the house. I needed to change his clothes, and he was bound to kick up a fuss.

As a scowling Emma reluctantly retook her seat beside me, I began the task of unwrapping my loudly protesting baby.

'Help me, Em.' I felt the glares and sighs of disapproval from my fellow passengers as Benny resisted my efforts to remove his soiled clothes.

'Can I do anything?' The woman seated across the aisle handed Tommy to her husband and rose. 'I'm Rachel. I know how hard it is to handle them when they're upset.'

'Thank you. I'm Janet.' I fought not to cry over this unexpected show of kindness.

'You play with my Tommy while I help your mum.' Rachel swapped seats with Emma. With her expert help, I wrestled Benny out of one outfit and into another.

'I hope he won't be sick again before we get to our stop.' I lifted Benny to my shoulder. He tucked his little blonde head under my chin, content at last to be safe in my arms. Frustration evaporated into pure love as Benny's tiny fingers curled around the neck of my cardigan. I cooed at him softly until he closed his eyes, surrendering to sleep.

'Tommy was a sickly baby in the beginning.' Rachel stuffed a packet of cotton balls into Benny's changing bag. 'He's growing out of it now. I'm sure yours will too.'

She clearly assumed Benny was much younger than nine months. Most people did because of his size, and I rarely had the energy to explain his epilepsy or lack of appetite. At least he hadn't suffered a seizure on the bus. I finally unwound and enjoyed a conversation with my undemanding companion, while Benny slept and Emma played with Tommy.

When we arrived at our destination, I placed Benny in his baby carrier and strapped him to my chest, while Rachel's husband carried our belongings off the bus before bidding us farewell and rejoining his family. Emma was tired and crotchety after the long journey, and Benny was stirring in readiness for his next feed. I hoped he'd be willing to wait until we got to my parents' house. I urged Emma to wrap a scarf around her neck and put her hood up. Although it was no longer raining, an icy December blast whipped at our hands and faces, making us glad of our winter coats.

'I don't want to walk,' Emma wailed as she stuffed her thumb into her mouth. 'I'm too tired!'

'It's not far to Grandma and Grandpa's house.' I injected an eagerness into my tone that I definitely didn't feel. Why couldn't David be here to collect us this time, when I really needed him? 'Anyway, you've got an important job to do. I need you to carry Benny's things.' I bent to hoist the holdall onto my shoulder, holding the smaller bag out to Emma.

'But I want you to carry me!' My daughter was having one of her rare stubborn moments.

'Don't be silly, Emma. you know I can't do that anymore. You're a big girl now.'

'I'm gonna stay here.' Emma plonked her little bottom down upon the pavement and set her jaw, reminding me of Ola. On a less stressful day, her dramatics might have been funny.

'You're a very naughty girl.' I wagged a finger at my sulky six-year-old. 'If you carry on like this, I'll tell Daddy when we get home, and he'll shout. You don't like it when Daddy shouts.'

'But Daddy's not here.' Huge tears rolled down Emma's cheeks, and Benny's cries joined his sister's. 'If he was, he'd carry me.'

'Come on, Em,' I pleaded whilst rocking Benny.

'You don't tell Benny he's naughty.' Emma's shoulders heaved. 'You always say he's good, even when he cries loads and he's sick everywhere.'

'He's a baby. He can't help it.' I tugged on her hand. 'I swear Emma Wellander, if you don't get up off the ground this instant, I'll carry on by myself and leave you here.'

'You wouldn't leave Benny.' Emma gave up the fight and followed me down the road, dragging her feet and grumbling with every step while I struggled with Benny and both bags. I attempted to cheer Emma by pointing out various festive window displays, but as the daylight faded and moisture fell from the sky, I quickened my pace, and Emma's short legs struggled to keep up.

'Not far now,' I encouraged. Why hadn't I just asked David to meet us? My parents still didn't own a car, and I guessed now they never would.

We arrived at our destination cold, tired and miserable, to a reception from my mother that was barely any warmer.

'Get in quickly so you don't let the heat out.' She ushered us into the hallway. 'Cost of fuel these days.' She didn't offer to take my bags, barely glanced at Emma and ignored Benny.

'Why haven't you got a Christmas tree, Grandma?' Emma stood in the lounge doorway, her eagle eyes taking in every detail.

'Why would we want to bother with a tree?' Mum was already heading for the kitchen to prepare warm drinks. 'There aren't any children in this house.'

'Lucy and Hannah come here a lot.' Emma danced into the kitchen in pursuit of her grandmother, while I followed more slowly with Benny, whose cries for milk became more insistent. 'And Uncle Malcolm's children do sometimes.' Emma turned back to me. 'Why haven't I met my other cousins yet?'

'I told you. Uncle Malcolm lives a long way away, so it's hard for us to visit Grandma and Grandpa at the same time.' I stood rocking Benny. He wouldn't wait much longer for his feed.

Mum glanced my way disdainfully. 'It sounds as though you'd better feed that baby. Will he eat a mashed-up banana?'

'I'll just give him milk for now.' I carried Benny into the lounge and sank onto the well-worn sofa. My health visitor was constantly badgering me about persevering with solid food, but the only thing Benny enjoyed was my milk. As he latched on, my eyes were drawn to the collection of family photographs on the sideboard. There were pictures of Malcolm and David with their wives and children, and one of me and Emma that David had taken during a summer visit. Ola was missing, and of course, there weren't any images of Sylvia. Did my parents and brothers ever think about her? Did they ponder what her future might have held, as I did?

If Sylvia was still alive, perhaps she would have been a mother by now. What kind of man would she have chosen?

Someone full of life, or a quiet, dependable man to balance her impetuous nature? Would he have been tall, dark, and handsome? Would Sylvia have cared about his outward appearance, or would she simply have sought someone to love her?

Benny whimpered, exhausted from the effort of sucking.

'Come on, sweetheart. You need to drink more than that,' I crooned.

He responded with a cry just as Emma burst into the room ahead of her grandmother, carrying a plate full of biscuits.

'Look, Mummy! Grandma bought me chocolate ones.' Emma brandished the plate like a prize in a contest.

'So you think she only bought them for you, do you?' I took a biscuit whilst patting Benny's back.

'He's gonna be sick.' Emma turned to her grandmother, who had followed her into the room carrying their drinks on a tray. 'Benny's always sick.'

Benny obliged his sister. Milk propelled out of his mouth, splattering me and the back of my mother's sofa.

'I'm sorry, Mum.' I stared helplessly at the stains, cheeks warming in humiliation. 'I don't know where it all comes from.' Benny threw up so much, I doubted there was anything left in his stomach, but I'd likely not get him to feed again. This was our constant battle.

'For a little person, he makes a lot of mess.' Mum sighed, setting the tea down and muttering as she left the room to fetch a cloth and some disinfectant.

'You'd never think Emma and Benny were related.' Sarah held out her arms, preparing to take my son. 'Hi, Benny. Are you going to come to Auntie Sarah for a cuddle?'

My sister-in-law had brought her daughters round for tea shortly after my father arrived home from work, excusing David by saying he was committed to playing in a darts match at the local pub. He would see us tomorrow.

'I wanted to hold him first!' Twelve-year-old Lucy rushed to her mother's side while her younger sister hung back.

'You can be next.' Sarah's expert arms cradled Benny. He gave a howl of protest, turning his head to search for me.

'He doesn't like anyone except Mummy.' Emma's tone was matter-of-fact.

'Hannah used to be like that.' Sarah relinquished my baby, who wrapped his little arms around my neck. 'She grew out of it.'

'Does that baby do anything except cry?' Dad tore his eyes away from the six o'clock news to glare at me and Benny.

Before I could answer, Benny's body stiffened, then convulsed.

'What's the matter with him?' Lucy's eyes widened, and I quickly lowered Benny onto the carpet as the seizure intensified, blocking the girl's view with my back.

'Mummy's here, Benny.' I swallowed my panic as I knelt beside him. 'It'll be over soon.'

The seizure ended, and as I lifted him, Benny projectile-vomited over both of us. At least this time, there was no cleaning up for my mother. It was all on our clothes.

'That's awful,' Sarah breathed. 'You must be terrified every time it happens.'

'Yes.' I headed for the door. 'I'd better clean us both up.'

'Tea won't be long.' Mum's emotionless voice followed us out of the room.

Lucy didn't ask if she could hold Benny again; her enthusiasm had clearly been dampened by the severity of his seizure. Perhaps she was afraid he'd be sick over her too. I toyed with the meal my mother had prepared without my help, while Emma chatted away with her cousins.

'If you're going to be here for a couple of nights, Emma can stay at our house tomorrow, can't she, Mum?' Lucy turned to Sarah for approval.

'Of course she can.' Sarah smiled at her niece. 'We'd love to have you. You and Hannah are only a year and a half apart, so you'll have fun playing together.'

'I can take you to the park.' Lucy leaned over to help Emma cut her meat. 'I'm allowed to go there by myself now, and I can look after you and Hannah.'

Emma was full of excitement when I bathed her in readiness for bed, after her aunt and cousins had left.

'I've never had a sleepover!' She splashed in the bathwater. 'It's gonna be lots of fun, Mummy. I love Lucy cos she's my big cousin, and she looks after me.' Emma paused, then added. 'I think I'd love Hannah too if she talked more. Maybe she will when Lucy takes us to the park.'

'Time to get out, Em.' I had left Benny sleeping on the bed we would all share, with a pillow on either side of him. He couldn't even roll yet, but I still feared leaving him alone, even for a few minutes.

'Can I stay in here longer? Please?' Emma covered her chin in bubbles. 'Look, Mummy. I've got a white beard, like Grandpa!'

I laughed, dipping a finger into the water to apply more bubbles to the tip of her nose. 'And now you've got a white nose.'

My little girl's giggles were infectious. How I longed to prolong this moment of fun. Bath times with Emma had always been a playful delight, but I couldn't afford to indulge. Benny might have another seizure and choke on his own vomit.

'Okay, Em. I'll let you stay in the bath for another five minutes.' I turned towards the door.

'I wish you'd play with me, like you used to.' Emma lay back in the water.

'You know why I can't.'

It was a relief when the following morning came, and I could hand Emma over to Sarah. My daughter went gladly, barely giving me and Benny a backward glance as Lucy enthused over the fun things they would do. Even Hannah seemed to have captured some of her older sister's excitement.

'Lucy's a proper little mother, like you were at her age.' Mum stood behind me in the hallway as I lifted Benny's hand to wave at Emma through the open front door, urging him to call 'bye-bye' to his sister even though he hadn't spoken a word yet.

'She is,' I replied. What more could I say without naming the little blonde girl I had loved to spoil? I closed the front door and focused on my baby. 'Shall we go for a walk, Benny?'

I could tell his constant fussing was getting on his grandparents' nerves. Neither of them had attempted to pick him up. They'd barely acknowledged his presence except to grumble about his noise, or to comment on how pale and sickly he was, and how underdeveloped for his age.

I yearned to be outside, away from their critical glances. I wrapped Benny up and prepared to take him on a tour of my favourite childhood haunts. I chattered as we walked, and Benny responded with contented little snuffles.

When we reached the park, it was empty. I sat on a swing, gently swaying with Benny lying on my lap, enjoying the meagre warmth of the winter sun on my face. Benny sighed and closed his eyes, lulled by my voice and the swing's rhythmical movement.

'This was your auntie Sylvia's favourite place.' It was the first time I'd dared to speak her name, but it felt safe in the empty park. Benny was too young to understand. 'I loved her so much.' I tilted my head to kiss him. 'Just like I love you.' I closed my eyes, surrendering to the relaxing jerking of the swing. 'I wish I'd stayed to look after her. I'm sure she must have cried for me, like she always did when she was ill.' Tears filled my eyes, and I didn't even try to fight them. 'I'm never going to let you cry like that.' I clutched Benny even tighter, snuggling him into my chest. 'I'll always be here when you need me, and I won't let anything happen to you.'

I hadn't been able to prevent his epilepsy. I couldn't stop his seizures, but I could watch over him, ensuring no harm came to him as a result. Under my watchful eye, my precious son wouldn't want for a thing. He would never doubt the depth of my love.

A squeak from Benny had me looking down at him with concern. Was he scared or in pain? My breath caught as he opened his eyes, and the corners of his tiny mouth lifted into a beaming smile.

'I love you, beautiful boy.' I lifted him until our faces touched. Benny smiled again, curling his fingers around a strand of my hair. 'I'm so glad I get to be your mummy.'

20

'Wow. I'm really starting to understand your relationship with Benny now,' Nettie said, leaning forward and squeezing Janet's hand. 'Thank you for opening up to me. It means a lot.'

The scraping of Nettie's chair against the cafeteria's wooden floor pulled Janet back to the present. 'I suppose we should get back to Benny and Beth. You finished your tea ages ago.'

'Yeah.'

Janet slung her bag over her shoulder before following Nettie along the maze of corridors to the children's ward. Nurses hurried between beds, taking temperatures and administering medication, while parents attempted to soothe their fretful infants. A toddler ran up and down the length of the ward, chased by her harassed mother, who apologised profusely to everyone she passed.

Beth was still resting, undisturbed by the noise. Benny hadn't let go of her hand. He sat in the chair beside the bed with his eyes closed, and Janet wondered if the oppressive warmth, coupled with the hum of activity, had lulled him to sleep.

'All right?' Nettie patted his shoulder, and Benny's eyes fluttered open.

'She hasn't woken up.' He gently released Beth's hand, yawned, and stretched.

'It's probably better if she sleeps.' Nettie leant down to kiss him. 'Thanks for giving me a break. I needed it.'

Benny relinquished his chair to Janet and sat on the bed beside Nettie, watching over Beth. Relief flooded Janet with every rise and fall of the little girl's chest. Her breathing seemed less laboured, with her face gradually returning to normal pallor.

When Beth woke, she graced them all with smiles and even allowed her mother to entertain her with a book. The doctor seemed more optimistic when he stopped by to check on her progress.

An hour after that, Janet returned from fetching Nettie another drink and a packet of crisps to find her son and his girlfriend cuddling while Beth slept more peacefully. Janet checked her watch and cleared her throat before addressing a red-faced Benny. 'It's getting late, my love. I need to phone your dad.'

'I'm gonna stay with Nettie.' He fought his girlfriend for a crisp as she playfully hid the packet behind her back. 'Don't be mean. You tell Beth to share, so you should too.'

Nettie relented with a cheeky grin and a toss of her hair.

'You can't stay here, my love.' Janet lightly stroked her son's back. 'They won't let you.'

'They only like one person to stay overnight.' Nettie gave up the last of her crisps. 'We'll both be okay now.' There was no mistaking the love that passed between the couple as their lips met in a tender kiss. 'I'm so glad you came,' Nettie said. 'You too, Jan.' She surprised Janet with a hug.

Benny remained unconvinced, but Nettie eventually persuaded him to leave with the promise of regular reports on Beth's progress. 'I'll phone you the next time she's sleeping,' she reassured him.

Janet and Benny waited under a canopy outside the hospital's automatic doors amid a sea of other visitors. Benny gripped his mother's hand, and she noted the tremor in his. Her son was physically and emotionally exhausted after the hours in the hospital. She worried he might have a seizure. Spotting Ola's car inching towards them, Janet urged Benny forward, opening the passenger door for him before climbing into the back.

'How's Beth?' Ola asked as Benny buckled his seatbelt.

'They reckon she's gonna be okay.'

As Ola swung his vehicle away from the hospital and into the traffic on the road leading home, Benny's head snuggled into the side of his seat, and he curled his arms round his stomach.

'She's a little fighter.' Janet retrieved a packet of mints from her handbag and reached between the seats to place one in her son's palm. She guessed he was feeling sick, and she hoped it would help.

They travelled home in silence. Darkness had fallen, so the roads were quiet. The lack of conversation in the car gave Janet too much time alone with her worrying thoughts, which flitted from Beth to Sylvia. If only her sister had recovered from her illness. Why had things turned out so differently for her when she'd only caught a cold? The more Janet pondered, the more she struggled to understand.

Despite his exhaustion, Benny couldn't sleep. He lay on his bed with the TV on, with no idea what was happening on the screen. Every half hour, he reached for his phone for an update from Nettie. Sometimes, her reply came quickly. Other times, he had to wait because she was busy with Beth.

'She's getting better. Giving me a load of cheek and everything.' Nettie had written the same words several times. However, Benny couldn't get rid of the knot lodged in the pit of his stomach. While he was with them, he'd forced himself to be calm. Now he was back at home, scared and alone. If he was really Beth's father, they might have allowed him to stay, but he was only Nettie's boyfriend. No one at the hospital understood the depth of his closeness to Beth.

His mum knocked on the door, bringing him a cup of tea on her way to bed, but Benny only sipped at it. As the night wore on, his stomach roiled until he found himself in the bathroom with his head hanging over the toilet. He hoped his mum wouldn't hear as he splashed cold water over his face, then stumbled back into his room, collapsing upon his bed in a flood of bitter tears.

This time, it was Benny who missed Nettie's text. He jumped when his phone rang at half past two, scrabbling to answer when he saw it was Nettie.

'Sorry,' she whispered. 'I guessed you were still awake.'

'I threw up.' He hid nothing from her. There was no point trying because Nettie always saw through him.

'Was it a seizure?'

'No.' He turned onto his side with the phone held to his ear. 'I throw up when I'm stressed.' His girlfriend's voice was having its usual calming effect. 'How's Beth?'

'She's sleeping.' Nettie yawned. 'I'm going to have a couple of hours in the chair by her bed before she wakes up again. That's why I rang. You'll worry even more if I stop answering your texts.'

'I'm glad you did.' Benny's stomach was finally settling. 'I know I'm being stupid, Nettie. I just wish I was with you. I hate being here by myself.'

'You're not going to school in the morning, are you?' She sounded concerned.

'Dad said I didn't have to.' Benny had been surprised by Ola's generosity. 'I reckon he knows I won't be able to learn nothing when all I can think about is Beth.'

'They said I can bring her home tomorrow if she keeps improving, so we can spend the day together.'

'That'd be good.' It was a huge understatement.

After saying goodnight to Nettie, Benny switched off the TV and fell into a restless sleep.

Benny slept late the following morning. His dad had left for work long before he appeared in the kitchen.

'Can I make you something to eat?' His mum rushed in, brandishing a duster and a tin of polish.

'No thanks.' Benny's mug of milk was already in the microwave.

'Your stomach will be empty because you were sick last night.' Janet put her cleaning items down to hug him, and Benny rested his head gratefully on her shoulder.

'How come you know everything?'

'I'm your mother.' She kissed his cheek, and he lingered in her arms, not quite ready to face the world yet.

'I'm okay,' he murmured, even though he wasn't sure it was true.

The microwave dinged, and Benny pulled free. 'It wasn't a seizure. I was worried about Beth.' He leaned against the draining board, sipping his drink. 'They're coming home soon. I'm gonna go round to Nettie's.'

'I'm so glad Beth's better. If they're not back yet, surely you've got time for a slice of toast?'

Benny relented with a nod. 'I'll make it cos you're dusting.' He was pleased when she didn't insist on making the toast for him.

'I wish we could do this tomorrow as well.' Benny sat beside Nettie at her parents' kitchen table, the two of them alternating mouthfuls of ice cream straight out of the tub.

'We could if you didn't have school.'

Benny laughed as their spoons clashed.

'I can't go back to work until Beth's less clingy.' Nettie leant against him with a sigh. 'The prospect of a day at home with her grizzling and my mum moaning at me isn't exactly filling me with festive joy.'

'I'll take another day off. It doesn't matter.' Benny shrugged.

'It'll matter to your dad. There's no way he'll let you because Beth's improving.' Nettie seemed to ponder her own words, then turned to him with a sly grin. 'Unless you don't tell him.'

'How am I gonna do that?' Benny gaped at her. 'He'll figure out I'm not going if I'm not up when he goes to work.'

'So, make sure you are.'

Benny's confusion increased.

'Get dressed for school like normal, and after he's gone, tell your mum you've got a headache.' Nettie plunged her spoon into the tub, coming out with a huge blob of ice cream which she stuffed into her mouth before continuing. 'That's all it'll take for her to give in and say you don't need to go.'

'If she thinks I'm ill, she'll tell me to stay in bed.' Benny's spoon hovered mid-air as he considered.

'Stay in your room for an hour, then tell her you're feeling better, so you might as well hang out here with me and Beth.' Nettie used the back of a hand to wipe the corner of her mouth.

'Okay.' Benny took no more convincing.

'We can only make that work for one more day,' Nettie cautioned. 'On Wednesday, I'll have to work, and you'll go back to school.'

'Stupid school.' Benny kicked the table leg.

'You still act like Beth sometimes.'

'When I've gotta go to school, I feel like Beth.' Benny grinned. 'I wanna lie in the middle of the floor and scream like her when she doesn't wanna do stuff.'

'If you did that, you'd probably end up having a seizure.' Nettie licked her spoon and put it on the table.

'Yeah, probably.' Benny draped his arm around her, and Nettie rested her head on his shoulder, allowing him to consume the last of the ice cream.

'At least there are only two more weeks before the Christmas holidays,' she said.

Benny nodded with a smile.

'Why didn't he go to school?'

Standing in the hallway the following evening listening to his father's raised voice, Benny realised he was in trouble. Nettie had urged him to sneak home before Ola arrived, but he'd misjudged the timing. His dad was early. Benny stood frozen to the spot, trying to decide what to do. Should he disappear up to his room and pretend to be ill again? Hopefully, his mother hadn't said he was at Nettie's, so his dad would presume he'd spent the whole day nursing an aching stomach or a bad head.

'Did he have a seizure?' That was Emma's voice. She was in the lounge with their parents.

'He said he had a headache.' Janet's tone was plaintive. 'And he looked pale.'

'Benny's always pale, Mum. It's his colouring.' Emma sounded irritated.

'So he's been in bed all day,' Ola barked.

Benny held his breath, praying his mother would cover for him.

'He said he was better after a while, so he went over to Nettie's.'

'Great. Thanks, Mum,' Benny muttered under his breath.

The living room door swung open, and Emma faced him.

'I thought I heard you.' Her eyes flashed, reminding him of their father.

'I didn't make no noise.' He knew he shouldn't have spoken as soon as the words slipped out. He sounded pathetic. Emma had her ways of making him act like a child.

'You don't know how to be quiet.' She wasn't smiling.

'Get in here, Benny Wellander!' Ola thundered.

Benny took a deep breath, squared his shoulders, and attempted to walk past Emma into the lounge with his head held high.

'What have you got to say for yourself?' Ola sat in his armchair, his face contorted with anger.

Benny's defences crumbled. 'I'm sorry, Dad.' He hung his head in defeat.

'Is that all you're going to say?' Ola rose to tower over him.

'I needed to be with Nettie and Beth.'

'When you should have been at school.' His father allowed time for his words to sink in before continuing his tirade. 'I thought we were past this nonsense, Benny.'

'I'm sorry.' Tears pricked at Benny's eyes and slid down his cheeks. He couldn't stop them.

'Please, Ola, don't upset him.' Janet rushed to Benny's side, her arms instantly going around him.

'It's always about him!' Ola turned on his heels and stormed towards the door, then spun around to inflict his final blow. 'Well, he's not getting away with it this time. You're grounded,

Benny. And you won't be missing another day of school before the end of term. Am I making myself clear?'

'He can't go if he's ill!' Janet protested.

'He can, and he will.' The living room door slammed, then his dad left the house, closing the front door with a resounding thud.

'He's not being fair.' Benny looked at Janet for support.

'He'll calm down, my love.' She guided him to the sofa, then wrapped her arm around his shaking shoulders.

'If I'm grounded, he won't let me see Nettie.'

'You should've thought about that before you lied to Mum and bunked off school.' Emma perched on their father's vacated chair.

'You don't know nothing, so shut up!' Benny glared at his sister.

His mother's eyes darted helplessly from him to Emma.

'He can't stop me seeing Nettie.' Benny was up again, and pacing. 'It's not fair.'

'You're always going on about what's not fair.' Emma shouted. 'You never consider how the way you behave isn't fair to the rest of us.'

'What do you mean?' Benny didn't want to listen, but once she'd started, there was no stopping Emma.

'You want to know what's not fair? I'll tell you.' Emma rose to block his path. 'Our lives have revolved around your selfishness, your spoiled little ways and your temper tantrums for the past 16 years. I couldn't do anything because of you. If I wanted to have friends round, Mum said it'd upset Benny. And if Benny got upset, he might end up in hospital. I got sick of hearing your name!'

'I can't help being ill.' Benny choked on a sob, all the fight having drained out of him. 'Do you think I want to have seizures? I hate them most cos I'm the one who's gotta put up with them.' He backed away from his furious sister. 'It's okay for you, Em. You can do loads of stuff. You always could.'

'That's not true.' Emma advanced on him again, and Benny had nowhere to go because his back was against the wall. 'Mum wouldn't let me in case you got upset or jealous. All I heard was "Benny needs us, Em." My needs didn't matter.'

'You had loads of stuff.'

'Like what?' Emma challenged.

'Like…' Benny searched frantically for an answer to silence her. 'Like how you stayed with our grandparents. They wanted you, but they didn't want me cos of my seizures.'

'Even if they had, you wouldn't have stayed.'

'Emma, please.' Janet forced her way between them. She reached for Benny, but he pushed her away. 'Benny love… You need to calm down or you'll have a seizure.'

'I don't care!' Benny barged towards the door.

'That's so typical of you.' Emma clearly hadn't finished. 'You don't care about anyone except yourself.'

'That's not true.' Benny stood in the doorway. 'I care about Nettie and Beth. That's why I wanted to be with them today. Nettie needed me.' Should he say more? 'I would've stayed at our grandparents' house with you, too, if they'd wanted me.'

'No you wouldn't.' Emma folded her arms, staring down her nose at him. 'You can't even spend one night away from home. You proved that on your Year 6 camping trip, remember?'

'I would've been okay if you were with me.' Once again, Benny was floundering. 'You always looked after me, Emmie.'

'Mum didn't give me a choice.'

Emma's words hit Benny like a punch to the stomach. He thought his sister was on his side. Had she just been pretending and putting up with him all along? Did she hate him as much as his father used to? Were they both going to turn against him because of one stupid mistake?

Unable to take any more, Benny climbed the stairs, blinded by tears, with his mum's cries for him to come back ringing in his ears.

21

Benny's frantic thoughts swirled as he stood in his bedroom gazing down at his schoolbag, stuffed full of useless books he had no interest in reading. If he threw them away, he could fill the bag with anything he wanted. It was big enough to hold spare clothes, his toothbrush, and his Bible. He could run down the road to Nettie's house and spend the night with her and Beth. He was 16, so no one could stop them from living together. His family might not want him, but Nettie did. She treated him like an adult because she loved him, and he'd helped her with Beth for the past two years.

They could get a place of their own if he left school and looked for a job. He didn't have to wait for his father's permission. His dad probably wouldn't want him working at the garage now, anyway. He'd do anything, as long as it paid the bills. They only needed to be together. Nettie hated living at home, so she'd jump at an excuse to move out. Benny would show Emma, and both sets of parents, how grown-up he was.

You're not acting like a grown-up now, are you, Benny?

Was that his dad's voice in his head, or God's?

'They don't let me!' he countered. 'They treat me like I'm stupid. I thought Emmie was on my side. Dad still hates me, and Mum wants me to be a baby cos she needs someone to look after.'

Benny threw himself face down on his bed.

You're not stupid.

The voice came again, firm but loving.

'No one gets me except Nettie!' Benny cried into his pillow. 'It's a waste of time going to school. I'm thick, and useless, and all the things Emmie said.'

Words scrolled through his mind as though they flashed across a TV screen. Recognition dawned, and he closed his eyes, whispering into his pillow the only Bible verse he'd learned by heart.

'For this is how God loved the world; He gave His one and only Son, so that everyone who believes in Him will not perish but have eternal life.'

Benny had learned to personalise that verse, to remind himself that Jesus would have died, just for him.

'For this is how God loved Benny Wellander; He gave His one and only Son, so that if Benny Wellander believes in Him, he will not perish but have eternal life.'

The truth dawned on him as Benny lifted his tear-stained face from the pillow. Jesus loved him with an everlasting love. He didn't see him as thick or useless, even when Benny acted like it.

Your family love you too. They want what's best for you.

Benny rolled over onto his back, desperate to believe what he'd heard. He reached for his Bible from his bedside cabinet, and a piece of paper fluttered to the ground. Leaning down to pick it up, he realised it was the list of the ten commandments Pastor Tim had given him during a Saturday study session. Didn't one of them tell him to honour his father and mother?

'I didn't do that today.' Benny sighed, closing his eyes in prayer. 'I'm sorry, Jesus. What am I gonna do now? Even if I say sorry to Dad, he still won't let me see Nettie and Beth.'

Benny's phone rang. It was Nettie. He was unable to disguise the sadness in his voice as he answered in his customary way.

'What's happened?' She got straight to the point.

'My dad found out I lied to Mum about being ill. He's really mad. He's grounded me, and… and…' Benny cleared his throat. 'We had a huge row. Emmie's here, and she said some mean stuff. I said some back. It's all a mess, Nettie. It's rubbish.' His voice cracked on a sob.

'It's my fault.' Nettie spoke with tender reassurance. 'I shouldn't have told you to go against your dad. I should've guessed you'd get found out and land up in a load of trouble. I'm sorry.'

'It's not your fault,' he protested. 'I was the one who did it. What are we gonna do now?'

'About you not being able to see me?'

Benny mumbled a response, and Nettie went on.

'We've been here once before, remember?'

He didn't, so she jogged his memory. 'When your dad found out about us. He grounded you then too. And it lasted longer than a couple of weeks.'

'I guess.' Benny still wondered how he'd survive their enforced time apart.

'Do what he wants,' Nettie encouraged. 'Go to school and do your best. I'll talk to him once he's had time to calm down. Your dad's usually okay with me. Perhaps I'll persuade him to change his mind.'

'What if he doesn't?'

'I'll phone you every night and I'll see you when he says I can.' Nettie paused. 'You're stuck with me, Wellander.'

Benny heard the smile in her voice. 'I want us to be together all the time.' He held the phone closer to his ear, longing to touch her.

'We will be one day.' She sounded certain. 'We've come this far, so we'll make it the rest of the way.'

'I love you so much, Nettie.' It was a doleful whisper.

'I love you too.'

After they hung up, Benny sat in contemplative silence until a knock on his bedroom door forced him to confront the harsh reality of the problems he'd created.

'It's me.' Emma's voice came through the crack in the door. 'Can I come in?'

He wanted to tell her to go away. However, he'd never refused his sister entry to his room.

'Yeah.' His half-hearted response gave Emma enough permission, and the door opened and closed behind her.

'I think we need to talk.' Emma leaned against the door.

Benny refused to make eye contact with his sister. The accusations she'd hurled at him downstairs still rang in his ears. Despite his poor memory, hurtful words had a nasty habit of imprinting themselves on his brain.

'I'm listening,' he mumbled. Emma needed to apologise, if she meant it. Or was she only backing down because of their mother? Benny pictured Janet fretting and pleading with her daughter to make things right. Would he be able to trust anything Emma said?

'I was hard on you.' Emma advanced further into the room, holding out a hand which Benny refused to take.

'Were you telling the truth?' He had to know. 'Do you really hate me?'

'I never said I hated you.' Emma seemed calmer.

'You said I'm selfish and spoilt.' Benny finally looked at her. 'I reckon that means you hate me.'

'You were.' Emma smiled cautiously. 'You're not so bad nowadays. Except when you do stupid things, like bunking off school and lying to Mum by pretending you're ill. That's the old Benny rearing his ugly head. And it's a shame because you can be a great kid when you try.' Her voice lowered as Emma covered his hand with one of her own. 'You're loving, and sweet, and funny. And you're the only little brother I'll ever want.'

'Do you mean that, Emmie?' He turned his head so she wouldn't see his eyes misting over. Would he ever stop crying today?

'I'm sorry if I hurt you, Pestie.' She sat on the bed beside him, and Benny didn't resist her hug.

'I'm sorry for the stupid stuff I said. I was mad cos of what Dad did.'

'Surely you expected it?' Emma pulled away, looking into his eyes.

'I guess I should've. Emmie?' He faltered. 'There's more stuff I need to know.'

'Okay. Let's talk.' Emma swung her legs onto the bed, making herself comfortable with her back against the headboard.

'When you stayed with Grandma and Grandpa...' Benny settled himself beside her.

'Why are we back to that?'

He gazed at her earnestly. 'Did you like going there to have a break from Mum fussing and me always getting my own way?'

'It was nice to get away from that.' Emma held his hand. 'But I always missed you after a couple of days. I knew there were things you couldn't help because of your epilepsy.'

'I could help some of it.' Benny sighed and rested his head on his sister's shoulder. 'It was hard. I only had you and Mum till I made friends with Damo and Nettie. Then Dad started acting like he wanted me.'

'He always wanted you,' Emma insisted.

'Not in the beginning.' Benny shrugged. 'I got on his nerves.'

'A lot of things went on when you were little.' A thoughtful expression settled on Emma's face. 'Before Mum had you, we were like every other family. Dad was moody, but we had fun. Especially me and Mum. She read to me and made-up games about my dolls and teddies. All that changed after you were born. Whenever I wanted her, she told me to play by myself because you were crying, or you'd had a seizure, or you'd been sick. You sulked if I had her attention for more than five minutes and you thought we were ignoring you.'

'And I didn't like playing games.' Benny stared up at the ceiling.

'You got bored.' Emma squeezed his hand. 'You just wanted Mum to hold you. So that's basically all she did unless she was gardening, cooking, or doing the housework. She wouldn't even put you down to play with me while you slept, in case you woke up.'

'I got scared, Em.' At his age, it felt embarrassing to admit. 'I hated loud noises, and lots of people, and my seizures. I never knew when they were gonna happen or how sick I'd be. And Dad was scary.' Benny hung his head. 'He shouted all the time.

I didn't think no one would ever love me except for you and Mum.'

'Well, they do.' Emma touched his shoulder.

Benny ran through the list of people whose love he gladly returned. There was Jesus, of course. Closely followed by Nettie and Beth, Pastor Tim, his parents and Emma. He no longer questioned Ola's love. One mistake wouldn't undo their growing bond. Would it?

Emma shifted on the bed. 'There is one more thing I need to tell you.'

Benny refocused on his sister. This was his chance to give back some of the love and attention she freely offered.

'I didn't just spend time with our grandparents because I needed a break. I didn't even want to be with them as they were really sad and distant. I guess now we understand why.' She reached for the pillow, placing it behind her. 'I actually loved going there in the summer to spend time with Uncle David's family. Our cousins were always really pleased to see me. Especially Lucy, the oldest one. Being with them felt normal. It was what I wished we had.'

'But we couldn't cos of what was wrong with me.' There was no petulance in Benny's tone. He was merely stating a fact.

Emma nodded.

'I'm sorry, Emmie.' Benny was ashamed to realise he'd never apologised to her before.

'It's okay.' She hugged him again and kissed his cheek. 'I'm glad we had this talk. Maybe I'm even glad we had the row. It pushed us into saying what we needed to.'

'I don't reckon it's gonna be so easy to sort stuff out with Dad.' Benny groaned.

'You might be surprised.' His sister stretched before climbing off the bed. 'He values your relationship, and he won't want to spoil it. You've got time though, because he isn't back yet.'

'I wish he'd let me leave school,' Benny complained. 'He knows I won't pass my GCSEs, so why's he making me do them?'

'He wants to give you a chance, I suppose.' Emma looked back at him from the doorway. 'Doing exams... Well, it's normal.'

'Yeah, but I'm not.' Benny grinned, and his sister laughed.

Emma said she needed to go home, and Benny promised to talk to their dad, although he had no idea where to begin.

'You've gotta help me, Jesus.' Benny was alone again. He considered waiting until the following morning, yet more of Pastor Tim's wise words niggled away at him. Something about not letting the sun go down when you were angry. Well, the sun had set before their row, but that didn't give him an excuse to go to bed without sorting things out. He would face his dad and apologise as soon as he got home, proving his maturity by accepting the punishment Ola inflicted.

22

The squeak of a loose floorboard told Janet her son was venturing downstairs. Emma had left half an hour ago, and Ola was watching the evening news, having returned home without explaining his whereabouts. He had taken the meal she'd prepared straight into the lounge on a tray. Benny's dinner sat on a worktop covered by tinfoil.

'Are you okay, my love?' Janet moved to Benny's side as soon as he appeared in the kitchen doorway, checking for signs of a seizure. 'Shall I warm your food?' She pointed at the covered plate.

'Can I have it later?' He advanced into the room, reaching for a glass and filling it from the tap. 'Emmie came upstairs to talk to me, so now I need to sort things out with Dad.'

'Is that a good idea?' Janet's shoulders tensed. 'Perhaps you should wait until tomorrow. Give him time to calm down.'

'I need to say sorry.' Benny placed his glass on the draining board, having merely sipped the water. 'And I've gotta say it to you too.'

'No, you don't.'

'Yeah, I do.'

As he returned to her side, Janet sensed an aura of peace surrounding him. The tension in her muscles eased.

'You're always looking after me. You stick up for me with Dad, even when stuff is my fault.' Benny held her gaze as he spoke.

'I love you.' A burning sensation rose in the back of Janet's throat.

'I love you too.' He kissed her cheek.

Janet ached to hold her son back, to prevent him from facing more of Ola's rage, but she needed to trust him. 'What did Emma say?' she asked.

When Emma announced her intention of talking to her brother, Janet had begged her to leave it for another day, but Emma wouldn't be put off. When Janet had questioned her afterwards in the hallway, her daughter simply said Benny was fine and she needed to go home to catch up on her studies.

'We sorted stuff out. She helps me understand when I'm being stupid.' A cheeky grin settled on Benny's face. 'Brothers and sisters argue all the time, Mum. It's normal. I bet you did it with yours.'

'I argued with Malcolm and David, yes.' Now Janet was smiling too. 'Never with Sylvie.'

'She was only young when she died. I bet you would've argued more when she got older.'

'Perhaps.' A frown replaced Janet's smile as Benny strode past her towards the door. 'Do you really want to risk your dad upsetting you again?'

'I upset him first.' Benny stopped in the doorway.

Janet was taken aback by his admission.

'I should've been straight with him and asked for another day off.'

'He wouldn't have let you.' Janet spoke softly.

Benny nodded. 'That's why I pretended until he left for work.' A cloud crossed his face. 'He won't want me working for him now. He'll say I'm lazy again.'

'He tells me you work hard on your evenings at the garage,' Janet encouraged.

'He's gonna think I only do stuff when I want to.' Benny looked unusually contemplative as his mouth opened and closed.

Janet waited, sensing he had more to say.

'Dad's gotta know I'll try, even when it's hard.' Benny tightened the buckle on the belt that was failing to hold up his baggy jeans. 'You can get away with stuff when you're Beth's age cos you're still learning. I reckon you let me get away with too much. You weren't so soft on Emmie.'

Protest rose in Janet's belly. 'You didn't understand.'

'Sometimes I pretended not to.' Benny looked her in the eye as he made his confession. 'I knew Dad wanted me to go to school today but you wouldn't make me.'

'You can't go anywhere when you're ill.' Janet still had the urge to defend him, even though he was admitting his faults with no trace of sulking. She was accustomed to drying his eyes when he felt everyone stood against him. Yet the boy standing before her now seemed calm and self-assured. Was this really her Benny?

'I could've gone today.' He even sounded more mature. 'Dad knew it, and I did too. He doesn't get cross when I'm really ill.'

Janet nodded. She had nothing more to say. Benny turned and headed for the lounge and his father, leaving her torn between pride and sadness. She was proud of the responsible young man her baby was becoming, and saddened over the fact that every step towards maturity meant he needed her less.

Benny stood in the living room doorway watching his dad, whose focus shifted from the TV to his newspaper and back again. If he was aware of Benny's presence, he wasn't showing it.

'Dad?' Benny drew closer, torn between wanting to act as though everything was normal and the urge to apologise. If he didn't say he was sorry, Dad would remain stony, and his barriers would go up. Although this had been normal during Benny's early years, it now felt cold and weird.

'What do you want, Benny?'

'To say sorry.' Benny watched his dad carefully. He wasn't great at reading people's moods. Nettie sometimes pointed at passersby, commenting on how that man was angry or that woman must be having a rubbish day. Benny saw none of those things, but Dad's anger had always been transparent. Once, when their relationship was still sour, Benny had asked Emma if

Dad ever stopped being angry. Emma had said, of course he did, but Benny thought that must be only for the daughter he loved. Definitely not the son he hated.

Facing him now, Benny reminded himself of the times Dad had said he loved him, even though he struggled to show affection. They could sort this out. They had to. They couldn't allow their relationship to go back to the struggle it once was.

'What are you apologising for?' His dad's tone was measured.

'I shouldn't have pretended I was going to school when I wasn't. And I shouldn't have told Mum I was ill.' Benny held his breath.

'Keep that up, and we won't believe you when you actually are. That would be dangerous, Benny.' His dad's stern expression didn't change.

'I'm sorry.' What else could he say?

'Are you only doing this because you want me to back down about grounding you?'

Benny's eyes widened. He genuinely hadn't considered that. He shook his head.

His dad must have believed him because he patted the sofa beside him. 'Sit down.'

Benny sat, perching nervously on the edge, ready to bolt if he needed to.

Ola switched off the television, then meticulously folded his newspaper before turning his attention back to Benny. 'Okay. I accept your apology.'

Was it going to be as simple as that? Benny was unsure.

'Is that it?' Ola asked.

'Maybe...' He faltered. 'I dunno, Dad. Is it?'

'You tell me. Is there anything else you need to say?'

'Lots of stuff,' Benny admitted. 'I just dunno how. It's sort of in my head, but it won't come out.'

'Why don't you try?' His dad leaned back against a cushion. 'You've surprised yourself before.'

Benny looked at him questioningly until he clarified.

'You didn't think you'd be able to work with me at the garage when I suggested it for your work experience. And you'd never travelled by yourself before you caught that bus to the hospital the day Beth was born. And what about Beth? Did you honestly think you'd be capable of caring for a baby?'

Benny shook his head, then followed his father's example, making himself more comfortable on the sofa.

'You've surprised us, son. Especially your mother. She was convinced you'd be dependent on her for the rest of your life. Only, I don't think that's true. Because it's not what you want, is it?'

'No.' Benny turned to face his father. 'You know what I want.' He scowled. 'But I reckon I've messed it up again.'

'By making one mistake?'

In response, Benny gave the slightest nod.

'You're a teenager.' Ola surprised him by putting an arm around his shoulders and drawing him closer. 'We all pushed the boundaries at your age. I'm proud of you for owning up and taking responsibility for what you did. That took courage, and it shows me you're growing up. Well done. The Benny I used to know would have sulked and blamed everyone else.'

'It was my fault.'

'That's why you're still grounded.' His dad gratified him with one of his rare grins. 'Apart from Monday and Friday evenings after school because I need you at work.'

'Okay.' Benny made to rise, then changed his mind. There was more he needed to say. With his dad's softened mood, he had the courage to say it. 'Me and Emmie had a long talk earlier.'

'Good.' Ola's eyes willed him to continue.

'She said stuff about when I was little. She…' Once again, Benny was struggling for words. 'She made me think about how I used to be.' He paused. 'I don't do it that much cos I hate remembering. Especially the bad stuff.' His voice dropped to a whisper. 'Lots of it was, wasn't it, Dad? I played up cos I wanted Mum to myself when she was doing stuff with Emmie.'

'Some people would argue that if I'd been a proper father, your mother and I could've shared the responsibility of caring for you.' Ola sighed.

'Like me and Nettie do with Beth?' Benny's courage was bolstered by his dad's willingness to listen. 'Nettie gets fed up sometimes when Beth's bugging her, so I bring her over here to give her a break. Or I just play with Beth to get her mind off stuff when she's sulking.'

'Those are the kinds of things I should have done.' Ola patted Benny's hand. 'I suppose I did, with Emma. I took her for walks, or we played board games. I didn't try with you, so of course you wanted your mother.'

'You did stuff with me sometimes.' Benny screwed up his face with the effort of dredging up examples. 'Did we go on holiday once by the sea?'

'We did, yes.'

'I think I remember being in the waves with you and Emmie. I went under, but you picked me up and stopped me getting scared. Didn't I ride on your shoulders at the fair too?'

'You remember that?' His dad's mouth fell open.

'I remember I had to go to the hospital. Then we came home.' Benny hung his head. 'I didn't understand why you and Emmie were cross about that until I was older.'

'What do you mean?' It was Ola's turn to look confused.

'Mum didn't tell me we were meant to stay all week. She just said we were going on holiday. I didn't know how long a holiday was cos we'd never had one. When I had seizures, we went to the hospital, then we came home. That's what I thought we had to do.'

'You need to have everything explained step by step.' Ola spoke slowly, like he was still thinking. Then his eyes seemed to light up. 'If we do that, you accept it, and you ask more questions if you don't understand.'

'I wish you'd explained, and we'd stayed there.' Benny smiled. 'I loved that holiday till I had the stupid seizure, and I would've liked it again when I was better. I wanted you to play with me more, but you never did.'

'I'm afraid we can't change the past.' His dad's words sounded like an apology. 'As much as I wish we could relive your early years, all we have is our future.'

'And I wish I'd let Mum do more with Emmie.' Benny sighed. 'I acted like a spoilt baby.'

'You don't anymore,' Ola confirmed. 'And you're applying what you've learned to the way you handle Beth.'

'It's good when we understand stuff, isn't it, Dad?' Benny's stomach rumbled loudly, reminding him of the meal his mother had saved. When his dad's eyebrows raised, Benny chuckled. 'Mum kept a dinner for me, so I'd better try to eat it.'

'Is everything okay?' Despite her efforts not to eavesdrop, Janet had overheard snippets of Benny's conversation with his father.

'Yeah.' Benny uncovered his meal and put it in the microwave. 'I'm still grounded, but Dad wants me to continue working on Mondays and Fridays.'

'What about youth group and your Saturday mornings with Pastor Tim?' Janet opened the cutlery drawer, took out a knife and fork, and placed them on the table.

'I guess I won't be able to do none of that till after Christmas,' Benny reasoned. 'I'll phone Tim and tell him why.'

'What will you say?' Janet asked.

'The truth.' Benny switched off the microwave, and Janet raised her eyebrows. 'I don't care about food being hot. I can't be bothered to wait for it.'

Janet cringed as Benny drenched his food in tomato sauce. She looked away when he pushed the vegetables to the back of his plate, knowing full well they were destined for the bin.

'Tim won't have a go at me if I tell him I said sorry.' Benny sat at the table, absentmindedly playing with his food. 'He'll probably say something good came out of it cos I learned how to sort stuff out.'

Janet picked up a cloth to wipe the worktop where her son had left a trail of gravy.

23

Janet lay in bed with a romance novel, her mind wandering over every line. Although she'd reread the same paragraph at least three times, the words might as well have been written in a foreign language. Too preoccupied to focus, she gave up and cast her book aside.

Closing her eyes against the glow from the bedside lamp, Janet sighed and turned over. It had been an emotionally draining evening. She hated conflict between those she loved, longing to smooth things over and keep everyone on an even keel. Thankfully, tonight's drama had resolved itself fairly quickly. Emma and Benny had sorted out their differences, and Benny had made his brave apology to his father, which Ola had accepted. So if all was well, why did Janet still have a sense of unease?

Was it because Emma's accusations weighed heavily on her heart, particularly since Benny had confirmed their truthfulness? Had Janet neglected her eldest in favour of her needy younger child? Didn't Emma know how much she loved her? Should she talk to her, or let it go?

Janet glanced at the clock on Ola's side of the bed. It was ten-30. Her husband would soon be beside her. Faint voices from the television in the room below made their way up the stairs, coupled with the sound of running water.

A while later, the bathroom door opened, and Janet heard the snap of the light cord.

'Are you off to bed, my love?' she called, hoping to entice Benny to her room for a hug and a goodnight kiss.

'Night, Mum.' He appeared in the doorway in his jeans and t-shirt. It amused Janet that her self-conscious teenager now refused to let anyone see him wearing pyjamas. Her days of caring for his needs and cuddling him to sleep were long gone. Benny now valued his privacy, and she was learning to respect that.

'Don't I get a kiss?' She held out her arms, smiling as he drew closer.

Benny leaned down, startling her with the strength of his hug. The familiar smells of shampoo and shower gel added to her melancholy. She missed taking care of him.

'Goodnight and sleep tight.' Janet reverted to a childhood tradition, wondering whether Benny would take it up where she left off.

'Watch the bedbugs don't bite.' He shuddered, and Janet laughed. 'Some things don't change.' She kissed his cheek. 'You were always scared of bugs.'

Benny headed onto the landing, meeting Ola at the top of the stairs. She heard them bid each other goodnight and was pleased by the warmth in their voices. Father and son had overcome yet another hurdle.

Ola strode into their bedroom purposefully, pulling the door closed behind him.

'I've been thinking, Jan.' His words tumbled out as he gazed at her intently. 'If you need answers about what happened to your sister, you deserve to find them.' He cleared his throat. 'So, I'll help you.'

Janet was taken aback by this unexpected announcement. 'What do you mean, and why are you saying this now?'

'It's been weighing on you more since last week.' Ola removed his wallet and a handful of loose change from his pocket, depositing them on the chest of drawers. 'You weren't yourself for a couple of days. I brushed it off and accused you of being dramatic.' He turned to face her, then spoke more softly. 'I shouldn't have done that.'

'You presumed once I'd talked about Sylvia, I'd be able to move on.' Janet's tone held no accusation.

'I suppose that's how I would handle things,' Ola said, sitting on the bed to remove his socks. 'To my way of thinking, you can't change the past. You've got to learn from it and make the best of your future. But you can't do that with something you don't understand.'

'Nettie brought it up again when we were at the hospital with Beth – how rare it is for a child to die from catching a cold.' Janet sat up, using her pillow to cushion her back from the slats in the wooden headboard.

'It is strange,' Ola agreed.

'Deep down, I knew there had to be more to it.' Janet sighed. 'I was afraid to ask because I wondered whether my family blamed me for being ill first. Perhaps that's why they became distant after we lost her.'

'Of course they're distant. We moved away.' Ola reached for her hand.

'No, it's more than that.' Janet leaned towards him. 'They'd changed long before I married you. My mother and I did everything together before Sylvia died. Afterwards, she shut me out.'

'You said she fell into a deep depression.'

'Yes.' Janet was comforted by his hand holding hers. 'She mostly stayed in bed for the first few weeks. When she finally got up, she did everything mechanically. She'd lost her joy.'

As Ola squeezed her hand, Janet was astounded by the depth of their conversation. These times were so rare. She expected him to pull away at any moment.

'You said your father changed his job.' Ola rose, gently releasing her hand.

Janet let him go, cherishing the warmth from his touch which remained on her skin.

'He found work in a factory,' she said. 'I didn't understand that either, because he loved working for the council.' Janet's eyes followed her husband as he reached for his pyjamas, which lay draped over a chair. 'Sylvie took after him, although she looked more like Mum. Our family mealtimes were loud and boisterous, with Dad and the boys teasing Sylvie, and Mum trying to keep them in order. Sylvie took all of that with her.'

'I'm sure you were very lonely.'

Janet was touched by his insight. 'I wouldn't have got through it without my love of reading,' she admitted. 'Even though I was always an avid reader, I became obsessive once I had our room to myself. I escaped up there all the time, only going downstairs when I had to.'

Ola inched towards the door, carrying his pyjamas. 'I remember how quiet you were when we first met.'

'Do you think that's what drew us to one another?' They had never discussed it but now seemed to be the right time. 'You were lonely too.'

Ola rested his hand on the door handle. 'In my case, it was more out of choice. I've never needed other people.'

'You enjoyed going to the pub with Peter Moss when we moved here,' Janet protested. 'You must have been looking for friendship.'

'I'd say Peter's friendship found me. And he's an undemanding sort. He doesn't ask too many questions. I've always hated a lot of questions.' Ola opened the door. 'You're different. You're more like Benny.'

Janet pondered her husband's words as she listened to him going through his usual routine in the bathroom. What did he mean? What were the similarities he saw between her and their son? And was he serious about helping her search for the truth behind Sylvia's death?

When he returned to their room dressed for bed, Janet was ready. 'What did you mean when you said I'm like Benny?'

Ola smiled wistfully, not looking annoyed about the extra question. 'He said something to me earlier. It really made me think.' He crossed to the window, pulling back the curtains to check on the garden below. 'We were talking about our holiday with the Mosses.'

'That was a disaster.' Janet frowned at his back.

'It didn't need to be.' Ola drew the curtains and turned back to face her. 'Benny told me he didn't realise we were staying in the caravan for the whole week. He presumed every time we took him to the hospital we had to bring him straight back home.'

'Of course we did. He needed to feel safe after a seizure.'

'He was enjoying our holiday. He would have been happy to stay if we'd explained things, but he presumed we had to come home because that was the only option.'

'He was crying and clinging to me!' Was Janet defending herself or Benny?

'He always did.' Ola climbed into bed beside her. 'He calmed down eventually if you stayed close.'

'Yes, I suppose he did.' Janet was ashamed of her outburst. Ola was trying to understand both her and Benny, so why risk antagonising him? 'I wonder why he hasn't mentioned this before.'

'You know how it is with Benny. He doesn't realise what he's thinking until someone draws it out of him. All he needed was a clear explanation. That's what made me realise how alike the two of you are. I bury things and move on; you and Benny need explanations.' Ola refocused his attention on Janet. 'So that's what needs to happen with Sylvia.'

'How?' Janet saw the sense in his words. Still, after all these years, was it too little too late?

Ola switched off the lamp and settled down beside her. 'I don't imagine your parents were able to fob your brothers off by saying she only had a cold, and they were at home while you were at your friend's house.'

'That's true.' Strangely, Janet had never considered her brothers' whereabouts on the weekend of Sylvia's death. 'I hardly ever contact Malcolm or David these days. I can't remember the last time I phoned either of them.'

'Does David still live near your parents?'

'Yes.' Janet repositioned her pillow and lay beside Ola. 'He's never moved, and Mum and Dad's retirement complex is still in the same village.'

'Then that's where you should go.' Her husband surprised her further by pulling her into his arms. 'You should talk to David. I'll take you this Saturday.'

Benny sat on the sofa, listening silently as his parents told Emma about their planned visit to Uncle David. They were probably telling him too, but long conversations usually went over his head. The evenings seemed never-ending since he was grounded. He missed Beth and Nettie.

'When will you go?' Emma asked from her seat next to him.

'On Saturday,' his dad said. 'I've advised your mother not to tell David we're coming.'

'What if he isn't there?' Emma asked.

'It's a chance we'll have to take.' Dad sounded resolute. 'If we give him time to prepare, he might wriggle out of telling the truth. If your mum surprises him by turning up out of the blue asking for answers, it might shock him into giving them.'

'I used to love spending time with Uncle David and his family.' Emma smiled. 'I'd like to see them again.'

'Come with us, then,' their mum urged. 'I could do with the moral support.'

'All right.' Clearly, Emma needed no persuading.

That wasn't the case for Benny. 'I don't remember Uncle David.' It was the first time he'd spoken since the start of their conversation.

'You wouldn't,' his mum said. 'You only saw him and your aunt Sarah a few times.'

Emma shuffled and turned to him. 'They've got two girls. Lucy's six years older than me and Hannah's closer to my age. I wish we'd kept in touch. I only saw them when I stayed with Grandma and Grandpa.'

'Can I come with you on Saturday?'

Three pairs of eyes widened in astonishment at Benny's words.

'Why would you want to come?' Emma asked with a nervous laugh. 'You hate long car journeys.'

His mum too was twiddling her fingers. 'You'll be sick, love. And you struggle with strangers. It'll be too much for you.'

'They're family,' Benny said.

That didn't seem to be good enough, for Emma patted his arm. 'It's best you stay here, Pestie. Mum won't need the extra stress of worrying about you working yourself up into a state and having a seizure.'

'I won't.' His hurt was probably spilling out too much, but he couldn't hide it. 'I mean, I'll try not to.'

He resisted as Emma tried to pull him into a hug. 'That's what you always say, Pestie. But it never works.'

Benny glanced at his dad, who leaned forward in his seat. 'If Benny wants to come, we should let him,' Ola said.

Benny couldn't believe Dad was on his side. He had expected the greatest resistance from him.

'But Ola!' His mum squeaked.

'No, Jan. The boy is right. If we're set on doing this, we need to do it as a family.' He addressed Benny. 'You'd need to cancel your study session with Pastor Tim because we'll be leaving early.'

'I already did that. You grounded me, remember?' Benny grinned.

'I wouldn't have stopped you meeting with Tim,' Ola said, drawing his brows together. 'He gives up valuable time to teach you, so the least you can do is show up.'

'I didn't think you'd want me to. I thought you'd be mad.'

'Thank you for the respect.' His dad rose, stopping to pat Benny's shoulder on his way to the door. 'We'll be leaving at eight o'clock sharp.'

'Would you like to join me for a cup of tea?' Janet asked, not wanting her daughter to leave.

Emma nodded, following her into the kitchen. 'Are you sure you want to do this, Mum?'

The time had come. Janet needed to clear the air.

'Your father is right.' She filled the kettle while Emma raided the biscuit tin. 'I deserve to know how Sylvia died.'

'What if it's as simple as they told you? What if her cold just got worse and turned into an infection?' Emma bit into a chocolate digestive. She held the packet, but Janet shook her head.

'If that's the truth, I'll have to accept it. There are still so many things that don't add up. If Sylvie died of natural causes, why did my parents change overnight?'

'I bet losing a child can do that to you.' Emma took one more biscuit before returning the packet to the tin. 'You would've gone to bits if we'd lost Benny. I remember how you were when the doctors couldn't control his seizures.'

'Even if the worst had happened, I would've still had you and your father.' Janet reached out, but Emma shrank back.

'We would never have been enough.' Emma turned and replaced the biscuit tin in its cupboard.

Her daughter's words cut like a knife. 'Of course you would. You were always enough.'

'Only until you had Benny.' Emma's eyes were steely. 'After that, it felt like I didn't exist. At least during the first few years. You got better when he started growing up, but in the early days, you only noticed me when I helped to calm him, or I let him sleep in my bed because Dad was fed up with him being in yours.'

'Emma, you're my daughter!' Janet fought the urge to cry as Emma shook her head.

'Everything changed after Benny. You stopped reading to me and telling me stories. You forgot how to play.'

'I was tired. I didn't always have the energy to play.' Though she knew Emma was right, Janet needed a distraction to prevent her emotions from spilling out. Crying never worked with Emma. As if on cue, the kettle switched off, allowing her to pour boiling water into the teapot.

'And when you did, you played with him.'

Janet blinked back tears and focused on getting the cups out. If Emma realised she was on the verge of crying, her daughter would accuse her of overreacting.

'I shouldn't have brought this up today.' Emma's tone softened and she moved closer, bringing a carton of milk. Janet ventured a look at her.

'There seems to be a lot happening this week,' Emma continued. 'First, I had the row with Benny, and now there's tension with you.'

When Emma's arms encircled her, Janet inhaled the musky scent of her daughter's favourite perfume and sank into her embrace.

'I love you, Mum.' Now it was Emma's turn to cry. 'And of course I know you love me. Even if I wasn't sure of it for a few years, I am now. All this talk about truth and honesty… Perhaps that's why I need to get these things off my chest. You couldn't help what happened with Benny, and Dad should've been more supportive.'

'You've always been an incredible big sister.' Janet stroked the chestnut hair that mirrored her own. 'I couldn't have coped without you. I'm sorry I neglected you, Em, and I'm sorry if you thought I loved Benny more.' She kissed her daughter's cheek. 'It's just… I was constantly afraid for his safety. If I wasn't vigilant, I was sure I'd lose him, like I lost Sylvia.'

'That makes sense, given what you've told us.'

Emma pulled away and Janet gazed into her eyes. 'Yes, although I couldn't voice it until now. The years of sadness and secrecy must have taken their toll.'

When Janet had finished the tea, Emma spoke again. 'I'm glad you're going to search for answers.'

'Only if Uncle David will give them to me.'

'He will.' Emma spoke with assurance. 'And if he tries not to, Dad and I will fight in your corner.'

'And Benny?' Janet still wasn't convinced about the wisdom of her son accompanying them.

'Benny will hold your hand.'

A smile of understanding passed between them, and Janet felt the stirring of a new bond with her daughter.

24

When Benny's phone rang late on Friday evening, he was baffled to see Tim's name on the caller display. Although they had exchanged texts on Wednesday when Benny admitted the mistake that had resulted in his grounding, he hadn't expected to hear from his pastor again.

'I just thought I'd check in with you since you couldn't come to youth group and I won't see you tomorrow,' Tim explained.

'Thanks…' Benny said. Hardly anyone phoned him except Damo or Nettie, and he wasn't sure what else to say.

'Are you still in your dad's bad books?' Tim sounded like he was smiling.

'He's been okay since I said sorry.' Benny turned the sound down on the TV. 'We're going to see Mum's family tomorrow. She wants to find out what really happened when her sister died.'

When Tim asked further questions about their trip, Benny answered without hesitation.

'It sounds as though tomorrow might be a difficult day,' Tim conceded. 'Especially for you. You'll have to face some of your fears.'

Benny nodded. 'Like meeting new people.'

'And the long car journey that will probably make you ill.'

'I've got tablets, but they don't always work.' Benny sighed. 'If I'm stressed, I throw up even if I take them.'

'I'll pray for you.' Tim paused before adding, 'I could do that now.'

'Yes, please.'

Benny switched off the TV, closed his eyes, and focused on Tim's words. He wished he could pray as confidently as his pastor. His simple prayers seemed childish by comparison. He fumbled over his thoughts, spinning from one idea to the next. He hadn't prayed out loud since the first day he prayed with Tim and Brian. Thankfully, Tim never pushed him. Benny wondered whether he might try it one day, in one of their Saturday morning study sessions.

Tim ended his prayer with an 'amen', adding, 'Let me know how it goes.'

'Dad said I can still go to church on Sunday, so I'll tell you then.'

Tim said goodnight, and Benny turned his attention to his Bible. He only managed one psalm, lingering over the words, 'Be still, and know that I am God.' Closing the book, Benny focused on the meaning of that simple phrase. Maybe knowing who God was meant trusting Him to help with the difficult things, the ones that stressed him out because he didn't understand. Despite the changes in his life, he still had so many fears and hangups. But God understood, and He wanted to help.

Returning the Bible to his bedside cabinet, Benny sent a goodnight text to Nettie, then kicked off his jeans, climbing under the covers in his T-shirt. His mum would never find out.

'Dad, I need you to stop.' Benny had managed over half the journey before nausea finally got the better of him. He was going to be sick, and there was no way he'd do it in the car, even though his mum was prepared with an empty ice cream container.

When the car pulled over, Benny jumped out, slamming the door in his haste to get away. He was glad they weren't on the motorway. He hated throwing up on the hard shoulder, with cars whizzing by. At least here it was quieter. Hopefully, no one would honk their horn or make fun of him by yelling out of the window.

Benny managed only a few steps before surrendering to the inevitable. He spluttered and choked, struggling to catch his breath. When it was over, he reached into his jeans pocket for a tissue and waited for the dizziness to subside.

'All right?'

Benny hadn't heard his dad following him out of the car. His father's comforting arm draped around his shoulders.

'Sorry, Dad.' As Benny leaned into Ola's strength, his father pressed a mint into his hand.

'To get rid of the nasty taste.'

As Benny made to retrace his steps, Ola held him back. 'There's no rush, son. A bit of fresh air might help with the sickness.'

Benny inhaled deeply while gazing into the sun-dappled sky. It was a crisp winter's day without a trace of rain. His mum had fretted about him not bringing a coat, but even though the temperature gauge on the dashboard had read two degrees, Benny wasn't cold.

'What are Mum's parents and Uncle David like?' He turned to face his father. 'I don't remember them. They only talked to Emmie and Mum.'

'I don't know them well either.' Ola sighed. 'I always got the impression they didn't approve of me.'

'Why?' Benny gaped.

His dad took several paces, then retraced his steps. 'I presumed they didn't think I was good enough for your mother, or perhaps they were angry because I took her away.'

'I don't reckon Nettie's mum and dad think I'm good enough for her neither.' Benny shrugged.

'Well, they'd better not hint at anything like that in front of me.'

Benny bristled with pride, realising his dad might actually stand up for him with the Thompsons.

'You've been a huge help to Nettie when most boys your age wouldn't want anything to do with a young girl with a baby.'

Benny didn't flinch. 'I love her, Dad.'

Ola patted his back. 'I know.'

Was this the first time his father had said it? If so, they'd reached another milestone.

'Let's get back to Emma and your mother.' Ola spoke over his shoulder, as he strode towards the car.

Janet's foreboding grew heavier as their vehicle ate up the miles towards her childhood home. Benny's travel sickness added to her tension until Janet herself considered asking Ola to stop. She'd never suffered from car sickness before, yet her stomach churned with every turn of the wheel.

Emma sat beside her in the back, while Benny rode in the front with his father. They had long since discovered a clear view of the road ahead made Benny ill less frequently. In the old days, he vomited two or three times in succession. Now it only happened once, if at all.

'Are you sure you don't need us to stop again?' Janet patted her son's shoulder as he shifted restlessly in his seat.

'There are loads of twisty corners.' Benny sounded weary.

Hadn't Janet warned Ola this was a bad idea? Why didn't he listen? The blame for her poor baby's suffering lay at his father's door. Ola still didn't understand Benny's limitations.

'Yes.' Ola swung the car around a tight horseshoe bend. 'These lanes are definitely narrow. I think that means we're almost there.'

Janet knew exactly where they were. 'Should be about another ten minutes.'

Ola offered Benny another mint while Emma distracted him with conversation.

'You'll like Uncle David and his family,' she encouraged.

'I doubt whether your cousins will be there.' Janet longed to relieve some of the pressure by reassuring Benny he wouldn't encounter too many new people. 'They're grown up now, like you, Em.'

As the country lanes gave way to tree-lined streets, Janet asked her husband to stop.

'What's the matter? Do you feel sick too?'

'No.' She pointed at a row of brick-built houses off to the left. 'I'd like to have one last look at where I grew up. Surely the people who live there won't mind us parking outside for a minute?'

Ola nodded and turned off the main road.

Janet pressed her nose to the window as they drove slowly past the house that had once belonged to Sylvia's friends, the Sloanes. The garden was no longer cluttered with the belongings of an overcrowded family. Screwing her eyes shut, she pictured her sister running down the street from the Sloanes' house to their own, her pigtails flying and her cotton summer dress billowing around her as she responded to Janet's familiar call.

'Sylvia Pew, where are you?'

Where was she? Why wasn't Sylvia waiting to welcome her home? Memories washed over Janet in waves. The tide came in, then went back out, and Janet swallowed down tears. She must reconnect with her family and ask for answers. No longer the 11-year-old child who needed protecting, Janet Wellander was a grown woman, capable of handling whatever the truth revealed.

'That was Grandma and Grandpa's, wasn't it?' Further down the road, Emma pointed at a house with a white car parked out front.

'Yes.' Janet gazed in horror at the gravel driveway that had replaced the lawn and her mother's flower beds. 'I lived there until I married your father.' She raised her eyes to an upstairs window framed by bright orange curtains, the likes of which Carol Pew had always detested. 'That was the room I shared with Sylvie.'

'I stayed in there with you.' Emma's eyes followed the direction of her mother's gaze. 'Why didn't you tell me about Sylvia, then?'

'Like I said before, after the funeral, we never even spoke her name.' The simple truth no longer satisfied Janet.

'I still reckon that was weird,' Emma mused. 'Even though it's sad, I bet other people who lose their kids don't act like they never existed.'

'That's why I need answers.' Janet rolled down the window, and an icy blast hit her in the face. 'I didn't know anyone else in our position, so I thought it was normal. Over time, it seemed easier to pretend it hadn't happened. But a wonderful little girl like Sylvia deserves to be remembered.'

'So, you're glad you told us?' Emma probed.

'Yes, even though it hurts.' Janet squeezed her daughter's hand and shut the window. 'It feels as though I'm grieving for her all over again.'

'You never really did the first time because you weren't allowed to.'

Emma's words struck a chord with Janet. She was right. The grief wasn't old, but fresh, as though Sylvia had only recently left them.

'Are you ready to go?' Ola's voice broke the silence.

Janet nodded, turning her attention to guiding him the short distance to David's house. Ola had never been there before, his brief encounters with her family always having taken place at her parents' home.

'What do you remember about Grandma and Grandpa?' Emma asked her brother.

'Nothing much,' Benny admitted.

'The few times we came, you were so ill and tired after the journey that you slept on my lap,' Janet said, making excuses for her son's lack of memories.

'Or you cried and threw up,' Emma added, chuckling.

'Well, I'm not gonna do that today.' Benny turned to offer them a genuine smile, whilst handing Emma the mints.

'You used to like those see-through fruit sweets, remember?' Emma popped a mint into her mouth as she spoke. 'You only liked the blackcurrant, and you moaned because there were hardly any of them in the bag.'

'And I didn't like him eating them on the move because I was afraid he'd choke.' Janet pointed Ola down another side road.

'All I can remember about family car trips is Dad yelling, Benny crying and throwing up, and you getting stressed.' Emma said.

Benny stretched round from the front. 'But it's been okay today, hasn't it, Emmie?'

Janet sensed Benny's longing for approval, and she prayed his sister wouldn't let him down.

'Yeah. It's nice, all of us being together.' Emma passed the mints back to her brother. 'You'll be fine, Pestie.' She swept her eyes over their surroundings. 'I wasn't sure when you wanted to come with us, but I'm glad you did.'

'Me too.'

Janet's heart melted as a loving smile passed between her two children.

'It looks like someone's home.' Ola gestured towards a silver Vauxhall as he pulled onto David's driveway.

'They're going to have a shock,' Emma said, reaching for Benny's hand as Janet opened the car door.

Soon they were gathered on the doorstep. Ola knocked. When the door swung open, Janet found herself face to face with her eldest brother.

25

'Jan?' David's face was a picture of confusion as he stood in the doorway, gaping.

'It's good to see you, David.' As soon as she spoke, Janet realised how stilted her words sounded. This encounter with her eldest brother threatened to evaporate the confidence she'd fought to find.

'You'd better come in.' David ushered them into his home.

Janet and Emma followed him through the hallway and into the lounge, with Benny and Ola following quietly. They formed an awkward huddle in the centre of the large room with a bay window at one end and a dining table at the other.

'Do sit down.' David gestured towards a sofa and two armchairs. 'Can I make you tea or coffee? Sarah's at Lucy's house babysitting the grandkids. She'll be back in a couple of hours.'

The rapid flow of her brother's words told Janet he was nervous. David had never been a talker, so his behaviour was completely out of character.

'I'm sorry we didn't tell you we were coming.' Ola's measured tones cut through the tension.

'We're family.' David held out a hand, and Ola shook it. 'Families don't have to make appointments.' This was a good sign. Might her family be warming to her husband?

'Perhaps they do when they haven't seen each other for years?' Emma caught her uncle's eye and smiled.

David's facial features softened as he locked gazes with Emma. 'You've grown, Em.'

Holding out her arms, Emma walked towards him.

Ever grateful for her easy-going daughter, Janet felt the tension in the room diffuse slightly as David returned the embrace warmly.

'Your cousins will be excited to know you're here.' David patted Emma's back before releasing her.

'I'm excited to see them again,' Emma said, sinking into one of the armchairs.

'Lucy works Saturday mornings. That's why your aunt's got her three kids. Perhaps later, I can take you over there.'

'She's a hairdresser, isn't she?' Janet asked. She was still standing in the centre of the room. Conscious of Benny hiding behind her back, protectiveness overtook her, and she reached for her son's hand. David hadn't yet acknowledged Benny. Would he?

'She is,' David replied, adding, 'So, what can I get you to drink?'

When she felt Benny's fingers slip into hers, Janet inched him towards the sofa where she sat and pulled her son down beside her.

Ola hesitated, then joined them, leaving Emma to answer David's question.

'Me, Mum and Benny like tea. Dad only drinks coffee,' Emma said.

'I won't be long.' David bustled from the room with barely a backward glance.

Benny felt like a sandwich, with his mum on his left and his dad on his right. Mum's hand shook as she maintained her vice-like grip, and Dad subtly patted his shoulder before folding his arms and straightening his back. The loving gesture might have been brief, but it sent Benny a message of courage in this strange new place.

Uncle David's hair and eyes were the same brown as Mum's, but he looked much older. Benny tried to remember his age. He was rubbish with numbers. His mum was 28 when she had him, so… Benny gave up. Their ages didn't matter.

'Are you all right, my love?' Mum turned worried eyes on Benny. 'Do you need anything?'

'He's fine, Jan,' Dad answered for him. 'If he needs anything, he'll ask.'

'Tell me if you feel sick.'

Benny allowed her to hug him, realising she needed the closeness more than he did.

'I always loved this house.' Emma swept a hand towards the bay window. 'Me and Hannah used to play over there with our dolls. When it rained, we pretended we were still outside.'

'It sounds as though you made some good memories here with your cousins,' Dad said.

'I missed them when I stopped visiting Grandma and Grandpa.' Emma rose, crossing to the sideboard to examine the framed photographs. 'I spent more time here than at their house.' She picked up a picture and pondered it. 'One time, Auntie Sarah let us pretend we were camping. We slept in front of the fire.' The memories brought a gentle smile to his sister's face. 'We ate our breakfast in the bay window, and we used this part for our imaginary tent.'

'You didn't tell me about that.' His mum sounded peeved, and Benny was a little bit too. He didn't have any nice memories with his cousins.

'You never asked.' Emma replaced the photograph and returned to her seat. 'You just banged on about how much Benny missed me, or how ill he'd been.'

'I missed you a lot.' Benny didn't mind talking now they were alone, and he could remember the feeling, if none of the details.

'I guess I missed you too.'

When Mum stroked his hand again, a longing for Nettie filled his chest. His girlfriend would know what to say to Uncle David. And she'd help him overcome his shyness. Nettie gave him confidence, prompting him when he fumbled over his words. She didn't fuss like his mum. He longed to slip outside to call her, but that would be rude.

Uncle David returned, carrying a tray filled with drinks and biscuits. Benny scowled at his dark brown brew in disgust, but a stern glance from his dad warned him not to complain. Still, he was surprised Mum didn't ask for more milk on his behalf. She usually did.

Janet's gratitude for the calming presence of her eldest child grew as Emma made small talk with David, leaving Janet to watch, listen and protect Benny. She hadn't realised the depth of Emma's bond with David and his family. Once again, her daughter's subtle dig cut her to the core. Despite their conversation on Thursday night, Emma was clearly still hurting. Janet needed to go further in her efforts to bridge the gulf between them.

Janet kept one eye on Benny while attempting to keep track of the conversation. David still hadn't spoken to her son yet, though perhaps it was just as well. She doubted whether Benny would be capable of answering.

Then Emma brought her up short by taking the conversation in an unexpected direction. When David asked about her love life, Emma laughed and tossed her head. 'I'm too busy for all that nonsense. I leave the soppy stuff to my brother. He's the one who's dating. And it's pretty serious, isn't it, Benny?' Emma's eyes twinkled with mischief.

Benny's response came slowly. Janet was about to jump in and rescue him by changing the subject, when Benny lifted his eyes from his lap and nodded.

'You started young.' David looked straight at Benny and the pressure of her son's hand increased as he fought not to spill his untouched tea.

'How old are you now?' David asked.

'He's 16.' Janet answered quickly.

'I was 16 when things started getting serious between me and your auntie.' David smiled, and to Janet's astonishment, Benny smiled back. 'What's your girlfriend's name?'

'Nettie.'

Janet knew how much that one word had cost him.

'She's three years older than him, and she's got a little girl,' Emma explained.

'You're a brave boy,' David said. Another smile passed between uncle and nephew, and Benny released Janet's hand. 'How old is her child?'

'Beth's two and a half,' Benny replied.

The conversation moved on, but instead of reaching for her hand again, Benny picked up a biscuit to dip in his tea.

Benny wondered when his mum would start talking about Sylvia. It felt as though they'd been at his uncle's house for ages, although a subtle glance at his watch told him they'd only been there for half an hour. He was bored and restless, but Uncle David seemed okay. Especially now they had something in common. Benny wondered if his uncle and aunt had experienced some of the same problems as him and Nettie. Had their parents also tried keeping them apart until they realised they couldn't? Maybe his grandparents hadn't minded because they were the same age, and Sarah didn't already have a baby.

Benny wished he could sneak outside to text Nettie an 'I love you.' He hadn't seen her since Tuesday, and he missed her like crazy. Was that how Uncle David had felt about Aunt Sarah? Was that how it had been for his parents too? Judging by the way they behaved, Benny didn't think so.

'You need to tell David why we're here.' Ola put an end to the stilted conversation by addressing Janet in a no-nonsense tone. 'I'm sure he must be wondering.'

Janet looked at her brother, who had fixed his gaze on her. 'I guess you would've phoned first if this was a casual visit,' he said.

Now the time had come, Janet longed for more delay tactics. If only Emma would step in to turn the conversation again...

'Is something wrong?' David's tone was pleasant, but his eyes gave away his impatience.

'I need to ask you something.' Janet broke eye contact to gaze down at her lap, unwilling to see his face when she mentioned Sylvia.

'Something serious, by the looks of it.'

A heavy silence followed as Janet focused on the chequered pattern of her blouse and played with her wedding ring. If she looked up, four sets of eyes would be upon her. 'It's about Sylvia.'

After a moment of silence, Janet heard David lower his cup onto the coffee table and shuffle towards the edge of his seat.

'It's been so long since I've heard her name.' He spoke in barely more than a whisper.

'Yes, too long.' When Janet forced herself to look at him, she noticed the unmistakable sheen of tears in his eyes.

'But we don't forget, do we, Jan?' Her brother cleared his throat.

'She was a huge part of our lives, even though we only had her for six years.'

'No one could forget about Sylvie.' He picked up his cup again, taking a long drink of coffee.

'I don't think we should. She'd want us to remember her and to talk about the things we did together.'

Janet's brave words earned a nod from her brother, and in that moment, she knew it would be okay. David would provide her with answers. He wasn't angry, just sad. For the first time, they were united in a grief that had silently gnawed at their family for over 30 years.

'In the beginning, I was sure you'd push for an explanation.' David gripped his mug more tightly. 'Yet you never did.'

'That wasn't my way.'

Benny's hand slid back into Janet's.

'When you came to the Grays' to tell me I couldn't come home, you made it pretty clear you didn't want me asking questions.'

'I thought you would afterwards. When you didn't, Malcolm and I wondered whether someone had told you.'

'Like whom?' Janet asked.

'Loads of people in the village found out. It was impossible to keep it hidden.' David drained his coffee, replacing the mug on the table beside his chair. 'You know how the rumour mill works.'

'No one said a word.' Janet realised she was stroking Benny's hand. 'Mum and Dad were completely broken. I couldn't ask them.'

'We all fell to bits.' David sighed. 'Malcolm and I were boys, so we didn't show it.'

'Did the two of you ever talk about her?'

'All the time when we were by ourselves.' David glanced towards the window. 'Never in front of our parents.' His gaze slid back. 'Or you.'

'I wish you'd let me in on those conversations.' Janet didn't want to antagonise him, simply to express her disappointment over being left out.

'We were protecting you.' Despite her intentions, David's tone was defensive.

'From what?' Janet's eyes pleaded for answers. 'Please, David, tell me.'

'Why now, after all these years?' His voice cracked.

'Because I'm fed up with pretending my sister didn't exist.' Janet paused. 'I don't know what made me do it, but a couple of weeks ago, I blurted everything out to my family. I realised how much I'd kept buried.'

'Mum and Dad never got over it.' David rose to walk the length of the room, stopping near the window.

'They might have if we'd talked about her.'

'They couldn't.' David paced back and forth, reminding Janet of Benny.

'Why?' Janet persisted.

'Because technically, it was Dad who killed her.'

26

'What do you mean?' Janet's chest tightened violently as she gaped at her brother. 'Dad adored Sylvia! We all did. He wouldn't have harmed a hair on her head, and he would've dealt with anyone else who dared to try.'

'People make mistakes, Jan.' David returned to his seat. 'Accidents happen.'

'You said our parents took her to the hospital because her cold got worse!' The volume and pitch of Janet's voice rose with her agitation.

'No, I didn't.' David sighed. 'You presumed, and I didn't argue. It was easier to let you believe that.'

'So you lied?' Janet's heart threatened to pound out of her chest, thundering in her ears until she wondered whether the others heard it too.

'No.' David gazed at the ceiling before refocusing on his sister. 'She was in hospital. They did their best, but they couldn't save her.'

'Was it some kind of accident?' Ola asked.

The muscles in David's throat constricted as he nodded. 'Dad hit her, coming home from work in his van.'

'He hit her?' Janet shuddered. The truth was worse than she'd feared. Did she really want to hear the ugly details? She reminded herself of the purpose behind this visit. 30 years of lies and misunderstandings were about to be unravelled, and although it would undoubtedly hurt, it was a necessary step on the road to healing.

'She was playing outside with the kids in the street, like she always did after school.'

Janet immediately jumped in to correct his mistake. 'No. Sylvie didn't go to school that Friday.' Did she think this would change the outcome of his story? Janet recognised her foolishness, even as she talked on. 'Mum kept her home because she'd caught my cold.'

'I didn't know that.' David sat back, pale and exhausted. 'I left for work before the rest of you got up, remember? And I went straight to Sarah's house afterwards. Will Sloane came pounding on Sarah's door, saying Dad had hit Sylvie and Malcolm was already on his way to the phone box to call an ambulance.'

'Did Will tell you how it happened?' Emma asked.

'I pieced it together once I'd calmed him down. He witnessed the whole thing, poor kid. He was shaking like a leaf. He kept yelling about how he'd tried to warn Dad, but he didn't see until it was too late.' David paused, then continued. 'You remember that cat Dad gave Sylvia for Christmas, don't you, Jan?'

Janet didn't trust herself to answer.

'Will said the cat ran out from under the hedge just as the van was reversing up the drive. Sylvie must've been afraid Dad would hit him.'

'So she wanted to save Mittens.' Janet could no longer stay silent. 'That was typical of Sylvie.'

'Dad didn't have a clue she was behind him. He just kept reversing, and…' David closed his eyes. 'Surely you don't need me to explain what happened next.'

'He ran over her,' Ola breathed.

Janet blinked, startled into remembering others were present. She'd been caught between David and the spectre of Sylvia's terrible death.

'Will said he and the other kids waved their arms and screamed for Sylvie to get out of the way, but it was already too late.' David took a tissue out of his pocket and pressed it against his streaming eyes. 'Dad probably didn't have enough time to see them, or if he did, he might've thought they were having him on. You remember what they were like, don't you, Jan?'

Janet sniffed. 'Mum called them wild and unruly. Mrs Sloane couldn't control them, and she kept having more.'

'The council found them two houses knocked into one in the end.' David gave a mirthless laugh.

'If Will and the others saw the accident, why didn't any of them tell me?' That part still made no sense.

'Malcolm and I threatened them.' The corners of David's mouth turned up in a wry smile. 'We didn't want you finding out how Sylvie died from the neighbourhood ruffians.'

'You presumed your parents would explain things properly.' Ola gave a nod of understanding.

'Yes, after they'd calmed down. Only they never did.'

Janet inhaled sharply as if she'd forgotten how to breathe. She'd believed a lie for 30 years. Everyone knew the truth apart from her. How had she missed it?

Emma crossed over and perched nearby on the arm of the sofa. 'Can you tell us more about what happened after the accident?'

'Malcolm and I didn't realise how bad Sylvia's injuries were until we got to the hospital. We were sure she'd wake up with nothing worse than a broken arm or leg.' David blew his nose. 'We didn't consider internal problems. Our parents travelled in the ambulance, and we followed with Mr Harris in his car.' He tossed his used tissue into a wastepaper basket. 'We sat in the waiting room for ages while they worked on Sylvie. Mum kept crying, and Dad stared into space with a dazed look on his face.'

Janet dropped her head into her hands as she felt the weight of her parents' torture. She knew all too well what it felt like, waiting in the hospital as the doctors worked on your child. Sensing her need, Benny stroked her arm.

'When did she actually die?' Janet needed to ask. 'Did Mum and Dad see her again?'

'A doctor came to talk to them a few hours after we got there. He took them into another room.' David folded his arms. 'When we heard Mum screaming, we knew it was bad. Dad was holding her up when they brought her back out. She kept saying she wanted her baby. She chanted it over and over, like a mantra. We couldn't get Dad to talk, but the doctor said everything we needed to know.'

Now David crossed the room to kneel in front of her, enfolding her shaking body into his arms. 'I'm sorry you found out this way, Jan. We shouldn't have kept it from you.'

'You still haven't said when she died,' Janet rested her head on his shoulder. She'd never been this close to her eldest brother.

'During the early hours of the following morning,' David replied. He tightened his hold as Emma pressed a tissue into her hand. 'They couldn't stop the internal bleeding, and some of her vital organs were crushed.'

Janet gasped, no longer conscious of anything except the image of her sister's broken body.

'That's horrible.' Emma exhaled deeply, pulling Janet back to the present. David slowly released her, then he rose on wobbly legs.

'Everything was a blur after the doctor spoke to us,' he continued. 'Mr Harris took us home, and Mum and Dad stayed with Sylvie till the end. We didn't hear them come back. When we woke up the following morning, one look at their faces told us everything. The police came in and out of the house all day. Somewhere in the middle of it, I remembered you were still at the Grays, Jan. I decided it would be better for you to stay there.'

'Did you tell the Grays the truth about Sylvia?' The confusing puzzle pieces of Janet's nightmarish past formed into a horrifying picture.

'I said she was ill.' David slumped into his armchair. 'If they sensed there was more to it, they didn't question me. They just said they were happy for you to stay.'

'I wish you'd brought me home.' Janet sobbed into her tissue.

'I didn't want you coming home to all that.' David rested his hands on his knees, a defeated expression settling on his face.

'What happened with your father?' Ola asked. 'I guess the police performed some sort of inquiry?'

'They had to, but there were enough witnesses to confirm the accident. Everyone could see Dad was in a state, so although he was formally charged, there was no talk of sending him to prison once the evidence was assessed. By the time Jan came home on Monday, things had quietened down at the house, and it was easier for us to hide what was going on behind the scenes.'

'I wondered why Dad never drove again.' Janet spoke wistfully. 'Now I understand.'

'He blamed himself,' David confirmed. 'He's never stopped.'

'It was an unfortunate accident.' Ola picked up his mug of cold coffee. 'No one should talk about blame.'

Janet still had so many questions. However, the walls were rapidly closing in on her as she struggled for every breath. Was she having a panic attack? She needed to be outside, inhaling clean, fresh air.

'I'm sorry…' She eased herself up off the sofa. 'I need to go outside.'

'You can't go by yourself.' Ola followed, putting a steadying hand on her back and ushering her into the hallway. Opening the front door, he allowed Janet to step outside ahead of him, then stood behind her with his arms around her shaking shoulders.

Janet took several deep breaths. In…out…in…out. Concentrating on her breathing steadied her racing heart. She leaned gratefully against her husband.

'I'm here for you, Jan.' Ola's arms caught her as spots danced in front of her eyes. They stood in silence as he gently massaged her shoulders.

'I'm sorry.' Janet was unaccustomed to so much tenderness. 'You're probably thinking I'm overreacting.'

Ola ran his hand lightly up and down her back. 'You've had a terrible shock.'

'I expected something bad. Perhaps I always sensed it deep down. Maybe that's part of the reason I hid away after Sylvia died.'

'I still can't get over no one telling you.' Ola shook his head. 'Accidents like that are rare. It must have been the talk of the village.'

'I do remember sympathetic stares from our neighbours.' Janet turned to press her face into his chest. 'There was a lot of shaking of heads and whispering around corners. I presumed they just felt sorry for us, and they didn't know what to say.'

'That's probably true.'

'I love you, Ola.' Janet raised her head to kiss his cheek. 'I couldn't have faced any of this without you and our children. Thank you for being by my side.'

'I'm your husband.' Ola pressed his lips against hers. 'And I love you too.'

Something at her core fluttered into life. In their 23 years of marriage, Ola had rarely spoken of love. Sometimes she doubted his feelings, especially during the difficult early years with Benny. The very survival of their marriage was a miracle. Her husband's words played on repeat in her head. She would never forget them. Ola's tender declaration acted as a rare and precious balm to soothe the pain of Sylvia's accident.

'Shall we go back inside?' he asked. 'Benny will be fretting.'

His words took her by surprise. Usually, she'd be the one to mention Benny. 'Actually, I'd like to go for a walk.' Janet squeezed his hand. 'Will you stay with him? Emma will be fine because she's used to David, but Sarah will be back soon, and a second stranger might be too much.' She hoped her eyes conveyed the love in her heart. 'He'll be fine with his dad.'

'I suppose I should be honoured you trust me to take care of him, considering our history.'

'The two of you are close now.' Janet rejoiced over that, even though Benny relied on her less.

'Benny will be fine.' Ola turned back towards David's front door. He opened it and moments later, returned with her coat. 'Where are you going?'

Janet was tempted to tell him she had no particular destination in mind. She simply needed time to walk and process the shocking information her brother had shared. However, Ola's question forced her to acknowledge the truth. There was only one place she needed to go, so she might as well admit it. 'To talk to my parents.'

Ola showed no surprise at her answer. 'I wondered if you might ask me to take you.'

'I need to do this by myself. The walk will help me sort myself out before I get there.'

'Fair enough.' Ola stepped into the hallway. 'Take all the time you need. The children and I will wait for you here.'

Janet watched her husband close the door and disappear into the house. She considered following him to share her intentions with David, then changed her mind. She didn't want to give her brother an opening to talk her out of it. Even though she'd received her answers, the healing journey wouldn't be complete until she'd spoken to her parents. There were still gaps only they could fill.

Turning her back on David's home, Janet ambled along the unfamiliar path towards the retirement complex where Bob and Carol now lived. It was strange to think of them being anywhere other than the home she'd grown up in, but she understood the reasons for their move. The three-bedroom house was far too big for an ageing couple.

As she walked, Janet replayed David's story, picturing each painful moment scene by scene. Sylvia's cold must have improved as the afternoon wore on. She'd probably worn their mother down with nagging until Carol gave her permission to go outside to play.

Sylvia and her friends loved hopscotch or running races up and down the street. They swung on gates and played with skipping ropes. Janet wondered what her sister was doing when their father's van turned into the street. His homecoming had always been a source of excitement. Sylvia must have been distracted when Mittens emerged from the hedge. Did the cat dart out, or did he move slowly? Either way, the prospect of her beloved pet being injured would have been too much for Sylvia.

In her mind's eye, Janet pictured her sister running to save the cat, seeing danger for Mittens but not for herself. When did she realise her father would hit her? Was it just before the van connected with her little body, or not until the moment of impact? What had she been thinking when he drove over her, if anything? What were her last words?

'Oh, Sylvie!' Janet groaned out loud, giving no heed to the passersby. 'Why weren't you more careful? We warned you about traffic. I taught you to stop, look, and listen before crossing the road. What made you think you could save Mittens without being injured yourself? Didn't you realise what it would do to us? Losing you destroyed our family. On the day you died, the sun went out.'

Janet shivered, wishing she'd remembered her coat. She gazed up, aware of the light the clouds concealed. Moments earlier, the sun's rays had taken the edge off the winter chill. Now they were completely hidden, and there was nothing to combat the wind's icy blast. It was like her own experience. Sylvia's death had drawn a huge cloud over the sun. Even when she'd met Ola, the cloud had remained, dappling her sky, allowing just a few rays of sunlight through.

She recalled the first day she'd seen him, serving behind the counter at the local petrol station. Tall and Nordic, Ola oozed the self-assurance Janet lacked. Yet underneath was a man just as lonely as she was. Something had drawn them together despite their differences. Was it desperation on her part, because Ola had offered her an escape from her miserable home life?

Perhaps Janet hadn't truly loved him then, but she did now. She belonged with Ola, Emma, and Benny. They were her life and had cleared enough of the cloud to keep the ice of Sylvia's departure at bay. Until this month – this revelation that had concealed her happiness once more. During the past two weeks, her past had collided with her present, and now it was time to face the two people who held the answers. Only after talking to them could this cloud move on forever, and the sun shine fully again.

27

Benny watched his parents' retreating backs with a growing sense of unease as he fought to unravel his uncle's complicated story. Surely his grandfather couldn't have killed Sylvia? If you killed someone, you went to prison, and his mum had never said her father had been in prison. Although Benny had only met his grandpa a few times, he'd never seemed like the type to hurt anyone. He dredged up vague and distant memories from his earliest childhood. No, Grandpa Bob definitely hadn't acted like a murderer. Uncle David must be wrong.

Benny wanted to follow his parents, but Emma must have noticed his eyes straying towards the door because she came and sat next to him, placing a restraining hand on his arm. 'Leave them alone to talk. Mum had a terrible shock.'

Although he understood his mother's need for fresh air, Benny wished she'd taken him with her.

'I hated upsetting your mum.' Uncle David addressed them with a weary sigh.

'She kind of forced you into it by turning up here.' Emma extended a reassuring smile. 'It was better for you to do it than Grandma or Grandpa.'

He nodded and made an offer of more tea.

'Thanks,' Emma said, adding, 'Benny likes his milky.'

Benny was grateful for his sister's willingness to speak on his behalf. His first drink remained untouched.

'You should've said.' Uncle David took his cup, and Benny looked away.

'He gets weird around strangers.'

Emma followed their uncle into the kitchen, leaving Benny convinced they were talking about him. Would Emma tell Uncle David how thick he was, or how he struggled at school? Benny scowled at the ceiling, mulling over the tragic death of the aunt who'd been killed by her own dad.

Sylvia was a child, not much older than Beth, and she hadn't been given the chance to grow up. That seemed cruel. Yet Benny knew God wasn't cruel. Why had He taken Mum's sister? They had been close. He knew by the way Janet talked about her. She'd loved Sylvia the way she loved him. Protective and patient, his mum had always taken his side, even when he didn't deserve it. That's why Emma had felt neglected.

When Emma and David returned, his uncle handed him a second cup of tea and a packet of chocolate digestives.

'Your sister said those are your favourites.' Rather than returning to his chair, Uncle David joined him on the sofa.

Benny shuffled nervously. His hand shook, and he was afraid he'd spill his tea. If he did that, Emma would be cross. She was always accusing him of clumsiness.

'It's nice to have this chance to meet you properly, Benny.' His uncle sounded sincere. 'Aunt Sarah and I often wished you'd visited us with your sister.'

Benny liked being treated as an equal. Whatever Emma had said in the kitchen, Uncle David was talking to him instead of going through her. Could Benny dare to look him in the eye? That was what men did. He'd been taking notice of his father and Peter. They always looked straight at one another when they spoke. Benny had learned to do it with Dad, but he still couldn't hold eye contact longer than a few seconds. It made him restless, giving him the urge to fidget until he looked away out of embarrassment.

'It's nice to see you too.' His words were weak and shaky, and he hoped he'd said the right thing.

'I imagine our conversation was a lot for you to take in.'

Benny was right - Emma had told their uncle about his struggles. Did that make things better, or worse? At least now he wouldn't have to pretend.

'Is there anything else you'd like to ask me?' Uncle David briefly patted his shoulder, and Benny forced himself not to shrink away from his touch.

What had he asked? Benny fought to remember. When he did, only one question came to mind. He blurted it out before he had time to consider how stupid it sounded. 'What happened to Sylvia's cat?'

The back of his neck warmed, and his hands were clammy. Benny put his tea down, sure he would spill it. He should've pretended he hadn't heard the question, or he didn't understand. He'd often done that when strangers tried to back him into a corner. His dad and Emmie called him ignorant, but his mum made excuses, covering over his shyness. Only she wasn't here now. It was just him, Emma, and Uncle David, and he'd given his uncle ample proof of his stupidity.

'Malcolm gave Mittens to his best friend's little sister.' Uncle David wasn't irritated or surprised. 'Keeping him would've been a painful reminder to our parents. Sylvie loved that cat more than anything, so we owed it to her to find him a good home. Your grandparents never asked after him, and strangely enough, neither did your mother.'

The door opened midway through the reply, and Benny breathed a sigh of relief as his dad walked in.

'How's Jan?' Uncle David said.

'She's visiting your parents.' Dad sat in the armchair, leaving Benny with Uncle David. 'I offered to go with her, but she said it's something she needs to do by herself.'

'I hope Mum and Dad will drop their guards and speak to her properly,' his uncle sighed.

'Have they ever done that with you?' Dad asked.

Uncle David shook his head. 'They've distanced themselves from all of us, not just from Jan. Obviously, I see them more because I live closer. Sarah and I made sure they saw plenty of the girls when they were little, but they never showed an interest. They locked up their emotions and threw away the key.'

Dad was frowning. 'We'll just have to hope Jan can help them find it.'

The conversation turned to lighter subjects. Uncle David asked about the work at the garage, and this time, it was his dad who drew Benny into the discussion.

'So you want to be a mechanic like your father?' When his uncle turned to him again, Benny nodded.

'He'll be a good one if he sets his mind to it and doesn't keep getting distracted by his girlfriend.' When Dad winked, Benny laughed nervously.

'I bet he's dying to phone her.' Emma grinned. 'They can't go more than a couple of hours without getting soppy.'

'That's true. You can go out to the car if you want to use your phone.' He tossed his keys, and in his surprise, Benny barely caught them.

'Thanks.' Although Uncle David didn't seem too bad, he was glad for a break and a chance to talk to Nettie.

'That's such a sad story.'

Benny sat in the car, revelling in the sound of his girlfriend's voice. The prospect of another two weeks without seeing her felt like an eternity. He wished his dad would back down, but he never did once he'd made up his mind. Well, that wasn't quite true. Dad had changed his attitude after their talk, so maybe there was hope.

'Mum's gone to see her parents.' He turned the key in the ignition so the heating came on.

'By herself?' Nettie sounded surprised.

'Dad said she wanted to.' Benny paused, and Nettie waited patiently while he formed his next sentence. 'It's really scary, Nettie. It made me worry about Beth.'

'What did?'

Benny realised his rapid change of topic had confused her. Although Nettie was brilliant at following his tangled threads, she had her limits.

'What happened to Sylvia....' Even talking about it made him want to curl up and cry over a blonde-haired, blue-eyed little girl he'd never known and the red-haired toddler with sparkling green eyes he loved and missed. 'What if something like that happens to Beth? What if we take her out one day, and she gets hurt when we're not looking?'

'We're always watching her,' Nettie said. 'We've got to because she's a typical two-year-old who doesn't understand danger.'

'Sometimes we're looking at each other.' Benny hung his head. 'Like when we're kissing and stuff. What if it happened then? I don't reckon I'd be able to forgive myself if Beth got hurt when I'm kissing you.' He spoke the last sentence in barely more than a whisper, and there was a catch in his voice as he continued. 'I know I'm not her dad, but I love her like I am. So if I let her get hurt, I reckon I'd feel as bad as my grandpa does about Sylvia.'

'Oh, Benny…' Nettie sniffed, then exhaled. 'Me and Beth are so lucky to have you. I love you so much.'

Benny wished he could hold her, but even if he hadn't been grounded, she was miles away.

'All any parent can do is their best,' Nettie reasoned. 'Just because we love our kids, it doesn't mean we should wrap them up in cotton wool like your mum did with you. If we did that, it wouldn't be fair to us or Beth. So we'll make sure she stays close, and when she's older, we'll teach her how to keep herself safe.'

'Sylvia was six, and she didn't stay safe.'

'It was a freak accident,' Nettie said. 'Those sorts of things are pretty rare.' Her tone changed, and Benny could tell she was smiling. 'And if you think I'll stop kissing you because it means I have to take my eyes off Beth, Benny Wellander, you can forget it. I'll never do that, and if you refuse to kiss me, then I'll… I'll…'

'You'll what, Nettie?' He was teasing her back and loving it.

'I'll think of something,' she warned.

'It's okay. I don't reckon I can stop kissing you, either.' He laughed. 'I'll just keep hold of Beth's hand if we're outside.'

'There has to be a way to get your father to change his mind about your stupid punishment,' Nettie groaned. 'Talking to you like this isn't enough.'

'I know.'

Benny closed his eyes as their easy conversation flowed. They never ran out of things to say. When Nettie put Beth on the line, the toddler chattered away nineteen to the dozen, begging Benny to come and play with her.

'I can't, Bethy. I'm grounded.' She wouldn't understand, but he enjoyed hearing her piping little voice.

'Benny come?' She blew kisses into the phone.

'Soon, okay?' He sent kisses back. 'I've gotta go. Love you, Bethy.'

He said goodbye to Nettie, then climbed out of the car, putting the keys in his jeans pocket. He should return to his uncle's house. However, like his mother, Benny longed to linger in the fresh air. He would go for a short walk. If he went too far, he'd get lost. Although he had no sense of direction, he'd be okay if he stuck to the main roads. If he messed up, he'd phone Emma, and she'd come find him.

Benny prayed silently for his mum as he walked, asking Jesus to help her accept the truth about Sylvia's death.

'Don't let her be angry with her dad. Nettie's right. Stuff happens, even when you're careful. Little kids have accidents. It's sad Grandpa blamed himself cos it wasn't his fault. And it stopped him from being a proper dad to Mum and her brothers. I guess it was like me and my dad.' Benny stopped to admire a garden display of Father Christmas on his sleigh, wishing he could show it to Beth. 'It's better now I'm working at the garage, so thanks for sorting stuff out, Jesus.'

He waited for a lorry to pass before crossing the road, waving at a little boy walking with his mother in the opposite direction. The child waved back, hollering a delighted greeting, and Benny responded. His shyness was never an issue with children.

'My mummy's taking me to see Father Christmas!' The boy could barely contain his delight as he swung his mother's hand, dancing along at her side.

'Tell him you've been extra good, so you need lots of presents.'

The mother laughed as she urged her charge forward. 'Come on, Harry, or we'll be late.'

It was time for Benny to turn back, or he really would get lost. He retraced his steps more slowly. There was no rush. His aunt might be home, meaning there'd be another stranger for him to meet. If she was like Uncle David, he supposed it would be okay. Perhaps having a bigger family wasn't so bad after all.

The truth about Sylvia was out. Would Mum get closer to her family now? Would they see more of Uncle David and his grandparents? And did he want more people in his life? Nettie was close to her grandparents. She took Beth to visit them every few months, coming back full of stories. Would Benny ever be able to introduce his extended family to Nettie and Beth? Would they care? Uncle David might because he'd seemed interested in hearing about Nettie.

During his growing-up years, Benny's life revolved around Mum and Emmie, with his dad acting the distant stranger. Even though they lived under the same roof, Dad only noticed him when he made him angry.

Now Benny's world was expanding to include his father, Nettie, Beth, and friends like Pastor Tim, Brian and Damo. He even had an uncle who didn't mind answering his stupid question about Sylvia's cat. Benny was learning to give and receive, to be loved and give love in return. He smiled whilst offering a silent prayer of thanks to the One who had made it all possible.

28

By the time Janet reached the retirement complex, she was more than ready to break down her parents' barrier of silence over the events surrounding Sylvia's death. Although David's devastating revelation was shocking, the basic facts hadn't changed. Sylvia had been gone for over 30 years. Nothing they did or said would bring her back. She wouldn't even want to come back, because she was in a better place. Meanwhile, Janet and her family needed to grieve, heal their strained relationships and move on.

A clear understanding of the truth brought Janet a new measure of freedom, absolving her of blame. It worked its way up through the core of her being, replacing anxiety with a sense of completion and peace. Janet longed to share this peace with her parents to begin their healing journey. Her arrival after a ten-year absence punctuated by obligatory phone calls would be unexpected, and she didn't know how they would react.

What were her hopes? It would be unrealistic to expect them to welcome her with open arms. Not once during their stilted conversations did her mother hint at a desire to see her. They skirted around safe subjects such as the births, deaths, and marriages of mutual acquaintances.

What would Janet have done if Mum pressed her to visit? She always had her answers prepared, just in case. Travelling made Benny ill, and she couldn't leave him to suffer a seizure without her. He would cry and pine for her. Although those were her excuses, Janet acknowledged them as a smokescreen to cover a deeper issue. Did her avoidance of her parents actually stem from anger and disappointment over the way they had treated her and her children?

She thought over their few visits after Benny's birth, the way Bob and Carol accused her of indulging him and enabling his bad behaviour. They hadn't wanted to allow for her son's limitations or to offer support. Couldn't they tell she lived on a knife-edge of fear and exhaustion? Yet they criticised, looked down their noses at Benny, and only tolerated Emma, waiting impatiently for them all to leave.

Now she needed to look past those things, to forgive them and move on.

The retirement community was housed in a tired-looking two-storey building behind the park. Although relatively new, the drab, featureless place appeared to be dark, foreboding and badly in need of a lick of paint. Janet hoped the interior would prove more cheerful than the exterior.

She stood in front of a locked door, studying an electronic panel, and pressed the number that would sound a buzzer in Bob and Carol's flat. A loud crackling made her jump, followed by a familiar voice.

'Hello?' Her mother sounded older. Or was it the distortion from the intercom?

'It's Jan, Mum. Can I come in?'

The crackling stilled, a beep sounded, followed by a click, and Janet pushed open the door. Finding herself in a dimly lit hallway painted an insipid shade of green, she felt momentarily disorientated until a stooped figure shuffled down a corridor towards her, familiar, yet altered by time.

'What are you doing here? Is something wrong? You didn't tell us you were coming.' Carol's tone carried a note of accusation.

'I'm sorry. No, there's nothing wrong.' Janet held out a hand which her mother failed to take.

It wasn't only Mum's voice that had aged. Her blonde hair had turned snowy white, her skin was wrinkled, she was painfully thin, and she walked with a limp. Janet experienced a stab of guilt. Despite their icy detachment, she shouldn't have avoided her parents for this long. She'd used Benny's illness as a convenient excuse.

'This is quite the surprise,' Carol said, running critical eyes over her. 'You're looking well.'

Unable to return the compliment, Janet offered a lame excuse for her visit. 'I thought I should come and see your new place.' It wasn't a lie, simply the safest option at this early stage in their reunion.

'You needn't have bothered. There isn't much to see.' Carol turned on her heel, heading back the way she came.

Janet ignored the pull to return to her family, even though her mother's cold dismissal suggested her departure would be welcome. Instead, she reminded herself of why she'd come, as she followed her mother down the narrow hall with its peeling paint and cobwebs dangling from the ceiling like unwanted Christmas decorations. They entered a sparsely-furnished square lounge. A tiny open-plan kitchen occupied the space to her left, and two closed doors faced her. The doors reminded Janet of her parents' hard and closed attitudes. They might not want to see her, but she had things to say, and she wouldn't leave until she'd said them.

Janet caught her breath as she recognised a worn armchair beneath the room's only window, and the frail man who sat in it. Her father looked even older than her mother.

'I told you it was small.' Carol closed the door behind them.

Janet's heart ached with the weight of the breakdown in their relationship. Gone was their perfect harmony. They were strangers.

'It's been a long time.' Bob prized himself out of the chair, tottering towards Janet while leaning heavily on a walking stick. He, too, was wrinkled and sallow-cheeked.

'You seemed to think phone calls were sufficient once Emma was old enough to travel by herself,' Carol said with a familiar tartness. 'And even she stopped coming when she had better options.'

Janet bridled. 'She was a teenager. She wanted to be at home with her friends.' She could excuse Emma's choice, if not her own. Janet had taught her children that two wrongs never made a right, yet when it came to her parents, she hadn't practiced what she preached, ignoring the wise advice of her old friend Mo to persevere with her visits.

'And that boy of yours consumed your every waking moment.'

Janet smarted at her father's tone. Anger fought against pity until she wasn't sure which emotion would gain the upper hand. She could handle whatever they said about her, but Benny didn't deserve their harsh words and derision. There was enough stacked against him without them adding fuel to the fire of his insecurities and low self-esteem.

'Can he talk properly yet?' Bob snorted. 'He didn't say a word the last time we saw him, and he had to be at least six.'

'Of course he can!' Janet couldn't stifle her irritation. This was why she had stayed away, why she had sheltered Benny from their disapproving stares and hurtful words.

'You can't blame me for wondering. He didn't do much.' Without greeting her properly, Bob returned to his chair, flopping down with a painful grunt. 'Just sat on your lap and either slept or cried. He wouldn't look at us or answer our questions.'

'He's shy.' Janet jumped to Benny's defence.

'You'd better sit down if you're staying.' Carol waved a gnarled hand towards the room's only remaining chair.

'Where will you sit?' Janet's eyes searched for more furniture but found only a small table and a footstool. 'I'll sit on that.' She crossed to the stool while her mother leaned her back against the door.

'You'll want a cup of tea.' Carol headed for the kitchen.

'I'm okay.' Janet inched the stool closer to her father and sat down. 'I had one at David's house.'

'You went to see your brother?' Carol whirled around to face her.

'I realised I've been avoiding my family.'

'Why now?' After making her way to the other chair, Carol sat down and picked up her knitting, her swollen fingers fumbling with wool and needles. Her hands were shaking. Was it nerves or something else?

Janet didn't have an answer, so they sat in awkward silence until another question from her father added to the tension buzzing through the room like electricity from a lightning storm.

'Does the boy still have those horrible fits?'

'His name is Benny, Dad.' The words came out sharper than Janet intended.

'How old is he now? Fourteen?' Bob propped his stick against the side of his chair.

'He's 16, and Emma is twenty-two.'

'A proper young lady.' Carol gave her first genuine smile. It softened her face, allowing Janet a glimpse of the mother she had loved. 'Is she still studying?'

'Yes. She'll complete her training to be a social worker next summer.' Janet beamed with pride, breathing an internal sigh of relief now they'd moved onto safer ground.

'That's good.' Bob rested his hands on his knees. 'There'll always be a need for social workers, what with the dysfunction in families nowadays.'

Janet resisted the urge to roll her eyes at the irony of his observation.

'And Benny?'

At least her mother had the decency to use his name.

'He's still at school, and he works part-time with Ola in the garage. He wants to train as a mechanic.'

'Is he capable?' Her father's face was a picture of astonishment.

'Ola is sure of it.' Janet indulged in a triumphant smile. 'And he's dating. Her name is Nettie, and she's got a beautiful little girl.'

'Your Benny got some girl pregnant?' Bob had no problem saying his name in anger.

'Beth isn't Benny's, but he loves her like his own.' Janet glanced from one parent to the other. 'Nettie's nineteen. She's been the making of Benny. She gives him confidence.' She sat up straighter on the stool, fixing her father with an assertive gaze. 'Naturally, Ola and I worried when they got together.

Especially with her having a child. But they're taking things slowly, and we're proud of the way they're handling it.'

'It's hard to believe.' Carol shook her head in bewilderment. 'Every time you brought him to our house, I thought he would never survive those awful seizures.'

'He still has them.' Janet frowned. 'The doctors say they'll always be a part of his life. He's learned to live with them and make the best of what he has.'

'Surely they've affected him mentally.' Bob arched his white eyebrows, clearly expecting confirmation despite what Janet had already told him.

'He has his struggles. Especially at school.' Janet's aching heart pleaded for her father to understand and accept her treasured child. 'He's a wonderful boy, Dad. I'd love for you to get to know him.'

'I'm glad he's making a life for himself, and it's good that he's learning a trade.' He sighed. 'As for getting to know him… You put paid to that when you stopped visiting.'

'I'm here now.' It was all she could say. Actions spoke louder than words, so only time would prove their truth. Healing wouldn't be possible unless her parents met her halfway, and they weren't ready for that yet. Perhaps they'd left it too late, and their relationship was beyond repair.

A beam of sunlight glinted through the window, drawing Janet's attention to a glass frame standing on the table. At first, she presumed it contained a picture of David or Malcolm's children, or Lucy's little ones. It wouldn't be Emma or Benny. However, something about the frame struck her as familiar, so she looked again, her breath catching in recognition.

'I made that for you!'

'For Christmas, when you were nine or ten years old.' Her mother looked up, then returned to her knitting. 'I found it when we were packing up to move.'

Janet leaned over to lift the frame off the table. Her mother was right. In the weeks leading up to her tenth Christmas, Janet had painstakingly hand-printed each word of the Lord's Prayer on a piece of pink card, drawing a border of hearts and flowers around the edge of her labour of love. She had asked her father to take her to the local shop, where she'd used her pocket money to buy the frame. Carol was thrilled with her simple gift, placing it on the sideboard and instructing Sylvia not to touch it because it was special. Of all the things for her mother to keep, why had she chosen this?

The printing had faded with age, yet Janet still made out the lettering. As she scanned the familiar words in her own neat handwriting, one sentence stood out bolder than the rest. 'And forgive us our debts, as we forgive our debtors.'

Janet replaced her artwork on the table with the realisation that their future was in her hands. She had no power over her parents' reactions or choices, but she needed to forgive their coldness and neglect, even if it continued for the rest of their lives. She must keep on loving, regardless of whether her love was reciprocated. Her mother's strange choice of a keepsake convicted her of her own unforgiveness while also offering hope. Was Carol, too, mourning their former closeness? Was that why she had kept the handmade gift?

An awkward silence fell, and Janet sensed her parents were waiting for her to break it. Should she introduce the subject of Sylvia slowly, or come right out and tell them what she knew? She momentarily wished she'd taken Ola up on his offer to accompany her. No, his presence would have made things worse.

'There's a reason I came here today, and why I visited David.' Janet fixed them both with a steady gaze. 'Ola and the children are waiting for me at David's house because I had to see you alone.'

'Is something on your mind, Jan?'

An interminable silence followed her mother's question, punctuated by the ticking of a wall clock that seemed to have increased in volume.

'I asked David to tell me the truth about Sylvia's death.'

Her parents gasped in unison, and Carol dropped her knitting upon her lap. The mere mention of Sylvia's name had sent them into a panic. Janet was struck afresh by their unhealed pain.

'You did what?' Carol squeaked.

'We never talk about her.' Her father was trying to shut down the conversation before it began.

'Well, it's time we did.' Janet waited for her words to hit their mark, then continued. 'It's been over 30 years. Surely that's long enough.'

'What did David say?' Janet noted the fear in her father's eyes.

'That it was a terrible accident, and you've blamed yourself every day since it happened,' she answered gently.

'What about you, Jan? Do you blame me? Has the truth changed your opinion of your father?' Bob's strangled words hung heavy in the air, and Carol reached up a hand to massage her temples.

'How could I blame you?' Tears pooled in Janet's eyes. 'You would never have intentionally hurt Sylvia. Or anyone else, for that matter. You were a wonderful dad.'

'Not for long.' He hung his head. 'I let you down because I couldn't live with my guilt. It was easier to pull away.'

'It might have helped if we'd talked. All these years I've blamed myself, thinking Sylvia died because she caught my cold. I should've heard the truth from you when you fetched me from the Grays, not 30 years too late from David.'

'I couldn't bear to say it... Just the thought of telling you I'd killed your sister! I was afraid you'd call me a monster. It was bad enough the boys knew what I'd done, and... and everyone else. I was petrified someone in the village would tell you.'

'I avoided talking to people, so I guess I never gave them the chance.'

'I'm ashamed to admit, I was relieved about that.' Bob's words were barely audible. 'I'm so sorry, Jan. I had no idea you blamed yourself.' His apology hung in the air, summing up the agony of a lifetime.

Janet could no longer stay seated. Compassion won the battle as she knelt at her father's feet and threw her arms around him. 'I love you, Dad. I always have, and I'll never stop. I missed you. I missed our family. We lost Sylvia but we didn't need to lose one another as well. It's not what she would have wanted.'

'She only ever wanted us to be happy.' Bob laid a shaking hand on her head. 'My carelessness ruined that.'

'David said you couldn't have known she was behind you.' Janet inhaled the long-forgotten scent of her father's spicy aftershave.

'I might if I'd used my mirrors properly.' Bob fidgeted nervously. 'I parked that van every night without thinking. Maybe I was distracted. It's all a blur. When I try to remember, I can't picture it clearly. There's a fog over the whole thing.'

'The police knew it was an accident.' Janet hadn't been this close to him in years, and she was in no rush to pull away.

'It didn't matter what anyone else said. I was the one who did it.' Bob's voice rang with self-loathing. 'I told her. That night, when we sat with her at the hospital, I told her I was sorry.' A tear rolled down his cheek, landing on Janet's hand. 'But it was too late. Our little Sylvie couldn't hear me. I pleaded with her to come back, but her organs were shutting down and she was already gone.'

The tear dissolved between Janet's fingers as she rubbed them. 'Did you blame him?' she asked, turning to her mother.

Carol screwed up her eyes. 'I said I didn't, but I pushed him away with the rest of you, so I suppose I did. It made sense to numb my emotions and keep doing what I had to. Over time, that became a way of life.'

'We all put the barriers up,' Janet conceded. 'David threw himself into his new life with Sarah. Malcolm focused on his schoolwork, and I hid away with my books.'

'Then you met Ola,' Carol folded her arms in her lap. 'I knew once you married him, we'd barely see you.'

'I might have come home more often if you hadn't treated me like an unwelcome intruder needing to be tolerated. That first Christmas after I had Benny, you saw I was struggling, and you never offered me an ounce of love and support.'

'I was afraid for you, Jan.' Carol's voice shook.

'Afraid of what?' Janet pulled away from her father to focus on her mother.

'That you'd suffer the same fate as me.' Carol looked directly at her. 'We're so alike. If I couldn't cope with losing a child, you wouldn't either. I couldn't bear to watch it.' Her eyes pleaded for understanding. 'Nor did I have the strength to let Benny into my heart – if I did, I'd have to go through losing a child again.'

'You thought Benny was going to die?' Janet gaped at her mother.

'He looked close to death's door from the beginning. And it didn't get better as he grew older. I was convinced one of his seizures would kill him, or he'd die of starvation because he couldn't keep anything down. I pictured him wasting away, with you fretting yourself into an early grave not long after him.' Carol turned her knitting needles around in her hand. 'You'd made him your whole life. You were obsessed. I had nothing to give you except my own pain.'

'All I needed was your love,' Janet whispered as her tears flowed. 'And for you to love my Benny.'

29

'I said I'd come back in the new year to help Mum get more things for the flat. Everything they had in the old house was too big. It's left them with next to nothing.' Janet and Ola stood at Sylvia's graveside in the fading light. Her heart rate was steady, so the cemetery had apparently lost its power over her. Was this, too, a symptom of her newfound freedom?

'It's good that they're willing to let you.'

Ola handed over a wreath of winter flowers, and Janet bent to lay the blooms on her sister's grave. 'Sylvie would definitely approve of those.' She straightened up, smiling at the vibrant shades of red and gold. 'She loved bright colours.'

'It sounds as though she was a bright little girl.' Ola took her icy hand, rubbing it between both of his.

'My parents and I have a long way to go.' Janet moved closer to her husband, enjoying his bulky comfort. 'Still, we've made a start, and I think Sylvie would be proud of us. We're going to keep in touch more by phone.'

'It's a shame it took 30 years.' Ola sighed.

'Dad was genuinely surprised that I didn't blame him.' The wind whipped at the collar of Janet's coat and one of the tall trees surrounding the graveyard let out a groan.

'Perhaps now he'll stop blaming himself.' Ola put an arm around her.

'Grief has a way of ageing people,' Janet mused. 'It eats away at your body and mind, especially when things remain unsaid.'

'Would you like a few minutes alone?' Once again, Ola's sensitivity startled her.

'Thank you.' She brushed a kiss on his cheek. 'I'll meet you back in the car. I'm sorry it's been such a long day.'

The sun was near to setting, causing the temperature to drop. Janet worried about Ola driving on the icy roads, but when she said so, he laughed.

'I'm Danish, remember?' He removed his arm, giving her back a gentle pat. 'I learned to drive in the ice and snow.'

Alone at her sister's graveside, Janet thought back over the events of the day. So much had happened in a short space of time, but she sensed a new beginning for her family. Although the hour she'd spent with her parents had started out strained, once the dam had burst, she'd seen glimpses of the mother and father she'd known as a child. Had they left it too late to find one another again? Only time would tell. Janet vowed to give it her best for Sylvia, for them and for herself.

'I wish you were with me today.' Janet whispered. 'We missed out, Sylvie. I thought we'd grow up together, that you'd be a bridesmaid at my wedding and me at yours. I wanted you to share your love of animals and zest for life with my children.' She bent to adjust a leaning flower. 'I'm sure they would have loved you. Especially Emma. When she was a child, I saw glimpses of you in her dancing and play, and I heard your echo in her laughter. She's a determined young lady. Maybe she gets that from her aunt too.'

Janet wiped dirt from the gravestone whilst continuing her conversation with Sylvia. 'I let her down, Sylvie. My worries about Benny and my need to protect him at any cost took over. I'd already lost you. I feared losing him as well, just as our mother did. I suppose I haven't really admitted that until now. I can, here, with you. You left your mark on us all, and we handled it badly. I blamed myself for your death, even though logic should have told me no one dies from catching a cold. And when Benny was born with epilepsy, I was scared I'd make a mistake with him too. That somehow, it was my fault. I was determined to be the perfect mother. No one would harm my baby as long as I was there to protect him. But I strangled him with my love. I tied us both up in knots until Benny was brave enough to break free. You'd love him too. It takes effort to break through his shyness, but I'm sure you would have done it. He wouldn't have been able to resist you.'

Another gust of wind whistled through the trees. It was time to go.

'I'll be back, Sylvie. I'm going to visit Mum and Dad more regularly. David and his family too. I'll bring you more flowers and tidy up around here.' It was obvious no one had done it for years. 'It's silly, really. You wouldn't care about moss and weeds. A mound of hard earth can't contain you. You were a free spirit, and you never stood still.' Janet closed her eyes, picturing Sylvia as she had been. 'I want to believe you're in heaven. Heaven felt so real when you were alive. Everything changed after you left us, even my faith.'

She whispered the words that had always summoned her sister. 'Sylvia Pew, where are you?'

A child's laughter floated to her on the wind. There was a playground nearby, but no one would be there so close to dark on such a bitterly cold evening. Janet turned, spotting a blonde-haired girl walking hand in hand with her mother. The child was wrapped up against the chill, and she clutched a teddy bear to her chest. As they drew closer, Janet heard her excited chatter.

'Can I tell her about it, Mummy? Can I tell my baby sister what Kelly Rose did?'

'Of course.' The mother laughed, obviously enjoying her daughter's excitement.

They walked past Janet and stopped beside a tiny white cross. The little girl knelt before the cross, unperturbed by the damp grass. Janet strained to listen.

'I've brought Rupert to see you, baby sister.' The child held out the bear, as though she expected someone to take it. 'I know you can't play with him cos you're in heaven with Jesus, but I still wanna share him with you. Mummy says it's good to share. And we would've played with him together if you hadn't died in Mummy's tummy.'

So this little girl had also lost her sister; a sister she had never even met. However, her faith was unwavering where Janet's had floundered. The child had no doubts that her unborn sibling was in heaven. Her innocence tugged at Janet's heart, taking her back to a simpler time before the scars of tragedy made their mark. Yet her words were also a timely reminder that the remedies of faith and hope could provide a healing balm.

Janet longed to stay and listen to more. However, her family waited. She left the mother and daughter to their privacy and headed for Ola's parked car.

Their homeward journey was painstakingly long, and they were all exhausted by the time Ola pulled into the driveway. Benny had fallen asleep after a seizure and a bad bout of sickness had forced them to stop at the roadside for half an hour. It wasn't unexpected after a day of new experiences.

Janet was out of the car as soon as it stopped, assuming her son would be disorientated and dizzy.

'Come on, my love. Let's get you inside and up to bed.' She opened the passenger door and reached in to unbuckle his seatbelt.

Benny had beaten her to it. 'I'm okay now, Mum. I feel better.'

He climbed out unaided, closing the door behind him, and Janet saw him sneaking a glance in the direction of Nettie's.

'Off you go then.' Ola briefly hugged their son's narrow shoulders and handed him a mint.

'Where?' Benny both looked and sounded confused.

'Where you're dying to go.' Ola smiled. 'Over to the Thompsons'.'

'Are you serious?'

Janet was as shocked as her son.

'You did well today, Benny.' Ola stood facing him. 'I know none of it was easy, so I'm proud of you for trying. As for what happened on Tuesday… There's no denying you made a huge mistake by skipping school and lying to your mother, but you faced up to it like a man and accepted the consequences. Perhaps my punishment was a little harsh.'

'Thanks, Dad!' Benny threw his arms around his father's neck, and Ola accepted his embrace. 'You're the best!'

'I doubt that. It's late, so don't stay too long.' Ola patted his back to send him on his way, while Janet resisted the urge to fuss.

Nettie had never looked more beautiful to Benny than she did that night. She opened her parents' front door and stood beaming at him on the doorstep, her long hair cascading in waves over her shoulders.

'What are you doing here?' She flew into his arms. 'I thought you were still grounded!'

'Dad changed his mind.'

She took his hand, drawing him into the empty lounge. 'My parents are already in bed, and Beth's been sleeping for hours.'

'I hope I didn't wake them up. Should I go?'

'No, please stay. Just for a bit. My parents aren't as strict as yours.' Nettie grinned and sank onto the sofa, pulling him down beside her. 'You're not looking great.' She faced him with concern in her eyes.

'I had a seizure on the way home.' Benny kissed her. 'I wasn't gonna let that stop me when Dad let me see you.'

As they held one another in the dimly lit room, Benny had to share the concern that weighed heavily on his mind. 'Can we always promise to tell the truth, Nettie? Even when it's hard.'

'What made you say something like that?' She stroked the back of his hand.

'I reckon not knowing the truth about what happened to Sylvia messed everything up for my mum, and for my grandparents and Uncle David. They all kind of blamed themselves, so they shut each other out. And that wrecked stuff for them. I don't want that happening to us, cos... I dunno... It's not how people who love each other should live. They should be able to talk until they sort stuff out.'

'I agree. So yes, I'll always be truthful with you.'

30

The final fortnight of the school term dragged by, with Benny counting down the days to the Christmas holidays. Janet fulfilled her promise to take him shopping, and he was pleased with the gifts they selected. He'd saved enough money to pay for everything himself, thanks to his part-time job.

On Christmas Eve, Benny sat on the floor alongside his sister in her lounge filled with second-hand furniture, surrounded by groups of carefully chosen photographs.

'I'm struggling to find decent ones of you,' Emma complained. 'Don't you ever smile?'

'I smile loads.' Benny gave her an exaggerated grin. 'Just not when I'm having my photo taken. It's weird when people tell you to smile if there's nothing to smile about. I don't get it.'

'You don't seem to struggle when you're with Nettie or Beth.' Emma held out an image of him holding Beth on his lap while they shared an ice cream in the park.

'Did Nettie give that to you?'

'She's given me quite a few.' Emma pointed at one of the piles. 'And I've got some of all three of you. It's the pre-Nettie photos I'm struggling with.'

'You don't need none of those.' Benny preferred not to think about the person he used to be. He'd talked to Tim about his selfishness, how he'd monopolised his mother and taken her away from Emma. Although his pastor had helped him repent and move on, Benny still wished he could change the past for his sister's sake.

'Mum won't want an album without photos from when you were little.' Emma focused on her sorting.

'Did they take any on our holiday to the seaside with the Mosses?' Benny asked.

'I think Karen might've given me one or two.' Emma rifled through another bunch. 'Here's one of us outside the caravan with Dale and Erin.' She laughed. 'I guess you're half smiling.'

The photo of Dale brought back memories of the boy who loved to taunt him and call him Weedy Wellander. 'Mum won't want photos of Dale.' He scowled as Emma held the glossy print out for his inspection.

'She'll have to put up with it.' She added the picture to her growing collection.

'You promised me hot chocolate.' Benny rose and stretched.

'Can't you focus on anything for over five minutes?' His sister glared up at him.

'I did. We've been doing this for half an hour.' He reached down to hoist her to her feet. 'Come on, Emmie.'

Emma sighed, then smiled indulgently. 'All right. But there's still more to do.'

'I'll do it better after we've had hot chocolate.' Benny flopped onto the worn sofa, a relic from Erin's parents.

'It's just as well I love you, little pest.' His sister pulled him into a tight hug. When she made to let go, Benny held her back.

'I'm glad you still do after the way I was.' He gazed deeply into her eyes.

'I've told you, Benny, it's all in the past. I shouldn't have brought it up.' Her tone was gentle.

'Yeah, you should.' He gave her a serious stare. 'You were telling the truth, and I reckon that's important.'

Benny exchanged texts with his schoolfriend Damian while Emma prepared their drinks. Damo was spending Christmas with his mother in London, and he'd already found a girlfriend. It wouldn't last because he'd be back in a fortnight. Benny struggled to understand the way Damo flitted from one girl to the next. Nettie was enough for him. She always would be.

'Don't say I never spoil you.' Emma returned to sit beside him, holding out a mug and a box of shortbread biscuits.

They chatted while enjoying their treat, laughing over memories from Christmases past.

'It's gonna be different this year.' Benny turned doleful eyes on his sister.

'Because of our grandparents?' Emma placed her empty cup at her feet. 'You're nervous about seeing them, aren't you?'

'How come you know?' He inched closer.

'I know you.' Emma patted his hand. 'It'd be bad enough if they were only visiting for a couple of hours, but it'll be harder because they're staying.'

'Mum's really pleased, so I'm trying to be happy for her.' He frowned.

'And you'll do your best to talk to them?' Emma raised an eyebrow. 'You need to try, Benny. If they sense you're uncomfortable, they'll be awkward back.'

'That's what Dad said.' Benny dropped his gaze to his feet. 'I told him I'll try.'

'That's all you can do.' She kissed his cheek. 'I promise, there's nothing scary about Grandma and Grandpa.'

'What if they don't like me?'

'They'll love you because we do.'

Ever the slave driver, Emma soon had him back on the floor, sorting more photographs. By the time he prepared to leave, they were both satisfied with their selections.

'I'll see you in the morning.' Emma hugged him in the hallway. 'I'm glad Mum invited Nettie and Beth for tea tonight. You'll feel more confident with them there.'

'Nettie always knows what to say. And Beth thinks everyone's her friend. I bet she'll love meeting Grandma and Grandpa.' Benny made to walk away, then turned back to his sister. 'Did Dad tell you he and Mum were at my school again before the holidays?'

She shook her head. 'Perhaps it was about your mocks.'

'Do you reckon they'll make me do them after Christmas?' The prospect of exams made Benny feel sick.

'It might be better for you if they did.'

He shook his head emphatically, and Emma held up a hand.

'Hear me out, Pestie. You'll need to get through the mocks before the final exams in May.'

'I can't!' Benny fretted. 'I'll throw up or have a seizure, and I won't know nothing.'

'You understand more than you realise.' Emma's brown eyes bore into his. 'You might surprise yourself if you actually tried.'

Benny mulled over his sister's words during the short walk home through the virtually empty park. A couple of excited children remained, whiling away the hours until bedtime and the promised visit from Santa. Benny usually covered the ground at a brisk pace, but today he dawdled on purpose, stopping to indulge in the children's animated chatter. It was a welcome distraction. He wanted to believe Emma was right, but he knew better. No matter how hard he tried, facts and figures slipped through his mind like the sand in his mother's egg timer. How come he remembered the things Dad taught him at the garage, yet he couldn't solve a basic maths problem?

Benny arrived home to find his father's car parked in the driveway. He took a deep breath as he reached into his pocket for his house key, only to realise it wasn't there. Had he left it at Emma's? Or had he gone out without it? He was forced to use the doorbell and wait for one of his parents to let him in.

'It's lucky we got back before you.' Ola stared at him with a fixed expression.

'Sorry, Dad.' Benny entered the house, pulling the door closed behind him. 'I thought I had my keys.'

'You left them by the kettle. You need to be more careful, Benny.'

'Yeah, I know.' He hoped he sounded sincere. 'You got back quick.'

'The traffic wasn't as bad as I expected.' His father's facial features softened as he placed a hand on Benny's shoulder. 'Are you ready to see your grandparents?'

Benny nodded bravely, relieved his father couldn't sense his rising heart rate.

He trailed Ola into the lounge where two elderly strangers sat on the sofa, each nursing a cup of tea, while Janet flitted about plumping cushions and adjusting ornaments.

'Here he is. Here's my Benny.' His mother rushed to his side.

'He's the spitting image of his dad.' Carol appraised him with the trace of a smile, and Benny fought the temptation to turn around and escape to his room. He was prevented from doing so by Janet taking a protective grip of his hand and pulling him forwards.

'Come spend time with your grandparents, my love,' she cajoled.

Benny was grateful when his dad moved closer, sandwiching him securely between his parents.

'You've grown since the last time we saw you.' Grandma eyed Benny warily while Grandpa remained silent.

'That's hardly surprising in ten years,' Ola said, with a laugh that sounded a little forced.

Benny hadn't been sure what to expect from this meeting. But Emma was right; the older couple sitting on the sofa weren't scary, just tired and sad. Could he pluck up the courage to act his age and greet them?

'Hi.' One word used up all the courage he possessed, but he accompanied it with what he hoped was a welcoming smile.

Benny knew his mum hadn't expected her parents to accept when she invited them. She had admitted to being both worried and pleased. There was still so much ground to make up. However, his parents and grandparents were trying, so Benny needed to do his bit and meet them halfway.

'Your father's been telling me about the work you're doing at the garage.' Grandpa spoke directly to Benny, and he noticed his mum's mouth open in surprise.

'I enjoy working with Dad.' Benny turned to his father for reassurance.

'Let's allow your grandparents to rest after their long journey. Why don't you call Nettie and let her know what time we'll be eating?' His dad was letting him off the hook.

Benny didn't need a second excuse to escape to his room until teatime.

Janet watched in delight as Beth scampered over to Bob straight after tea. She'd taken to him immediately and he'd relaxed as he'd eaten the meal, unable to resist Beth's antics and chatter.

'She's a little character, Nettie,' Bob said.

'And she talks well for her age,' Carol affirmed, moving her husband's cup of coffee out of the toddler's reach.

'She never stops.' With a sigh, Nettie abandoned her attempt to prevent her daughter from clambering onto Bob's lap as Beth plonked her bottom down like she belonged there and tugged on his glasses.

'Oh no you don't.' He captured her flailing hand with a smile.

'It looks like our Bethy's made a new friend.' Janet smiled warmly at Nettie, who responded with a tinkling laugh.

The evening had gone more smoothly than Janet could have hoped. Her mother had even helped with the meal, soothing Janet's panic over the food. Nettie and Beth had arrived on time, and Janet was gratified by the way Benny's girlfriend instinctively drew him into their conversations. Beth was a safe subject, guaranteed to make Benny talk.

'Your Benny really loves that little girl.' Carol followed Janet into the kitchen carrying a tray of empty mugs.

Was it Janet's imagination, or had her mother's posture improved with her mood?

'He has since the day she was born.' Janet had briefly filled her in on the facts of Benny and Nettie's unconventional history. 'He'll do anything for her.'

Nettie joined them to help with the washing up, while Benny followed Beth in and out of rooms and up and down the stairs, and Bob made a concerted effort to chat to Ola. The pleasure of having her whole family under her roof filled Janet's heart.

Later, Janet sat beside Ola in front of their glittering Christmas tree. Nettie had gone home to put Beth to bed, and her parents had settled for an early night.

'It was a lovely evening, wasn't it?' Janet said with a contented sigh.

'I'd say it was a bit much for your parents.' Ola unfolded his newspaper. 'They're not used to handling an inquisitive toddler and her chatty mother.'

'Nettie always has plenty to say.' Janet rose to wipe Beth's sticky finger marks off the glass-topped coffee table. 'Still, she broke the ice for Benny.'

She turned as her son sauntered into the room, surprised to see him wearing his Sunday best jeans and sweater.

'I'm gonna go now.' Benny jingled his house keys at Ola with a triumphant grin.

'Where are you going?' Ola looked up.

'To church. It's Christmas Eve.'

'I'd forgotten about that.' Ola put down his newspaper. 'Do you want a lift?'

'I don't mind walking. It's not raining.' Benny moved closer to Janet and reached for her hand. 'Do you wanna come with me?'

'Me?' Janet gaped at him.

'Brian said it's a really nice service, with carols and candles and stuff. I thought you might like it cos of what you told me about taking Emma to church on Christmas Eve when she was a baby.' Benny squeezed her hand, then spoke more quietly. 'I'd love it if you came.'

'I'd love to go with you, sweetheart.' Though she was emotionally tired, Janet's assent was surprisingly easy. She wasn't just doing this to please Benny. It was for her too.

31

Benny laced his fingers through his mother's as they sat in the back row of the candlelit church, mesmerised by the music and Pastor Tim's retelling of the Son of God being born into the world as a tiny infant. Janet's voice had rung out strong and clear as she sang the familiar carols. She seemed to have a new layer of joy and peace. Benny had felt a nudge to invite her, and he was glad he'd obeyed, though he wished Nettie held his other hand. That would be perfect, but Nettie wasn't ready for church. Her lack of faith saddened him, and he prayed every day for her to find Jesus.

When Tim spoke about Mary and Joseph's arduous trek to Bethlehem, likening it to the trouble-strewn pathway of life, Benny considered his own life's journey. It had taken some surprising turns. He'd presumed things would become simpler after he gave his life to Jesus, and Nettie chose him over Beth's father. Then his mum opened up about Sylvia, adding another twist. This one had brought his grandparents back into their lives. Hopefully, that would be a good thing. Despite everything she'd learned about her sister's death, his mum seemed happier. Nettie told him she'd seen a new peace in Janet's eyes, and studying her now in the candlelight, Benny saw it too.

'I love you, Mum,' he whispered.

'I love you too.' Janet blinked back a tear before standing to sing *Silent Night.*

During a moment of quiet prayer and reflection, Janet opened her eyes to gaze at the flickering candles. Beside her, Benny's eyes remained closed. Who was he praying for - himself, Nettie,

Beth or her? Janet wished she could pray in the old familiar way, but how should she begin?

Once, prayer had been as natural as breathing. She had started and ended each day by talking to Jesus. With childlike faith, Janet had assumed her Heavenly Father would always be eager and willing to listen and help. But if that were true, where was He on the day Sylvia died? Why didn't He stop the cat running into the road, or delay their father, even for a minute? One red light on the way home, and her sister would still be alive.

Did she blame Jesus for Sylvia's death? She'd stopped talking to Him, so perhaps she did. It wasn't a conscious decision. At first, her family needed her to take over at home. Later, she couldn't face attending Sunday school without her sister. Yet here was her Benny, having found a faith of his own, and he'd done it without her help.

Janet recalled that other Christmas Eve when she'd sat in a different church with baby Emma in her arms and Mo at her side. Mo had offered friendship and support during a critical period of adjusting to life as a new mother. The passing of time had distanced them as letters and calls became less frequent. Mo said she understood – Janet's time was consumed by caring for her needy child – but Janet felt she could have made more of an effort to keep in touch.

She vowed to introduce Benny to Mo one day. In hindsight, she realised her friend was a Christian, so she and Benny would find common ground. If anyone could put him at ease, it would be Mo. He would love her gentle motherliness, and she would welcome him with open arms. Janet knew Mo was still alive because her Christmas card stood in pride of place on their sideboard.

They rose to sing the final carol, after which Pastor Tim stood in the doorway, wishing his congregation a Merry Christmas as they filed out into the chilly night air.

'It's lovely to see you here tonight, Jan.' Her neighbour Louise Brooks touched her arm.

'It was a beautiful service.' Janet meant every word.

'See you on Friday, Benny,' Brian said, grinning at Benny, who shook his head in bewilderment.

'Is youth group still happening? I didn't think it would cos it's Christmas.'

'There's an outreach games night,' Brian confirmed. 'Everyone's welcome. Why don't you bring Nettie?'

'Maybe.' Benny looked unimpressed. 'If she won't come, I'm not going by myself. I hate games and stuff.'

'Why?' Brian asked.

'I'm rubbish. I never know what to do. I get it wrong, and I bug people if I make their team lose.'

'Me too. So let's be rubbish together.'

The easy interaction between the two boys filled Janet's heart with pleasure.

When Benny stubbornly shook his head, Brian laughed. 'If I've got to make a fool of myself, you should too.' Brian patted Benny's back and left with his family.

'You've made good friends here.' Janet looped her arm through Benny's as a brown-haired girl waved and mouthed a greeting.

'That was Heather.' Benny waved back as she guided him through a gap in the throng.

Janet assumed her son would avoid Tim's receiving line in the doorway, but the pastor caught his eye.

'Merry Christmas, Benny.' Tim shook his hand, and Janet observed the warmth with which Benny returned his gesture.

'Nice to see you too, Mrs Wellander.' It was her turn to receive the pastor's handshake.

'That was a special service.' She smiled. 'It reminded me of going to church when I was a little girl.'

Tim's expressive eyes radiated love and peace. 'You're welcome here any time.'

'Thank you.' Janet paused, then added, 'You've been so good to my Benny.'

'We're friends.' Tim was in no rush to dismiss them.

'Those chats the two of you have on a Saturday...' Janet swallowed the dryness in her throat, wishing she'd made space for the next person in the line. However, Tim's expectant gaze gave her the courage to press on. 'Would you mind if I came too? Only once.' She blushed. 'I wouldn't want to spoil your time with Benny. I just have a few questions...' Had the church suddenly grown warmer? And was Janet's face as red as it felt?

'We wouldn't mind at all, would we, Benny?'

'Course not.' Her son tightened his hold on her arm.

'You'd better go to bed.' Janet sat with Benny at the kitchen table. She'd made cocoa, which they drank while sharing Benny's favourite chocolate digestives. It was like old times as they indulged in one of his childhood pleasures.

'Nettie's gonna phone me when Beth wakes up so I can see her opening her presents,' he enthused.

'That'll be special.' Janet reached across the table to cover his hand. 'She's old enough to understand this year.'

'She's really excited.' He rolled his eyes. 'Nettie said she didn't wanna go to bed.'

'She'll be up early.' Janet grinned. 'Emma always was on Christmas morning.'

'I don't mind.' Benny yawned and rubbed his eyes. 'I won't make loads of noise and wake Grandma and Grandpa.'

'Thank you.' His consideration of their needs touched Janet's heart. 'You seemed more comfortable with them after tea.'

'That was cos of Beth.' He laughed. 'She wouldn't leave Grandpa alone.'

'I saw glimpses of the man he used to be when he played with her.' Janet leaned back in her chair. 'He was like that with Sylvia. Full of nonsense. It all changed after she died.'

Benny looked down at his hands, then up at Janet, and over at the door. He fidgeted restlessly, and she sensed he had something important to say.

'What is it, my love?' She was reminded of her little boy, who'd become overwhelmed and frustrated over his inability to convert thoughts into words. How he'd matured this last year...

'Me and Tim were talking on Saturday about all the stuff that's happened.' Benny's eyes zipped around the room, unable to focus. 'I hope you don't mind. I told him about Sylvia.'

'Of course I don't,' Janet reassured him. 'You can trust Tim.'

'I wanted to ask him about the truth.' Benny rose to pace the kitchen.

'The truth?' Janet followed him with her eyes, longing to make this easier.

Benny stood with his back to the closed door, poised in readiness to bolt should the need arise. 'It's important, isn't it, Mum? I mean, the truth matters.'

Janet waited for him to continue.

'I reckon loads of stuff would've been different if you'd known the truth about Sylvia.'

'Possibly so.' Janet held out a hand to her agitated son. 'Come here, my love. It's okay. I'm not angry.'

He inched away from the door.

'Take your time,' Janet spoke tenderly. 'I'm listening.'

Benny's facial features softened. Then he positioned himself behind Janet's chair with his arms around her shoulders.

'What do you think would have been different?' she asked.

'You wouldn't have had to pretend you never had a sister,' he whispered. 'You and your parents would've talked about stuff more, and you could've told Grandpa it wasn't his fault.'

Janet nodded slowly.

'And you wouldn't have blamed yourself every time I had a seizure.'

His final words pulled her up short. 'What do you mean?' Janet's voice quivered.

'When I was having them, you cried and said you were sorry.'

'I didn't realise you could hear me.' She sniffed.

'I can hear stuff, even when I can't talk.' Benny walked around the table to stand facing her again. 'It scared me when you cried and you kept saying sorry. I didn't know what you were on about. It wasn't your fault I had epilepsy. But I get it now. You thought Sylvia died cos she caught your cold, and you were worried you made me ill.'

Janet gaped at him, hit by the force of his insight.

'You were afraid I'd die like her.' Benny picked up their empty mugs, crossing to the sink to wash them under the tap. 'You tried to make sure nothing bad happened. Well, it already did, and we can't do nothing to stop it. God can, if He wants to. If He doesn't, I'll always be epileptic. And if I am, I can live with it. I'm okay.'

Janet stared at her son wide-eyed. This confident young man was nothing like the child who cried and clung to her whenever he faced something new or scary.

'You, Grandma and Grandpa have talked about the truth, and it's started making things better.' Benny put the mugs on the draining board. 'You know how Sylvia died, and Grandpa knows you don't blame him, even though he hit her.' He leaned against the sink unit, his arms folded against his chest. His face took on a serious expression. 'Tim told me about a verse in the Bible where Jesus says when we know the truth, it'll set us free. He's talking about knowing the truth about who He is, but Tim said it's the same with everything. I've told Nettie I always want us to tell the truth, even if it's hard. And I've said sorry to Emma about how I used to be. I was selfish for wanting you all the time. She needed you too. We were both your kids.' He paused, paced, then stopped behind Janet with a hand on her shoulder. 'If me and Nettie have more kids, we're gonna make sure Beth knows we still love her, even if one of them is ill.'

'It sounds as though you've done a lot of thinking.' Janet turned her head with a loving smile.

'It's hard for me,' Benny confessed. 'I never thought about stuff till I started believing in Jesus and reading the Bible.' He shrugged. 'I'm trying.'

'And your dad and I are very proud of you. I'm sure Tim is too. And Nettie.' Janet squeezed his hand. 'You've given me a lot to mull over, and more questions to ask when I have my chat with Tim.'

'He's good at answering questions.'

Benny bade her goodnight with a hug.

Janet glided around the silent house, plumping cushions, tidying away Beth's discarded toys, and switching off the lights on the Christmas tree before climbing the stairs. On the landing, she listened to the gentle rhythm of her father's snores, smiling as she headed into her bedroom, where Ola waited.

'How was church?' Her husband leaned over to switch on the bedside lamp.

Janet picked up her night gown. 'I'm glad I went.'

She undressed in the lamplight before climbing into bed beside him. Ola switched off the light and turned over. Moments later, when he reached for her in the darkness, she went to him willingly.

32

Benny slept with his phone under his pillow, ready to answer the moment it rang.

'She's awake, and she's already found her stocking.' It was 5am, and Nettie's voice was thick with sleep.

'I'll be there soon.' He was already out of bed and pulling on his jeans in the darkness.

Nettie let him into her parents' house less than five minutes later with her hair hanging limply down her back, wearing her dressing gown and fluffy pink slippers.

'Don't worry.' Benny kissed her in the hallway as she gazed self-consciously into the mirror. 'I'm gonna see you like that every day when we get married, so you might as well get used to it.'

'I haven't agreed to marry you yet.' She poked her tongue out at him, a twinkle of mischief in her eyes.

'Benny!' Beth darted out of the living room, a huge grin on her face and arms outstretched in greeting.

'I wish she'd let me have an extra hour.' Nettie groaned, leaning heavily into his hug.

'It'd be mean to make her go back to bed.' Benny turned his attention to the bouncing two-year-old. 'What have you got, Bethy?' He swept her up into his arms, tickling under her chin.

'Toys!' Beth squealed with laughter, a bundle of unbridled joy.

Benny carried her into the living room with Nettie following, and the child pointed at a collection of brightly coloured parcels under the tree.

'Mine!' She beamed, and Benny and Nettie laughed.

Beth's gifts were simple due to Nettie's limited income, yet she exclaimed over each discovery in wide-eyed wonder. When everything was opened, her favourite proved to be a baby doll. The little girl cradled it in her arms, calling it Nettie.

Benny stayed for a while, braving the frostiness of Nettie's mother. He knew she didn't think he was good enough for her only daughter. However, after much soul-searching during the hardest months of Benny's life, Nettie had chosen him. She loved him. She was ready to commit to their future, and Benny's world slid into place.

When he left them to return to his family, Benny extracted a promise from Nettie that she and Beth would join them later that afternoon.

'You've got more presents at my house,' he whispered to Beth before sauntering into the street. In the pre-dawn light, Nettie picked her child up to prevent her following. Benny turned back, and they both blew him kisses.

'It's a lovely clear morning.' Janet stood in the lounge window as Benny joined her. 'Merry Christmas, my love.' She held out her arms. 'I heard you sneaking out. Was Beth excited?'

'She got Nettie up at five.' Benny hugged her willingly.

'I warned you.' Janet smiled.

'I didn't mind.' He pulled away. 'I'm gonna make tea. Do you want one?'

'Thank you.' Janet followed him into the kitchen and started removing items from the cupboards while Benny switched on the kettle. 'I've heard movement from upstairs, so I know your dad and your grandparents are awake. But while I still have you to myself...' Janet crossed to the table, picked up a flat package wrapped in shiny green paper, and held it out with a flourish. 'There are other presents under the tree.' She placed the rectangular object in his hand. 'But this is something special from me.'

Peeling back the wrapping, Benny found a book of illustrated Children's Bible stories, worn from use, with a picture of Noah's ark on the cover.

'It was my childhood Bible,' Janet explained. 'Grandma gave it back to me when Emma was a baby. I'd hidden it away because I used to read it to Sylvia.'

'Did you read it to Emmie?' He leafed through the pages.

'No.' Janet sighed. 'Half of me wanted to, but the other half just couldn't. So I hid it away again. That was silly, and a terrible waste. I thought you should have it, to read to Beth when she's older.'

'I'm rubbish at reading.' Benny frowned. 'It'd be better if you did it.'

'You've got plenty of time to practice,' Janet encouraged. 'Start getting used to the stories now, and you'll know them by the time she's ready.'

'Yeah, maybe I could.' He scanned the contents page. 'I've heard some of them at church. And Beth will like the pictures.'

'This one was Sylvia's favourite.' Janet turned to a page depicting Jesus surrounded by a crowd of small children. 'She said it looked like He was having fun.'

'I reckon Jesus liked kids.' Benny closed the book with a grin.

'He had something in common with you, then.'

Janet gathered the ingredients for an omelette, explaining it had always been her father's favourite breakfast treat. Benny offered to help. He grated cheese and chopped onions, barely flinching when his grandmother entered the room clad in her dressing gown.

'I was going to help you, Jan.' Carol smiled at Benny. 'But it looks as though someone else beat me to it.'

Benny returned his grandmother's smile. 'I hate onions. They make you cry.' He scowled as a stray tear ran down his cheek, and Ola and Bob filed into the room side by side.

Janet's enjoyment of a morning spent exchanging gifts with her family was complete when Emma arrived soon after breakfast. Her parents had gone for a quick sit down when Emma handed Benny his present and he unwrapped his sixth box of chocolates.

'How come you all give me so much sweet stuff?' Benny glanced down at his growing pile.

'Because you're a nightmare to buy for, and we know it's the one thing you'll enjoy. At least Mum didn't buy you anything babyish this year,' Emma teased before crossing the room and fetching a large gold-wrapped package from her bag. 'Should we give this to Mum now?'

Benny nodded.

'What's this?' Janet took her gift with a girlish giggle.

'There's only one way to find out.' Emma's eyes were sparkling.

Janet gasped as she opened the wrapping then slowly turned each page of the photograph album, marvelling over the carefully selected catalogue of their family's history. She paused over a picture of Sylvia as memories flooded back. This was the first time she'd seen her sister's expressive eyes and cheeky grin since the last morning they spent together. Sylvia looked so alive. At first, Janet wondered whether she might cry. Instead, as the years slipped away, she smiled at the blonde-haired sprite she had loved so dearly.

'She was cute.' Emma pressed a kiss to her cheek.

'How did you...?' Janet breathed.

'Uncle David kept them. When I phoned to tell him what we were planning, he sent them to me.'

'It's amazing.' Janet put the album down carefully to pull her children into a hug. 'And so are my son and daughter. I love you both, and I'm so proud to be your mother.'

'We love you too, Mum.' Emma's voice caught on a sob. 'You're the best. And it was fun because Benny and I worked on it together.'

'We're all in there, just as we should be.' Janet held on tightly. 'Grandma and Grandpa, Sylvia, David and Malcolm, plus their families, me and your dad, and my beautiful children.'

'And Nettie and Beth,' Benny insisted.

'Oh yes, them too.' Janet gave him an extra squeeze. 'I'm going to show this to your grandparents later because they need to see it.'

'Do you think they're ready?' Emma's eyes clouded with concern.

'Yes.' Janet nodded resolutely. 'It will help them move forward in their healing.'

Benny discovered that having Christmas dinner with his whole family was different, but fun. Crackers were pulled, with Grandpa Bob taking responsibility for reading the corny jokes. Benny even ate most of his meal once Emma snuck some of his vegetables onto her own plate while their parents' backs were turned.

His grandparents seemed happier today. Grandpa let out a few booming laughs that made Benny jump, then blush with embarrassment over his skittishness. Though Benny said little while they ate, he responded confidently when spoken to.

'I'll help with the washing up.' Grandma rose as crockery and cutlery were passed down the table and gathered into a pile.

'You both deserve a rest,' his dad replied. 'Benny and I will do it, won't we, son?'

'Okay.' Benny groaned inwardly at the magnitude of the task awaiting them while outwardly, he smiled and nodded at his father.

'There's so much of it,' Mum protested.

'We're used to working together,' Dad said from the doorway. 'We'll get it done in no time.'

The words put a spring in Benny's step, and he strolled into the kitchen and filled the sink, while his dad organised things into piles.

'We're going to have to get used to this.' Dad didn't look up from scraping unwanted food into the dustbin. Most of it was Benny's.

'Doing dishes?' Benny was confused.

'Not exactly. I meant working together. I mean, we're going to be doing a lot more of it.' Dad dropped the first pile of plates into the sink.

'Not till after my exams.' The plate in his hand felt heavier.

'Well, about that… It might be sooner than you think.'

'What do you mean?' Benny scrubbed the plate and slotted it into the drainer.

'I've been waiting for the right moment…' Dad deftly dried the plate and put it away. 'Your mother wanted me to tell you as soon as we decided, but I left it until today, thinking it would make an extra Christmas present. A special one from me to you.'

Benny waited for him to continue, unsure where this was going. Dad seemed to be enjoying drawing it out.

'You know we were called to the school again before the holidays, don't you?'

'Was it about my mocks?' Benny frowned.

'Not exactly.' Dad dried a handful of cutlery and tossed it into a drawer. 'Your teachers don't think you'll be ready to sit your GCSEs in May. They suggested giving you an extra year, with more tuition in the special needs unit.'

'But I'm already a year behind!' Benny couldn't believe what he was hearing. Another 18 months of school would be torture.

'That's what I said. So, I asked where we'd stand if we took you out of school before the exams.'

Benny's hands stilled in the water. He held his breath, both scared and desperate to hear what his father would say next.

'Hey, stop your shirking.' Dad patted his arm. 'I won't allow for shirkers at the garage. It's going to be non-stop nine-to-five work every day, with a couple of short breaks in between. Do you think you can handle that, Benjamin Ola Wellander?'

'Are you gonna let me leave school?' Benny couldn't look at him. What if he'd misunderstood?

'You've already left.' Dad put an arm around him, and as the reality hit, Benny released tears of relief, resting his head on his father's broad shoulder. 'That's one of the advantages of being a year behind your peers. We could pull you out legally because you're already 16.'

'Thank you! I love you, Dad.' Those two short sentences meant more than a lifetime of words. Finally, Dad saw him as a man, as a son to be proud of. Benny wouldn't let him down.

Benny couldn't wait to tell Nettie the news when she arrived with Beth an hour later. He pounced on her the moment she came through the front door.

'No more school, Nettie! No more teachers, and tests, and getting stuff wrong, and worrying about how rubbish I am.'

'You're not rubbish,' she scolded.

'I won't be a rubbish mechanic. I'm gonna try really hard and show my dad he did the right thing.'

Their eyes locked, and a current of love and desire radiated through him.

'I bet he already knows that.' Nettie reached for his hand.

As they kissed, Beth muscled her way in, eager for her part in their affection.

'Do you fancy a walk so we can have some time by ourselves?' Nettie asked.

'I bet my mum won't mind looking after Beth.'

'Perhaps she'll be able to persuade her to have her afternoon nap.' Nettie sighed. 'She's definitely over-excited.'

Janet was happy to help. However, as Benny made to follow Nettie out of the house, he suddenly turned back.

'I won't be long,' he promised. 'There's something I forgot, and it's important.'

'You'd forget your head if it wasn't screwed on,' Nettie said, following him back inside.

In the lounge, Benny grabbed Emma's arm, hoisting her up off the sofa.

'What do you want now?' She rolled her eyes.

'Will you come up to my room?' She made to protest, but Benny put up a hand. 'Please, Emmie? Just for a minute.'

His sister nodded with a scowl and followed him up to his untidy bedroom.

'This had better be good, Pestie.'

'It is.' Benny handed over a cardboard box.

'What is it?' Emma peered inside, her face a study in confusion. 'Wait. I remember this.'

'I bet you remember him best of all.' Benny picked out the headless shepherd, holding him out to his sister.

'It's Ed!' Emma gasped. 'How did you…?'

'Mum gave it to me. I said I wanted a nativity set for Beth.' He draped an arm around his beloved sister's shoulders. 'I couldn't let her have this one. It's yours, Emmie. And I reckon…' He faltered, choosing his next words carefully. 'I reckon I've taken enough of what was yours, so it's time for me to give stuff back.'

Janet sat in her favourite chair, cradling Beth on her lap. Once again, the toddler was reluctant to surrender to her need for sleep. Beth made her displeasure known at full volume as she cried for her mother and Benny.

'Sylvia used to get like that when she was over-tired.' Carol sat on the sofa nearby while Ola dozed in an armchair. Bob had retired upstairs for his own afternoon nap. 'You were the total opposite. Such an obedient little girl. When I told you it was time to sleep, you closed your eyes, and that was that.'

'It was the same for me with Benny and Emma.' Janet's tone was reflective. 'He loved cuddles, whereas she was convinced if she closed her eyes, she'd miss out on something important.'

Beth screamed with gusto, attempting to struggle free, and Janet held her back. 'It's no good, Bethy,' she crooned. 'You won't feel better until you've had a rest.'

'Want Mummy! Want Benny!' Her wails became a pitiful whimper.

'You'll see them soon.' Janet stroked the little girl's tear-stained cheek. 'They've only gone for a walk. When you wake up, Mummy and Benny will be back.' She adjusted Beth to lie across her lap. 'Shall Auntie Jan tell Bethy a story to help her go to sleep?'

'Okay.' Beth sniffed.

Janet's voice took on the singsong tone she'd used so many times with Sylvia. 'Let's make our story about two little girls, one redhead, and one blonde.'

Carol shifted her position on the sofa, placing a cushion behind her back.

Janet dropped a kiss on Beth's forehead. 'We'll call one of them Beth and the other Sylvia.'

The lights on the Christmas tree twinkled and the gas fire bathed them in its warm glow as Janet spun her tale. Beth's eyes closed, and the toddler drifted into a peaceful sleep.

Acknowledgements

Mam, you are everything I could wish for in a godly mother and so much more. Thank you for a lifetime of love, patient nurturing, gentleness and understanding. Most of all, thank you for sharing your faith.

Nanna Dil, thank you for passing on your love of books, and for the hours you spent reading to me. Thank you for cheering me on and helping me through many dark seasons. You were my best friend. I miss you so much and I can't wait to hug you in heaven.

Auntie Pat, you taught me to dance and to knit. You were full of fun, encouraging my imagination through play, and you influenced my fashion sense with your love for floaty skirts and dresses.

Auntie Linda, your heart and home were always open to me, and your children felt more like siblings than cousins.

And Auntie Gloria: we shared midnight feasts, soppy films, and vivid imaginations. I'm sure I inherited my story-writing gift from you. I'm so glad we also shared our faith, as this assures me we will meet again.

There aren't enough words to describe how much I love you all, and how grateful I am.

Charm is deceptive, and beauty does not last; but a woman who fears the Lord will be greatly praised. Reward her for all she has done. Let her deeds publicly declare her praise.

Proverbs 31:30-31

About the Author

Alex Banwell lives in the beautiful Forest of Dean with her husband, Jonathan.

As a child, she made up stories on the swings at the park. Later, she began writing them down, firstly on a Perkins Brailler, then later on a typewriter, and finally a laptop computer.

In 2021, she felt led to take the plunge, adapting some of her earlier writings into a full-length novel. It began as an experiment, a secret project between her and her Saviour. She had no idea it would lead to where she is now, a published author of contemporary Christian fiction.

You can connect with Alex at
https://alexbanwellauthor.com

About Broad Place Publishing

Broad Place Publishing is a new Christian imprint whose aim is to bring Jesus-centred books to the market. We want to see good-quality books, inspired by the Holy Spirit, brought to life and made available across the world.

We work in partnership with the Holy Spirit at every step, encouraging our writers to listen to Him in their creativity, asking our editors to trust Him as they strive for excellence, and seeking Him for finances and marketing strategy.

We also strive to be an accessible publisher, using dyslexic friendly fonts and making the book available in multiple formats. Please contact us if you see any ways we can improve in this.

If you wish to support us in this missional work, either in prayer or financially, please see the website, or email us directly support@broadplacepublishing.co.uk

You can find out more about our work at
https://broadplacepublishing.co.uk

Also from the Publisher

Who is Benny Wellander?

To his mother, he's her precious baby, forever in need of protection. To his sister, he's 'Pestie', the kid who destroyed her happy childhood. To his classmates, he's the quiet loner plagued by seizures. To his father, he's barely visible; a constant disappointment.

Caught in a web of insecurity, Benny defines himself by his illness and the damage it's wrought on his mind. But is he truly rubbish at everything? Or could he be worth loving?

Join Benny on a poignant journey of self-discovery as he seeks to understand his own worth. What will it take for him to break free from his labels and embrace the person he truly is?

Just Benny is contemporary fiction available at Broad Place Publishing now.

https://broadplacepublishing.co.uk/shop

"Adah and Tzillah, hear my words!"

Adah lives trapped between the life she longed for and the life she chose. Childless and desperate, she has failed to produce an heir for her once devoted husband, Lamech.

As Lamech becomes increasingly unpredictable and domineering, Adah is drawn to legends about the mysterious Wanderer.

When Lamech takes a second wife, Adah's world shatters, sending her fleeing to her family home. There, a fragile sense of freedom awakens long-buried hopes. But a secret grows within her – a secret that will propel her back into the heart of danger.

With survival a daily struggle, can a legend offer Adah salvation? Or does someone else hold the power to help her dwell in safety?

The Wanderer's Legacy is biblical, historical fiction available at Broad Place Publishing now.

https://broadplacepublishing.co.uk/shop